Mackenzie Bell

Christina Rossetti

A Biographical and Critical Study

Mackenzie Bell

Christina Rossetti
A Biographical and Critical Study

ISBN/EAN: 9783337099138

Printed in Europe, USA, Canada, Australia, Japan

Cover: Foto ©Raphael Reischuk / pixelio.de

More available books at **www.hansebooks.com**

CHRISTINA ROSSETTI

A BIOGRAPHICAL AND CRITICAL STUDY

BY

MACKENZIE BELL

AUTHOR OF 'SPRING'S IMMORTALITY, AND OTHER POEMS'
'CHARLES WHITEHEAD, A BIOGRAPHICAL AND CRITICAL MONOGRAPH' AND
'PICTURES OF TRAVEL, AND OTHER POEMS'

WITH SIX PORTRAITS AND FIVE FACSIMILES

Fourth Edition

COMPLETING TWO THOUSAND FIVE HUNDRED

LONDON

THOMAS BURLEIGH

370 OXFORD STREET

1898

First Edition published January 7, 1898
Second Edition published January 26, 1898
Third Edition published February 18, 1898
Fourth Edition published November 19, 1898

TO MY FRIEND

WILLIAM MICHAEL ROSSETTI

I DEDICATE A BOOK

WHICH

WITHOUT HIS UNCEASING KINDNESS

AND DEEP INTEREST IN IT

COULD HARDLY HAVE BEEN WRITTEN

PREFACE

THE writing of this book has given me peculiar pleasure. But far greater than the pleasure of its composition has been that of considering the various aspects of Christina Rossetti's work, and of contemplating her character as revealed therein. Perhaps my study may serve to some readers as an introduction to the writings of Christina Rossetti both as a poet and as a prose writer. Remembering this I have for the most part relinquished the functions of a critic and assumed the easier functions of an exponent.

Whatever are the shortcomings of my book—and none can feel these shortcomings more than myself—it may at least claim to be correct as to biographical fact, and further to be a useful guide to Christina Rossetti's voluminous writings, for it contains, in a series of chapters, a detailed analysis of all her books of poetry and prose. In these days of hurry and high pressure the work of a writer, however eminent, who, like Christina Rossetti, has produced no fewer than fourteen separate books (irrespective of the privately printed 'Verses' of 1847, and of her 'New Poems' and 'Maude,' both published posthumously, in 1896 and 1897), almost necessarily fails to command attention proportionate to its merit, if for no other reason than that readers do not allow themselves, time to examine it thoroughly. In the case of Christina Rossetti there are reasons why such considerations should have especial weight. If, therefore, my volume be the means of increasing the knowledge of those whose acquaintance with her work is now imperfect, or of drawing the attention of readers for the first time to her depth of thought (the fruit of a rare experience), and to her beauty of expression (the fruit of a rare spiritual strength), one of its chief purposes will be gained.

My task could hardly have been accomplished without the unwearied sympathetic co-operation and unvarying kindness of my friend, Mr. WILLIAM MICHAEL ROSSETTI, Christina Rossetti's literary executor ; and I take this the earliest opportunity of expressing my deep and abiding sense of gratitude to him. I have also to thank him warmly for having thrice read my study through with that care which he gives to everything. I have availed myself freely of his written replies to my numerous inquiries as to many points in his sister's life, or concerning her opinions, about which I sought enlightenment from his fuller knowledge. Thus many autobiographical allusions, especially in ' Time Flies ' and ' The Face of the Deep,' have been made clear. Very often, to insure greater accuracy, I have quoted his actual words.

At his suggestion I have, whenever occasion arose for mentioning the poet-painter, usually referred to Dante Gabriel Rossetti as Dante Gabriel.

The biographical material has generally been used in order of date, though sometimes, when such a course seems more desirable, it has been arranged rather as to subject. Christina Rossetti rarely dated her letters fully. Indeed it is often by internal evidence alone that the date can be inferred. Fortunately it has appeared unnecessary to follow the chronological order absolutely, though whenever such an order seemed to conduce to clearness, or to serve any other good purpose, it has been adopted when possible. Some of the letters included may be deemed by some readers too slight for publication ; my endeavour has been however not to exclude anything slight if it seems to possess personal or other interest or to have felicity of phrase. Her punctuation has been carefully preserved.

I am indebted to Mr. FREDERIC SHIELDS for much assistance, and I am under obligations to the late WILLIAM MORRIS, Mr. THEODORE WATTS-DUNTON, Mr. HOLMAN HUNT, the BISHOP of DURHAM, Mr. ARTHUR HUGHES, Mr. JOHN R. CLAYTON, Dr. CHARLES J. HARE, the Rev. Dr. GROSART, Messrs. MACMILLAN, Messrs. JAMES PARKER & Co., the Society for Promoting Christian Knowledge, Mrs. GEORGE HAKE, Dr. RICHARD GARNETT, Mr. WILLIAM SHARP, the Rev. J. J. GLENDINNING NASH, the Rev. ALFRED GURNEY, Mr. THOMAS WEBSTER, Mr. JOHN H. INGRAM, Mr. GARRETT HORDER, Mr. FAIRFAX MURRAY, Mr. and Mrs. PATCHETT MARTIN, Mr. SYDNEY MORSE, Mrs. WRIGHT, and others, to all of whom I tender my heartiest thanks. I am grateful also to Mr. JOHN P. ANDERSON of the British Museum for the exhaustive bibliography, appended to my volume, to which I have added some items.

MACKENZIE BELL.

LONDON, *January* 1898.

CONTENTS

CHAPTER III

BIOGRAPHICAL—*continued*

(Mainly 1874–1886)

CHAPTER IV

BIOGRAPHICAL—*continued*

(Mainly 1886–1893)

CHAPTER V

BIOGRAPHICAL—*continued*

(Mainly 1893–1894)

CHAPTER VI

GENERAL POEMS

CHAPTER VII

DEVOTIONAL POEMS

CHAPTER VIII

CHILDREN'S BOOKS AND PROSE STORIES

CHAPTER IX

DEVOTIONAL PROSE

CHAPTER X

CRITICAL SURVEY

CHRISTINA ROSSETTI

CHAPTER I

BIOGRAPHICAL

(Mainly 1830–1853)

NEVER does a writer feel so keenly how weak are words—at the best inadequate makeshifts for expressing conceptions or for conveying impressions—as when he strives to show to others in some measure the sweetness and irresistible fascination of such a personality as that of Christina Rossetti—a personality whose unique charm is well-nigh untranslatable into words. Time, skill in word-painting, and, above all, much preparatory thought are needed before any success, however small, can be attained in such an endeavour. And the difficulty is no less great when I turn to another aspect of my present undertaking.

One evening when I was in the company of Christina Rossetti's intimate friend, Mr. Frederic Shields, the painter, the talk turned on the relative merits of two other poets and Dante Gabriel Rossetti, and I ventured to point out certain respects in which these poets excelled the last named. At first my companion demurred entirely to the opinions I put forward, and maintained that Dante Gabriel Rossetti surpassed those with whom he was being compared in all the particulars I had mentioned. Suddenly, however, he turned to me and exclaimed : 'You may be right—it is so hard to criticise when one loves.'

' It is so hard to criticise when one loves !' Ah, thought I, that expresses exactly my chief feeling as I attempt a critical study of Christina Rossetti's work. It is always hard to criticise adequately the work of any poet for whom we have personally a feeling akin to affection. And, if this is true as a general rule, it is particularly true in relation to Christina Rossetti, whom to know at all personally was almost to love.

Her life was outwardly uneventful : it is, however, possible to put too much emphasis on this. Very rarely has a life so lacking in incident as hers been passed amid such noteworthy surroundings, and in such constant touch with eminent persons. When we think of the families who, as families, have enriched English literature during the present century, we probably think first of the Tennysons. The late Laureate, who, by his commanding genius, has conquered and dominated the English-speaking people in a way which has been equalled by no other writer of the century, with the possible exception of Sir Walter Scott, is largely responsible for this. It seldom happens that a family which has produced so illustrious a poet as the late Laureate should include among its members such poets as Mr. Frederick Tennyson and the late Charles Tennyson-Turner, both of whom are admirable in their degree ; while Mr. Frederick Tennyson shares with Landor the almost unparalleled distinction of having produced a volume of fine poems at the venerable age of eighty-eight. In the case of the Brontës also we see conspicuous gifts ; we see the genius of Charlotte Brontë, and the more limited genius of her sister Emily. Nevertheless, much might be said in favour of the assertion that the Rossetti family are in some respects well-nigh unexampled. Sufficient time has now elapsed since the death of Dante Gabriel to enable us to realise in a large measure the legacy of memorable work which he has left to the world both as a poet and as a painter ; Maria Francesca showed in 'The Shadow of Dante,' and elsewhere, rare powers; William Michael, by a life of scholarly labour, has won for himself a notable place among contemporary critics ; while the present volume is designed to exhibit the many excellences of Christina as a writer in poetry and in prose, as well as to give a survey of her life.

Unquestionably, the natural endowments of Christina Rossetti were very great, but her powers were largely developed by the remarkable training she received, and her character largely influenced by her circumstances. Her father, we are told by his younger son, 'always spoke Italian in the family, never English ; and the children from the earliest years, as well as his wife, answered him in Italian.'

Though some prominent critics have held a contrary opinion, I clearly trace in her writings the effect of her descent and youthful environment. It has enriched her vocabulary and increased that underlying sensuousness which is so marked a characteristic of all her poetical achievement. She was an exquisite lyrist, but she was not dramatic in the sense that some great lyrists—for example, such as Burns (who, though he lived in peaceful domestic times, has given us ' Scots wha hae,' one of the supreme war-songs of the world) —were dramatic. Much of her finest work both in verse and prose is the veiled expression of her own individuality. She was deeply religious, and carried her convictions into every detail of life, and her clearly-defined religious opinions gave a special interest to her religious verse. Hers was emphatically a character that it was needful to know personally in order to understand : I doubt if anyone who had not the privilege of knowing her can understand in its fulness, in all its sweetness, in its profundity, and in its fascination, her personality, and the effect of that personality both on her poems and on her prose. She conformed her life to a high standard of duty and conduct, and in the serene atmosphere where her soul dwelt she was unsullied by the petty meannesses, and, in her later years at least, almost incapable of being ruffled by the petty worries of existence. But she was intensely human and full of sturdy common sense. Her habitual serenity had not come to her naturally; it had been acquired by constant, though perhaps partly unconscious effort. And this was one reason why the study of her personality became so interesting.

Christina Georgina Rossetti, the younger daughter

and youngest child of Gabriele and Frances Mary
Lavinia Rossetti, was born on December 5, 1830, at
38 Charlotte Street, Portland Place, London, where her
parents then resided, their other children being Maria
Francesca, born in 1827; Gabriel Charles Dante, born
in 1828; and William Michael, born in 1829.

Gabriele Rossetti was eminent in more than one
respect. Besides winning repute as a poet, and as a
student of Dante, he was an ardent reformer, and, owing
to his support of Liberal ideas, he became, when still
young, obnoxious to the then Government of Naples,
where at the time he lived. He fled from the city under
romantic circumstances. Eventually he settled in
London, where he became a leading teacher of Italian,
and also Professor of Italian at King's College. In
1826 he married Frances Mary Lavinia Polidori, sister
of that Dr. Polidori so well known as physician to Lord
Byron.

Christina Rossetti manifested and evidently felt the
deepest love and reverence for both her parents, but the
ties of affection which bound her to her mother were
peculiar and passionately strong. All of Christina's
books, except two, were dedicated to her mother. Mrs.
Rossetti was more than usually gifted in telling stories
to her children, and this is commemorated in Christina's
dedication of ' Speaking Likenesses.'

To My

DEAREST MOTHER,

IN GRATEFUL REMEMBRANCE OF THE

STORIES

WITH WHICH SHE USED TO ENTERTAIN HER

CHILDREN.

Mrs. Rossetti survived until April 1886, and during fifty-six years Christina was rarely absent from her.

Christina, on her father's side, was wholly of Italian extraction, but her mother was English on the maternal side. Her father, educated as a Roman Catholic, did not in England 'openly abjure' that creed. Nevertheless, according to his son William, 'in religion he was mainly a freethinker, but tending in his later years towards an undogmatic form of Christianity.' His attitude towards Christianity in the later years of his life is shown by the interesting and touching volume of Italian religious poems, called *L'Arpa Evangelica* ('The Evangelic Harp'), which he published in 1852, two years before his death. His wife was a devout adherent of the Church of England, and brought up all her four children as Protestants. Her younger daughter's godmothers were Lady Dudley Stuart and Miss Georgina Macgregor. Lady Dudley Stuart was one of the Bonaparte family, several members of which family, particularly Prince Pierre Bonaparte, and occasionally even Prince Louis Napoleon, afterwards Napoleon III., were visitors in the Rossetti household. Mr. W. M. Rossetti has given me some interesting information about Lady Dudley Stuart :

' My knowledge of Lady Dudley Stuart is not minute, but the following is more or less correct. She was a daughter of one of the brothers of the great Napoleon— Lucian—and must originally have been called Princess Christina Bonaparte. She married a Swedish Count, Arvid de Possé, and subsequently Lord Dudley Stuart. My father knew her well, and, I think, liked her : she, I suppose, offered to be godmother to the infant born on December 5, 1830, and he assented. She died in 1847.'

Miss Georgina Macgregor was the daughter of Sir

Patrick Macgregor, to whose children Mrs. Rossetti had been governess until the latter's marriage. The names of Christina and Georgina were given to the child in compliment, respectively, to her first and second godmother.

The touching little poem by Gabriele Rossetti, reproduced below in facsimile with a line-by-line translation from the Italian by his younger son, was sent to me by the latter with the following remarks:

'The enclosed verses by my Father about Maria and Christina ... are very pretty in their simple way, especially in sound. Their date would, I suppose, be towards 1834, when C[hristina] was three years of age.

Cristina e Maria	Christina and Maria,
Mie care figliuole	My dear daughters,
Son fresche viole	Are fresh violets
Dischiuse all'albor.	Opened at dawn.
Son rose nudrite	They are roses nurtured
Dall'aure novelle,	By the earliest breezes;
Son tortore belle	They are lovely turtle-doves
Nel nido d'amor.	In the nest of Love.'

About 1836 the family removed to 50 Charlotte Street. There, partly owing to the father's conspicuous ability, partly to his growing celebrity as a leader of the movement in favour of Italian freedom, his house became a meeting-place of Italians, some of them exiles like himself. Christina and her surviving brother have told me something of their father's kindness to his compatriots even when his own means were of the

narrowest. Very naturally these compatriots had a
great fascination for the children. Gabriele Rossetti
had a high estimate of the talents of one of them named
Filippo Pistrucci, a painter and teacher of Italian, and
also entertained a cordial liking for the man himself.
Pistrucci was often in money straits, the result of family
conditions. Gabriele Rossetti, in some degree because
of his sympathy for Pistrucci on this account, in some
degree because of his appreciation of his powers, set him
to paint portraits of all his children. Maria he painted
twice; Dante Gabriel twice; William once; and Christina
twice. The portrait of Christina, a water-colour on
paper, was executed when she was about seven years
old. It is reproduced here, and
represents a thoughtful face—a
face even then betokening the
qualities which made her what she
ultimately became. The loftiness
of the brow is perhaps greater
than was apparent in later life,
and the mouth and the lips are
perhaps set with greater determination. The portrait as a whole
fully justifies the opinion of most
of her early friends that in youth
Christina was beautiful. William
Bell Scott, probably about 1860, did an etching from
this water-colour, and produced, in her younger brother's
judgment, a satisfactory result, though he thinks that
the upper lip is too long. A son of Filippo Pistrucci
succeeded Gabriele Rossetti as Professor of Italian at
King's College, London.

Prominent among the Italian refugees who used to

CHRISTINA ROSSETTI

Reproduced direct from the water-colour by Filippo Pistrucci 1838, in the possession of Mr. W. M. Rossetti

frequent Gabriele Rossetti's house almost every evening was a 'tall gaunt man' named Benedetto Sangiovanni, a capable modeller in clay. He was a special source of interest to the children, as it had been reported of him, whether rightly or wrongly it is impossible now to say, that he had stabbed some one in Calabria. He had lived in Naples under the protection of Murat, and after the latter's downfall had come to England. He designed a little oiled clay letter-weight which stood above the clock in Christina Rossetti's dining-room and this relic she retained till her death.

Among the great pleasures of Christina's early childhood were her visits to the cottage of her grandfather, Gaetano Polidori, at Holmer Green, near Little Missenden in Buckinghamshire. This cottage was about thirty miles from London, and in those days could only be reached by a stage coach journey of six hours' duration. The novelty of this journey to the town-bred and town-immured little girl may be imagined, more especially as surrounding the cottage was a garden, small in actual extent, but large in her idea. To her this garden was a revelation of the beauty of nature, and she spoke to me frequently respecting the exquisite delight she had derived from her rambles in it—a delight which came to an end before she was nine years old.

In Chapter IX. I shall deal with her volume, ' Time Flies : a Reading Diary, being short Devotional Essays for every day in the year.' A notable example of her later prose work (it was first published when she was in her fifty-fifth year) this book contains many personal allusions, though there are rarely any definite indications as to place or as to time. I am able, nevertheless, to furnish particulars concerning many of these allusions.

The first reference to Holmer Green is under date March 4, where she tells, in a few simple words, of her first knowledge of death :

'So in these grounds, perhaps in the orchard, I lighted upon a dead mouse. The dead mouse moved my sympathy ; I took him up, buried him comfortably in a mossy bed, and bore the spot in mind.
'It may have been a day or two afterwards that I returned, removed the moss coverlet, and looked . . . a black insect emerged. I fled in horror, and for long years ensuing I never mentioned this ghastly adventure to anyone.'

She speaks (July 6) about two frogs she had seen in the same garden. One of the frogs had startled her by jumping unexpectedly, while she, all unwittingly, had startled the other frog. On the little incident she remarks :

' Is it quite certain that no day will ever come, when even the smallest, weakest, most grotesque, *wronged* creature will not in some fashion rise up in the Judgment with us to condemn us, and so frighten us effectually once for all ? '

On July 17 and 18 we read how she and another ' little girl ' (somewhat older in years) watched a wild strawberry grow on a hedge-row bank, visiting it daily to see how it throve. Not the least of her childhood's disappointments was that which befel her when she discovered that a snail had made it 'good for nothing.' With the wisdom of maturity she deduces the moral that even snails have their rights, while ' man, alas ! finds it convenient here to snap off a right and there to chip away a due.' ' The little girl,' somewhat older in years, was her sister Maria, and the hedge-row bank was at Holmer Green.

But in some respects the most interesting reminiscence of her days of childhood occurs under date June 19, where she says :

' I know of a little girl who not far from half a century ago, having heard that oil calmed troubled waters, suggested to her mother its adoption for such a purpose in case of a sea storm.

' Her suggestion fell flat, as from her it deserved to fall. Yet nowadays, here is science working out the babyish hint of ignorance.'

' The little girl ' was herself.

Mr. William Sharp, in an admirable essay contributed to ' The Atlantic Monthly ' for June 1895, entitled ' Some Reminiscences of Christina Rossetti '—an essay full of sympathetic discrimination—has narrated how she told him once of her first visit to the Zoological Gardens, made in the company of her brother Gabriel. The two children amused themselves in a manner worth recording. Christina felt that the captive birds should be celebrated by ' plaintive verses,' while her brother entertained her by laughable biographies of them. Mr. Sharp tells further of a singular dream which Christina Rossetti had in early life. She thought she was ' in Regent's Park at dawn,' while, just as the sun rose, she seemed to see ' a wave of yellow light sweep from the trees.' It ' was a multitude of canaries, thousands of them,' all the canaries in London. They had met, and were now going back to captivity. Her brother Gabriel, to whom she spoke of her vision, thought to make a picture of it, but never did so.

Mr. W. M. Rossetti, in his ' Dante Gabriel Rossetti :

his Family Letters ; with a Memoir,' gives some distinctive particulars respecting the children's amusements in the Rossetti household. Besides the inevitable rocking-horse, and the almost equally inevitable ' blind-man's buff' and ' puss-in-the-corner,' the children early identified themselves ' in a sort of way with the four suits of cards,' clubs being appropriated to Maria, hearts to Dante Gabriel, diamonds to Christina, and spades to William. But they were trained to 'dislike . . . gambling,' and never throughout life ' played for money.'

Christina was deeply affectionate, and had, besides, much fondness for animals, a trait perhaps first exemplified in the lines ' On the Death of a Cat : a friend of mine aged ten years and a half,' written when she was sixteen.[1] The lines, though creditable enough when the author's age is remembered, are without much poetical merit. Some of them may be quoted here, however, as showing that, child of genius as she was, Christina Rossetti was not unduly precocious, or uninfluenced by her practical commonplace surroundings.   In the second stanza is an exceedingly neat allusion to the proverb that a cat has nine lives :

> Come, ye Muses, one and all,
> Come obedient to my call ;
> Come and mourn with tuneful breath
> Each one for a separate death ;
> And, while you in numbers sigh,
> I will sing her elegy.

Christina's mother (originally belonging to the Evangelical School, though at a later period she adopted somewhat High Church opinions) taught all her four

---

[1] This poem appeared in the privately printed volume of 1847 shortly to be mentioned.

children the Church Catechism, besides imparting to
them Biblical knowledge; and Christina soon showed
deep religious feeling and aspiration.

She was educated at home, and, as her younger
brother forcibly said to me, 'owed *everything* in the
way of early substantial instruction to our mother.'
One result of never going to school was constant
association with her sister and brothers. As a child her
temper was quick, and it is strong evidence of her
force of will that in later life scarcely any trace of this
quickness of temper seemed to remain.

Christina told Mr. Sharp that she was the ill-
tempered one of the family ; and 'my dear sister used
to say that *she* had the good sense, William the good
nature, Gabriel the good heart, and I the bad temper of
our much-loved father and mother.'

Indeed, it is no more than the fact that Christina had
naturally an irritable strain in her disposition—a juster
way of putting it, perhaps, than to say that she was ill-
tempered in the ordinary sense of the term. The irritable strain may partly have been the result of physical
causes ; in later life it was altogether conquered, and this
conquest strengthened her character, as moral conquests
ever do strengthen the character.

Like many children possessing incipient genius, she
was desultory in her habits of study. But this disposition in her case (as in the case of so many others
similarly endowed) was compensated for by much wide
general reading.

About the age of nine she appreciated Hone's
'Every Day Book.' In this compilation she first saw
the name of Keats, and read extracts from 'The Eve of
St. Agnes' which naturally impressed her. In common

with her brothers and sister she liked also ' John Gilpin,' ' Casabianca,' and ' Chevy Chase,' nor were ' Robinson Crusoe' and ' The Arabian Nights' neglected. Pope's ' Iliad' was soon placed in her hands ; so were books descriptive of Irish life, for she read both Carleton's ' Traits and Stories of the Irish Peasantry,' and the tales of Maria Edgeworth.

She was early acquainted with Shakespeare and Sir Walter Scott ; about 1844 she read Anne Radcliffe, perhaps chiefly that writer's ' Mysteries of Udolpho,' and about 1847 Maturin's stories.   Nevertheless, her brother informs me that, ' as compared with the rest of the family, she read very little, and only what hit her fancy. . . . From 9 to 14 one of her most constant companions was Metastasio, the operatic poet. My sister can have read very little of Burns in childhood. I question whether she *ever* knew much of him. Though from infancy speaking Italian almost as well as English, she did not study Dante till about 1848.'

Mr. W. M. Rossetti once showed me an early sonnet of his sister's on Lady Montrevor in Maturin's novel ' The Wild Irish Boy,' remarking : 'When Gabriel, Christina, and I were young we used to read Maturin's novels over and over again, and they took great hold of our imaginations. '[1]   He has since published the sonnet in her posthumous ' New Poems '[2] which he edited in 1896, adding a valuable series of notes that elucidate many points in regard to her work.

In 1842 occurred the well-remembered war with China, and one of Mr. William Rossetti's schoolmasters

[1] Students of Sir Walter Scott will recollect that, in a published letter, he describes Maturin as ' a man of great, but eccentric genius.'

[2] This collection of verse is more fully referred to in Chapter VI.

requested him to write a composition on the theme.
Christina, knowing that he was at work, herself produced
a set of verses, pentameter in measure, called 'The
Chinaman.' These, however, were not the first verses
she wrote, for they were written later than April 27,
1842, the date of the two stanzas commemorative of
her mother's birthday, which her grandfather printed
on a card. The original MS. of these verses is now in
the British Museum, and the childishness of the handwriting betokens their early date. There is a very early
attempt at humour in a couplet quoted in the 'memoir'
of her elder brother.

'Come, cheer up, my lads, 'tis to glory we steer !'
As the soldier remarked whose post lay in the rear.

The late William Bell Scott tells in his autobiography
how he met Christina for the first time in the company
of her father :

'By the window was a high narrow reading-desk, at
which stood writing a slight girl, with a serious regular
profile, dark against the pallid wintry light without.
This most interesting to me of the two inmates turned
on my entrance, made the most formal and graceful
curtsey, and resumed her writing, and the old gentleman
signed to a chair for my sitting down.'

The date of William Bell Scott's call was probably
December 1847, or January 1848, when Christina was
just seventeen. In the first-named year her grandfather,
Gaetano Polidori, printed privately her first volume,
entitled 'Verses.' Mr. William Rossetti possesses a
copy which is curious and especially interesting because
illustrated in water-colours by Christina herself, the
date of the illustrations being somewhat later, though
not much later, than 1847. He has dealt with these

illustrations in some detail in his notes to ' New Poems.'
It may be said, however, that these drawings are in
no sense remarkable except as being Christina's work.
Perhaps the best is that of the line

Lay a kitten by her side,

in 'The Death of a Cat,' a poem already referred to.
Another copy was given by Christina, when twenty-four
years of age, to her mother, and some years after her
mother's death it was presented by Christina to Mr. W.
M. Rossetti on his sixty-first birthday. It contains a
frontispiece portrait of the author, besides illustrations
of the poems by her brother Gabriel.

We have seen already that Christina Rossetti began
early to paint in water-colours, and at a somewhat later
date we find her one of Ford Madox Brown's pupils
in a drawing-class he conducted at Camden Town on
rather novel principles—a class in which the members
of the Præraphaelite Brotherhood (to which allusion
shall elsewhere be made) were much interested. Dante
Gabriel averred frequently that had she continued her
artistic efforts she might have reached excellence.

Probably she was Dante Gabriel's first model, and
there is a portrait of her by him, executed in 1848,
when she was seventeen. It used to hang in the back
parlour at 30 Torrington Square, formerly her sitting-
room. It is described by Mr. W. M. Rossetti as ' the
very first finished painting ' Dante Gabriel produced.
Probably her brother executed it as a preliminary study
for her portrait in 'The Girlhood of Mary Virgin.' It
has many qualities of beauty—chief among which is
the lovely spiritual expression of the eyes, and the
firmness of the mouth, revealing strength as well as

CHRISTINA ROSSETTI.

(From the oil painting by James Collinson. In the possession of Mr. W. M. Rossetti, and reproduced here for the first time.)

sweetness of character. There is also a portrait painted about 1849 by James Collinson, now remembered mainly by his association with 'The Germ' and the Præraphaelite Brotherhood. It is reproduced here for the first time. She sat, as stated above, for the Virgin in Dante Gabriel's picture of 'The Girlhood of Mary Virgin.' This, originally exhibited in 1849, is so well known, and has been so often spoken of and reproduced, that a detailed reference to it need not be attempted.

About a year afterwards Christina again sat for the Virgin in her brother's picture called 'Ecce Ancilla Domini,' better known, perhaps, as 'The Annunciation.' This picture, now in the National Gallery of British Art, given to the nation by Mr. Tate, has been often minutely dwelt on, and has also been reproduced. So I need only say that the tender, almost deprecating look mingled with simplicity, the almost childlike beauty on the Virgin's face, was, I am informed by more than one early friend of Christina Rossetti, very characteristic of her in girlhood and in opening womanhood.

To Mr. John R. Clayton, the artist, who knew her well about 1849–51, I am indebted for an anecdote which will be new to my readers. At this period he was on very intimate terms with Dante Gabriel, and privileged to enter the latter's studio in Newman Street at any time. When he first saw 'Ecce Ancilla Domini' there the head of Christina alone appeared on the canvas.

After the picture had nearly reached completion, Mr. Clayton found his friend 'busily engaged in painting, from the "snap-dragon" effects of ignited spirits of wine in a saucer, the flames under the feet of the angel Gabriel.' The painter explained to Mr. Clayton his dilemma from the impossibility of obtaining at that time of the year (for it was the month of March) a real lily from which to paint the flower symbolically represented in the hand of the angel. Mr. Clayton having no study of his own, such as his friend sought to borrow of him, suggested that something to serve his friend's purpose might be obtainable at Foster's artificial flower shop, then in Wigmore Street. His friend immediately went there, bought an artificial lily for two shillings, and used it as a substitute for a real one.

Mr. Clayton differs from the early friends, to whom allusion has been recently made, as he does not regard the portrait of Christina in 'Ecce Ancilla Domini' as a portrait seriously intended or true to fact. He considers it merely as a delineation of the mystery of expression in the face. He has pointed out to me, as an instance of the painter's 'indifference to scholastic antiquarianism,' that the angel in the picture is represented as 'indicating Benediction with the *left*! instead of the right hand.'

Concerning Christina's personal appearance, Mr. Watts-Dunton wrote in 'The Athenæum' (No. 3,506, January 5, 1895):

'In most things, Christina Rossetti seemed to stand midway between Gabriel and the other two members of her family, and it was the same in physical matters. She had Gabriel's eyes, in which hazel and blue-grey were marvellously blent, one hue shifting into the other, answering to the movements of the thoughts—eyes like the mother's. And her brown hair, though less warm in colour than his during his boyhood, was still like it. When a young girl, at the time that she sat for the Virgin in the picture now in the National Gallery, she was, as both her mother and Gabriel have told me, really lovely, with an extraordinary expression of pensive sweetness. She used to have in the little back parlour a portrait of herself at eighteen by Gabriel, which gives all these qualities.'

One or two of her still earlier friends whom I have met have agreed in describing her as beautiful in youth —beautiful, that is, with a ' pensive ' beauty. Admirers of Mr. Ruskin will remember his warm praise of ' Ecce Ancilla Domini ' in ' The Three Colours of Præ-raphaelitism.'

What follows is part of a conversation about Christina Rossetti with which Mr. Holman Hunt honoured me :

' When I was painting " The Light of the World," ' said Mr. Holman Hunt, ' Christina, at my request, came ' to me with her mother to my little studio in Chelsea, ' and sat for me for the face. I had several other sitters ' for it, and eventually I modelled the head in clay.   I ' can hardly remember now whether Christina came to ' me early, or just before the cast was made.'

In the summer of 1848 Christina visited Brighton, and while there wrote several *bouts rimés* sonnets, to be mentioned hereafter. She was incited to this work by the example of her brothers, both of whom at that time were addicted to this metrical exercise.

We · learn from a touching note by Mr. William Rossetti on ' Looking Forward,' a poem dated June 8, 1849, that the MS. is in his mother's handwriting, and he adds that when Christina was seventeen or eighteen years old her health was so uncertain as to lead none of her family to suppose she would attain an average length of life.   Christina placed her ' Looking Forward,' though without title, as the work of the heroine in her prose story ' Maude.' [1]

---

[1] Some extracts from ' Maude ' are given in Chapter VIII. beginning at p. 281. This story has been published with a preface by Mr. W. M. Rossetti.

It is generally unwise to endeavour to identify too closely the habits of an author with the incidents described in his or her work, when that work is presumably of fiction. But in the portrayal of the heroine in ' Maude ' allusions occur that one cannot doubt are personal. Sometimes, for example, Christina makes Maude go to ' St. Andrew's Church '—probably intended for St. Andrew's, Wells Street, W.—because of the finer music there than at her ' parish church.'

Both her brothers, but especially Dante Gabriel, were ' adorers ' of their sister (to quote Mr. Clayton's phrase in conversation with me), and Mr. Clayton is convinced that it was from ' the fascinating mystery and soft melancholy of his sister's eyes,' that Dante Gabriel gained that impulse towards the sad female face so noticeable in the pictorial work of his whole career.

It must not be supposed, however, that Christina's early life was without brightness. Even as a child she had humour, and, although it is true that gifted natures endowed with a sense of humour are often melancholy, in reality her youthful years were full of quiet joy of various kinds.

Dr. Charles J. Hare first attended her professionally in November 1845, and she remained ' more or less constantly ' under his care until 1850. He permits me to quote part of the first memorandum he made concerning her :

' Fully the middle stature ; appears older than she really is—15 ; hair brown ; complexion is brunette ; but she is now pale (anæmic). Conformation good.'

From subsequent memoranda by the same gentleman the two following brief extracts are taken :

'She had been under the care of several very distinguished physicians before I saw her—Drs. Locock and Watson, and, I think, Dr. Latham. . . . In 1848 she had a sharpish attack of bronchitis.'

When he was good enough to talk to me on the subject, Dr. Hare said that what chiefly impressed him was Christina's deep love for her mother—a feeling shown by every word and look. In the whole course of his life he had never known an instance of affection more absorbing in itself or more touchingly evinced. Evidently in these early days she thought with especial favour of the lines 'Looking Forward,' for among Dr. Hare's most cherished possessions is a copy of them in her own handwriting which she gave to him at the time. In Dr. Hare's opinion she was sweet and interesting, but not strictly beautiful.

As to Christina Rossetti's grandfather, Gaetano Polidori, Dr. Hare writes :

'At eighty-four, when I first attended to him professionally, he was a very hale, hearty, fine-looking old man, full of enthusiasm, and not the least so as regards his estimate of the talents and character of his grandchild Christina.'

Christina reciprocated the affection of Gaetano Polidori, for Mr. W. M. Rossetti writes thus in his notes to 'New Poems' :

'To her grandfather especially Christina was most warmly attached.'

Here is Dr. Hare's description of Mrs. Rossetti at the time of which we are now speaking :

'A face full of beautiful expression as her heart is full of faith, hope, and love.'

One of the most pleasing of the poems in Christina

Rossetti's 'New Poems' is that addressed 'To Lalla, the favourite name of her cousin Henrietta Polydore. The latter was only three years old when the poem was written. Her father, Henry Polidori, had Anglicised his name. The lines incidentally point the moral that wisdom of the heart is better than knowledge of the head. It is a trite moral, but rarely has it been better expressed than here.

> Read on : if you knew it
> You have cause to boast :
> You are much the wiser
> Though I know the most.

During many of her early years Christina Rossetti attended Christ Church, Albany Street, Regent's Park —a plain, somewhat unattractive building in external aspect. Mr. Clayton has told me that he frequently encountered her and other members of her family after service. On such occasions she would say little, but what she did say was sometimes memorable. When meeting her elsewhere about the same date, she would sometimes speak with great vigour and energy, though usually she was very reticent, hardly giving utterance to more than the usual commonplaces. This fitful energy and power in conversation, coming as a contrast to her habitual reserve, was one of the reasons why, in my informant's opinion, she came to be regarded, even in her early years, as a marked personality. Mr. Clayton does not think that at this time she was lovely in the exact sense, although about her face there was always an interest that excelled the charm of mere loveliness. There was likewise an indescribable but prevailing sadness that constrained the onlooker to regard her with deep attention. This sadness partly resulted from several ailments from which she then suffered, and which she then thought might terminate fatally. In this connection two of her early poems, 'Looking Forward,' recently alluded to, and 'Life Hidden,' dated respectively June 8 and July 23, 1849, which appeared first in 'New Poems,' may be referred to. These pathetic lines from the first-named poem give utterance to a melancholy too deeply felt to be uttered superficially :

> Sweet thought that I may yet live and grow green,
>   That leaves may yet spring from the withered root,
> And buds and flowers and berries half unseen ;
> Then, if you haply muse upon the past,
> Say this : poor child, she has her wish at last ;
>   Barren through life, but in death bearing fruit.

Several of her early friends say that about this period a certain degree of restraint and pride was observable in Christina's demeanour. She herself alludes to this in 'Is and Was,' written in the spring of 1850, and first printed by her brother William in 'New Poems.' He there informs us that a lady told Christina she

'seemed to do all from self-respect, not from fellow feeling with others, or from kindly consideration for them. Christina mentioned the remark, with an admission that it hit a blot in her character, in which a certain amount of reserve and distance, not remote from *hauteur*, was certainly at that time perceptible. She laid the hint to heart, and, I think, never forgot it,'

and he adds in a communication to myself, ' Afterwards Christina wrote the poem, and this verse

> Doing all from self-respect

in it.'

Our interest in the poem is increased when we thus find it contains autobiographical touches.

In 1851 the family left 50 Charlotte Street, and went

to reside at 38 Arlington Street, Mornington Crescent. For some years before and after this date their means were much straitened. The father's emoluments had been considerably reduced, for German had become at the moment more popular than Italian, while his failing sight, and of late even his failing general health, continued a source of further anxiety. Dante Gabriel had as yet achieved not much pecuniary success as a painter and none as a poet, while William Michael, now in the Civil Service, was only at the beginning of his career as a literary and artistic critic.

The need had therefore arisen for augmenting the family pecuniary resources, and Mrs. Rossetti, assisted by Christina, opened a day school at 38 Arlington Street, while Maria Francesca went out as a daily governess, chiefly giving lessons in Italian. The day school was not altogether prosperous, producing 'very little income' (I quote from a private communication from her surviving brother), and in April 1853 it was deemed advisable that Christina with her father and mother should go to reside at Frome Selwood (better known merely as Frome) in Somersetshire—Maria, Dante Gabriel, and William remaining in London. At Frome also Mrs. Rossetti kept a day school, in the management of which Christina took part ; but the result was no more satisfactory than in London.

The eleven months during which Christina Rossetti lived at Frome were the longest period she ever spent out of London. Probably she then acquired, through observation, some of the considerable knowledge she possessed of country objects. Mr. Watts-Dunton has said in the obituary notice contributed to 'The Athenæum,' to which I have before referred :

'It is, of course, a great disadvantage to any poet not to have been born in the country : learned in Nature the city-born poet can never be, as we see in the case of Milton, who loved Nature without knowing her. It is here that Miss Ingelow has such an advantage over Christina Rossetti. Her love of flowers, and birds, and trees, and all that makes the earth so beautiful, is not one whit stronger than Christina's own, but it is a love born of an exhaustive detailed knowledge of Nature's life.'

Doubtless Jean Ingelow excelled Christina Rossetti in 'exhaustive detailed knowledge of Nature's life.' But though sharing to some extent Mr. Watts-Dunton's opinion, I cannot altogether concur in it. For it seems to me that Christina Rossetti's actual knowledge of Nature was greater than he here supposes. It must not be forgotten, however, that he speaks from actual knowledge of Christina while staying in the country.

Christina did not look back with any pleasure to her sojourn at Frome. If I mistake not, once or twice she alluded incidentally to it in talking to me, though never appreciatively. Concerning it Mr. W. M. Rossetti writes to me :

'I can remember that the part of the town in which Christina lived was called Fromefield (I was there once, or perhaps twice). This, according to my recollection, was an integral part of Frome, but not in the centre of the town, which is a hilly up-and-down sort of place. At that date (at any rate) it was a regular countrified sort of town—not absolutely small, but certainly not much marked by traffic or shop-display.'

Possibly the somewhat untoward family circumstances had to do with the feeling she may have had on the subject. Perhaps also Frome was too considerable a town to be sufficiently 'countrified' for Christina's taste.

In 'Time Flies,' under date of April 2, she narrates
an incident referring to Frome. She tells us how in
one of her country walks, being then entirely ignorant
of its rarity, she lighted upon a four-leaved trefoil. She
goes on to say :

'Perhaps I plucked and so destroyed it : I certainly
left it, for most certainly I have it not.

.   .   .   .   .   .

'*Now* I would give something to recover that
wonder : *then*, when I might have had it for the
carrying, I left it.
'Once missed, one may peer about in vain all the rest
of one's days for a second four-leaved trefoil.
'No one expects to find whole fields of such : even
one, for once, is an extra allowance.
'Life has, so to say, its four-leaved trefoils for a
favoured few : and how many of us overlook once and
finally our rare chance !'

Some time after the publication of 'Time Flies,' one
of her admirers on reading the above passage sent to
her a four-leaved trefoil which she preserved carefully.

During Christina's residence at Frome her brother,
Dante Gabriel, was at work in London on his picture
called 'Found,' about which so much has been written,
and speaks thus in one of his letters to his mother, dated
Arlington Street, September 30, 1853 :

'I believe I shall be wanting to paint a brick wall,
and a white heifer tied to a cart going to market.
Such things are I suppose to be had at Frome, and it
has occurred to me that I should like if possible to come
and paint them there. There is a cattle-market, is
there not ? Have you ever seen such an article as the
heifer in question, and have you or Christina any
recollection of an eligible and accessible brick wall ?
I should want to get up and paint it early in the
mornings, as the light ought to be that of dawn. It
should be not too countrified (yet beautiful in colour)

CHRISTINA ROSSETTI.

(From the pencil drawing by Dante Gabriel Rossetti, October 1852. Now in the possession of Mr. W. M. Rossetti, and reproduced here for the first time.)

as it is to represent a city-wall. A certain modicum of moss would therefore be admissible, but no prodigality of grass, weeds, ivy, etc. Can you give any information on these heads? I suppose Christina's pictorial eye will by this time have some insight into the beauties of brick walls—the preferability of purplish prevailing tint to yellowish, etc.

'I suppose Christina has not been working much at the Art? Will you tell her that I am quite ashamed of not being able yet to tell her anything positive about "Nick"? I am constantly remembering it when Hannay is not in the way, and always forgetting it when he is. I have now resolved to remember it the next time I see him, and, if I am baulked again, to write to him the next time I think of it.'

Dante Gabriel, however, painted the 'brick wall' not at Frome, but at Chiswick, as we learn from his characteristic letters to William Allingham, edited skilfully by Dr. George Birkbeck Hill.[1] 'Hannay,' referred to in Dante Gabriel's letter, was James Hannay, the novelist, and 'Nick' was a tale, to be mentioned by-and-by in connection with Christina's 'Commonplace and Other Short Stories.' Presumably Dante Gabriel intended to recommend it to Hannay for publication.

A drawing of Christina was made by Dante Gabriel in October 1852, and by the permission of her brother William is reproduced here for the first time. I quote what follows from a communication made by the latter to me:

'Towards 1852 (perhaps) C[hristina]'s illness was considered to be essentially *angina pectoris*. . . . Dr. Crellin was called in, and he set her fairly right as regards those particular symptoms.

'C[hristina]'s knowledge of Sir W[illiam] Jenner began towards 1854. In 1853, when C[hristina] with

[1] *Atlantic Monthly*, May—August, 1896.

our parents went to Frome, Maria and I took lodgings in Albany Street (not the same house wh[ich] we all afterwards occupied as a family residence), over a chemist's shop, occupied by a Mr. Burcham—who turned out to be also an amateur painter of still life of considerable merit. There Maria and I first met [Sir William] Jenner, not yet a man of professional celebrity, and afterwards C[hristina] did. She liked him, thinking his manner not unpleasantly scrutinizing, or "formidable"—a point as to which she was rather sensitive in medical concerns. I am not clear that she ever consulted him professionally until her terrible illness, exophthalmic bronchocele, beginning in 1871. He pronounced her then to be "a very interesting case"—the malady being far from a common one. After that she always consulted him (until he retired from practice) at the more important crises of her illnesses ; Dr. Stewart (who attended my Mother and Aunts) being also employed by C[hristina] in the ordinary course of events. C[hristina] had a particular dislike if a doctor "looked surprised" when she mentioned her symptoms. Her liking for [Sir William] Jenner was partly because he did not look surprised.'

Mr. Ford M. Hueffer, in the exhaustive life of his grandfather, Ford Madox Brown, writes in allusion to 1852–1855 concerning one of the latter's chief religious paintings, 'Christ Washes Peter's Feet' :

' Apart from the intrinsic worth of the picture, it has an historical interest of its own, in that it contains portraits of several of the members of the P. R. [Præraphaelite] circle.

' The head of Christ is a literal transcript of that of Mr. F. G. Stephens ; of the Apostles, omitting Judas, the first on the left is Mr. W. M. Rossetti ; the second, Mr. Holman Hunt; the fourth, Mr. Hunt, sen. ; the fifth, C[harles] B[agot] Cayley ; the sixth, D. G. Rossetti, and the seventh, St. John, is, I believe, Miss Christina Rossetti. Mr. William Rossetti is, however, rather of opinion that it was Deverell, the P. R. [Præraphaelite] who sat for the head.'

However, ' The Athenæum ' for February 27, 1897, in a review of Mr. Hueffer's life of his grandfather, states :

' He [Mr. Hueffer] errs . . . in thinking that the head of St. John in Brown's " Christ Washes Peter's Feet," now in 'the National Gallery, was painted from Christina Rossetti. There was excuse for this belief before the lady found herself unable to remember sitting for the head ; but Mr. W. Rossetti is certainly mistaken in supposing Deverell, whom it does not at all resemble, sat for it.'

Christina addressed to Henrietta Polydore another lyric some years afterwards, the beautiful poem entitled ' Next of Kin,' dated February 21, 1853. But here both motive and subject are more in accordance with her usual manner than is the case in ' To Lalla.' The poem also betokens an expectation of speedy death, which runs through many of her early verses. She addresses her cousin as

You, white as dove or lily or spirit of the light :
I, stained and cold and glad to hide in the cold dark night :
You, joy to many a loving heart and light to many eyes :
I, lonely in the knowledge earth is full of vanities.

It may, perhaps, be permissible to say here, parenthetically, as showing how early fears may be falsified by fact, that while Christina herself lived an average length of life, and died from a disease far other than that which, in early years, seemed to threaten her, the young lady to whom these poems were addressed died twenty years before her of consumption, the very disease Christina feared for herself when she wrote the poem last named.

The piece of the same date, entitled ' Portraits,' is possibly not very poetic in quality, but is very interesting autobiographically. It consisted originally of three stanzas, the first descriptive of her brother

William ; the second of her brother Dante Gabriel ; and
the third containing a sisterly reference to both brothers.
Most readers will share her brother William's regret that
the MS. of the second stanza is lost, having presumably been destroyed of set purpose by Dante Gabriel.
According to the same authority, Christina was a diligent
correspondent, and knew well Miss Macdonald, now
Lady Burne-Jones, corresponding with her ; and was
also acquainted with Lady Burne-Jones's two sisters,
now respectively Mrs. Lockwood Kipling (mother of
the celebrated writer) and Lady Poynter, though the
latter she knew only slightly.

Sometimes in these early years Christina was asked
to write verses for friends, and these were not always
very appropriate to the occasion, as when she contributed the mournful lines beginning—

> Do you hear the low winds singing,
>   And streams singing on their bed ?
> Very distant bells are ringing
>   In a chapel for the dead—

to the album of a youthful friend, Miss Orme, afterwards
the wife of Professor Masson of Edinburgh.

Readers of 'New Poems' will recollect the delicately
touched lyric called 'What ?' dated May 1853, and
ending with the lines :

> Glorious as purple twilight,
>   Pleasant as budding tree,
> Untouched as any islet
>   Shrined in an unknown sea :
> Sweet as a fragrant rose amid the dew :—
>   As sweet, as fruitless too.
> A bitter dream to wake from,
>   But oh how pleasant while we dream !
> A poisoned fount to take from,
>   But oh how sweet the stream !

This poem is the first of several in that volume, to depict
what her younger brother has called 'an unhappy love-
passage' in his sister's life. During 1849, or possibly late
in 1848, she was sought in marriage by a painter very well
known in her circle. She regarded him with favour. But
he was a Roman Catholic, and she determined to decline
his suit owing to 'religious considerations.'

CHAPTER II

BIOGRAPHICAL (*continued*)

(Mainly 1854–1876)

Returns to London—Death of Gabriele Rossetti—Straitened circumstances
—Miscellaneous writings—Literary income up to 1890—Hastings —
Newcastle-on-Tyne —Brookbank, Shottermill, Haslemere—Chelten-
ham—Second offer of marriage—Foreign travel—Switzerland—Italy—
Dr. Gordon Hake—The Rev. Dr. Littledale—Chalk drawing by Dante
Gabriel, 1866—Penkill Castle, Ayrshire—Removal to 56 Euston
Square, now 5 Endsleigh Gardens—Serious illness—Meads, East-
bourne—Devotion to her family—Her sister's ' Shadow of Dante '—
Her own papers on Dante—Dante's Lucifer and Milton's Satan
contrasted —Her sister's influence upon her in religious matters—Her
sister and Mr. John Ruskin.

IN March 1854 Christina returned to London with
her father and mother, and went to reside at the house
of her brother William, then 45 Upper Albany Street,
but now 166 Albany Street, Regent's Park.   Here, only
a month afterwards, in April 1854, her father died.

For a while there was no material alteration either
in the circumstances or in the prospects of the family.
Christina wrote, though she did not publish, much
poetry, and also some prose.

Respecting some of her miscellaneous writings
Mr. W. M. Rossetti has written to me :

' There are *many* articles by C[hristina] on Italian
writers and other celebrities in a cyclopædia called
the " Imperial Dictionary of Biography " and edited by
Dr. Waller.   She undertook something (and may pos-

sibly have executed it) for [the Rev. Dr.] Grosart's edition of Spenser. . . . Towards 1855 a Translation was published of the " Memoirs of Mallet du Pan ": part of this was done by C[hristina], much more by myself and another [Mr. Benjamin H. Paul]. Also at some date, wh[ich] may have been tow[ards] 1865, C[hristina] certainly did some translating-work in connection with a book in Italian about Architecture—I forget the details, but *may* possibly light upon them some time—and she revised (say a little earlier) an edition (may have been [that of the] S.P.C.K. [The Society for Promoting Christian Knowledge]) of Diodati's Italian New Testament, in very small print —I recollect Gabriel remonstrated with her for over-working her eyes.'

Regarding Christina Rossetti's share in his edition of Spenser, Dr. Grosart has written to me :

' Miss Rossetti's intention to trace Italian poets in Spenser fell through from her ill-health, as I understood. She sent me at the outset two pages of note-paper with a few Dante and Boccaccio references taken, I think, from Todd's Spenser, with one or two of (possibly) her own. . . . I need hardly say that even though so slight I would gladly have sent you her notes had they been of sufficient value.'

From the diary of Ford Madox Brown comes this glimpse of her in 1856 :

Christina Rossetti called ; she is reading Carlyle with her mother.

When Arthur, the child of Mr. and Mrs. Madox Brown, died in 1856 or 1857, Christina wrote to his mother :

' Mamma unites with me in affectionate sympathy with you on the loss of poor Arthur : indeed I was quite grieved at the news Lucy brought us this morning ; and cannot forbear telling you so, though it seems almost a mockery to talk of *my* sorrow to his parents. I hope we shall all follow Nolly's [Oliver Madox Brown's] advice, and go and see him some day—Yet it is a relief poor little dear to think he is now out of all his pain for ever.'

The little incident narrated at April 10 of ' Time Flies' has no date assigned to it in that volume. It occurred, however, at the Botanical Gardens, Regent's Park, about 1860. Such an incident, if told by an ordinary narrator, would be commonplace—told as she knew how to tell it, it becomes most fascinating :

'One day long ago I sat in a certain garden by a certain ornamental water.
' I sat so long and so quietly that a wild garden crea- ture or two made its appearance : a water rat, perhaps, or a water-haunting bird. Few have been my personal experiences of the sort, and this one gratified me. I was absorbed that afternoon in anxious thought, yet the slight incident pleased me.

.　　.　　.　　.　　.　　.　　.

' Many (I hope) whom we pity as even wretched, may in reality, as I was at that moment, be conscious of some small secret fount of pleasure : a bubble, perhaps, yet lit by a dancing rainbow.
' I hope so and I think so : for we and all creatures alike are in God's hands, and God loves us.'

The next few years of Christina Rossetti's life, though not outwardly eventful, were yet important. They witnessed a gradual increase of the family pro- sperity, and they were also years in which she began to gain repute as a noticeable poet. For although her first mature volume, ' Goblin Market and Other Poems,' did not appear until 1862, a great deal of the verse composing it was written earlier. Despite the favour- able reception of her books, they did not until about 1890 bring her much money—her average income from literature up to that date hardly amounted to £30 or £45 a year. After 1890 her income from literature became relatively large.

She generally resided in London, but spent notwithstanding some time both in the country and at the seaside, her visits to congenial friends being especially sources of enjoyment to her. She first saw the sea at Herne Bay, and among other marine resorts she visited were Clacton and Deal. Her Italian poem 'Lisetta all' Amante' was written at Folkestone in August 1846, and she was again at the same place in August 1871.

She was always delicate, but more particularly so in her early years. In opening womanhood and even up to 1863 she was troubled with symptoms which, it was supposed, as has been said before, pointed to phthisis. Hence anything of the nature of a cold was always regarded with some measure of anxiety. For the benefit of her health she spent the winter months, which closed 1864 and began 1865, at Hastings, with her mother and her cousin Henrietta.

It was either during this residence at Hastings or during one of the four or five shorter visits she paid to that place that the incident occurred she recounts so excellently in 'Time Flies' under date of May 15. She there says how, when one of a luncheon party, she heard a General who was present relate that, when returning from shooting one day, he observed 'a speck in the sky.' Taking it for a wandering bird he aimed at it 'his last random shot,' but he felt no surprise at no result following when he remembered the considerable distance between him and the object. The General had at home a robin—originally wild and still allowed to go at large —a bird that had acquired a certain degree of tameness through the kindness shown to it.   To this 'free familiar bird' the General was greatly attached, but it 'never came again' after the day just mentioned, and ever afterwards he was of opinion that, on the occasion referred to, he had himself unwittingly shot it, and when he told the anecdote he was unable to do so 'without emotion.'   This is Christina's comment :

'Let us have mercy on each other and forgive : even a wronged robin's silence and absence were hard to bear.'

The officer just referred to, General Ludlow, married Miss Leigh Smith, sister of the lady who, as Mrs. Bodichon, became favourably known through her close connection with Girton College.   A portion of the winter·of 1864 was also passed by Christina Rossetti at Hastings with her uncle and cousin.

In a pleasant article entitled, 'A Poetic Trio,' contributed by 'M.' to 'The Athenæum' (No. 3,641, August 7, 1897), we find a rather amusing account of a 'great sewing competition,' in which Christina, Jean Ingelow, and Dora Greenwell engaged, in 1863–4.

Christina stayed at least on three occasions with Mr. and Mrs. Bell Scott at Newcastle-on-Tyne with especial pleasure.   Here she met Dora Greenwell, who, it will be remembered, addressed to her the fine poem beginning :

> Thou hast filled me a golden cup
> With a drink divine that glows,
> With the bloom that is flowing up
> From the heart of the folded rose.

Concerning the friendship of these two, Mr. W. M. Rossetti has written to me as follows :

'Dora and Christina met several times [at Newcastle-

on-Tyne] and liked one another much : the acquaintance may have begun towards 1858, and continued on
and off till D[ora]'s death : . . . they did not meet *often*.
I myself met D[ora] two or three times, when she was
getting on towards 40 : a slim dark rather tall woman,
of an elegant-serious type ; there was something particularly pleasing in her tone of voice and mode of elocution
—a graceful sweet tripping delivery.'

Christina visited Clifton, and Darlaston in Stafford-
shire.   On more than one occasion she stayed with her
attached friend, Anne Gilchrist, when the latter lived
at Brookbank, Shottermill, near Haslemere, a charmingly situated and most picturesque house afterwards
associated with George Eliot, for there the novelist
wrote a good deal of ' Middlemarch.'   In a published
letter Anne Gilchrist thus describes Christina after the
conclusion of her first visit to Brookbank : [1]

' We were both altogether charmed with Miss
Rossetti—there is a sweetness, an unaffected simplicity
and gentleness, with all her gifts that is very winning—
and I hope to see more of her.   She was so kind to the
children and so easy to please and make comfortable
that, though a stranger to me, she was not at all a
formidable guest.'

This sojourn was in summer, and owing to the residence at Hastings, already referred to, she was unable to
go to Brookbank in the ensuing winter.   Her fondness for
children and some of her theories about education are
both referred to in the following extract from a letter
addressed to Anne Gilchrist :

' What a great girl the little Grace of my admiring
memory has become.   Pray ask your " nurse " and your
" sunshine " to accept my love.   As to a stand in their

[1] For this, and other quotations from the same source, see *Life and
Letters of Anne Gilchrist*.

education surely they may gain more by tending a beloved mother than by a great many books ; though for all your sakes it will indeed be a joyful day when you can take your old place amongst those who love you.

'My mother and sister and William join me in all the affectionate good wishes which this season calls out. William also joins me in a return-offering of photographs, though you will notice that what represents myself is not taken from me direct but from a great drawing Gabriel did of me in 1866. This must account to you for its unblemished smoothness and finish.'

'The little Grace of my admiring memory'—Miss Grace Gilchrist, now Mrs. Frend—contributed to 'Good Words' for December 1896 an article about Christina Rossetti full of sympathetic discernment. Two extracts may be made descriptive of Mrs. Frend's early reminiscences of her :

'My first recollection of Christina Rossetti hovers in the sunny dreamland of earliest childhood, and in this, it may be, the ethereal grace of her rare poet's nature finds its most appropriate setting. For then it is that I have a vivid impression of playing a game of ball with her one summer afternoon upon a sloping lawn, under the branches of an old apple tree in the garden of a tiny hamlet among the Surrey hills. It was in the June of 1863 that Miss Christina Rossetti came upon her first memorable visit to my home there ; she was then a dark-eyed, slender lady, in the plenitude of her poetic powers, having already written some of her most perfect poems—"Goblin Market" and "Dream Land."

'To my child's eyes she appeared like some fairy princess who had come from the sunny south to play with me. In appearance she was Italian, with olive complexion and deep hazel eyes.. She possessed, too, the beautiful Italian voice all the Rossettis were gifted with—a voice made up of strange, sweet inflexions, which rippled into silvery modulations in sustained conversation, making ordinary English words and phrases fall upon the ear with a soft, foreign, musical

intonation, though she pronounced the words themselves with the purest of English accents.   Most of all
I used to wonder at and admire the way in which she
would take up, and hold in the hollow of her hand,
cold little frogs and clammy toads, or furry many-legged
caterpillars, with a fearless love that we country children
could never emulate.   Even to the individual whisk of
one squirrel's tail from another's, or the furtive scuttle of
a rabbit across a field or common, nothing escaped her
nature-loving ken ; yet her excursions into the country
were as angels' visits, " few and far between " ; but when
there, how much she noted of flower and tree, beast and
bird !

   .   .   .   .

   ' As a quaint instance of her shyness which was
wholly charming, I can recall one little incident of her
first visit to my mother.

   ' Upon her arrival she was shown to her room, to
prepare for the simple meal of the household.   She
arrived by an afternoon train, and it must have been a
late tea-supper.   My mother, finding after the lapse
of some time that she did not appear in the drawing-
room circle, went upstairs in search of her, and, tapping
at her door, found Miss Rossetti ready, but waiting, in
some trepidation, too shy to venture down alone, or to be
formally announced by the servant, into the expectant
group in the drawing-room.'

Christina visited Cheltenham and Gloucester on four
or five occasions as the guest of her uncle, Mr. Henry
Polydore, who resided in both of these places at different
times.

Intense symbolism was an inherent attribute of her
mind, and shows itself both in her poetry and in her
prose. notably in ' Time Flies.'   In the last-named, she
tells us of the pleasure she experienced from examin-
ing the lovely tints of some ancient Venetian glass, and
how one day, when in the country, she found in a
ditch a broken bottle, which, having been oxydised, also

displayed 'in a minor key . . . a variety of iridescent tints, a sort of dull rainbow.' · She ends quaintly thus :

'If it is well for the few to rejoice in sun-rise and moon-rise it is no less well for the many to be thankful for dim rainbows.'

The fine collection of old Venetian glass she had seen at the house of Mr. Virtue Tebbs ; the broken bottle she had found near Cheltenham.

During one of these sojourns at Cheltenham she visited Malvern, and in the course of a letter addressed to Anne Gilchrist calls it ' very delightful with its grand old priory church and view-commanding hills.'

A little note from his mother to Dante Gabriel, now living at 16 Cheyne Walk, Chelsea (then called Tudor House) may be introduced here as showing the somewhat curious mixture of respect and affection with which he was regarded by his family circle.

June 27th, 1864.

' My dear Gabriel,—May I have the heartfelt pleasure of your presence at tea at 8 o'clock on *Thursday*, when a few of our friends will be assembled ?

'Pray give your ultimatum to Christina and know that I am for ever and ever

' Your affect^e mother
' FRANCES ROSSETTI.'

Christina Rossetti received a second offer of marriage —her suitor, in this instance, being a man of letters and pre-eminently a scholar. Again she was favourably disposed towards her suitor, and again, actuated by religious scruples, she was constrained to reject his offer, for, in the words of her surviving brother, he was ' either not a Christian at all, or else was a Christian of undefined and heterodox views.' This incident, which terminated about 1866, was more deeply felt by her than was her first attachment, and it is to this that the touching poem entitled 'Il Rosseggiar dell' Oriente' relates. This incident, and the other incident of a similar kind, make clear many allusions in her poetry, particularly the fine lyric called 'Memory.' <u>Both of her suitors</u> pre-deceased her.

Here are inserted some letters and extracts from letters addressed to Miss Lucy Madox Brown, afterwards Mrs. W. M. Rossetti. What immediately follows is of an earlier date than June 1865. 'Nolly' is, of course, Oliver Madox Brown; 'Golden Deeds' is presumably the work with that title by Miss Yonge; and 'Clemenza di Tito' is one of Metastasio's operatic dramas.

166 Albany St. N.W.
Wednesday Evening.

'My dear Lucy,—I am in fact only Maria's pen. Yesterday she sought but failed to find an opportunity of asking you "unbeknown" whether Nolly happens to possess 'Golden Deeds,' a little book which she thinks might interest him and also supply him with pictorial subjects. Will you accept her love and oblige her by an answer, as she proposes to herself the pleasure of giving it him in case he has not got it?

'In thinking about my "Clemenza di Tito," I have no reason to believe that when I lent it Mrs. [Madox] Brown it was anything but a perfect copy; and I very much regret the loss of its leaf, as it is a present of my mother's and much valued by us. If by chance the missing leaf can be found I shall be particularly glad; probably we might have the volume bound, but of course not if it remains imperfect. I shall look for the leaf amongst the other music when this comes back to me; but of course it cannot be helped if it is really lost.

'I won't send kind regards, because Maria's message is somewhat in the nature of a "private."

'Always your affectionate
'CHRISTINA G. ROSSETTI.'

'Again I am Maria's pen. This time to ask your acceptance of her long-promised carte : she received it from Harrogate only this morning, and loses not a moment in sending it with her love ; only she does this by proxy because she had to go out early on a melancholy teeth expedition.

'Thank you most warmly for having done me so kind and great a service as to hunt up the missing leaf of " Clemenza " ; Mamma is as pleased as myself at its recovery.

'I saw Sir W. Jenner again to-day ; and don't feel on the high road to your pleasant party, though he says I am better.

'Mamma, William and I think of going to the Rifle soirée to-night at University College : we have a spare half ticket, and if you will like to go also, pray join us and appear under our venerable wing. Please be with us not later than a quarter before 8, as Mamma wishes not to go very late.

'I hope this will reach in time : of course if we do not see you, we must conclude you are prevented coming. (I confide to you my private opinion that William will not start before 8.)'

July 19th.

'Dear Lucy,—The enclosed knobbed bodkin will remind you of me, and is accompanied by my affectionate wishes that you may enjoy many happy returns of this day.

'With Christina's love, believe us both
'Your truly attached friends,
'FRANCES ROSSETTI.
'CHRISTINA G. ROSSETTI.'

Mr. Edmund Gosse, in the excellent article on Christina Rossetti in his admirable 'Critical Kit-Kats,' says :

'Gabriel Rossetti, both as poet and painter, remained very Italian to the last, but his sister is a thorough Englishwoman. Unless I make a great mistake, she has scarcely visited Italy, and in her poetry the landscape and the observation of Nature are not only English, they are so thoroughly local that I doubt whether there is one touch in them all which proves her to have strayed more than fifty miles from London in any direction. I have no reason for saying so beyond internal evidence, but I should be inclined to suggest that the county of Sussex alone is capable of having supplied all the imagery which Miss Rossetti's poems contain. Her literary repertory, too, seems purely English ; there is hardly a solitary touch in her work which betrays her transalpine parentage.'

Surely, however, the critic's statement here is somewhat needlessly emphatic. It is true that according to our modern notions Christina Rossetti had not much foreign travel. Yet she was not wholly without this experience ; its influence has left abiding traces on her writings ; and, even in her poetry, once and again she described aspects of Nature not to be seen in England. Although the opportunity for travel possessed by her brother William was necessarily limited to an annual summer vacation, owing to his professional duties at Somerset House ; yet on two occasions he travelled with Christina on the Continent of Europe. In 1861 he took his mother and herself to Paris and Normandy, returning by Jersey, the sojourn abroad occupying about six weeks. Her second and most important tour, though only filling the same space of time, occurred in 1865. With the same companions she then proceeded through France and by Basle, the Lake of Lucerne, and the St. Gotthard to Italy. The party visited Como, Pavia, Brescia, Bergamo, and Milan, taking on their way northwards the Splügen, Schaffhausen, Freiburg in the Black Forest, and Strasburg. Mountain scenery delighted Christina inexpressibly ; pictures, and such matters of fine art appealed to her much less. There is a most interesting hint as to her feelings in Switzerland in 'Time Flies,' under date June 10. She there speaks of what she aptly calls the 'saddening influence of mountain scenery.' For this she does not seek to assign a definite cause, suggesting, however, that because the ' mass and loftiness ' of high mountains far exceed the ' physical magnitudes ' —magnitudes mainly of sea and sky—to which our eyes are accustomed, therefore ' their sublimity impresses us like want of sympathy.'

This is, I think, a very just explanation of a mood of mind which many of us who have lived much amid high mountains must have often known. The truly great poet, by subtle discrimination, often reveals to us the secrets of mental phenomena. In the passage just referred to she goes on to tell how she was ' saddened and probably weary.' (Readers of Mr. Ruskin will remember his experience in like circumstances as to the Alps.) Then she ' passed indoors, losing sight for a moment of the mountains.' But here let me supplement the narrative, and tell what happened subsequently, from information given me by Mr. W. M. Rossetti, who was present. By-and-by, when she entered the large saloon of the Hôtel Schweizerhof at Lucerne, where she was staying, she beheld suddenly, from a window, ' with apparent ecstacy,' the magnificent panorama of the Righi towards sunset. She makes an eloquent reference to this incident in Sonnet XXII. of ' Later Life,' where she says :

> The mountains in their overwhelming might
> > Moved me to sadness when I saw them first,
> And afterwards they moved me to delight ;
> > Struck harmonies from silent chords which burst
> > Out into song, a song by memory nursed ;

> For ever unrenewed by touch or sight
> Sleeps the keen magic of each day or night,
>   In pleasure and in wonder then immersed.

An equally interesting allusion to this tour is seen in Sonnet XXI. of the same fine series, where she gives a most charming reminiscence of Como.   She says :

> A host of things I take on trust : I take
>   The nightingales on trust, for few and far
>   Between those actual summer moments are
> When I have heard what melody they make.
> So chanced it once at Como on the Lake :
>   But all things, then, waxed musical ; each star
>   Sang on its course, each breeze sang on its car,
> All harmonies sang to senses wide awake.

She adds, after a few lines of further vivid description,

> For June that night glowed like a doubled June.

Another incident of this tour worthy of record is mentioned in 'Time Flies' under date September 16. Christina there expresses her regret that, when descending a mountain, she did not turn to look at a foambow on the mountain torrent seen by her companion, and she evidently felt poignant disappointment at having accidentally missed the beautiful sight.   Her companion was her brother William, and she was descending the Splügen.   As a sequel to the foregoing remarks an extract from a letter to Anne Gilchrist may be quoted, more especially as it brings into pleasing prominence some of her marked traits, her love for her mother and her love for children :

' Our small continental tour proved enjoyable beyond words ; a pleasure in one's life never to be forgotten. My mother throve abroad, and not one drawback worth dwelling upon occurred to mar our contentment.   Such unimaginable beauties and grandeur of nature as we beheld no pen could put on paper ; so I obviously need not exert myself to tell you what Lucerne was like, or what the lovely majesty of Mount St. Gotthard, or what the Lake of Como, with its nightingale accompaniment, or what as much of Italy as we saw to our half-Italian hearts.   Its people is a noble people, and its very cattle are of high-born aspect.   I am glad of my Italian blood.   I don't say a word about art treasures : the truth being that I far prefer Nature treasures, but we saw glorious specimens of both classes.   Our longest stay was at Milan ; where we witnessed a rather interesting ceremony, the unveiling by Prince Omberto of a statue of Cavour.   At Milan, too, we went over a most in-teresting institution, the Ospedale Maggiore ; the children's ward was quite a pretty sight with its population of poor little patients.'

Christina says above that she will not attempt to describe Mount St. Gotthard.   Yet she did so on two occasions.   In one of the sonnets in ' Later Life ' she thus speaks :

> St. Gotthard, garden of forget-me-not :
> Yet why should such a flower choose such a spot ?
> Could we forget that way which once we went
> Though not one flower had bloomed to weave its crown ?

And some time afterwards she wrote in ' Time Flies ' under date of June 13 and 14 :

'Years ago a small party of us crossed the Alps into Italy by the Pass of Mount St. Gotthard.

'We did not tunnel our way like worms through its dense substance.   We surmounted its crest like eagles.

'Or, if you please, not at all like eagles : yet assuredly as like those born monarchs as it consisted with our possibilities to become.

.   .   .   .

'At a certain point of the ascent Mount St. Gotthard bloomed into an actual garden of forget-me-nots.

'Unforgotten and never to be forgotten that lovely

lavish efflorescence which made earth cerulean as the sky.

'Thus I remember the mountain. But without that flower of memory could I have forgotten it?

'Surely not: yet there, not elsewhere, a countless multitude of forget-me-nots made their home.'

These last two quotations are made not only for their intrinsic value, but also because they constitute a marked example of a poet putting the same ideas both into verse and into prose.

Even yet the references to her foreign travel are not exhausted. The two extracts about to be given from 'Time Flies,' under date August 4 and 22 respectively, show how keenly she could observe:

'When I was in north Italy, a region rich in sunshine, heat, beauty, it struck me that after all our English wild scarlet poppies excelled the Italian poppies in gorgeous colour.

'I should have expected the direct contrary; the more sunshine, surely the more glow and redness: yet it appeared otherwise when I came to look.

'Perhaps sheer stress of sunshine tended to bleach as well as to dye those poppies.

.   .   .   .

'In north Italy I observed that whilst the cattle are grand and beautiful beyond our English wont, the pigs are exceptionally mean and repulsive.

'Thus in one characteristically lovely land what is fair shows at its fairest, what is ugly shows at its ugliest.

'And if thus in the natural sphere, thus likewise in the spiritual sphere.'

In her last book, 'The Face of the Deep, a devotional commentary' on the Book of the Revelation (which I shall deal with fully in Chapter IX.), concerning the Biblical passage—

**And the heaven departed as a scroll when it is
rolled together ; and every mountain and island
were moved out of their places—**

she writes :

'Once, years ago in Normandy after a day of
flooding rain, I beheld the clouds roll up and depart and
the auspicious sky re-appear.   Once in crossing the
Splügen I beheld that moving of the mists which gives
back to sight a vanished world.   Those veils of heaven
and earth removed, beauty came to light.   What will it
be to see this same visible heaven itself removed and
unimaginable beauty brought to light in glory and
terror ! auspicious to the elect, by aliens unendurable.'

Her poem 'En Route,' dated June 1865—probably
one of the most beautiful, as being one of the most
personal of her poems—contains these lines :

> Farewell, land of love, Italy,
> Sister-land of Paradise :
> With mine own feet I have trodden thee
> Have seen with mine own eyes :
> I remember, thou forgettest me,
> I remember thee.
>
> Blessed be the land that warms my heart,
> And the kindly clime that cheers,
> And the cordial faces clear from art,
> And the tongue sweet in mine ears :
> Take my heart, its truest tenderest part,
> Dear land, take my tears.

About them her surviving brother has written :

' The passionate delight in Italy to which the second
section of " En Route " bears witness suggests that she
was almost an alien—or, like her father, an exile—in
the North.   She never perhaps wrote anything better.
I can remember the intense relief and pleasure with
which she saw lovable Italian faces and heard musical

Italian speech at Bellinzona after the somewhat hard
and nipped quality of the German Swiss.'

Long before I came to know Christina Rossetti
personally, towards the close of her life, through the
kindness of the late Dr. Gordon Hake, I had been on very
intimate terms with the late Rev. Dr. R. F. Littledale,
the noted Anglican theologian and controversialist.
Dr. Littledale had first met Christina Rossetti at the
house of William Bell Scott in Elgin Road, Notting
Hill, soon after the latter's return to London in 1864.
She had become much attached to this clergyman,
with whom, indeed, she had had constant and close
intercourse of a religious kind. My own relations with
him were not the same, being none other than those of
ordinary friendship. But I had seen much of him, and
had loved him, and I think it was her knowledge of this
fact that caused Christina Rossetti to place me immediately on a widely different footing with herself than
she would otherwise have done. In truth my acquaint-
anceship with her at once became friendship—if I may
use such a term to characterise my relations with one so
eminent. From the very first she treated me not only
with a courtesy that had something peculiarly winning
about it, but with a degree of confidence and unreserve
which is rare, and which, coming from such a woman,
was singularly fascinating.

As to Dr. Littledale, she wrote in 'Time Flies' under
date of April 21 :

'Once in conversation I happened to lay stress on
the virtue of resignation, when the friend I spoke to
depreciated resignation in comparison with conformity
to the Divine Will.

'My spiritual height was my friend's spiritual hillock.

' Not that he reproved me : standing on a higher level he made the way obvious for others also to ascend.'

On more than one occasion she talked to me about Dr. Littledale at some length, and she quite agreed with me when I averred that the bursts of merriment that would break forth, despite his constant bad health and unending pain, were quite irresistible. In 'Time Flies' she has further written about him thus, though in neither case does she refer to him by name.

'He was a man . . . hindered and hampered in his career by irremediable ill-health. And moreover he was in occasional social intercourse one of the most cheerful people I ever knew.'

In 1866 Dante Gabriel made a chalk drawing of his sister. She is represented as seated at a small table. A book is before her, and her face, in profile, rests on her folded hands. Mr. Shields (than whom surely none could be a better judge) greatly admires this drawing. From what she herself said to me I am strongly of opinion that of all her brother's portraits of herself, this was her favourite. A reproduction forms the frontispiece to this volume.

Christina Rossetti knew a little of Scotland, residing once or twice with the late Miss Alice Boyd at Penkill Castle in Ayrshire, but she never went further north. She was there in 1866, and, somewhat later, she tells Anne Gilchrist :

'If the end of my Penkill sojourn deprives me of seeing you, its beginning mulcts me of a visit to the Isle of Wight in which I was promised to meet Tennyson—poor me! This invitation was only given me yesterday, too late to be closed with : however I am not certain that in any case I should have screwed myself up to accept it, as I am shy amongst strangers and think things formidable ; '

while in 1870, to the same friend she thus writes :

' Even Naples in imagination cannot efface the quiet fertile comeliness of Penkill in reality : and when, beyond the immediate greenness, a gorgeous sunset glorifies the sea distance one scarcely need desire aught more exquisite in this world.'

Mr. Arthur Hughes, in the course of conversation, has described to me in a very vivid manner the little four-cornered window of Christina Rossetti's bedroom at Penkill, which commanded a view over an old-fashioned garden, and in which, according to Miss Boyd, as quoted by my informant, she used to stand, leaning forward, ' her elbows on the sill, her hands supporting her face '—the attitude in which she is represented in Dante Gabriel's drawing of 1866, just alluded to. ' The little window exactly framed her,' added Mr. Hughes, ' and from the garden she could be seen for hours meditating and composing.' Christina Rossetti's opinion of Miss Boyd is expressed in the following words from a letter to Anne Gilchrist :

' My more than seven weeks in Scotland proved a thorough success, and have sent me home to receive friendly congratulations on my looks and *fat*. I think my dear hostess at Penkill Castle, Miss Boyd, might charm you if you knew her : perhaps she is the prettiest handsome woman I ever met, both styles being combined in her fine face ; and Mr. and Mrs. Scott, who shared the long visit with me, are tried old friends . . . and now I am well content to be at home again, and to take my turn at housekeeping.'

In February 1867, her aunt, Margaret Polidori died.

For this lady, Dante Gabriel designed a memorial window now in Christ Church, Albany Street.

In June of the same year, with her mother, her sister Maria Francesca, and her brother William, Christina removed to 56 Euston Square, now 5 Endsleigh Gardens. Her aunts, Eliza and Charlotte Polidori, also lived there—the latter, however, who was at the time companion to the Dowager Marchioness of Bath at Muntham, near Arundel, only intermittingly.

At this time Christina Rossetti occasionally went into society. In 1868 Ford Madox Brown writes to his wife about one of the 'At Homes' where he gathered round him so many famous men and women :

'The Martineaus, and the Rossettis, and the Streets, can't come. However, Christina, if well enough, may.'

In April 1871 Christina was seized by 'Dr. Graves's Disease '—or ' Exophthalmic Bronchocele,' to give the complaint its technical name. As almost invariably happens with this disease, a long and serious illness followed, accompanied by great suffering, and, until 1873, her life was in constant danger. As soon as possible she was removed to Hampstead for change of air, and the 'Family Letters' of Dante Gabriel at this period bear ample testimony to his constant and affectionate solicitude on her behalf.

I might not have deemed it necessary to give precise details respecting this illness, had not the complaint unhappily left its usual traces, and modified her appearance. This was chiefly noticeable in a certain protruding of the eyes, though never, when I knew her, so pronounced as to be disagreeable ; but her brother informs me that at a much earlier date, particularly about 1872, the effects of this malady were more visible. When I first met her she had acquired much of the portliness of middle age, and her face in repose was sometimes rather heavy and even unemotional. But her smile was always delightful, and sometimes irresistibly sweet, and, when in animated conversation on some especially congenial theme, her face to the last was comely.

It is this marked difference between the comparatively unattractive aspect of her features in repose, and the great change which came over their lineaments during animation, that make her photographs taken in later life seem so unsatisfactory. There is considerable fidelity to external fact in a full-face photograph taken by Messrs. Elliott and Fry, well known through reproductions (which represents her with a book in her lap), but in it her soul's beauty, so to speak, is altogether lacking. It may be as well to quote what she herself said about this photograph, and her portraits generally, in a letter to Mrs. Patchett Martin, dated January 4, 1892 :

'The photograph I spoke of is one on sale (I believe) at Elliott and Fry's, Baker Street, and as I do not think I have a copy by me I must refer you thither. Of course if you aimed at beauty rather than at aught else, there are photographs on sale at Mansell's, 271 Oxford Street, from beautiful drawings by my brother D. G. R : but what between his being my brother and his overmastering love of beauty I dare not recommend these as equally faithful with Elliott and Fry's stern transcript. This last, and the last of the drawings, were taken I believe in the same year 1877.'

Once, when she was so good as to write her name on one of her photographs now in my possession, she mentioned Messrs. Elliott and Fry as having produced,

on the whole, perhaps the most satisfactory photographs
of her in later life. It was agreed that I was to go to
Baker Street, procure specimens of the two photographs
obtainable there—that just mentioned, and another with
the face in profile—and to submit them for her inspection,
retaining the one she most approved. I determined
beforehand not to express my own opinion as to their
relative merits, but I cordially agreed with her when she
chose unhesitatingly that in profile with downcast eyes.

On four or five occasions, in the years between 1870
and 1883, Christina Rossetti lived for a while, though not
herself a patient, at the Convalescent Hospital, Meads,
Eastbourne, connected with the Anglican Sisterhood of
All Saints, Margaret Street, London. Maria Francesca,
deeply imbued with devotional feeling and allied by all
her religious sympathies with the Anglo-Catholic school
in the Anglican Church, had entered this community as
a novice in 1873, and in 1874 had joined it finally as a
fully professed Sister. Hence Christina, who had not
only a deep love, but a profound reverence, for Maria in
all things, was much *en rapport* with this Sisterhood.
Her brother has written to me :

'She was (I rather think) an outer Sister—but in no
sort of way professed—of the Convent which Maria afterwards joined—Also at one time (1860 to '70) she used
pretty often to go to an Institution at Highgate for
redeeming "Fallen Women"—It seems to me that at
one time they wanted to make her a sort of superintendent there, but she declined—In her own neighbourhood, Albany Street, she did a deal of district
visiting and the like.

'One thing which occupied C[hristina] to an extent
one would hardly credit was the making-up of scrapbooks for Hospital patients or children—This may
possibly have begun before she removed to Torrington

Sq[uare] : was certainly in very active exercise for several years ensuing—say up to 1885. When I called to see her and my mother it was 9 chances out of 10 that I found her thus occupied—I daresay she may have made up at least 50 biggish scrapbooks of this kind— taking some pains in adapting borderings to the pages etc. etc.'

At Meads the incident took place narrated under June 26 in 'Time Flies,' and readers of that book will remember in what a vivid manner it is related. She tells how 'one summer night' she saw 'a Parable of Nature' :

'The gas was alight in my little room with its paperless bare wall.'

On the wall there was a spider. He perceived his shadow without understanding what it was, and 'was mad to disengage himself from the horrible pursuing inalienable presence.' She brings the whole scene before us concisely in a few well-chosen words, and to her 'this self-haunted spider' is a symbol of an 'impenitent sinner who having outlived enjoyment remains isolated irretrievably with his own horrible loathsome self.' To another mind such an occurrence might have seemed trivial or have passed unnoticed. To her with her genius for symbolism it appeared most noteworthy.

The following letter refers to a later visit to East- bourne with her mother :

111 Pevensey Road—Eastbourne.
Friday Afternoon.

'My dear Gabriel,—We got down comfortably yes- terday, but then ensued not very short of 3 hours' lodging seeking ! However, at last we settled where you see us to be ; and here we are very comfortable tho' by no means in the quarter of Eastbourne we aimed

at, & with a repulsive prospect of having to remove
about August on account of heavy rise of rents. All
this makes it very possible that we may devote part of
this initial week to further researches, in hopes of finding
something more permanently promising than our actual
rooms ; which meanwhile are spacious, commodious &
much to our taste. Our mother sends you love, & I
rejoice to say that the extra fatigue of these last few
days she has borne admirably. This morning we were
out, seated very comfortably most of the time, for
not much less than 3 hours, the morning being bright
and neither too hot nor too cold. Eastbourne is
enlarged and altered since my recollection of it. We
have some thoughts of driving over to the Hospital [at
Meads] one day, & seeing whether in that neighbourhood we might light upon aught eligible. But unless
you hear from us again, please conclude us to be staying
just where we are.

'Always your affectionate sister,
'CHRISTINA G. ROSSETTI.'

Much of Christina Rossetti's life was devoted to
ministering to her near relations, and once and again,
in the opinion of some of her friends, she showed towards
them a greater ardour of devotion than was compatible
with her own health, abandoning, for instance, for their
sakes, without a murmur, visits to the country that
otherwise she would have relished greatly. She soothed
her father in his last illness ; she ministered unceasingly
to her brother Gabriel, to her sister Maria, and to
her aunts, the Misses Polidori, the last of whom only
pre-deceased her by eighteen months ; but the chief
ministration of her life was her ministration to her
mother. Anyone who knew her, even after her mother's
death, could not fail to be aware of the sweet influence
that mother had exercised, and still continued to
exercise over her. Mr. Sharp tells touchingly how, at

her mother's request, she read to him Southwell's poem
'The Burning Babe,' and, on a subsequent occasion, her
own lines beginning :

Heaven's chimes are slow, but sure to strike at last.

Mr. Sharp says that Christina was in the habit of remarking that if Maria Francesca had been her younger
instead of her elder sister she would have become celebrated, and that she was prevented from achieving fame
only by 'religious scruples' and domestic cares. Certainly
it is true that Christina had the very highest opinion of
her sister's gifts, and was never weary of speaking in
their praise. One afternoon, in the last year of her life,
I called upon her. After some conversation on quite
other subjects, she said, with an eagerness unusual to her,
and which surprised me, as I did not then understand it,
'Do you admire and study Dante?'

I answered that although of course I admired him,
and had some general knowledge concerning him, I
could scarcely describe myself as a student.

'Ah then,' she exclaimed with renewed eagerness,
'I have just the book to help you. Messrs. Longmans
have just issued in their Silver Library a new edition of
my sister's book on Dante. They have just sent me a
copy, and I should be much pleased if you will be kind
enough to accept it.'

Whenever Christina Rossetti wished to confer a
favour, her manner of doing so was as if she were about
to ask one.

On my next visit, nothing seemed to give her greater
pleasure than the information that I had read the book
and admired it.

Over and above her deep concern for all that pertained to her sister, she was herself a student of Dante, though not in so profound a sense as her father, her sister, Dante Gabriel, or William. As to this aspect of her character Mr. Sharp reports a very interesting utterance :

' I wish [she said] I too could have done something for Dante in England ! Maria wrote her fine and helpful book, William's translation of the " Divina Commedia " is the best we have, and Gabriel's " Dante and his Circle " is a monument of loving labor that will outlast either. But I, alas, have neither the requisite knowledge nor the ability.'

Her brother William, however, desires me to mention at this point that Christina considered the translation of Dante in *terza rima* by Charles Bagot Cayley a 'far more important and satisfactory achievement' than his.

In 'The Century Magazine' for February 1884 she wrote a study of Dante, calling it 'Dante : The Poet Illustrated out of the Poem.' It is an essay written in that quiet manner peculiar to much of her prose : as far as I am aware, it has not been reprinted. Not confining herself to the literary aspect of her subject merely, she dwells at some length on Dante's spiritual relations with Beatrice Portinari and his earthly relations with Gemma Donati. An article from her pen on the same subject, entitled 'Dante : an English Classic,' appeared in the 'Churchman's Shilling Magazine' in the latter part of 1867.

She did not confine the expression of her high opinion of her sister's ' Shadow of Dante ' to conversation merely. She expressed it in her writings, and some of these references are so intrinsically worthy of record that I make no apology for quoting them. In her commentary on the text—

And they had a king over them which is the angel
of the bottomless pit, whose name in the Hebrew
tongue is Abaddon, but in the Greek tongue hath his
name Apollyon—

(' The Face of the Deep,' p. 264) she writes :

'" And they had a king over them . . . whose name
. . . is Abaddon, . . . Apollyon."—Whether named
King Abaddon or King Apollyon, his English equivalent
is King Destroyer. Whatever we call him he remains
the same : were we to call him King Preserver it would
modify neither his nature nor his office. Being a
destroyer, our safety lies in recognising, acknowledging,
fleeing him as such. And further : so far as we are
constituted our brother's keeper, our brother's safety
similarly lies in our plainly calling him a destroyer ;
and never toning him down as a negation of good,
or even unloathingly as an archangel ruined ; which
last suggestion I cull from my sister's *Shadow of
Dante*, where she contrasts Milton's Satan with Dante's
Lucifer.

'" Sins for like reason should be spoken of simply as
what they are, never palliatingly or jocosely. Lies and
drunkenness should bear their own odious appellations,
not any conventional substitute. But some sins "it is a
shame to speak of" : true : so let us not speak of them
except under necessity ; and under necessity even of
them truthfully. "Woe unto them that call evil good,
and good evil ; and put darkness for light, and light
for darkness ; that put bitter for sweet, and sweet for
bitter !" '

And again, in the same book, in reference to the
text—

And the great dragon was cast out, that old ser-
pent called the Devil, and Satan, which deceiveth the
whole world : he was cast out into the earth, and his
angels were cast out with him—

she exclaims somewhat naively :

'Whilst studying the devil I must take heed that my
study become not devilish by reason of sympathy. As

to gaze down a precipice seems to fascinate the gazer towards a shattering fall ; so is it spiritually perilous to gaze on excessive wickedness, lest its immeasurable scale should fascinate us as if it were colossal without being monstrous. A quotation from my sister's *Shadow of Dante* speaks to the point :—

'" Some there are who, gazing upon Dante's Hell mainly with their own eyes, are startled by the grotesque element traceable throughout the Cantica as a whole, and shocked at the even ludicrous tone of not a few of its parts. Others seek rather to gaze on Dante's Hell with Dante's eyes ; these discern in that grotesqueness a realised horror, in that ludicrousness a sovereign contempt of evil. . . . They remember that the Divine Eternal Wisdom Himself, the Very and Infallible Truth, has, not once nor twice, characterized impiety and sin as Folly ; and they feel in the depths of the nature wherewith He has created them that whatever else Folly may be and is, it is none the less essentially monstrous and ridiculous. . . . A sense of the utter degradation, loathsomeness, despicableness of the soul which by deadly sin besots Reason and enslaves Free Will passes from the Poet's mind into theirs ; while the ghastly definiteness and adaptation of the punishments enables them to touch with their finger the awful possibility and actuality of the Second Death, and thus for themselves as for others to dread it more really, to deprecate it more intensely, Dante's Lucifer does appear " less than Archangel ruined," immeasurably less ; for he appears Seraph wilfully fallen. No illusive splendour is here to dazzle eye and mind into sympathy with rebellious pride ; no vagueness to shroud in mist things fearful or things abominable. Dante's Devils are hateful and hated, Dante's reprobates loathsome and loathed, despicable and despised, or at best miserable and commiserated. . . . Dante is guiltless of seducing any soul of man towards making or calling Evil his Good."'

And yet once more, in the same work, in allusion to the text—

And here is the mind which hath wisdom. The

seven heads are seven mountains, on which the woman sitteth (Revelation xvii. 9)—

she says :

'Dante in the DIVINA COMMEDIA (*see* my sister's *A Shadow of Dante*) tells us how he "dreamed of a woman stammering, squinting, lame of foot, maimed of hands and ashy pale. He gazed on her, and lo ! under his gaze her form straightened, her face flushed, her tongue loosed to the Siren's song." '

Concerning her sister's conduct when invited to look at some prints from Blake, she writes in ' Time Flies,' under date of April 15, though without giving names of person or artist :

' I have never forgotten the courageous reverence with which one to whom a friend was exhibiting prints from the Book of Job, avowed herself afraid to look at a representation which went counter to the Second Commandment, and looked not at it.

' A host of us talk " as seeing Him Who is invisible " : she so acted.

' Blessed she who then set to her seal that God is true, and since then has " died in faith." '

There was a vein of strong practical commonsense in Christina Rossetti, as shown in the entry of ' Time Flies ' appertaining to May 7 :

' A lovely young woman (not then of my acquaintance) went one evening to a concert, her face swollen and bound up, observing that she went not to be seen but to hear. She had, I believe, a methodical brain in that charming head of hers. Certainly on this occasion she drew the line accurately between what is and what is not essential to a listener. Thus, despite her swollen face, she went with a fair prospect of enjoyment.

' Half the mortifications of life (many of them lifelong mortifications) spring from a confusion in our own minds as, to what the particular occasion, connexion, circumstance, demands of us.

'We insist on being attractive, when all that is required of us is to be attracted, edified, or it may be merely entertained.'

The young lady referred to here, Miss Rosetta Wood, was one of her sister's pupils in Italian.

There are several other allusions to her sister in Christina Rossetti's writings. Evidently these allusions are all spontaneous, and in truth reveal a beautiful feature of Christina's character, the passionate fervour which underlay her usual calm demeanour.

In her remarks in 'Time Flies,' under date July 2, regarding the Feast of the Visitation of the Virgin, she tells us how long ago a 'dear speaker' suggested that 'Righteousness and peace have kissed each other' would be a suitable passage 'for the Salutation.' The 'dear speaker' was her sister Maria. Again, under date of July 4, which has reference to the exhumation of the remains of St. Martin, after some wise observations respecting the usual undesirability of such practices, she tells us how 'one no longer present with us, but to whom I cease not to look up,' would not enter the Mummy Room of the British Museum because she realised how the general Resurrection might happen even as she looked at 'those solemn corpses turned into a sight for sight-seers.' That 'one' was again her sister Maria. Still further in 'Time Flies,' under date April 22, she tells this characteristic anecdote :

'One of the most genuine Christians I ever knew, once took lightly the dying out of a brief acquaintance which had engaged her warm heart, on the ground that such mere tastes and glimpses of congenial intercourse on earth wait for their development in heaven.

' *Then* she knew Whom she trusted : *now* (please God) she knows as she is known.

I am permitted to say here that the ' brief acquaintance which had engaged' the 'warm heart' of Maria Francesca was with Mr. John Ruskin. In the Prefatory Note of Christina's ' Face of the Deep' she once more mentions her sister, though not by name :

' A dear saint—I speak under correction of the Judgment of the Great Day, yet think not then to have my word corrected—this dear person once pointed out to me Patience as our lesson in the Book of Revelation.
'Following the clue thus afforded me, I seek and hope to find Patience in this Book of awful import. Patience, at the least: and along with that grace whatever treasures beside God may vouchsafe me. Bearing meanwhile in mind how " to him that knoweth to do good, and doeth it not, to him it is sin."'

CHAPTER III

BIOGRAPHICAL (*continued*)

(Mainly 1874–1886)

Kelmscott Manor House—Removal to 30 Torrington Square—Cheyne Walk
'—Bognor—Hunter's Forestall—Death of her sister Maria—Letters to
her brothers—Walton-on-the-Naze—Mr. Frederic Shields—Discusses
religious problems—Her opinion of Elizabeth Barrett Browning, Adelaide Procter, and Anne Radcliffe—Autobiographical allusions ' Time
Flies'—Memorial window to Dante Gabriel at Birchington, designed
by Mr. Shields, and correspondence with Mr. Shields about it—Her
suggestions for decoration of chapel at Eaton Hall—Interest in social
questions—Correspondence with Mr. Shields respecting her mother's
last illness and death—Mr. Watts-Dunton on her mother's influence
on Christina, and Christina's influence on her elder brother.

DURING her elder brother's long residence at Kelmscott Manor House, beginning in 1871, and continuing
with interruptions until July 1874, Christina was a guest
there, and Mr. Theodore Watts-Dunton, who was also
a guest, has pointed out a noteworthy contrast between
the brother and sister in the way in which they regarded
Nature.   Speaking of Dante Gabriel, he says :

' At Kelmscott, for instance, nothing would make
him more surprised than to see Christina and myself
lingering over a patch of those lovely many-coloured
mosses upon the old apple-trees in the garden, which
look as if embossed with miniature forests in jewel-
work.'

On Mr. William Michael Rossetti's marriage in March 1874, to Miss Lucy Madox Brown, the Misses Polidori went to live at 12 Bloomsbury Square, and Christina and her mother visited them frequently. In October 1876 Christina, her mother, and the Misses Polidori settled at 30 Torrington Square, though Miss Charlotte Polidori, being still companion to the Dowager Marchioness of Bath, was at first not constantly there.

Admirers of Mr. Watts-Dunton are looking forward to his promised volume of reminiscences, in which they hope he will tell them much about Christina Rossetti during her sojourns at Cheyne Walk; at Kelmscott; at Bognor; at Hunter's Forestall, near Herne Bay, in 1877; and at Birchington-on-Sea in the spring of 1882. These sojourns were chiefly on account of, or because she was in attendance on, Dante Gabriel. Dante Gabriel spent the Christmas of 1875 at Aldwick Lodge, near Bognor, in the company of his mother, his two aunts, his sister Christina, Mr. Watts-Dunton, Dr. Gordon Hake, and the latter's sons, Mr. George Hake, Mr. T. St. E. Hake, and Mr. Henry Hake.

What follows, addressed to Mrs. W. M. Rossetti, may be quoted because of its allusion to Bognor:

Aldwick Lodge-near-Bognor —
Tuesday 28th. [Dec. 1875.]

'My dear Lucy,—Oddly enough, I have to send back again to London an "at home" which came to me this morning for you; happily not too late even for the earliest evening in question.

'Our party here has been very pleasant. To-day it breaks up in the main, tho' I suppose our section will not return to Bloomsbury before Thursday. Please, accepting family loves and best seasonable wishes, let William

F

also have a share of them ; and tell him that Dr. [Gordon] Hake appears gratified at the prospect of an Academy review from his pen, tho' I was not so rash as to announce one positively.

'As many kisses as will not burden you to Olivia [at that date her only niece]. Mamma charges me to hope for her that the poor little arm has recovered from its vaccination: poor little plump arm, beginning its troubles so early.

'If Mrs. Bromley is still with you, will you please offer her my remembrances. I hope your family gathering proved an enjoyable one, but I suppose the Hüffers (*sic*) could not be with you. I wonder if our connexion has become enlarged since we left Euston Sq.

'Your affectionate sister,
'CHRISTINA G. ROSSETTI.'

At this point is introduced a letter addressed to her brother Gabriel. All her letters dated from 12 Bloomsbury Square were written between April 1874 and September 1876 :

12 Bloomsbury Square—W.C.
Tuesday Afternoon. [September 1874.]

'My dear Gabriel,—Mamma thinks, with her own dear love to you, that Maria's remarks on the Sacred Picture may interest you, & will at least show you how your kind thought is appreciated. To direct your eye to the passage concerning it and you, I have drawn an initiatory & a final *hand*; which will show you how great has been my profiting by early art-lessons from great Masters. But of course the whole letter is open to you.

'Please observe my address. Mamma and I are paying a visit here to my Aunts, & it strikes Mamma that we 4 should enjoy paying a visit to you at Chelsea, if there were any morning when without trenching on your business engagements you could devote an hour to us. If then you can lay finger on such an hour any day for a fortnight or so to come, please notify it to us : of course Aunt Charlotte's stays in Bloomsbury are never *very* long, & the duration of this present one is uncertain.

'Lucy has made steady progress, though still she is somewhat invalided : To-day Mamma & Aunt Charlotte called in Euston Square, & found it so. The distance deters me from making a call, but I saw Lucy as lately as yesterday before coming here.

'Your affec. sister

'Aunt Charlotte's love to you.'

In 1874 Christina Rossetti wrote thus to Oliver Madox Brown, the 'too-lifelike albatross' being an allusion possibly to a sketch of his inspired by Coleridge's 'Ancient Mariner':

12 Bloomsbury Square—W.C.
Wednesday.

'My dear Nolly,—I have the pleasure of redeeming my promise, & offering you my first essay in mitten making. I fear my crimson is not crimson enough : yet pray do not reject it from sometimes warming the hand which harrowed me up by a certain too-lifelike albatross.

'With cordial remembrances to Mr. & Mrs. Madox Brown

'Very sincerely yours'

The letters to Dante Gabriel that follow immediately belong to 1875, or possibly 1876.

56 Euston Square—N.W.
Friday 29 [1876.]

'My dear Gabriel,—Let me renew my thanks for the poor dear " Elephant " book, whose pathetic ending is truly painful and goes to one's heart. Delicious is the prosperous Elephant ladling out rice to mendicants : I wish all Elephants were prosperous.

'A few days ago I saw Mme. Bodichon, who sends a cordial message of remembrance to you, and would like some afternoon to pay your studio a visit "between lights" —so very likely she will do so. What a fine looking personage she is. She let me look at a number of her paintings, too, which make up quite an interesting gallery, from Algiers, Sussex, &c.

'I saw Mr. [Madox] Brown's Sheffield portrait the other day. He is invariably cordial and kindly—the man, I mean, not the canvas—and even now it might be the sitter ! ! '

56 Euston Square—N.W.
Thursday morning.
[Probably written in 1875 or 1876.]

'Dear old Gabriel,—Mamma is so impressed with the beauty of to-day for you as a long working day, & all is so doubtful as to the hour at which we may leave the [Bell] Scotts, that with her very best love she announces that we will *not* have the pleasure of visiting you & your studio this afternoon ; but will look forward in a general way to the same indulgence on some future occasion.

'Have you ever noticed the large modern clematis in blossom ? Mamma and I saw a house full of it at the Botanic Gardens the other day, & I really think it must be a flower adapted to pictorial purposes. The old-fashioned garden clematis—tho' indeed these new ones also profess to be all hardy,—beautiful as it is, is beautiful in really quite a different style.

'Affectionately your sister'

[Written about 1876, or perhaps later.]

'My dear Gabriel,—My spirits rose like quicksilver at the news in your letter.

'Since we spoke together of Fiammetta's bower I have recollected *clematis*, not a tree certainly but a climber attaining any height you please. The old-fashioned clematis was so far as I know limited in blossom to purple or white ; but nowadays you see it with much larger flowers, and these of many tints, deep and pale, of lilac and rose colour ; besides of course white. The Xmas Rose in number and arrangement of petals, as well as in their shape and in the central tuft of the blossom, does strongly assimilate with many a modern clematis. The foliage, however, is very different. I just tell you this in case it may suggest anything. I think, but I cannot remember with certainty, that I may have seen the clematis house in the Botanical Gardens in full bloom as early as about Easter.

'Always your affec. sister'

'If you like to lay in a bottle of *dye*, I will try my hand on toning your slippers on Boxing-day morning ; if, as I expect, Mamma and I dine & sleep at your house the night before. Or why not try sending to a dyer's ?'

30 Torrington Sq.—W.C.
Wednesday.

'My dear Gabriel,—The grouse have proved eatable, and this is proved by their having been eaten. Our mother's love to you in commemoration of the event, and mine after the same exceptional feast. So never hope to see those birds again !

'Some of the London directories have " Rossetti "—: I did not know the Post Office D. was a defaulter. *I*, however individually do not figure in such prominent pages, but consider myself sufficiently represented by the insertion of Mamma. I do not want to notify to all whom it may and whom it may not concern my private and personal habitat.

'Affectionately yours
'CHRISTINA G. ROSSETTI.'

The next letter, written in 1875 or 1876 to Mrs. W. M. Rossetti, has reference to a domestic difficulty. 'Mr. Cayley' is Charles Bagot Cayley:

56 Euston Square—N.W.
Wednesday morning.

'My dear Lucy,—Thank you for your note of news, —yet not literally of news—as William had already written. Mamma and I feel sufficiently at ease in our hermitage not to care to vacate it : you, with a baby, are quite differently situated from our sober selves. I hope the Board of Works will act as becomes it ; tho', so common is scarlet fever, that I am not inclined to connect this particular instance of it with the condition of.

the enclosure.   I hope the poor invalid next door, which-
ever of the family it may be, will do well.

'Pray remember us both very cordially to Mr. &
Mrs. Madox Brown, giving our loves to William.   Mr.
Cayley owes you thanks for the prospectus of "confér-
ences," & thinks to pay them through me : permit us !'

From a marginal note in her own handwriting in a
copy of 'Time Flies,' now in the possession of her
younger brother, it appears that the incident described
in the following passage occurred at Eastbourne :

'I remember rising early once to see the sun rise.
'I rose too early, and waited wearily and impatiently.
'At length the sun rose.
'At length ?   Scarcely.   The sun kept time, though
I kept it not : the sun lagged not because I hurried.'

This somewhat bald and matter-of-fact way of alluding to so interesting a phenomenon has no doubt been
occasionally disappointing to those who remember her
loving eye for Nature.   They will observe, however, the
central idea in her mind here is that 'the sun kept time,
though I kept it not,' applied as an emblem of the second
coming of Christ.   Possibly, also, she would have
devoted more attention to the physical aspects of the
sunrise had it not been in all likelihood a disappointing
one, such a one, for instance, as when the sun mounts
above the horizon in a colourless watery haze.   A
correspondent, in a letter to 'The Daily News' that
appeared shortly after her death, narrates how Christina
told her once (at a period later than this visit to Eastbourne) that she (Christina) had never seen a sunrise —
by which she of course meant a sunrise rich in the
'tasselled hangings of the clouds' such as a poet thinks
of almost involuntarily, whenever the word 'sunrise' is

mentioned.   Such a sunrise she saw afterwards at
Hunter's Forestall in the company of Mr. Theodore
Watts-Dunton, to whom she also had said that she had
never seen a sunrise.   In his usual concise and original
manner Mr. Watts-Dunton described what happened in
'The Nineteenth Century' of February 1895.

'I believe that it [a sunrise] is a phenomenon not
commonly observed by poets, and that is why it so
commonly occurs that a poet's description of the cloud-
pageantry of a sunrise is evidently borrowed from his
recollection of the sunsets he has seen.   No doubt, as I
said to Christina, the two are alike in many ways, and
yet in many ways they are extremely different.
'Upon a certain occasion she made up her mind that
a sunrise she would see, and one morning we went out
just as the chilly but bewitching shiver of the dawn-
breeze began to move, and the eastern sky began slowly
to grow grey.
'Early as it was, however, many of the birds were
awake, and waiting to see what we went out to see, as
we knew by twitter after twitter coming from the
hedgerows.   Christina was not much interested at first,
but when the grey became slowly changed into a kind
of apple-green crossed by bars of lilac, and then by
bars of pink and gold, and, finally, when the sun rose
behind a tall clump of slender elms so close together
that they looked like one enormous tree, whose
foliage was sufficiently thin to allow the sunbeams to
pour through it as through a glittering lacework of
dewy leaves, she confessed that no sunset could sur-
pass it.
'And when the sun, growing brighter still, and falling
upon a silver sheet of mist in which the cows were
lying, turned it into a sheet of gold, and made each
brown patch on each cow's coat gleam like burnished
copper, then she admitted that a sunrise surpassed a
sunset, and was worth getting up to see.   She stood
and looked at it, and her lips moved, but in a whisper
that I could not hear.'

The most touching of all Christina's references to her sister is to be found in ' Time Flies ' under date November 7. Maria Francesca had expressed an aversion to the old style of funeral, with its rigid ceremonial and its paraphernalia of grief, and had said in answer to some plea of Christina's in favour of it, ' Why make everything as hopeless looking as possible ? '

' And at that moment which was sad only for us who lost her, all turned out in harmony with her holy hope and joy.

' Flowers covered her, loving mourners followed her, hymns were sung at her grave, the November day brightened, and the sun (I vividly remember) made a miniature rainbow in my eyelashes.

' I have often thought of that rainbow since.'

Maria Francesca was interred in Brompton Cemetery in November 1876, according to the simple rules of the sisterhood of which she was a member.

Here may be given some letters addressed to her brother Gabriel from Torrington Square. The ' John Gilpin ' referred to in the succeeding letter was illustrated by the late R. Caldecott.

January 1, 1879.

' My dear Gabriel,—This is my first letter this year and carries you our dearest mother's and my own love and very best wishes for your health and prosperity. We hope—we so wish to hear—that your throat and cough are better.

' I am indulging in sending you the " John Gilpin " we talked about. I hope you will not despise our taste, but we are quite amused by it. The expressions are surely consummate in some of the faces. Aunt Charlotte sends you her love. She came up yesterday, but we fear we shall keep her for only a week. Yesterday also William, going out for the first time, came here—

looking quite as well as can be expected, but of course
pulled down.   He was in one large gouty shoe, and was
still taking colchicum

' Always your loving sister '

The ' critic ' referred to in what follows was the late
Ashcroft Noble, and the probable date of the letter was
1879.

30 Torrington Square—W.C.
Saturday.

' My dear Gabriel,—I take it most kindly of you that
among other interesting matter you put forward to my
critic what you conceive to be my claim on name and
fame.

' What an interesting and intelligent letter his is : I
will, as you suggest, keep it till we meet.   But before
it came mamma and I were already planning a visit to
you next week, yourself and all else permitting.   Shall
it be next Tuesday towards 3 o'clock as usual?   If we
do not hear from you, we will conclude Tuesday ; but
if your afternoon is then preoccupied, please propose a
different day ; Thursday would suit us just as well.
Our Mother's love, as ever '

The ' sealskin which warms her heart as well as her
person,' a phrase in the letter that succeeds, alludes to
a present given by Dante Gabriel to his mother.   Signor
Maenza ' and his wife an Englishwoman '—old friends of
the Rossetti family—had Dante Gabriel as their paying
guest for his health's sake twice during his boyhood, at
Boulogne-sur-Mer, where they resided : [1]

Thursday morning.
[Probably written in 1879.]

' My dear Gabriel,—We are quite grieved to hear of
your continuing ill and weak, and fear that the many
dark days we have had of late must have tried you in
more ways than one ; but we are glad to hear of friends
who chase away loneliness.

[1] *See* Dante Gabriel Rossetti's *Family Letters*, vol. ii. p. 19.

'Our mother, with one of her three best loves, quite deprecates the idea of your coming round to see her during the conjunction of such health with such weather. She, however, ensconced in that seal-skin which warms her heart as well as her person, is not afraid to look forward to dining with you on Xmas Day. Our plan is as follows. We shall be four in number, both Aunts included. After Church, we have promised, all of us, to lunch with William and his party, at what I believe is to be their early dinner. About 5 o'clock we will be taken up there by our own fly, and go straight on to you ; thus reaching you, we trust, early enough for a good chat before dinner. The only moot point is,—shall Mamma and I, as you kindly proposed, accept a bed at your house ? She inclines to think that as we shall be 4 old ladies in a safe fly with a responsible driver, we had better all go home in a clump: but if you like better to say " Good morning " to her next day instead of " Good night " the same evening, then she and I will profit by your hospitality. Not hearing from you again, we will settle to go home in a fly.

'Mamma is delighted with the "Maenza" letter, and as you do not want it back, means herself to preserve it. Its special value to her is its tribute to you.

'Looking forward to our pleasant Xmas party, always '

Concerning ' the " Maenza " letter ' her brother has written to me as follows :

' *Mrs.* Maenza survived her husband several years— When she died she bequeathed her small funds (say £100) to Gab[riel], who had been the main support of herself, also her husband, for some 15 years—The *letter* was, I think, written by herself not long before death, or possibly the letter announcing her death, &c.'

The work of Mr. William Davies, author of ' Songs of a Wayfarer,' whose etching is referred to in the succeeding letter, was much admired by Dante Gabriel and Christina :

30 Torrington Square, W.C.
Tuesday Evening. [Probably 1879.]

'My dear Gabriel,—Mamma is delighted at the lovingness of your thought for her and for us all, but on the whole we agree in thinking it wise to wend our way home the same night : weather might play us false the next day, if we became as dilatory as my " Prince " in his " progress."—

' All our loves to you.   Aunt Charlotte highly values the welcome you extend to her, and reciprocates to the full its goodwill and affection.

' I have just received an etching by " William Davies," endorsed as sent me by your suggestion.   I like it very much, and when I have seen you perhaps you will tell me of some address—none accompanies it—whereto I may thankfully acknowledge it.'

Under dates of October 20 and 21 in ' Time Flies ' she relates, and moralises upon, another ' parable of nature,' though without stating that the circumstance upon which it is founded came under her notice at Walton-on-the-Naze about 1880 :

' Once at the seaside I recollect noticing for some time a row of swallows perched side by side along a telegraph wire.   There they sat steadily.   After a while, when some one looked again, they were gone.

'This happened so late in the year as to suggest that the birds had mustered for migration and then had started.

' The sight was quaint, comfortable looking, pretty. The small creatures seemed so fit and so ready to launch out on their pathless journey : contented to wait, contented to start, at peace and fearless.

' Altogether they formed an apt emblem of souls willing to stay, willing to depart.

.   .   .   .

' That combination of swallows with telegraph wire sets in vivid contrast before our mental eye the sort of evidence we put confidence in and the sort of evidence we mistrust.

'The telegraph conveys messages from man to man.

'The swallows by dint of analogy, of suggestion, of parallel experience, if I may call it so, convey messages from the Creator to the human creature.

'We act eagerly, instantly, on telegrams. Who would dream of stopping to question their genuineness?

'Who, watching us, could suppose that the senders of telegrams are fallible; and that the Only Sender of Providential messages is infallible?'

Here may be quoted two letters having reference to Walton-on-the-Naze:

30 Torrington Square—W.C.
Wednesday evening.

'My dear Gabriel,—My post-card CROSSED your first letter; otherwise I could not excuse myself for not having answered you. Dear Mamma and the rest of us got home perfectly successfully on Monday night. She is grieved and I am vexed that you should have taken kind and useless trouble for us, troubling, moreover, a friend : but it was only this morning that a letter from Muntham arrived, setting Aunt Charlotte free (at least for a few days) from the likelihood of any immediate recall, and at the same time showing us that it beseemed us to make haste out of town and waste not a day if she wished—as she does wish—to accompany us. This combination of her convenience with ours it was which led to our sudden resolve; and *then* I did not lose an hour in writing to let you know : still, the result has been annoying to you, and I truly am sorry. Mamma sends you a dear love. We have fixed upon Walton-on-Naze not from any decided preference, but at any rate it does not face the baking south, and it is nearer than most of the east coast watering-places. I suppose we are very likely to be away for a month; and I count on letting you have our address when we have one, all favoring.'

2 Lombardian Place Walton-on-the-Naze.
14th August.

'My dear Gabriel,—We have reconsidered and I hope bettered our plans, and are staying on here: a little more prudence on my part may I dare say check neuralgia, etc., and at the worst these are very bearable. Our dearest Mother seems fairly suited by this air : and such being the case, Walton becomes highly desirable as she is often upset and oppressed by the seaside. I don't know that we any of us dislike the surroundings ; I, certainly, do not. Aunt Charlotte is not yet recalled, but from day to day I fear the letter may arrive to deprive us of her company : meanwhile we wage nightly rubbers, and I think repeated practice has somewhat improved my play.

' Mamma's love to you.

' Walton seems a fairly agreeable place and has a fine open sea. We have not yet taken any drives. There are 2 piers, and I dare say there may be good pickings on the shore for any one with available legs.'

30 Torrington Square—W.C.
Monday Evening.   [Written about 1880.]

' My dear Gabriel,—Thank you for two kind little letters come to hand, in the course of to day.

' Aunt Charlotte also has just come to hand,—and she, and Aunt Eliza, and, most of all, our Mother renew the expression of their love to you, and assure you (I, too, of course) that this propitious change of weather makes us hope and trust to be with you without fail in the course of Xmas afternoon. We shall be quite disappointed if our plan fails. But on no account will we trouble you to provide us with a vehicle : we will engage one from the livery stables close by, which will take us to and fro quite comfortably, as it did last year ; every now and then we hire a highly satisfactory "trap" thence. Mamma, noticing the thoughtfulness of your offer, yet cannot wish to accept it.

' Thanks for unfailing brotherliness negociating between Mr. Watts[-Dunton] and me. And truly grateful am I to him, whether or not any act ensues ; the friendly goodwill commands my thanks in either case

I do sincerely. hope to soar above the level of THAT despised poem,—if ever I can scrape a fresh volume together: and at present I am very hopeful of so doing at no very distant date.

    'Very affectionately, your sister
     'CHRISTINA G. ROSSETTI.

'So now observe, please, that we shall *not* write again, except in the deprecated contingency of being unable to come.'

The ' friendly goodwill ' and ' THAT despised poem ' in the preceding letter refer to an incident well told in the same vivid essay by Mr. Watts-Dunton in ' The Athenæum,' to which allusion has already been made.

'On one occasion,' he says, . . . 'she expressed a wish to have some of her verses printed in the " Athenæum," and I suggested her sending them to 16 Cheyne Walk, her brother's house, where I then used to spend much time in a study that I occupied there. I said that her brother and I would read them together, and submit them to the editor. She sent several poems (I think about six), not one of which was in the least degree worthy of her. This naturally embarrassed me, but Gabriel, who entirely shared my opinion of the poems, wrote at once to her, and told her that the verses sent were, both in his own judgment and mine, unworthy of her, and that she " had better buckle to at once and write another poem." She did so, and the result was an exquisite lyric which appeared in the " Athenæum." '

       Tuesday Morning.

'My dear Gabriel,—It seems doubtful whether the roads will be passable to-morrow, because of slipperiness : Aunt Charlotte writes that she cannot come up from Muntham, because of this. Of course London roads are less formidable than country d°, but our Mother desires me to write to-day, in case we find it too hazardous to start for Chelsea to-morrow. Her dearest love to you, and warmest seasonable wishes ; and mine with them. She is so sorry not to be with you on

Xmas Day, that I still will not despair; yet I fear it will be unmanageable. As you see, Aunt Charlotte is now out of the question; and Aunt Eliza of course will do as we do.'

Friday Night.

'My dear Gabriel,—Aunt Charlotte, with love, anticipates the pleasure of seeing you and your 'Pia,' and hopes that when we write actually to propose an afternoon (which I hope will be early next week) we may secure a milder moment,—I say *we* because I hope to accompany her. At the worst, however, we can face a fair amount of cold, for this day we were cabbing and shopping about together for just 3 hours!

'Your grand Sonnet,—our Mother to whom (tho' not to me) the incident was new, is delighted with it. She sends you her love, and I was able to cheer her up a little after my glimpse of you yesterday. Aunt Eliza, too, returns love.

'As to "Buonarruot*i*"[1] surely the play upon words is obvious despite the vanished gender.'

'Pia' in the previous letter means Dante Gabriel's oil-painting 'La Pia' from Dante's 'Purgatorio'; while Mr. William Rossetti informs me that the 'grand sonnet' refers to Dante Gabriel's

'"Tiber, Nile and Thames": the incident being that of Fulvia, who ran her needle through the tongue of the truncated head of Cicero—C[hristina]'s [letter] w^d thus be an answer to the one from G[abriel] which was printed in my volume [Dante Gabriel Rossetti : His Family Letters, with a Memoir], vol. ii. p. 367.'

Thursday.

'My dear Gabriel,—Your letter received this morning relieves our Mother *immensely* (her own word) and me

---

[1] The reference to 'Buonarruot*i*' alludes to Dante Gabriel's use of it in Sonnet 94 in 'The House of Life,' concerning which Mr. William Rossetti has a learned note at p. 254 of his 'Dante Gabriel Rossetti as Designer and Writer.' As to the matter he has also written to me:

'The particular point raised by C[hristina] is that ruot*e* shows the *feminine* plural termination, whereas Buonarruot*i* shows the masculine plural termination.

in proportion. I trust nothing very bad can accrue from so good a friend.

'Perhaps while Winter is in its depth the best chance for getting a sight of you and "la Pia" will be for my independent self to take my chance of finding you at leisure any afternoon when weather and all other influences favour my starting. At the worst—and that will be by no means bad! I can combine a visit to Mrs. [Bell] Scott with my own visitation of you : and as Scotus has been ill, my so doing would be obviously neat and appropriate.'

'I fear to dwell upon your brightening business horizon, lest gloom should return ; but meanwhile am thankful—I am glad you have had another fine Sonnet in the " Athenæum " : " poets' corner " is desirable in my eyes, not cloyed by success quite (!) to the degree of yours.'

The other 'fine sonnet in the " Athenæum "' refers to Dante Gabriel's 'The Holy Family' (by Michaelangelo, in the National Gallery) beginning 'Turn not the prophet's page, O Son! He knew,' which originally appeared in that journal for January 1, 1881.

The ensuing brief note may be quoted as showing Dante Gabriel's affectionate interest in his mother's health :

Wednesday.

'My dear Gabriel,—I can thoroughly reassure you. Our dearest Mother is extremely well, and keeps indoors without variation : she has not stirred out since *before* the day I saw you last week. Indeed she does on the whole keep very fairly warm, despite cold which even keeps hardy Aunt Charlotte indoors day after day. She sends you a dear love, and my Aunts join with her. I really begin to fear this overwhelming cold will prevent Aunt Charlotte getting to your studio, when I meant to accompany her : however, I won't despair yet.'

The letters ensuing were written from London or from Sevenoaks in the late summer or autumn of 1881. Signor Gamberale, mentioned in the first of these, published in Italy in the same year a volume entitled 'Poeti Inglesi e Tedeschi moderni o contemporanei,' which contains Italian translations from poems both by Dante Gabriel and by Christina. The 'Cumberland plan,' alluded to in the first letter, relates to Dante Gabriel's visit to Fisher Place, near Keswick. 'Mr. Caine's book' refers to Mr. Hall Caine's 'Sonnets of Three Centuries.' Her 'Pageant and other Poems' appeared about August of the same year.

Thursday.

'My dear Gabriel,—Thank you for a helpful feeler put out in the direction of Felixstowe. But two things (alas!) prevent our profiting thereby. First, our Mother very wisely has contracted her radius, and now seeks places not remote from London, thus avoiding the exhaustion of long journeys. Secondly, as we are making a sociable family party this year, we must avoid the glaring seaside on account of poor Aunt Eliza's eyes. The green refreshing country promises to suit us all, and this morning a friend has sent us an address at Tunbridge Wells, to which I am about to write. We still hope to get away on Saturday.

'Signor Gamberale's letter is interesting: I recollect the fact of your " Last Confession " being translated, tho' the translator's name had escaped me. I wonder which of my books he has got. I wonder also if you and William will condescend to his (somewhat costly perhaps) request for books: if so, I think I must emulate you with at least some one of mine; and in any case Aunt Charlotte will bestow upon him a copy of dear Maria's "Shadow of Dante." But of course I shall make no move yet awhile in his direction. I re-enclose his letter, and am curious to see myself in travestie.

'Our Mother rejoices, and so do I, in the hope that you will carry out your Cumberland plan; for it sounds

G

pleasant and promising. Is Mr. [Hall] Caine's book
out yet, I wonder.   Mine ["A Pageant and other
Poems "] was printed long ago—at least, the final sheets
passed thro' my hands, and in this month's " Macmillan "
it was announced " immediately," and still I see and hear
nothing of it. Your two, I suppose, by what William
says, are wisely waiting for October·: and mine perhaps
may be doing the same, tho' I fancied it might have
been issued ere this.
   ' With a dear love from a most dear Mother,
       ' Your affectionate
           'CHRISTINA G. ROSSETTI.'

The letter which follows was written in September
1881.   Under date of September 4 of that year Dante
Gabriel, in the course of a letter to his mother (see his
'Life and Family Letters,' by his brother, vol. ii. p.
385), says :

' I wish C[hristina] would write me a line in answer
to this (not taxing yourself), and say how she liked
[Mr. Hall] Caine's little notice [of "A Pageant and
other Poems "] in " The Academy." '

Here is Christina's answer :

' My dear Gabriel,—Our Mother has been enjoying
the article which you lent me, which I return, and
which, to own the truth, I have copied out at full length !
She sends you a dear love, and is very grieved at your
weak and suffering state, and with me looks forward to
coming to see you next Tuesday. I am glad to have
met Mr. Watts [-Dunton] again, and to have made
acquaintance with Mr. [Hall] Caine.
       ' Affectionately your
           'CHRISTINA G. ROSSETTI.'

In a postscript to a letter written about this date, she
speaks thus concerning Dante Gabriel's sonnet 'Raleigh':

' " Raleigh " is indeed fine, and its end a grand
climax.'

Friday Night.

'My dear Gabriel,—After all I stopped short at Sevenoaks instead of reaching Tunbridge Wells. And at Sevenoaks I have secured what promise to be charming lodgings (Fayremead) whither we trust to betake ourselves to-morrow.

'Mamma's love and Aunt C's, by

'Your tired sister,

'C. G. R.'

Fayremead—Sevenoaks.
Friday Evening.
[Written in 1881.]

'My dear Gabriel,—I dropped in at the agents' this morning ; and this afternoon all except myself (for I had a headache) drove to Seal, a village (say) $1\frac{1}{2}$ or 2 miles out of Sevenoaks, to inspect the following small house.

'It stands in its own grounds, with garden back and front. Has 3 sitting-rooms, that is, a dining-room, drawing-room, small extra room. 4 bed rooms (2 large, 2 small) besides servant's room at top of house. Rent £2 15 0 per week ; but will be vacant not till 2nd September, from which date it can be had for any term proposed. It is of course furnished, but no servant remains : lodgers must provide their own. As I say, it is detached : but next to it (tho' separate) is the Vicarage : and this cottage belongs to the Vicar. Within 5 or 10 minutes is Wilderness Park, a fine looking place either for driving or walking, and open to the public. The water, by the bye, is good, but there is a filter to boot! The garden is rather picturesque and wildish, full of greenery, has walks and three grassy steps, and is of a good size. . . . If any question further seems to you worth asking, the agents' address is Messrs. Cronks, Sevenoaks.

'Perhaps we may hear of something else promising, & I will be on the alert.'

What follows refers to Dante Gabriel's project of leaving 16 Cheyne Walk permanently :

G 2

' My dear Gabriel,—Getting home, we found our old friend Henrietta Rintoul waiting for us; and she mentioned in the course of chat that Mr. Topham's (the artist's) house is she believes now to let, a house in a part of Hampstead with a capital look-out towards Cricklewood, if she is not mistaken.

 . . . . . .

'[I lose not a] moment in letting you know the little I know, on the bare chance of its availing.'

' Francesca' in the succeeding letter refers to a translation by Christina's elder brother of a well-known passage in Dante, and ' elder ' and ' modern ' allude to Amelia B. Edwards's two volumes of poetic selections, the first of ' elder ' the second of ' modern ' poets.

30 Torrington Square—W.C.
Saturday.

' My dear Gabriel,—Our Mother sends you her love, and announces that some of the best news she could have received is of improvement in your health. D°. I.

'She has enjoyed reading in 2 following " Athenæums " your nice letter of contradiction, & your fine " Francesca," and has bought both.   We only heard of them by a side chance.

 . . . . . .

' Mamma suffered from a similar attack [of influenza], but rallied much more rapidly, and is now fairly her dear self again.   I cough wofully, but I dare say there is no great point amiss ; and am taking a mixture of Sir W[illiam] J[enner]'s.

'Thank you for writing to Miss Edwards.[1]   Mamma was so disturbed at the misstatement that I wrote to correct it ; but I am very glad Miss E. should receive collateral evidence, and should be aware that my family noticed the point.

'My comfort in the business is, that the error is so broad I think it will in a measure neutralise itself.

---

[1] In *A Poetry-Book of Modern Poets*, edited by Amelia B. Edwards, published in 1879, Christina Rossetti is described as born in 1816.

' I have scarcely as yet glanced at the " elder " and " modern " volume, but I understand from Mamma that both are good.'

Soon after the publication of her ' Pageant and other Poems,' she writes to her brother Gabriel :

' I trust Mr. Watts [-Dunton] received his own " Pageant " so know not why he confiscated yours ! There seems (I am sorry to say) to have been some hobble at the " Saturday Review " office, tho' a copy was sent in due course : now, I fear, they will not notice me, and at any rate Mr. Gosse is off for a holiday and cannot " do " me. But I am not going to worry myself over this trifle, tho' I should like it to have happened otherwise. I rather wince in prospect of Mr. Watts [-Dunton] and Mr. [Hall] Caine.
' Mamma's dear love to you.

' I have been reviewed in the " Tablet," fair average, —and more favourably in the " St. James's Gazette." '

Mr. Shields was one of the small band of those who, together with Dante Gabriel's ' friend of friends,' Mr. Watts-Dunton, ministered to Dante Gabriel during his closing year of life. In this connection a Christmas letter from Christina written from London becomes deeply interesting. The ' medical man ' was Mr. Henry Maudsley :

December 16, 1881.

' Dear Mr. Shields,—Your letter comes like balm. My dearest Mother thanks you with a warm heart, and so do I, for the hope you help us to keep up. I need not dwell on our grief and anxiety on poor Gabriel's account ; yet with you I do hope that under the absolute authority of a medical man he may yet be weaned from that fatal chloral, and that even now much which has been lost may be retrieved. You and Mr. Watts [-Dunton], and every unwearied friend who is kind to him now, earn our deepest gratitude.

' Let me wish you and Mrs. Shields a bright and blessed Christmas, a wish my Mother most truly unites in.

'Always gratefully yours,'

Christina handles two of the deepest problems of religion—that of predestination and free will—in 'Time Flies' under date January 31, where she says :

' A friend once put it to me that the choice of each man's free will must be unknown beforehand even to God Omniscient Himself. To foreknow would involve to preordain, and that which is ordained is not free :—so, I suppose, my friend might have gone on to argue, handling a mystery far beyond my comprehension.

' Limited Omniscience is a contradiction in terms. A being any one of whose attributes is limited, cannot be our Infinite Lord God.'

The friend mentioned above was the Rev. W. Garrett Horder, well known as the editor of ' The Poets' Bible,' ' an attempt to set forth the great scenes and characters of Holy Scripture in the words of the Poets.' To this work Christina Rossetti contributed several poems. Mr. Horder has been good enough to place at my disposal correspondence, dated from London, from which extracts shall be made. The first letter, in answer to inquiries made by Mr. Horder, expresses some opinions respecting other poets, and contains also one of her rare flashes of self-criticism :

July 11, 1881.

' Dear Sir,—Thank you for all the interesting information you are so good as to afford me. I have admired fine work by Canon Dixon ere now, tho' I have not the advantage of being acquainted with him. But another of your contributors I do know—Dr. Littledale : not to speak of my own brother !

' If any of my own pieces could find place in your

proposed volume, they would be quite at your service. But they are so prevalently in <u>a subjective</u> vein that I fear they may not repay you for a sifting of the collected edition. The fresh volume announced just now by Messrs. Macmillan will (I conjecture) be open to the same objection. Do you happen to recall a poem by Carrington on the Nativity? He, I suppose, may be a poet not universally known; and even I tho' with a vivid certainty of my early admiration of the piece in question, cannot at this much later day feel sure whether my judgment was then correct. Yet I venture to name the poem to you. Another, presumably not widely known, occurs to my memory—a blank verse poem of some length on the " sorrowful mysteries " of our Lord's life, written by James Collinson, an artist not long deceased, and published in a now rare Magazine entitled " The Germ," about the year 1849. " The Germ " lived only through 4 nos., and in the course of its brief career changed its name to " Art and Poetry "—but I think it was " The Germ " when the poem I speak of appeared in it.

'If any other poem should occur to me as worth naming I will count on your permission to write to you again. Could I help forward a good work I would gladly see you or hear from you again,—I should be fortunate in so doing.
                    'Very sincerely yours,

'Yet I think there may be one or two of mine which might perhaps accord with your scheme, for instance one called " By the Waters of Babylon "—Oddly enough I do not possess a copy of the volume which contains it, or I should feel tempted to count on your leave to lend it you.'

In the following year Mr. Horder was writing a volume entitled 'Intimations of Immortality,' and wrote to her requesting permission to use her sonnets beginning

The Wise do send their hearts before them to

and

> If I could trust mine own self with your fate,

demurring, however, to the line

> Whose knowledge foreknew every plan we planned

in the latter sonnet, as 'indicating such a fore-know-ledge that no space was left for the action of the human will.'   To this she replies :

July 29. 1882.

'Dear Mr. Horder,—I am very glad if you can utilise " The Wise do send. . . ."   I heartily wish I could answer quite the same as to " If I could trust. . ."—but here you have already (have you not ?) felt that con-victions and principles are involved—I cannot unsay what I hold to be absolutely true, even if originally I might have expressed myself better.   And if one of the illogical sex may without offence argue with one of the logical, I would venture to illustrate my point by observing that my prescience that you will take all kindly does not *compel* you so to do ! '

Apropos of Mr. Horder's demur she wrote the remarks in 'Time Flies.' On its publication she sent him a copy of the book, and, in answer to a letter of thanks, wrote to him :

May 20. 1885.

'Dear Mr. Horder,—I have no doubt we differ on some points, but I rejoice over those points on which we agree.   Thank you for kind words about my new little book.   Be sure. that not one of my readers would be more genuinely pleased than myself if I could always write poems !

'But just because poetry *is* a gift, I scarcely dare to follow your allusion to prophets in company with poets —I am not surprised to find myself unable to summon it at will and use it according to my own choice.'

Early in 1882 Mr. John H. Ingram was projecting his ' Eminent Women Series,' and was desirous that Christina Rossetti should undertake one of the volumes.

After he had broached the subject to her younger brother, the latter spoke to his sister on the subject. From Birchington (where she was in attendance on Dante Gabriel during his last illness) Christina commenced a somewhat lengthy correspondence with Mr. Ingram, from which, by Mr. Ingram's permission, some extracts are made:

'My absence from London puts me out of the way of books of reference such as of course would be essential to any practical attempt to ascertain whether I could meet your requirements : could I do so it would be of advantage and satisfaction to myself, and the £50 you mention (I fully understand without pledging yourself to any defined sum) would I anticipate fully repay me. One point in which, I fear, I should conspicuously fall short of your wishes is as to rapid production of a life ; I am but a slow worker, and could not prefix a time for sending in ; this premised, it might (might it not ?) suit us both better if instead of one of the *earlier* lives of the series being assigned to me one of the *later* should be selected. You propose Adelaide Procter—I should very willingly make my essay on her biography but have so long dropped out of literary society that I mistrust my ability to get at private sources of information altho' many years ago I met her and I daresay her mother and certainly one or two of her intimate friends. Your stating that copyright difficulties will not hamper the transaction is very good news, as (I suppose) a great part of the volume of from 150 to 200 pages must in the case of a quiet life, such as I suppose Miss Procter's to have been, be made up of quotations from her unpublished verse or of available correspondence should such come to light.

'My response does not, I fear, read very promisingly, and pray feel no scruples at turning elsewhere. How long I shall continue in the country I have no means of foreseeing as my movements do not depend upon myself in this matter. So if nothing else comes of our overtures let them at least lead up to my remaining
'Very sincerely yours,'

Mr. W. M. Rossetti subsequently suggested that the monograph on Adelaide Procter had better be written by Mrs. A. A. Watts, as that lady had had a more intimate acquaintance with her than had Christina. Christina Rossetti's next letter, dated Birchington, March 13, 1882, sets forth this, and states that, owing to her present circumstances, she was unable at the moment to take up definitely any literary occupation. With characteristic thoughtfulness she names 'with warm commendation' Mrs. Bell Scott, Mrs. Gemmer (Gerda Fay), Mrs. Edgecombe, and Miss Rintoul as very suitable for such work.

In the early part of 1883, again through her brother, Mr. Ingram once more approached Christina Rossetti, asking her to undertake the life of Elizabeth Barrett Browning, which Mr. Ingram himself subsequently wrote, and I quote a portion of a letter, written from Torrington Square, shortly afterwards :

'My brother has showed me that obliging letter in which you express good will that I rather than some others should undertake a life of Mrs. Browning. I should write with enthusiasm of that great poetess and (I believe) lovable woman, whom I was never, however, so fortunate as to meet. But before I could put pen to paper it would be necessary for me to know what would be Mr. Browning's wish in the matter,—and by his wish, whatever it might be, I should feel bound ; both because he as her husband seems to me the one person entitled to decide how much or how little concerning her should during his lifetime be made public, and because having long enjoyed a slight degree of acquaintance with him I could not but defer to his wish.'

After some delay Christina abandoned the thought of the proposed study of Elizabeth Barrett Browning, the reason being indicated in a letter dated May 8 of the same year :

'Do you know, I do not feel courage to embark on the memoir of E. B. B. ; it seems to me clear that without Mr. Browning's co-operation the thing cannot (at least during his lifetime) be thoroughly executed : besides which, I strongly sympathise with his reticence where one so near and dear to him is concerned.'

Dating from Torrington Square, April 24, 1883, she says to the same correspondent :

'My brother tells me you are kindly thinking of me for "Mrs. Radcliffe." She takes my fancy more than many, altho' I know next to nothing about her. And I will try my pen upon her, if you please. Are any hopes to be indulged of private letters, journals, what not, becoming accessible to us? or must I depend exclusively on looking up my subject at the British Museum ?'

In a few days' time, when acknowledging a list of authorities and British Museum readers' slips made out by Mr. Ingram for her use, she wrote to him as follows :

'Will you add one more favour? letting me have a *page* of the edition you edit, that so I may copy it out and form an idea of about how much of my own MS. will go to the 180 or 200 (is it not?) pages of print required.'

And again :

'I find I can get the four books in question at Mudie's, and I will do so if you are so good as to assure me that my contingent publisher will not "time me." I am not strong, and working under pressure is too formidable. But I hope this time the difficulty will not compel me to forego my undertaking, tho' were it insisted on I must secede.'

Informed that she would have what she termed her 'weak point'—time—she replies under date of May 28 :

' 50*l.* is all I wish for, and if I succeed in finding sufficient material I shall be very pleased with my earnings.'

It may here be mentioned that Mr. Ingram never had the smallest intention of inconveniencing Christina Rossetti by insisting on the prompt production of a biography, or upon its consisting of a given number of pages.

In Christina Rossetti's opinion the great difficulty that stood in her way in the case of Anne Radcliffe was lack of material. She wrote a letter on the subject to ' The Athenæum,' and also wrote privately to Professor Masson of Edinburgh, who recommended Dr. Richard Garnett of the British Museum. The latter gentleman and several others were applied to, but, the result being in Christina Rossetti's opinion inadequate, she communicated her final decision to Mr. Ingram in a letter written from London, dated September 17, 1883 :

' Returned from the seaside I can only say I have done my best to collect Radcliffe material and have failed. Some one else, I daresay, will gladly attempt the memoir, but I despair and withdraw. Pray pardon me for having kept you so long in suspense. . . .

' Apologising for all that has been disappointment in my doings and not-doings,

' I remain, etc. etc.'

This correspondence has much intrinsic interest, because it reveals Christina Rossetti's opinion of two very different women poets of the century, and the wide range of her literary sympathies. It also reveals incidentally some of her own habits of work.

At a much later date (September 23, 1891) she wrote concerning Elizabeth Barrett Browning to Mr. Patchett Martin, who had then just published an article in which he had stated as his opinion that she herself was 'the greater literary artist' of the two :

'Yet all said, I doubt whether the woman is born, or for many a long day, if ever, will be born, who will balance not to say outweigh Mrs. Browning.'

Mr. Shields was with those who gathered round Dante Gabriel during his last days at Birchington, and he is the 'friend' mentioned in 'Time Flies,' under date of April 28, as having told Christina how he had observed, in the course of a walk,

'cobwebs shaped more or less like funnels or tunnels, one end open to the road, while deep down at the other end lay in wait the spider.'

And she adds, somewhat naively,

'I walked a little about the same country, and failed to observe the spider ; fortunately for me I was not a fly.
'The spider was on the alert in his sphere, my friend was on the alert in his higher sphere ; I alone, it would seem, was not on the alert in either sphere.'

With that vivid symbolism which is so marked a feature of her genius, she gives us a homily on the little incident that, in its own way, both in insight and in style, is one of the finest passages of her prose. But only in a mind like Christina Rossetti's could so trivial an incident have evoked so remarkable a sequence of ideas. Truly it is one of the prerogatives of genius sometimes to see the much and the little.

The following letter was probably written in 1883 :

30 Torrington Square W.C.
Thursday 7th.

'Dear Mr. Shields,—My Mother and I have thought of you very often since our common loss drew us all to Birchington. Will you and Mrs. Shields come to see us one evening, say Monday or Tuesday? We shall be quite by ourselves. You know we do not achieve late dinners, but we would have a solid tea at any hour suited to your convenience, half-past eight or nine,—it would make no difference to us, and we recollect how precious daylight is to an artist. Please remember us cordially to Mrs. Shields : we shall welcome you both. My Mother thinks you will like to look at one treasure she possesses, a medallion of our dear Gabriel done when he was eighteen by John Hancock : this is the solitary attraction we put forward to induce you to come !—but do *not* come if health or aught else interposes a bar.

> ' Yet hopeful of your saying *yes* I remain
> ' Very truly yours
> ' CHRISTINA G. ROSSETTI.'

On April 9, 1883—the first anniversary of Dante Gabriel's death—I went down to Birchington with my friend, Mr. Hall Caine, to visit the poet-painter's last resting-place. To Mr. Hall Caine, Christina and her mother had entrusted some choice flowers to be placed on the beloved grave.

30 Torrington Square W.C.
April 15.

' Dear Mr. Shields,—My friend Miss Heaton is in London and reminds me of my promise to introduce her to your beautiful works and gracious self,—so I, in my turn, remind you of your sanction accorded to our scheme. Would next Tuesday (21st) morning, about noon I mean, suit your convenience as well as our pleasure ? If not, please kindly propose any other morning whatsoever.

.   .   .   .   .   .

' Please write your *yes* or *no* on a CARD, which is a modern luxury among friends.

' I wonder whether you are an anti-Vivisectionist, and I wonder whether you are a Minors'-Protectionist. I am trying to get signatures on both subjects to Petitions to Parliament.'

Mr. Shields is an anti-Vivisectionist, and he signed

that petition, and also one in favour of the Minors' Protection Bill—a proposed measure dealing with the 'age of consent.' She was a strong anti-Vivisectionist, and in another letter thanked her friend 'very warmly' because of his zeal in the same cause.

One of the windows in Birchington Church, to the memory of Dante Gabriel, was erected solely at the expense of his mother, and this she confided to Mr. Shields. Christina conducted the necessary correspondence, which is beautiful and touching as revealing anew her affection for both Dante Gabriel and her mother. It also shows Christina's assured belief in Mr. Shields as an artist, and the high esteem in which she held him as a man. These letters, as all such letters between tried friends should be, are direct transcripts of character. To read them is to seem to hear her speak.

Concerning the window in Birchington Church the following extract from remarks addressed to me by Mr. Shields may here be given :

'My original proposition was that both the subjects should be copies of Rossetti's designs, and I consented that one of the lights should be filled by a design from my own hand, only in deference to their will (which touched me much) because, said they, I was his friend.'

Mr. Shields first selected for the memorial window Dante Gabriel's own design of ' Mary Magdalene at the Door of Simon the Pharisee,' but this was ' disallowed ' by the incumbent of the church. Hence, with the approval of Dante Gabriel's representatives, Mr. Shields adopted finally Dante Gabriel's design, ' The Eve of the Passover.'

'We, too,' in the following letter refers to the acquiescence of Mrs. Rossetti and Christina in Mr. Shields's suggestion to use 'The Passover' design in place of the rejected one.

30 Torrington Square W.C.
Wednesday.

'Dear Mr. Shields,—We, too! Stirred up by your note I have just written to Mr. Wheeler of Oxford—I suppose " Oxford " suffices for his address—to ask after this much-wished-for photograph.

'My poor Mother salutes you with a weary disappointment fully equal to your own, and I remain in harmony.'

Concerning 'this much-wished-for photograph' Mr. W. M. Rossetti has written interestingly to me :

'I feel confident that the photograph wanted must have been one from Gabriel's own drawing of the Passover in the Holy Family, which drawing (first bought by [Mr.] Ruskin) had been presented by him to, or deposited in, the Art-Gallery of Oxford.'

Mr. Shields had exceptional trouble as to this window, but the result is a very fine example of his work. At the outset he felt some uncertainty as to which were the bitter herbs eaten at the Passover. He consulted Christina, who in her turn inquired of Dr. Littledale. Her reply may be given for the sake of the playful humour of the postscript :

30 Torrington Square W.C.
Friday afternoon.

'Dear Mr. Shields,—I return Dr. Acland's letter. My Mother read it with interest, and I wrote our joint answer. Thank you for it and for all the toils encountered in our cause.

'Dr. Littledale answered my query so immediately that here is his answer. Lettuce and endive are so familiar that it may tempt you to avoid the other two!

'The above ill-constructed sentences shall veil themselves behind motherly remembrances, while I remain

' Very truly yours

 'CHRISTINA G. ROSSETTI.'

'Don't remark, " I had better have borrowed the Thesaurus ! "—don't let him, my dear Mrs. Shields.'

Concerning Dante Gabriel's 'Eve of the Passover,' Mr. Shields has written to me :

'The drawing (one of Mr. Ruskin's precious gifts to the Oxford Museum) is unfinished, in which state Mr. Ruskin bore it away from the painter, in mistaken enthusiasm, declaring he would spoil it in finishing. Hence a vacuity—which I was loth to supply from myself—I ascertained that Dr. Acland had the original pencil sketch, and there I found the entire motive sufficiently indicated to enable me to complete the design according to the beautiful purpose of its inventor. To Dr. Acland's kind permission to make notes from the precious sketch, the reference in the letter applies.'

Several of the letters that follow immediately were written during somewhat lengthy sojourns which she and her mother made at Birchington in 1883 and 1884.

The letter given below is valuable, as it contains a tentative suggestion of Christina's for the design of the window.

Church Hill, Birchington-on-Sea
July 25, 1883.

' Dear Mr. Shields,—My mother joins me in thanking you for the warm reception you accord to her wish, and bids me explain the 100*l.* is not necessarily the extreme limit of her offering. *Less* she does not propose—something *more* she is quite willing for.

'Mr. Seddon was here the other afternoon, seemed to think her window quite feasible, and promised himself to write to you : so I hope all will be made accurate and intelligible. The window in question consists of

H

2 lights only: its companion window equally of 2 lights would be abandoned entire to friends and admirers who of course would please themselves as to what artists should be called in : but my Mother's window she wishes (if so it may be) to secure exclusively from yourself. We wonder how you will devise a design which can at all express the man and the work : I am quite unable to think of anything nearer than the inadmissible combination of 2 incongruous figures, St. Luke and the Archangel Gabriel ! A quite different treatment of our dear subject had occurred to me, and had for the moment approved itself to my Mother : a Raising of the Widow of Nain's Son. We considered that as Baptism is " a death unto sin, and a new birth unto righteousness " an instance of Resurrection might be viewed as typically appropriate to a Baptistery ; while Gabriel (tho' not an only son) was a beloved, loving, conspicuous son of a widow, who cherishes among her dearest hopes that of receiving him back at the general Resurrection by the overflowing mercy of God. But I tell you this so freely because you always invite confidence—not because you need prompting, or we are wedded to our own idea.

.   .   .   .

'We hope Mrs. Shields will yet get better, and brighten your heart and home again. Our love to her, please. I wonder whether Birchington would suit her : it is coldish at present, yet we—who in age might more than be her grandmother and mother !—are revived in this fine air. Welcome will you be on Monday, or Tuesday, or any other day. We dine at 2, and would have tea at any hour to suit you ; but we would not grudge you livelier entertainment at Dilkoosha or the Vicarage, if such were to offer. And never make excuses for not calling, please ! It is a friendly favour when you drop in, it is no omission when you forbear.'

The following letter and its ' separate sheet ' will show both the practical side of Christina Rossetti's character, and how she spared herself no trouble, even as to the minutest particulars, when the comfort of the friends who formed her inner circle was concerned.

Church Hill, Birchington-on-Sea
August 1.

' My dear Mr. Shields,—How I hope that Birchington —if Birchington prove to be your bourne—may revive you and your wife. Our love to her, please, and our very best wishes for her recovery and enjoyment,—if she rallies, you will brighten up, and I hope throw off that very painful besetment neuralgia.

' On a separate sheet I send you what particulars I have unearthed. By far the largest and best room of all I have seen is the *one* room at the pastrycook's, but very likely such a make-shift is not admissible. The whole group of lodgings I send you are more or less near the church,—this, need I remind you? involves their being at some distance from the sea, and accounts for the comparatively low rents demanded. Near the sea I am not aware of anything to be had, short of an entire house.

' If there is anything more I can do, command me. I called on Mrs. Seddon before commencing my round of apartments-hunting, and it was in fact thro' her that I heard of *the cottage* in my list ; so there can be no doubt of the respectability of this said cottage— for, it is let by people who she thought might have rooms to let.

' The weather here varies between summer and winter ! To-day is of an intermediate temperature.

' Be sure you will find my dear Mother ready and anxious to set forward the memorial. To-day I re- visited the dear old bungalow and brought away a bunch of flowers from its garden and conservatory.'

[Copy of separate sheet]

Mr. Tapsell—pastrycook, Station Road (which is a
sort of village High St.)

ONE only but really large room seeming thoroughly furnished as bed and sitting room in one.
25ˢ/ per week.

Gas 1ˢ/6 do.
Boots 1*d*.
Washing linen either at a small charge or perhaps for a fortnight gratis.

A square landing outside the room door large enough for a small table and chair would do to write a letter or what not, if the real room were occupied at the moment.

Mrs. Harris, Jessamine Cottage, Church Street.
Stands in a row of a few cottages.

Fronts towards the Church: back looking into own garden or kitchen garden
Sitting room ground floor, bedroom above.
25ˢ/. per week with attendance.
Boots 1*d*. per pair.
Cruets &c., 6*d*. per week.
Kitchen fire 1ˢ/ do.
Washing of linen *about* 2ˢ/ for a fortnight, if that is the whole term.

Mr. D. Golder, Ironmonger, Park Lane.

A cottage, furnished, could be entered at once but must be vacated not later than the 13th. 2 guineas for the above short term. Occupant must provide his own attendance, plate, linen.
3 bedrooms
2 sitting-rooms
Kitchens &c.
The cottage looks into its own little piece of garden front—it stands in a row—and at the back towards other premises.

Mrs. Jakes, 10 Prospect Villas.

Sitting room and bedroom on first floor. (Stands in a row of lodging-letting houses.)
30ˢ/ per week
Kitchen fire 1ˢ/6 per week
No other extras.

When I saw these rooms *both* had beds in them, but one would be cleared and turned into a sitting-room

C. G. R.

The succeeding letter has characteristic touches :

5
6 Station Road Birchington-on-Sea
Monday.

' Dear Mr. Shields,—I return with many thanks the letter which shows how readily you oblige us. Its substance I have forwarded to my Aunt and I hope it will open to her a great pleasure. If when the window is completed it will be " on view " for a day or two, I have a very old friend—an admirer too of Gabriel's—who would greatly like to look at it : in case of such a chance I venture to send you her address :

' Mrs. Heimann
' Rolandseck
' 25 Mayflower Road
' Clapham Road '

' But I selfishly hope the window will not be detained long " on view " in London.

' For my Mother and I nurse the hope of seeing it ourselves before we leave this place. To-morrow, however, we have arranged to change our lodgings to *next door :* so henceforward our number will be 5, all else continuing as at present. Kindly note the petty change in our address.'

This passage from a letter to the same correspondent, written from the same place at a somewhat earlier date, gives an almost pathetic glimpse of her mother's disposition :

' Even your personal love of Gabriel weighs less with her [Mrs. Rossetti] in this quest than your personal love of Christ.'

As to the above quotation her brother William writes to me :

' I consider the meaning must be that Mrs. Rossetti, in addressing to Shields her *quest* for a memorial window (and not for instance to Madox Brown), was influenced by Shields's love of Christ, even more than by his love of Gabriel.'

This one, written from London, shows in what spirit her mother and herself approached financial considerations when dealing with friends :

Oct. 4.

'Dear Mr. Shields,—The paragraph in a recent Athenæum which announces your forthcoming window upbuilds our hope of seeing that beautiful work.

'My Mother salutes you with true friendship and—begging your excuse if we violate artistic etiquette—desires me to ask whether this is the moment for offering you a " retainer "?—either 50*l.* or 100*l.* as you shall dictate. If you will favour her with a prompt reply she is just now about to have an account-settling, in the course of which and without any great delay she will have the pleasure of transmitting to you either sum you may prefer. Not that she forgets that the beloved window remains at liberty to exceed 100*l.* : every detail will be cheerfully gone into at a future moment ; but this proposal is, perhaps, what applies to the present time. I daresay you saw or at least heard of the letter in a " Times " not long ago, which stirred up all our family feeling for the cherished grave, if it needed stirring up.'

Evidently Christina and her mother found the end of their stay at Birchington a little wearisome.

5 Station Road Birchington-on-Sea
October 14.

'Dear Mr. Shields,—Alas! the weather took a wintry turn some days ago, and has only partially recovered itself since. So my Mother desires me to announce that unless the beloved window can fill its nook by *the end* of *this month* she resigns herself to return home, and gaze at it—next best—in London when the happy moment shall arrive. Birchington cold, when it does come, is no trifle.

'We hope this will find your wife and you at least

pretty well, and that both will accept our very friendly salutations, and that you will not begin quite to hate
'Your tormenting correspondent
'CHRISTINA G. ROSSETTI.'

This reveals her mother's character as well as her own :

5 Station Road Birchington-on-Sea
October 22. 1884.

'Dear Mr. Shields,—Your *red letter* to-day turned into a " red letter day " for us. I wish to-morrow may turn out one for you by finding Mrs. Shields better and so your load of care lightened. Pray give her our love and accept our friendliest remembrances.

'Now indeed we look forward to admiring the beautiful window. It will always remain your labour of love—but my Mother begs you as soon as possible to let her have an exhaustive list of her money debts to the Glass Firm and much more to yourself: that she may as quickly as she can meet her liabilities. At 84 she feels that to-day's duty had more than ever better be performed to day and not postponed till to-morrow. Please recollect the St. Mary Magdalene Cartoon along with all the rest. We hope to go home next Tuesday, on which day our ninth week at Birchington expires. I rejoice to see Mr. Seddon's name and Mr. [the Rev. Alfred] Gurney's—not to speak of William's—among the gazers [" gazers " refers to those who had been privileged to see the memorial window at Mr. Shields's studio]; I wonder if Mr. Dunn was included. Mr. Watts [-Dunton] we knew already you meant to summon, and truly that staunch friend is not one to be omitted on such an occasion.

'With warm thanks for all you have done for us and an earnest wish that the results may enhance your fame
'Very truly yours '

Mr. H. Treffry Dunn alluded to above is more than once mentioned by Mr. W. M. Rossetti in his 'Memoir' of Dante Gabriel. With the latter Mr. Dunn was at one time much associated, as his 'art-assistant,' and resided with him. Dante Gabriel had a high opinion of Mr. Dunn's artistic gifts especially as a colourist, and it was with Mr. Dunn as companion that the poet-painter made his memorable pilgrimage to Stratford-on-Avon.

Mr. Shields has told me that he was so much touched by the sympathetic and delicate tact of Mrs. Rossetti in connection with the negotiations for this window, that, on its completion, he gave her, as a mark of his appreciation, a copy of his drawing 'The Good Shepherd' to be mentioned hereafter.

This is individual :

30 Torrington Square W.C.
Friday afternoon.

'Dear Mr. Shields,—We awaited you last night and you did not come. Did this arise from my not having answered that we should be at home? I thought my silence would speak, but if I ought to have written pardon me. Or was it that you were not well enough to come? If so, sad is the cause : but the result shall not be sad, so far as my calling on you can forward business matters. Any evening we shall be at home, if still you like to come : or if I call at your studio I will (not hearing from you to the contrary) do my best to appear next Tuesday before about 1.o'clock.

'My Mother greets you and your wife cordially, and I act echo. The beautiful window abides in our mental eye, even if our corporeal eye see it never again.

'Truly yours '

'P.S. I had just written the ERASED pages when I found your card in the post box. Do pray take care of your precious self. I will try to call to-morrow (Saturday) towards noon ; but if you are out or engaged do not feel kindly anxious, as I can quite easily return another time.'

The ensuing letter shows Christina's conscientiousness; her tact in dealing with one of the occasional *contretemps* of social intercourse; and her views on a difficult subject that is often discussed, views which, coming from one with her artistic surroundings, are particularly noteworthy, though it must be remembered that her brother, the famous painter, was no more a 'dealer in such wares' than was his friend Mr. Shields.

30 Torrington Square W.C.
Tuesday.

'Dear Mr. Shields,—I must beg your patience and favourable construction for this letter, for it may appear clear to you that I ought not to write it. Even if so, you are one to make allowance for a conscientious mistake.

'I think that last night in admiring [Miss]——'s work I might better have said less unless I could have managed at the same time to convey more. I do admire the grace and beauty of the designs, but I do not think that to call a figure 'a fairy' settles the right and wrong of such figures. *You* (so far as I know) are no dealer in such wares. Therefore I think it possible you will agree with me in thinking that *all* do well to forbear such delineations, and that most of all women artists should set the example and lead the way.

'I ought not now—I fear—be having to say awkwardly what should not have been so totally ignored in my tone last night: but last night's blunder must not make me the slave of false shame this morning.

'Do not answer this: I am not afraid to have offended you.

'My mental eye is fixed on fetching the dear photograph, I hope possibly to do so to-morrow and then quickly to send it to you. But if a longer time elapses do not think I am forgetful: sometimes I am hindered.'

The 'dear photograph' in the above extract alludes to a photograph of Dante Gabriel she herself brought to Mr. Shields.

Here is an extract from a letter to Mrs. Frederic Shields written on December 26, 1883. The 'dear friend' referred to was probably Charles Bagot Cayley, the translator of Dante, whose work, as I have mentioned, Christina admired greatly, and whose literary executrix she became :

'. . . . Pray thank your husband for sympathy. Our Xmas has indeed been saddened by the loss of so dear a Friend. " They shall perish, but Thou remainest," —one ought to be able to say so even when Death does its momentary work, but how easy the words are to utter and how difficult their meaning to attain. I hope your near and dear circle will remain long uninvaded.'

Apropos of a visit to Brighton in 1885 she writes two letters to Mrs. W. M. Rossetti giving hints as to the habits of the household in Torrington Square, and as to her sentiments towards Birchington :

'Do you happen to recollect the direction of *your* lodgings? If so I am sure you will kindly let me have it, but I will only trouble you to do so if you judge that the house is one likely to accommodate our party of four. Not that we want anything exceptional : four beds in either 2 or 3 bedrooms, and a sitting-room. Ground floor or 1st floor preferred,—not, that is, any of the rooms higher up than the 1st floor. Cooking nice, and proper attendance. If possible we should be quite glad to pay for *board* as well as lodging : do you think there would be a chance of this ?—for not one of us feels any fancy for the housekeeping department. If I do not hear from you I shall understand that you do not see a likelihood of our suiting the lodgings in question.

.　　.　　.　　.　　.　　.

'Our rooms are on the ground floor, which for some reasons suits us best. I don't think I have stayed at Brighton since 1850 (!) so my recollections of locality are not very vivid ; and were they so, doubtless many of them would be obsolete . . . We cannot be accused of being *children* ! . . Our loves to sensible Olive and studious Helen [her second niece] ; please tell the former that it would do *me* a great deal of good to spell certain words over and over again . . . The short journey is a boon, otherwise I should hanker after Birchington.'

Mr. Shields had promised to design a cover for 'Time Flies,' but, owing to illness, was unable to carry out his intentions. Hearing of this Christina wrote to him thus :

April 20.

'My dear Mr. Shields,—My Mother and I join in hearty hopes that you are rallying by the sea and are storing strength for a happy return to London and to congenial work. Whether your wife is or not with you our love to her and our best wishes.

'Meanwhile "Time Flies"! Pray do not bestow another thought on the beautiful work you meant to do for me, and of which the good will is more precious to me than the handicraft however choice that might have been. I beg you to ease your mind of any further care on the subject. Will you write to Mr. McClure or shall I ? My book must trust for success to its inner graces and not to the mantle of your name and fame.'

April 22.

'Dear Mr. Shields,—We are so sorry, my mother and I, to know that you are ill and suffering,—for we have just seen your kind letter to the S.P.C.K. But I will not forego associating you in some degree with my book, for I am sure you will give me pleasure by accepting a copy when I hope the cover will seem to you not amiss as a humble substitute. I who have just been shown the design, think it not at all unpleasing, and as I am quite incapable of figuring to myself what I have missed I may rest contented. I hope " Time Flies " will interest you more rather than less, because on 2 of the days you will recognise thoughts of your own : you threw light on ' Cleansing of the Temple " one evening, this furnishes the substance of one paper [" Time Flies," January 23] ; and another owes its origin to your vivid description of certain wayside spiders at Birchington [see p. 93 of the present volume]. Mr. McClure tells me the book is to come out on May 1st, so I hope it will not be very long before I offer you your copy.

'Always your obliged friend
'CHRISTINA G. ROSSETTI.'

What follows was written in 1885. Dr. Olivieri, in the words of her surviving brother, 'was an estimable and cultivated Italian, much afflicted by ill-health and other troubles. . . . He died some years ago.'

30 Torrington Square W.C.
Saturday evening

'My dear William,—Dr. Olivieri has given Mamma and me the tickets I enclose to you with our loves. Can you make any use of them? . . . best of all *yourself*, but this I dare not anticipate. The prospectuses I add, thinking it not quite impossible you might mention the 3 lectures in an Athenæum "gossip" paragraph but of course there is no time to lose, if kindly you bestow a thought on the matter. Mamma and I— who really *cannot* attend—are going to purchase 2 tickets apiece, and I must think (if I can) of the best people to give them to. Mamma was tired with a long drive yesterday, and to-day we have stayed at home, but we hope to get to church to-morrow. Mr. John Walker writes that he has got "Time Flies" and mentions with admiration the roundels in general and "If love is not worth loving" in particular. Your blushing sister
'C. G. R.'

'I saw the first quotation from "Time Flies" in a parish paper by Mr. Gurney [see pp. 120–6].'

The Duke of Westminster commissioned Mr. Shields to decorate the chapel at Eaton Hall. He talked over with his friend possible subjects for designs, and soon afterwards she sent him the following memoranda. Concerning these Mr. Shields has written to me.

'These notes generously sent to me by Christina Rossetti after a talk with her over the subjects are most interesting—that on Love particularly so—though none concurred with my own subsequent designs, they manifest a clear beautiful power of vision in the writer.

'The suggestion of heartsease on the floor of the figure of "Obedience" caused me to wreath the yoke he bears with the floral emblem of rest.'

The original MS. of the memoranda was written on sheets of blue paper quarto size. From the manuscript it would seem that she had, subsequently to its being written, gone through it again, renumbering her notes, and italicising certain of her phrases, in red ink.

1. '(*You told me*) 1 Adam and Eve, Angels like birds in trees. *Praise.* Revelation xv. 2, 3 : vii. 9. Some in white robes, 2 Palms and harps in hand, standing and singing on sea of glass and fire.

'2. 3 *Nativity.* Canticles ii. 1 (applied to our Lord). B. Virgin seated in sky-coloured robe sprinkled with flames (as a symbol of God the Holy Ghost : St Luke i. 35) our Infant Lord on her knee, He wearing the 3-flame Glory. Background of upper portion of design *trefoils* as symbols of the Holy Trinity—lower background and floor roses and lilies (see *ante* Canticles ii. 1).

'4 *Obedience.* Proverbs xxiii. 26 Youthful figure kneeling, elevating and offering a flaming and smoking censer, of heart-shape, golden and set with rubies (perhaps some reference might be made to Job xxviii. 17, 18).

'Quote St. John xiv. 15 and Romans xiii. 10. The floor of heartsease flowers . . . their being *floor* hinting how often if we offer our heart to God we must also trample earthly affection under foot.

'3. *Crucifixion.*

'5 *Faith.* Canticles ii. 3. Apple tree full of fruit and foliage branching crosswise. Female figure expressive of joy and sorrow (seated in tree-shadow which "signs her with the sign of the Cross") and gazing upwards.   Ground of lilies amid thorns.

'6 4. *Ascension.*   Ascends with visible ascending action, and in attitude of benediction : St. Luke xxiv, 50, 51.

'7 *Hope* (this I merely add, knowing it is not wanted) Hebrews vi. 19.   Man in boat <u>casting anchor</u>.   Above, sky <u>with rainbow</u> : below, fainter rainbow in water, into which anchor strikes.

'5. *Pentecost.*

'8 *Love.*   Romans xii. 20, 21.   Man feeding enemy, with *warm* mess.   Fire at which he has cooked it, whence revives phœnix.   Taken in connection with compartment above, I want the thread of fire (so to say) to descend (in idea) from the Divine fountain of Love, through the Twelve, to the love-kindled symbolic figure, to kindle finally the "enemy,"—whose life re-kindled by his benefactor's "coals of fire" is emblematized by the phœnix.

'9 6. *Judgment.*   Same action precisely as in No. 4, only *descending* instead of *ascending.*   The clouds (Rev. 1. 7) dimly lighted up by returning saints (1 Thess. 4, 14, 16), and the Archangels, one shouting the other sounding the trumpet.

'10 *Vigilance.* (as you said) the Wise Virgins.

'The *three top lights* if *Angels,*—I think a *moon* might accompany each,—the first *crescent*, the second *full*, the third *waning*, to correspond with the course of the Dispensation figure and symbolised below.

'I have fancied that the balance of colour, &c., is in some measure observed in the details as above.'

To the same correspondent she says some time afterwards :

'Dear Mr. Shields,—Do you recollect in old days signing an anti-Vivisection Petition to Parliament?   A Memorial is now preparing for presentation to the Home Secretary beseeching him not to licence a so called "Institute of Preventive Medicine" which will establish Pasteur's treatment and I suppose other horrors in our midst.   I am procuring a few signatures.   If you share our anxiety, and will favour us with a post card, I will send the memorial to you for signature for yourself and (if it were so) by any other grown-up English man or woman within your influence. If on the contrary I do not hear from you I will understand your silence as negative.'

Mr. Shields gratified Christina by signing the petition. In truth she paid more attention to social questions than one would be apt to suppose, and respecting them her attitude was often highly individual.

Augusta Webster, one of the most eminent of women poets, was also a trenchant prose writer. A vigorous and eloquent advocate of Women's Suffrage, she wrote on this subject in 'The Examiner,' then under the editorship of Professor William Minto. Her contributions were subsequently reprinted by the Women's Suffrage Society in leaflet form, and were forwarded to Christina Rossetti. Mr. Thomas Webster has most courteously placed at my disposal the correspondence that ensued, and from two of Christina Rossetti's letters to Augusta Webster I make the following extracts :

'You express yourself with such cordial openness that I feel encouraged to endeavour also after self-expression —no easy matter sometimes. I write as I am thinking and feeling, but I premise that I have not even to my own apprehension gone deep into the question ; at least, not in the sense in which many who *have* studied it would require depth of me. In one sense I feel as if I had gone deep, for my objection seems to myself a fundamental one underlying the whole structure of female claims.

'Does it not appear as if the Bible was based upon an understood unalterable distinction between men and women, their position, duties, privileges ? Not arrogating to myself but most earnestly desiring to attain to the

character of a humble orthodox Xtian, so it does appear
to me ; not merely under the Old but also under the
New Dispensation.　The fact of the Priesthood being
exclusively man's, leaves me in no doubt that the
highest functions are not in this world open to both
sexes : and if not all, then a selection must be made and
a line drawn somewhere.—On the other hand if female
rights are sure to be overborne for lack of female voting
influence, then I confess I feel disposed to shoot ahead
of my instructresses, and to assert that female *M.P.'s*
are only right and reasonable.　Also I take exceptions
at the exclusion of married women from the suffrage,—
for who so apt as Mothers—all previous arguments
allowed for the moment—to protect the interests of
themselves and of their offspring ?　I do think if anything ever does sweep away the barrier of sex, and make
the female not a giantess or a heroine but at once and
full grown a hero and giant, it is that mighty maternal
love which makes little birds and little beasts as well as
little women matches for very big adversaries.

'Nor do I think it quite inadmissible that men should
continue the exclusive national legislators, so long as
they do continue the exclusive soldier-representatives of
the nation, and engross the whole payment in life and
limb for national quarrels.　I do not know whether any
lady is prepared to adopt the Platonic theory of female
regiments ; if so, she sets aside this objection : but I am
not, so to me it stands.'

And again :

'Many who have thought more and done much more
than myself share your views,—and yet they are not
mine.　I do not think the present social movements
tend on the whole to uphold Xtianity, or that the influence
of some of our most prominent and gifted women is
exerted in that direction : and thus thinking I cannot
aim at "women's rights."

'Influence and responsibility are such solemn matters,
that I will not excuse myself to you for abiding by my
convictions : yet in contradicting you I am contradicting
one I admire.'

Christina was deeply interested in the concerns of her nieces and nephew. One of her names for them was 'the Four.' Writing to Mrs. W. M. Rossetti one Sunday morning of 1883, she says :

'Reconsidering the great question of Olive's birthday, it strikes me very strongly that I would rather give her Motley's book than the other. So if she has taken no steps in the matter, please tell her so : but if on the faith of my word she has actually procured the other, then I will pay for it as I said at first. Of course should there be something else which she would prefer to either, I am cheerfully open to " a bid." My love to her and to her juniors if they are all at home again. Please tell Arthur that Aunt Eliza liked his flowers particularly.'

And in July 1885 she writes to the same correspondent then at Bournemouth :

'Welcome was the triple letter of this morning, especially as it tells us that you appear to gain ground and that your children are well. To you Mamma sends a maternal love, and to them a grand maternal. I add my modest greeting. Mamma values Olive's sensible letter and notices the improved handwriting, and little Mary's funny composition with its spirited account of the dogs and monkeys greatly pleases her. We should very much like to see Bournemouth with its shade and its charms : but such delights are no longer for us. Meanwhile we find London extremely bearable.

'We had the pleasure of seeing Mr. [Madox] Brown and William on Sunday afternoon ; and we brought out portraits of Gabriel, amongst which 2 photographs may perhaps prove useful [for Ford Madox Brown's bust of Dante Gabriel at Chelsea]. Dr. Littledale dropped in before they left and renewed acquaintance. . . .'

The phrase 'such delights are no longer for us' alludes to her mother's determination to avoid railway journeys of any great length.

I

The three succeeding beautiful letters, addressed to
Mr. Shields, have reference to her mother's final illness
and death.

30 Torrington Square W.C.
Monday Afternoon.

' My dear Mr. Shields,—On our part good news.   My
precious Mother is better, is out of danger, says to-day
her doctor, if only her strength suffices for the rally.
God grant it, if it be His merciful Will : more than that
I dare not say or even wish.   But you may think what
the hope is to me.

' Meanwhile you have been in trouble and sorrow for
your one nearest and dearest.   Our love to her, and our
very best wishes for her present ease and speedy recovery.
She has youth on her side, that beautiful and delightful
thing youth.   May she soon rejoice you by restored
health.

' Yours very truly,'

And later on she says :

30 Torrington Square W.C.
Monday.

' Dear Friend,—I must not hear of the inestimable
boon of your prayers without writing to thank you for
us both.   May your dear wife grow strong.   For me
there is no earthly hope,—but far better, a heavenly.

' Always truly yours,'

Characteristically unselfish is the remark which
closes what follows, written after her mother's death
in April 1886 :

30 Torrington Square W.C.
Saturday.

' Dear Friend,—Thank you for every word which
shows how my dearest Mother was honoured and beloved.
I am glad it is I and not she that is left sorrowful and
lonely.

' Gratefully yours,'

Constantly did she speak, both in her correspondence

and in her published work, about her mother. Indeed the thought of her mother seemed rarely absent from her mind. ' The Face of the Deep ' contains this delicate piece of analysis of opposite feminine qualities :

' Eve exhibits one extreme of feminine character, the Blessed Virgin the opposite extreme. Eve parleyed with a devil : holy Mary " was troubled " at the salutation of an Angel. Eve sought knowledge : Mary instruction. Eve aimed at self-indulgence : Mary at self-oblation. Eve, by disbelief and disobedience, brought sin to the birth : Mary, by faith and submission, Righteousness.

' And yet, even as at the foot of the Cross, St. Mary Magdalene, out of whom went seven devils, stood beside the " lily among thorns," the Mother of sorrows : so (I humbly hope and trust) among all saints of all time will stand before the throne, Eve the beloved first Mother of us all. Who that has loved and revered her own immediate dear Mother, will not echo the hope ? '

Nor is it possible to help reading into these opening lines from a noble sonnet in the same book an allusion both to her sister and to her mother.

> Our Mothers, lovely women pitiful ;
> Our Sisters, gracious in their life and death ;
> To us each unforgotten memory saith :
> ' Learn as we learned in life's sufficient school.'

When reviewing in ' The Athenæum ' of February 15, 1896, Christina Rossetti's ' New Poems,' Mr. Watts-Dunton had some touching remarks respecting her mother's influence on Christina, and Christina's own influence on Dante Gabriel :

' Christina Rossetti's peculiar form of the Christian sentiment she inherited from her mother, the sweetness of whose nature was never disturbed by that exercise of the egoism of the artist in which Christina indulged, and

without whose influence it is difficult to imagine what
the Rossetti family would have been.

'All that is noblest in Christina's poetry, an ever-
present sense of the beauty and power of goodness, must
surely have come from the mother, from whom also
came that other charm of Christina's, to which Gabriel
was peculiarly sensitive, her youthfulness of temperament.

'It was the beauty of her life that made her personal
influence so great, and upon no one was that influence
exercised with more strength than upon her illustrious
brother Gabriel, who in many ways was so much unlike
her. In spite of his deep religious instinct and his
intense sympathy with mysticism, Gabriel remained
what is called a free thinker in the true meaning of that
much-abused phrase. In religion as in politics he
thought for himself, and yet when Mr. W. M. Rossetti
affirms that the poet was never drawn towards free-
thinking women, he says what is perfectly true. And
this arose from the extraordinary influence, scarcely
recognised by himself, that the beauty of Christina's life
and her religious system had upon him.'

CHAPTER IV

BIOGRAPHICAL—(*continued*)

(Mainly 1886-1893)

Letters to Mrs. W. M. Rossetti—Correspondence with the Rev. Alfred
Gurney—Her humour in a letter to Mr. Shields and in letters to
Mr. and Mrs. W. M. Rossetti—Poem on the death of the Duke of
Clarence—Article on Tudor House in ' Literary Opinion.'

CHRISTINA ROSSETTI often spoke to me about her
mother, less frequently about her sister Maria and her
brother Gabriel, though respecting them, and even the
latter, she was by no means reticent, mentioning without
reserve 'that fatal chloral' which had done so much to
mar and to shorten her brother's life. She herself did
not suffer from insomnia. She told me she never knew
what it was to be sleepless, and she told another friend
that her brother Gabriel's sleeplessness had a mysterious
fascination for her. In a letter which she describes as
'dismal,' written soon after her mother's death, she
says :

'Life is full of anxieties . . . I fluctuate, but neither
far above nor far below my level.'

On the sudden death of Dr. Hueffer, the brother-in-
law of Mrs. W. M. Rossetti, she wrote to her. Mrs. W.
M. Rossetti was then at Biarritz :

30 Torrington Square—London—W.C.
January 21. 1889.

'My dear Lucy,—I cannot hear of such bereavement among almost your nearest circle without writing to remind you of my love and sympathy. Aunt Eliza unites with me in good will and sympathy and in love to our nieces and nephew. I had not the slightest idea such a blow was imminent. Poor Cathy! [Mrs. Hueffer] I ventured to send her a few flowers to-day. William came this morning looking as you may suppose, much concerned, and anxious on your account. Dear Lucy, reassure us by bearing the shock bravely and resignedly. Something led me to mention the death to Mr. Stewart (my Aunts' medical man) and I found he had already seen it announced in the 'Times.' I hope the children are affectionate to their sorrowful mother—tho' Ford is no "child" indeed, and Oliver, perhaps, scarcely to be reckoned one: so I will rather say, I hope the sons and the little daughter are affectionate to their mother. Poor Dr. Hueffer, I recollect the special love he lavished on his little girl, his "Poppy."

'We have just been in much doubt as to Aunt Charlotte; however, she has rallied once more. The attack seemed to begin with a chill, but happily this did not fasten on the lungs.

'She is very weak, but not perhaps what I ought to call very ill.

'I hope Biarritz retains all its charms and even develops fresh ones. *Of course* you and yours will dip into Spain when under William's escort! I am the more impressed by your triumphant achievements of economy, because I had understood [1] Biarritz to be particularly dear.'

Christina could still be quietly cheerful, as is seen in this extract from a letter to her sister-in-law dated 1890, which refers to Christina's first prospective visit to 3 St. Edmund's Terrace, Regent's Park, where her brother William and his family had now gone to reside:

[1] Ah perdona! [On account of a blot.]

'Thank you for the love which sends me so beautiful a present even more than for the present itself. But it must lie by : it must wait till energy combines with cash to refurbish my drawing-room decayed in chintz and cushions. At present I am in the mood to feel hurried—not to say alas! to feel *worried*—with the various things which must be done. Laugh at your inert sister in law, my dear Lucy: and erect her as scarecrow to frighten Helen and Mary from such moods and ways ; Olive seems not to need the warning.

'I had been secretly hoping I might see William yesterday, and he came.

'Thank you affectionately for kindly wishing me to see you all in your new house. Some day I hope to do so, though I fear I must forego William on account of Sunday. Neither can I dream of coming before the stair carpet completes your splendours ! '

What follows from a letter to her sister-in-law, written early in 1890, refers to certain articles formerly the property of Miss Charlotte Polidori who had recently died. It is given here as perhaps being the only glimpse in this volume of Christina Rossetti in relation to matters merely feminine :

'Encouraged by you I send you a very miscellaneous selection, yet I assure you it *is* a "selection," not a higgledy-piggledy all at random.

'The 2 coloured pockethandkerchiefs and the white kid gloves look as if possibly they might avail for William, to whom all love. The little pair of white woollen sleeves (the one which has an *edge*) please hand to Helen the beloved, as good old Aunt Charlotte had a fancy for her to have them. There is a very odd looking article in velvet and fur—but perhaps you are familiar with such—which properly arranged resolves itself into a hood and throat-guard, for over-bonnet-wear in driving,—perhaps suitable to "opera " wear in London ; I mean for transit, of course. The other items explain themselves.   I am no adept in lace, so if some rubbish has crept in please condone the error to ignorant good will.'

Here is a letter, penned in April 1891, to Mrs. W. M. Rossetti, then at Broadstairs.   Some time before, Christina had planted an acorn in a flower-pot, from which had sprung the ' oak tree ' alluded to :

30 Torrington Square, London, W.C.
Monday.

' My dear Lucy,—Thank you for remembering— — — I just discover that I am writing the wrong way of the paper, but I am sure you will not mind— — — for remembering the stay-at-home.   I like always to have the address of " my family," and thus to feel that I can get at you in case of need.   Aunt Eliza has had a drive in her chair this morning, and sends that all-embracing love in which I unite.   I hope your Broadstairs day is as sunny as ours.   Admirable and triumphant was your sudden flitting : I hope 8 *The Paragon* is the paragon it professes to be.   I bear in mind that if William has to be at home on the evening of the 4th, *my* second Wednesday will not be interfered with.
' Perhaps the most tender-hearted of your children will bestow a (figurative) tear on the announcement that my own carelessness in repotting broke of[f] the *lateral branch* of the oak tree the other day : I can but comfort myself inasmuch as the *trunk* looks still alive.'

For some years between 1883 and 1893 Christina Rossetti corresponded at intervals with the Rev. Alfred Gurney, vicar of S. Barnabas, Pimlico, and her letters to that gentleman, all written from Torrington Square (which by his courtesy it has been my privilege to peruse), are full of characteristic touches.   Probably the first of these letters is in answer to one of his, in which, presumably, he had supposed her to have joined the Anglican Sisterhood of All Saints, Margaret Street, London.

5 December.

'Rev^d and dear Sir,—I must strip off my halo!
It was my dear sister, not I, who felt drawn to the
noble vocation *I* have never attempted to fulfil : and
she (I trust) is now an inhabitant of a yet holier and
more blessed Home than the one in Margaret Street.
We both met you years ago at Mitcham [at a 'hay-
making party'], before several gaps had been made in
either family.

'The advantage and pleasure are mine whenever
what I have written can be turned to good account :
your utilising the Xmas carol lays me under obligation.'

And again at a later date she writes to the same
correspondent :

' I have just been re-reading your sonnets, and finding
them more beautiful than I at first perceived. Thank
you for them, and for the kind and valued sympathy of
your letter : the " respect " I return in deep earnestness
to the Priest, and the cordiality to the Friend.

'Thank you too for the " Book of Strife." Indeed
I did not possess it, and glancing within I see beauty.
Not that I always like [Dr.] George Macdonald's utterances, but sometimes I do : and even when I do not, the
fault may sometimes (!) be in me and not in him.'—

How quaintly pretty is the turn of this phrase :

' May no wearier weariness beset me than the recognising a handwriting which confers favours.'

What follows is interesting as showing her predilec-
tions with regard to two of Dante Gabriel's pictures,
and also her thoughtfulness for those who needed her
help :

' " Veronica Veronese " is one of my prime favorites,
tho' not so " La Bella Mano." "Beata Beatrix " [pre-
sented some years ago by Lady Mount-Temple to the

National Gallery] will repay a call in Stanhope St. some day.

'Since we saw you we have been down at Birchington, —and now we are hoping————wishing that the tomb-stone and my mother's own window near the porch would arrive at completion. Mr. Shields has undertaken the latter, so it is certain to be beautiful at last.

'I am going to beg a favour. It is that you will harbour not literally in the waste-paper basket but if possible in your obliging memory the name of Miss——. I do not know her personally, but I do know with absolute certainty that she is a *deserving* candidate for a pension from the Governesses' Benevolent Institution. The next election is in May. Not that I suppose you have votes, but you must have so much influence that I cannot bear to let slip the chance of your being ready to help by a word should occasion offer.'

To the same correspondent :

March 5.

'Dear Mr. Gurney,—If I may volunteer an opinion I cannot but think Mr. Watts [-Dunton] will regard your pamphlet with due interest, and an author's presentation copy has such an unique value that I will not suggest he has a second chance of seeing it thro' my brother,— I would by no means deprive him of his *best* chance, otherwise I could—thanks to your kindness—send it him myself. Very much do we like to hear of your good will towards " Hand and Soul " ; but none the less we fully understand the difficulty of finding time for such extra work, so we must not dwell too fondly on the prospect. We are very glad to see, and proportionately to you for showing us, Mr. Ruskin's sympathetic sentence.

'I need hardly say with what interest *we* have read our friend's article [" The Truth about Rossetti " by Mr. Watts-Dunton] in the " 19th Century."'

As to ' Mr. Ruskin's sympathetic sentence' men-tioned above Mr. Gurney has written to me :

'Mr. Ruskin's letter referred to by Christina Rossetti

was a letter to [Mr.] George Richmond, acknowledging an essay of mine sent to him by the latter, in which I discussed (not at all from the art-critic's point of view) some of Rossetti's pictures exhibited at Burlington House.   Mr. Richmond and Mr. Ruskin both were good enough to commend it.'

Concerning Mr. Watts-Dunton and her brother's ' Hand and Soul' she wrote :

' Thank you truly for letting us see Mr. Watts [-Dunton's] interesting letter.   All that comes from that Friend is worth our reading, and I ventured to keep the letter which now I return long enough to show it to my brother.   " Hand and Soul " is rich in beauty and power : *that* even my anxious eyes see and admit ; and I hope others wiser than myself see as you do.   Please do not leave off giving us pleasant surprises from time to time, disgusted by my density !
' The Mission almost over I trust I may congratulate you on some response to your loving invitations.'

The following quotation from a letter written by Mr. Gurney to myself will explain the foregoing allusion to ' Hand and Soul ' :

' Her critical faculty, almost as remarkable perhaps, though not so rare and precious as her artistic, comes out in an interesting and characteristic manner in one of the letters [to himself] about an essay of mine on her brother's " Hand and Soul "—an essay which I had the pleasure of reading to her and her mother and Mr. W. M. Rossetti.'

February 4, 1885.

' Dear Mr. Gurney,—My Mother joins me in thanking you for the permanent form of your paper on our dear Gabriel.   I waited to receive it before thanking you, and now I have reread it.   How much you see in his work, and how earnestly do I hope that what you see is truly there to be seen.

'Thank you not least for your beautiful mission address : may it bear fruit "an hundredfold "—
            'Very truly your obliged
                    'CHRISTINA G. ROSSETTI.'

Her comments respecting Wagner's 'Parsifal' are individual :

'What shall I say of "Parsifal"? I will make an avowal : I would not on any account see it performed. I should not dare witness such a treatment of such a subject. That it is rich in beauty, charm, I do not doubt,— in loftiness, I will not question : but I cannot think it would edify myself.'

This also is individual :

Saturday.

'Dear Mr. Gurney,—Thank you for prolonged kind remembrance and for such a charming poem : it conveys the very sentiment one wants at 55! So I venture to hope that you enter into it a little less deeply than I do, and that 1886 may fairly bring you a more buoyant joy than would befit me.   I never told you how much I enjoyed seeing "Time Flies" quoted in one of your Parish Papers : allow me to tell you so now, remaining as I do' [etc.].

With respect to the 'charming poem' Mr. Gurney tells me :

'I cannot remember sending Christina Rossetti any detached poem.   If I did, it was probably one of 2, both of which are published in my little Christmas volume—"A Xmas Faggot"—one for New Year's Eve, the other for New Year's Day (called "The Victim").'

She could be appreciatively critical respecting a friend's work :

Friday.

'Dear Mr. Gurney,—It is a pleasure to hear from you again, and to read and to return the agreeable "Academy" critique, for which I thank you.

'Nor am I silenced by your condescending appeal to my taste.   As whole poems perhaps my favourites are " Bethlehem Gate "—" St. Joseph " :   Next if not on a par with these (I am not certain) the 1st and 3rd " Epiphany " and the " Nunc Dimittis."   But then there are little bits elsewhere by no means to be set low down : as the stanza beginning ' Oftentimes a sleepless infant ' and that strictly lovely line " Love is of loveliness the root."

'Do you know that our dear friend Mr. Shields is ill at Brighton ? so at least we heard a day or two ago, and my mother and I are grieved for him.   I find your " Xmas Faggot " cover is his handiwork.   What an enviable cover.

'Pray receive my Mother's remembrances and let me trust always to remain ' [etc.].

About ' The Academy ' critique mentioned in the foregoing letter Mr. Gurney sends me the following communication :

' I think the critique in " The Academy " was a short review of the same volume [" A Christmas Faggot "] in which the writer spoke of me as being powerfully influenced by D. G. Rossetti, and under his influence numbered with the mystics, more however on the spiritual than the æsthetic side.'

This letter of Christmas salutation shows how she could give freshness to a trite subject by her graceful and ever present fancy :

December 20.

'Dear Mr. Gurney,—Faggots of wood warm our hearths, and your " Christmas Faggot " warms our hearts, my Mother and I sending you back a responsive glow of good will and good wishes.   Thank you for the taking little volume you devote to your Godchildren : I hope they themselves will prove an impregnable " faggot " (according to the old story) bound together by " the very bond of peace and of all virtues."

'Thank you most of all for our pleasure in seeing Gabriel's name once more graced by your pen.

'Of course I have dipped and glanced already, but I have some idea of not reading steadily before Christmas Day.   Not long to wait for now.

'I have pleasure—for it is so pleasant to be thought of!—in remaining

'Again your obliged
'CHRISTINA G. ROSSETTI.'

Here is a glimpse of her habits:

June 6.

'Dear Mr. Gurney,—Thank you for all the kind thought you take to give us pleasure.

'Your call for any purpose and at any time will be a favour.   I am generally at home.   To which circumstance please attribute (at least in part) my not having yielded to the attraction of your Lecture last night, an attraction to which I was not insensible.

' . . . I am glad Mr. Watts [-Dunton] interested you.   He ranks high amongst our friends.'

What follows was written in acknowledgment of a copy of Mr. Gurney's book ' The Story of a Friendship ':

Christmas 1893.

'Dear Mr. Gurney,—Thank you indeed for your " Vita Nuova," sweet and tender and full of regret and hope.   May each Dante join his Beatrice, and each Beatrice be or become worthy of her Dante.

'This scarcely reads like a Christmas letter until it offers you my deepest best wishes.

'Always gratefully yours,
CHRISTINA G. ROSSETTI.'

Regarding the foregoing Mr. Gurney has written to me thus:

'The letter [that dated Christmas 1893] about Dante and Beatrice is I think a very lovely little bit of aspiration. . . . . . She was a genius, robed in grace.'

If Christina Rossetti's occasional humour was the exception that proved the rule it was none the less present. She could be quietly droll concerning her own habits as will be seen in this extract from a letter to Mr. Shields, written probably in 1888 or 1889.

'What a kind letter from what a kind friend! I am better again, thank you, altho' still subjected to extra care, and amongst precautions is early bedtime,—but for this it would seem possible that I might get a glimpse of you some day. Bedtime however is not so early as to suppress me before 9 o'clock.'

The following excerpts from letters to Mrs. and Mr. W. M. Rossetti attest the same quality :

' Please wink at ugliness, as I have lost my pen.'

' Thank you for thinking my austere presence would be "nice." '

' *I* am not conspicuously in bloom :—but let us hope I resemble the trampled chamomile which "yields more sweets the while—." '

' I fear all 3 *stamps* are unworthy of Arthur. To whom and sisters love.

'Your faithful old friend and sister '

''My dear Lucy,—William asked me to dine with you next Thursday—shall I come? I know that at times with the kindest good will one guest more is one too many, and I shall not doubt your kindness if you frankly tell me it is not convenient.

'With loves all round
'Yours always

'William conjectured 7 o'clock to be the hour : but if I like to arrive a little beforetime I think you will *wink* at the freedom————that is, if you ask me!'

'My dear Lucy,—Thank you heartily. I was aware of the fact, and had foreseen the possibility, and am very glad indeed that your kind thoughtfulness makes

it easy for me to avoid the difficulty. It happens too
that I am just so unwell at present as to invite me to
keep quiet ; I have had to miss one or two little family
expeditions already.
> 'Lovingly and gratefully
> 'Your sister'

'We all unite in a general *yes*, with love and thanks—
tho' Aunt Eliza asks for 10 minutes law, as she cannot
be quite punctual.
'So till to-morrow—and not merely *till!*—
> 'Your affec. sister'

'If you think the "Chronicles" not alarmingly dry
for immature Arthur, pray oblige me by securing such
on my account,—unless you achieve some improved
afterthought. I own I do not think they would have
enraptured me at a more advanced age : qu., indeed,
what would happen now?'

'I hope we shall so soon see you that there is no
need to hammer out a letter. "Certainly not" you
respond alacritously to
> 'Your affec. sister
> 'C. G. R.'

'Why waste ink on stating that I am always glad to
see you ?
'Your destitute—of—news *

> C. G. R.

* or at least not regurgitant.'

'Miss Wilson writes : "I am very grateful to Mr.
and Mrs. Rossetti for all their details—please tell them
so"—and thus tell I them, adding my own particular
thanks for *your* valuable a*dd*enda—(I hope all those *d*'s
are right ?).'

'To my regret, the poetry of impulse has been succeeded by the prose of calculation.'

'I am writing with the paper in my lap, so excuse
degradation. Poor Mr. Turner will, I think, undergo
another paper from me to-morrow, which * transcends my
wits—*the paper*,* I mean.'

'Thanks in proportion to my density : I recall to memory the British farmer who equipped himself for the Rhine apparently by divesting himself of his wits !

'With returning reason I propose to act thus. Monday or Tuesday (Office days) next, to send 11/6 in compliance with this demand of my country, asking no questions and awaiting whatever may next occur. Short of your *veto*, thus I trust to act.'

. . . .

'Last night I got a few words from Lucy asking me to send name of Publisher of " Sing Song " to a Bookseller who failed to unearth that obscure tome. So of course I did. But thus you see I am groping in an atmosphere of befogment, and my renown is under eclipse.'

. . . .

'Bye-the-bye, the other day in the " St. James's Gazette " there appeared a chaffy allusion to " My heart is like a singing bird "—not ill natured rather amusing, not naming author.'

. . . .

'Padrone ! Questa tua casa !

'You are welcome on the most *cupboard love* terms, always and every way welcome. You shall have a cup of tea, and I will show you a book or two if you care to look at them. . . . Why not always come here on Shelley nights [meetings of the Shelley Society] ?

'My dear William

'Your affectionate old sister '

'My dear William,—The accompanying 16ˢ 3ᵈ stands for our share up to January 8, but if you deem yourself entitled to additional pennies I will honour your view— my arithmetic is not a prime article.'

When, on January 14, 1892, the death of the Duke of Clarence was announced, Mr. Patchett Martin, who was at that time editing ' Literary Opinion,' asked her to write a poem on the subject for his next number (though with considerable diffidence, remembering her unwillingness to be hurried). At once she consented verbally and a day or two afterwards, in time for his February issue, he received one of the most beautiful of her later poems, 'A Death of a Firstborn,' accompanied by the following little note, dated January 21 :

'I enclose a few lines. Please accept or return them with absolute freedom.'

She wrote as follows to Mrs. Patchett Martin when forwarding a receipt for three guineas, her honorarium for the poem :

Wednesday, February 10, 1892.

'Dear Mrs. Patchett Martin,—Will you kindly hand the enclosed receipt to Mr. Martin with my thanks for the handsome cheque. And I thank you especially for the pleasure of reading Miss Caldecott's letter : you may be sure I enjoy such verdicts,—yet the being so often "spoken well of" ought to make me the more wary not to offend. . . . "Literary Opinion" has much good in its power. I am glad to have appeared for once in its pages, but my pen being partly at the mercy of impulse I can never count on a second such moment ; and at 61 one can neither wish nor expect to be as impulsive as at 16!

'Will you excuse my shabby envelope, but it happens to be my only one of the right size and shape.'

'Italy's greatest living Novelist' alluded to in what follows was Signor Verga, author of 'Cavalleria Rusticana' :

Wednesday, [March 28, 1892.]

'Dear Mr. Patchett Martin,— . . . My best wishes accompany every effort to send forth high-minded criticism, and I hope you will be every way happy in your venture. It is not in my power—at least, not in conformity with the way in which I have mainly used such powers as are mine—to promise you original articles on approval : but if ever you received a "Dante" book for review and cared to entrust it to me I would gladly try my hand on it ; perhaps enthusiasm for my subject might make up for scant learning.

Miss Helen Zimmern's name I recognise : but I actually do not know who it is she records as " Italy's greatest living Novelist ! "—so obsolete am I.'

She did not however write on Dante in ' Literary Opinion.'

When her poem ' Faint, yet Pursuing,' was sent to her in proof she found, owing to a printer's blunder, that the tenth line had been omitted ; whereupon she wrote to Mr. Patchett Martin on April 16, 1892, as follows. Before returning the proof revised, &c., she had with great elaboration attended to the indentation. A fac-simile of this proof is given on p. 132.

' Let us hope that merit will perpetuate the demand [for Literary Opinion] which curiosity may in part have initiated.

' Is it conceivable——I hope it is inconceivable that I sent you a 13 line Sonnet !! My rough copy assures me that it was not so written. I dare say you will make sure that the missing line is properly put in ; and perhaps you will not deem unworthy of revision the *inning and outing* of both pieces. I hope I have not overlooked any error.'

Having been desired to contribute the article respecting Tudor House, (quoted from at p. 134), she writes to Mr. Patchett Martin on May 6, 1892 :

' I do not feel myself the proper person to review D. G. R.'s " Dante and his Circle," and very likely might break down even over some other writer on a kindred subject as I am not an expert in such articles. Have I any associations with the old Cheyne Walk House ? Indeed I have, some of them very agreeable : if I succeed in jotting anything down to any purpose I shall feel disposed

"FAINT, YET PURSUING."

1.

Beyond this shadow and this turbulent sea,
  Shadow of death and turbulent sea of death,
Lies all we long to have or long to be :—
  Take heart, tired man, toil on with lessening breath,
Lay violent hands on heaven's high treasury,
  Be what you long to be thro' life-long scathe :
A little while hope leans on charity,
  A little while charity heartens faith.
A little while : and then what further while ?
  For ever new whilst evermore the same :
All things made new bear each a sweet new name ;
Man's lot of death has turned to life his lot,
And tearful charity to love's own smile.

2.

Press onward, quickened souls, who mounting move,
  Press onward, upward, fire with mounting fire ;
Gathering volume of untold desire
  Press upward, homeward, dove with mounting dove.
Point me the excellent way that leads above ;
  Woo me with sequent will me too to aspire ;
  With sequent heart to follow higher and higher,
To follow all who follow on to love
  Up the high steep, across the golden sill.
Up out of shadows into very light,
  Up out of dwindling life to life aglow,
  I watch you, my beloved, out of sight ;—
Sight fails me, and my heart is watching still :
  My heart fails, yet I follow on to know.

CHRISTINA G. ROSSETTI.

[FACSIMILE OF PROOF OF SONNETS 'FAINT, YET PURSUING']

to submit my reminiscences to you in case you should
care for such text to accompany Miss Thomas's drawing.

'The May " L.O.," thank you, came duly to hand and
certified me of the correct issue of my 2.   I am glad you
approve of them.'

'My 2' alludes of course to the two sonnets 'Faint,
yet Pursuing' mentioned above.   Miss Margaret
Thomas, who illustrated the article by a woodcut, is
best known by her bust of Henry Fielding at Taunton.

The extracts immediately succeeding, from letters
addressed to Mr. Patchett Martin, written in May 1892,
refer to the article on Tudor House.   The 'bracketed
clause' was the Italian poem, beginning 'O Uommi-
batto,' given below :

'Please do not delay the woodcut on my account :
the trifle I hope to submit to you will I trust be in
your hands next week, very possibly on Monday.   If
you can supersede it by something better, pray do.
For I feel myself not the right person to write " Rossetti"
articles, only this matter of the house seemed unobjec-
tionable.

'So many portraits of D. G. R. have appeared that I
know not whether you would easily find a fresh one.   I
wonder if a sketch of the Drinking Fountain associated
with Tudor House might sufficiently interest some of
your readers ?

'Here is the slight sketch we projected, in case you
may judge it to be worth appending to the drawing.
You will notice that I have conspicuously bracketed
one clause : possibly it is too irrelevant to the matter
in hand, or possibly space will run short : in either
event it can be excised by merely concluding what
precedes it by a *.   It is such a long time since I
last saw Tudor House that perhaps my hints as to
its actual outside appearance are no longer correct : Miss
Thomas will oblige me if she considers this point.

'I think my note of Saturday answered other suggestions in your last kind letter, and I should not wonder if in truth you agreed with me that I am not the fit person for a Rossetti tome.'

An extract from Christina's remarks descriptive of Tudor House during Dante Gabriel's tenancy may suitably be reproduced here, more especially as the article has not been reprinted.

'There were, as has often been stated, various creatures, quaint or beautiful, about the house and grounds, some of them at liberty. I particularly recall Bobby—a little owl with a very large face and a beak of a sort of egg-shell green ; a woodchuck, a deer, and a wombat, nameless, or of name unknown to me. Gabriel (his family never called him Dante, Gabriel being indeed his first Christian name), was amused by some lines I wrote on that wombat :—

> O Uommibatto
>   Agil, giocondo,
> Che ti sei fatto
>   Liscio e rotondo !
> Deh non fuggire
>   Qual vagabondo,
> Non disparire
>   Forando il mondo :
> Pesa davvero
>   D'un emisfero
> Non lieve il pondo.

But far from " liscio " the wombat turned out rough, and I altered l. 4 to :—" Irsuto e tondo."

' With such inhabitants, Tudor House and its grounds became a sort of wonderland ; and once the author of " Wonderland " photographed us in the garden. It was our aim to appear in the full family group of five ; but whilst various others succeeded, that particular negative was spoilt by a shower, and I possess a solitary print taken from it in which we appear as if splashed by ink.

' Allowing for long lapse of years and consequent possible defects of memory, such as these are my recol-

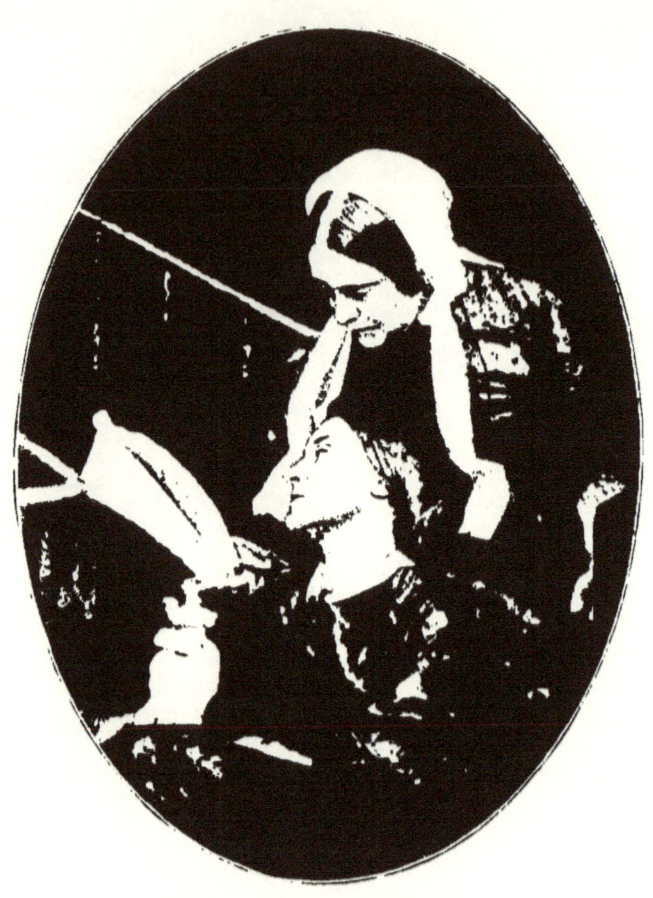

CHRISTINA ROSSETTI AND HER MOTHER.

*(From a photograph, now in the possession of Mr. W. M. Rossetti, taken by
' Lewis Carroll ' (Rev. Charles Lutwidge Dodgson) in the garden of
Tudor House, 16 Cheyne Walk, Chelsea, towards 1863.*

lections of happy days when family or friendly parties used to assemble at Tudor House there to meet with an unfailing affectionate welcome.   Gloom and eccentricity such as have been alleged were at any rate not the sole characteristics of Dante Gabriel Rossetti : when he chose he became the sunshine of his circle, and he frequently chose so to be.   His ready wit and fun amused us ; his good nature and kindness of heart endeared him to us.'

By the kindness of Mr. W. M. Rossetti, a photograph of Christina and her mother taken by ' Lewis Carroll ' (Rev. Charles Lutwidge Dodgson), one of those which ' succeeded ' as mentioned above, is reproduced to face this page.

CHAPTER V

BIOGRAPHICAL—*(continued)*

(Mainly 1893–1894)

Her appearance—Wishes to remove to neighbourhood of Regent's Park—
Reminiscences of London—Mr. Watts-Dunton's and Mr. W. M.
Rossetti's remarks respecting her attitude towards animals—Description
of 30 Torrington Square—Habits of work—Her handwriting—Her books
—Her drawing-room—The garden of Torrington Square—Mr. Shields
as artist—His Good Shepherd—Mrs. Garnett, Miss Lisa Wilson—Her
goddaughter, Miss Ursula Hake—Her opinion as to cremation—Her
political proclivities—Her consciousness of evils in our social system—
Her practical habits—Her appreciation of poetry—Her reading of
poetry—Her admiration of Augusta Webster's drama 'The Sentence,'
and of Jean Ingelow—Personal habits—Her voice—Her household—
Prayers—Her attitude towards music—Christ Church, Woburn Square
—Increasing illness—Relinquishes attendance at church—Dr. Stewart—
Dr. Abbot Anderson—Closing days—Her aspect after death—Spiritual
disquietude towards the end—Widespread regret occasioned by her
death—Letter from the Bishop of Durham to Mr. W. M. Rossetti—Her
funeral—Preliminary service Christ Church, Woburn Square—Highgate
Cemetery—Mr. Theodore Watts [-Dunton's] 'Two Christmastides'—
Memorial service.

I SHALL never forget Christina Rossetti's appearance
when first I called upon her. She gave me the impression of being tall: I thought then, as I do still, that none
of her portraits sufficiently indicate the commanding
breadth of her brow. She looked unquestionably a
woman of genius, and it is not every woman or man of
genius that so looks. Her voice attracted me at once:
never before had I heard such a voice. It was intensely
musical, but its indefinable charm arose not alone from

that cause ; it arose in a large measure from what Mr.
Watts-Dunton has aptly called her ' clear-cut method
of syllabification,'—a peculiarity which he thinks, no
doubt rightly, attributable to her foreign lineage.   Indications of her foreign lineage were very noticeable on
the occasion I am describing.   Not of course that it was
discernible in accent, nor even in mere tone or inflexion
of voice, certainly it was not markedly observable either
in her modes of speech or in her ideas.   It was something
assuredly there, but, like many of the things we perceive
with life's subtler perceptions, it eluded precise definition.
Perhaps the nearest approach to an illustration of my
meaning would be to say that the effect produced was
as though a highly educated foreigner, thoroughly acquainted with the grammar and the vocabulary of the
English language, were to speak English, and continue
to do so for years, although English was not his mother
tongue.   No one, I think, can fully understand Christina's many-sided personality without taking into account
that foreign origin, and there can be no doubt that under
some circumstances the blending of races has much to
do with the possession of certain gifts.

Demurely attired in a black silk dress she wore
no ornaments of any sort, and the prevailing sombre
tint was only relieved by some simple white frilling
at the throat and wrists.   Her hair, still abundant, had
by this time a hue which was almost black, and the
intermingled grey strands, though visible, were not
conspicuous.   Her cap, of some dark material, was
extremely plain and unobtrusive.

It has often struck me that one of the great tests
of genius is whether the writer or speaker deals with
ordinary subjects in such a manner as to reveal his or

her own personality. For both in literature and conversation the manner is much.   And if this be true
then both on the day to which I am at present alluding
and on every subsequent occasion when I saw her,
Christina Rossetti talked like a woman of genius.
Naturally at our first meeting the conversation was on
ordinary subjects.   Yet it lives with me still because of
her incomparable manner and the distinction of her
phraseology.   I may add that she conversed in that
calm measured way which, I fancy, often conceals real
shyness.   In Mr. Sharp's able article before referred to
he describes vividly his first meeting with her at an
earlier date than that to which I allude :—

' In some ways she reminded me of Mrs. Craik, the
author of " John Halifax, Gentleman " ; that is, in the
Quaker-like simplicity of her dress, and the extreme
and almost demure plainness of the material, with, in
her mien, something of that serene passivity which has
always a charm of its own. She was so pale as to
suggest anæmia, though there was a bright and alert
look in her large and expressive azure-gray eyes, a
colour which often deepened to a dark, shadowy, velvety
gray ; and though many lines were imprinted on her
features, the contours were smooth and young. Her
hair, once a rich brown, now looked dark, and was
thickly threaded with solitary white hairs, rather than
sheaves of gray. She was about the medium height of
women, though at the time I thought her considerably
shorter. With all her quietude of manner and self-
possession there was a certain perturbation from this
meeting with a stranger, though one so young and
unknown. I noted the quick, alighting glance, its swift
withdrawal ; also the restless, intermittent fingering of
the long, thin double watch-guard of linked gold which
hung from below the one piece of colour she wore, a
quaint, old-fashioned bow of mauve or pale purple
ribbon, fastening a white frill at the neck.'

In one of his family letters Dante Gabriel expressed much surprise that his mother and sister would continue to reside in Torrington Square at a rental of 100 guineas per annum,[1] which he regarded as exceptionally high, when they could elsewhere obtain at a less rental, even in London or in the immediate vicinity, a house more convenient, and probably with a garden. And I cannot but think that, in making this remark, the poet-painter gave a proof of that strong practical common-sense which, when allied to great imaginative power, is itself an evidence of genius. In truth the house seemed hardly the most suitable for his sister. She herself came to think so, even in the last year of her life, and when I called upon her so late as June 5, 1894, she told me with her usual cheerfulness of manner that she had determined to leave it at the following Michaelmas. She remarked further, that when she had come to live at 30 Torrington Square eighteen years before, there had been 'quite a large family,' and now there was only herself, and the house was 'mostly shut up.' Her intention, as stated to me, was then to take a little house in or near the Regent's Park, if possible with a garden, and in close proximity to No. 3 St. Edmund's Terrace, as she wished to see more of her brother and of his family. In relation to this project her brother informs me :

'After Lucy's [Mrs. W. M. Rossetti's] death on April 12 1894 there was some suggestion on my part that C[hristina] sh^d become an inmate of my house 3 St. Edmund's Terrace, but that did not seem really feasible —I then proposed to her whether she would like to take

---

[1] *Vide Dante Gabriel Rossetti: His Family Letters, with a Memoir,* p. 343.

the house No. 1 [St. Edmund's Terrace] vacated by Madox Brown's death.'

In response to this 'suggestion' Christina wrote to him on a postcard, postmarked 'April 21. 1894 ':

'Thank you for your post card received yesterday, but short of the solace of amalgamating with yourself, such a house would be both too large & too expensive.'

On my calling again, shortly after June 5 of the same year, she told me that her physician, Dr. Stewart, imperatively forbade any project of removal with its inevitable attendant inconveniences in her present state of health. So it came about that the project was abandoned, and that her last days were spent in Torrington Square.

Sometimes in conversation she would give me vivid reminiscences of the changed aspect of London. Once, I remember, she gave me a full account of a walk she had taken in early days—I think about 1852-3—to visit Mr. and Mrs. Coventry Patmore then living in Kentish Town in a house they had taken over from her uncle, Mr. Henry Polydore. Kentish Town was then still rural, and the stroll quite partook of the character of a country walk, though perhaps it ought to be added that (as I am informed by Mr. William Rossetti) their residence was in a district of Kentish Town a ' long way up which might almost be termed Highgate Rise.' When Kentish Town was reached, other friends were met, and there was a further walk in the fields, Mr. (now Dr.) Richard Garnett being of the party. She had clear recollections of Regent's Park as it was in earlier days before it was railed in as at present. There was one nook in it presenting to her childish eyes some of the features of a cavern, of which she was especially fond. She also remembered wild flowers in a secluded place close to where there is now a railway tunnel. Miss Proctor, in an interesting brochure entitled ' A Brief Memoir of Christina G. Rossetti,' tells us that the impulse for the beautiful lines beginning

> I wonder if the spring-tide of this year
> Will bring another spring both lost and dear;

came to her when walking in the outer circle of Regent's Park, and to the last her memories of that locality seemed always pleasurable—a fact not to be wondered at. For even yet there are spots in it which present as much quiet, almost sylvan beauty as is to be found in any part of London.

Mr. Theodore Watts-Dunton has well said about Christina that she spoke of wild animals ' sometimes as though they were human beings and sometimes as though they were fairies.'   Indeed there is no doubt that her attitude towards animals had something very remarkable in it. She had a predilection for all animals—even mice not being thought of with disfavour. But any animal which was closely associated with her seemed to be viewed, in some sense, as a friend by her. She was much attached to ' Muff,' her cat, and when she found that I was not unsympathetic in this matter she talked to me a good deal respecting ' Muff's ' habits, revealing keen observation in everything she said. She was gratified when I saluted ' Muff,' and used to exclaim : ' How condescending you are to that pussy.' Once she remarked : ' Like ourselves, creatures have their friends.'

I remember that Christina once said to me in her gentle way, ' Perhaps you go into the country in August to kill something ? '

'I never go into the country to kill anything,' I answered.

I shall not cease to remember what pleasure she showed in my avowal. It was as though she had been inclined to take back the gift of her friendship had she found that I really went 'into the country to kill something,' and was relieved to find that she was not obliged to do so.

Number thirty Torrington Square, Bloomsbury, where Christina had lived since 1876, in no wise differed in external aspect from many thousands of other houses in the same part of London. Torrington Square is really oblong in shape, and according to Mr. Sharp, Dante Gabriel used to call it 'Torrington Oblong.' Probably the ordinary dull-coloured bricks used for so many London houses were employed for the erection of Christina's home. But Time, weather, and soot had so completely done their work that it was impossible to know precisely what the original colour had been. The house, of three storeys above the ground floor, appeared even higher than it was on account of its narrowness. The small windows were of a usual shape. The front door, slightly raised above the level of the square, was approached by stone steps. There was the inevitable area (which, however, served one useful purpose in giving apparently excellent light to a pleasant-looking kitchen window), and the hardly less inevitable verandah, opening from the first floor.

The entrance-hall was narrow, and had on the left the room which had once been the dining-room and concerning which I am about to speak more fully. The staircase was not steeper than was to be anticipated in such a house. From a window on the half landing (the small yard space behind could hardly be termed a back garden) a glimpse was obtainable of one or two plane-trees. Several pieces of old furniture, some of it Chippendale, were scattered through the rooms. The drawing-room, immediately over the dining-room, was comparatively spacious, and always struck me as being not only the largest, but, by far, the most cheerful room in the house. It also had a bedroom behind it. There were no other sitting-rooms. The narrow entrance-hall, with decoration and wall paper somewhat faded in appearance, calls for no especial mention. The plainness and simplicity—almost the bareness of the furniture and appointments in the dining-room were however relieved by one or two objects of interest, such as a letter-weight designed by Benedetto Sangiovanni mentioned previously. There were also several family pictures, but not of such importance as those in the drawing-room to be mentioned hereafter. At the time of which I speak the little room behind the dining-room was arranged as a bedroom, though, somewhat earlier, it had been Christina's sitting-room.

The bareness of furniture in the dining-room was accounted for by the fact that the room had ceased to be used for dining. In or about 1887 it had become the bedroom of Miss Eliza Polidori, who from that date was mostly bed-ridden. On that lady's death in June 1893, (subsequent to which date my description of the house must be understood to apply) it was arranged once more as a sitting-room. But, as a matter of fact, it was unused except by the servants who were allowed by their mistress to use it whenever convenient to themselves.

I have always felt that when houses are inhabited

by persons of marked idiosyncrasy, or, it may be of genius, they acquire in some inexplicable way some of the characteristics of their occupants. And in using the word characteristics, I mean something far more subtle and indefinable in words than can be brought about by any mere material arrangements which are of course entirely dictated by the convenience or by the caprice of the inhabitants. And never has this feeling come upon me more strongly than in respect to Christina Rossetti's residence. About much of her best work there is a quietude, a controlled and well-ordered sadness (gloom would not be the correct term), and I trust I shall not be deemed unduly fanciful when I say that I seemed to feel a like atmosphere whenever I entered her abode. I forgot the prosaic character of my external surroundings ; I forgot the whirl of the streets ; I forgot even the comparative lack of silence in the square itself. I seemed to have passed into an atmosphere of rest and of peace.

Her work with all its noble—its unsurpassed qualities, with all its faults too, was her own. It was original, it was unborrowed. She was too great a writer even to be ' bookish.' Her impulse to write was spontaneous, it came from the deeps of her own soul, it was not derived even in the most perfectly justifiable and noblest sense from the achievements of others. Hence it was probably that, though none valued really great books more than she, books were not conspicuous in her home. She did not require them as tools. She had no room set apart and arranged for a study. I am told by an intimate friend that in her mother's lifetime she did much of her writing—wrote many of her lovely poems descriptive of Nature—in the small upper back bedroom whose only outlook was to the tall dingy walls of adjacent houses.

Afterwards, as Mr. W. M. Rossetti informs me, she wrote whatever she wrote in her drawing-room. In truth her inner vision was so keen that she was well-nigh independent of external influences.

She was always reticent respecting her habits of work or methods of composition, and even to her intimate friends sought to avoid reference even to her published work. Rarely has there been an instance of high poetic genius so spontaneous in character. As will be seen by examples I cite in subsequent chapters she did occasionally recast passages. Nevertheless the statement about her work which I am about to quote from Mr. Glendinning Nash, her friend and clergyman, is substantially correct. Mr. Nash says in a private letter to me, which I am permitted to quote :

'Christina Rossetti told me that there were times when the power to write had apparently passed away, and at others she wrote for hours with no mental effort or fatigue. The poetic flow was spontaneous and often she wrote on themes which she had not previously decided to write on. She seldom revised her work.'

Her brother William has himself written about her in this connection :

'Christina's habits of composition were eminently of a spontaneous kind. I question whether she ever once deliberated with herself whether or not she would write something or other, and then, having thought out a subject, proceeded to treat it in regular spells of work. Instead of this, something impelled her feelings, or "came into her head," and her hand obeyed the dictation. I suppose she scribbled the lines off rapidly enough, and afterwards took whatever amount of pains she deemed requisite for keeping them right in form and expression—for she was quite conscious that a poem demands to be good in execution, as well as genuine in

L

impulse ; but, (strange as it may seem to say so of a sister who, up to the year 1876, was almost constantly in the same house with me), I cannot remember ever seeing her in the act of composition. (I take no count here of the *bouts rimés* sonnets of 1848.) She consulted nobody, and solicited no advice, though it is true that with regard to her published volumes—or at any rate the first two of them—my brother volunteered to point out what seemed well adapted for insertion, and what the reverse, and he found her a very willing recipient of his monitions.'

Since Christina's death Mr. Shields has told me that he thinks, before she wrote a poem, she shut her eyes, and called up all the scene—especially all the natural objects in it.

She began to compose verses, as we have seen, in April 1842. From that time until about 1866, when she published her ' Prince's Progress and Other Poems,' her pieces were copied into note-books by her sister Maria until November 17, 1847, and thenceforward by herself, the date of composition being given in each case. These note-books, small and very neat, are variously bound in green, red, and black leather. From 1866 she discontinued the practice of writing in note-books and afterwards generally wrote on ruled blue paper, often quarto size.

Christina's handwriting is an interesting study. At the age of eighteen (as will be observed from the fac-simile of the original MS. of the lovely song ' When I am Dead, my Dearest ' appearing at p. 147) it was clear and small, but essentially characterless. Subsequently, while continuing equally legible, it became strong and full of character, and did not, like the handwriting of so many literary workers, deteriorate. Mr. Shields, when conversing with me, once advanced the plausible theory

Song.

When I am dead, my dearest,
  Sing no sad songs for me:
Plant thou no roses at my head,
  Nor shady cypress tree:
Be the green grass above me
  With showers and dewdrops wet:
And if thou wilt, remember,
  And if thou wilt, forget.

I shall not see the shadows,
  I shall not feel the rain:
I shall not hear the nightingale
  Sing on as if in pain:
And dreaming through the twilight
  That doth nor rise nor set,
Haply, I may remember,
  And haply, may forget.
          —12th December 1848.

FACSIMILE OF THE MS. OF THE SONG 'WHEN I AM DEAD,
MY DEAREST']

that Christina's handwriting[1] grew in evidence of strength as gradually she became conscious of her own powers.   Certainly it remained strong and full of character even after her last illness had become serious, as two examples in my own possession, written as late as August 1894, clearly show.   Then it became shaky, and probably about the end of September 1894 she ceased to write, her last attempt to sign a cheque, made towards November 10th of that year, being quite illegible.

On entering the room which had once been the dining-room one saw to the left and near the window a small bookcase of some plain inexpensive wood.   It contained only a few books.   Many were novels, and these were mostly English classics, Scott and Maria Edgeworth, for instance, and Dickens.

In a sympathetic essay, contributed to 'The Bookman' soon after her death, Katherine Tynan (Mrs. Hinkson), after saying how fond Christina was of Mrs. Gaskell's 'Cranford,' goes on to tell how

'when she found I had not read it she pressed upon me her own copy, an old one bound in the original brown cloth, and with an inscription, "from her affectionate uncle." '

In the drawing-room (the only sitting-room used by Christina Rossetti after the death of Eliza Polidori) there were two bookcases.   Many of the volumes were religious and devotional, though by no means all; but it should be understood, as her brother informs me, that

'Christina's library consisted scarcely at all of books of her own choosing—certainly not one volume in twenty— they were principally her mother's books.'

[1] In his work on the philosophy of handwriting Mr. John H. Ingram has given a careful analysis of her calligraphy based on a minute examination.

The drawing-room, lit by two cheerful large windows overlooking the square, always impressed one as the most agreeable room in the house. On entering it one saw in the centre of the wall on the left hand the chalk drawing of Christina by Dante Gabriel, done in 1866, elsewhere referred to. Opposite to it at the other side of the room, and over the chimney-piece, was a most beautiful portrait of her mother also by Dante Gabriel. This picture was flanked on either side by portraits of Dante Gabriel and William, while on the same wall, but hanging further from the window, was a portrait in oils of that Dr. Polidori who was Byron's physician. This picture is now in the National Portrait Gallery. On the table was an Empire enamel and ormolu inkstand of delicate workmanship which had been in her family for three generations. After her death it was given by her brother to Mr. Theodore Watts-Dunton as a fitting memorial of old friendship.

Close to one of the windows, and opposite to the door, was a miniature glass-house containing ferns. These particular ferns were especial favourites, and as long as she was able to do anything, she saw to them herself. Doubtless due to the care lavished upon them they were excellent specimens when their somewhat artificial mode of existence is borne in mind. They have now passed into the possession of her brother, who hopes to be as successful as his sister in their cultivation.

Unlike her friend, the late Dr. Littledale, who though passionately fond of flowers in the abstract, was compelled by a curious physical disability—he turned faint in any room with flowers—to banish them from his chambers, she was not only fond of flowers but much appreciated their presence in the rooms she

inhabited.   In a letter quoted by Miss Proctor, Christina
says :—

'As I no longer go to the country from time to
time, I may say the country very graciously comes to
me, for friends send or bring me flowers.'

She expressed always particular pleasure in receiving
flowers from her friends, often remarking when I brought
some : ' It is delightful to get flowers which one knows
have not been bought, which are from a garden, and
therefore really fresh.'

As a centre picture, on the wall facing the drawing-
room window, was the copy of the autotype of Mr.
Shields's lovely drawing which, under the circumstances
previously alluded to, had been given by the artist to
her mother.   On either side were photographs of Dante
Gabriel's ' Hamlet [1] and Ophelia ' and ' Cassandra.'   It will
be remembered that to bring out the significance of the
last named, Dante Gabriel wrote two sonnets.   Christina
Rossetti's couch (on which she usually lay during the
last year of her life, scarcely rising even when visitors
were announced) was generally placed near to, and in
full view of ' The Good Shepherd,' by Mr. Shields.
Often, however, on summer evenings, it was wheeled
closer to the windows which, facing the west, admitted
the afternoon sun.   Mr. W. M. Rossetti reminds me that

' one of the features of the drawing-room was a rather
elaborate glass chandelier for candles—bought by Gabriel,
—say towards 1864, and given to his mother, I suppose
in 1876—When there was a strong low sun the pendants
of this chandelier made extremely vivid prism reflections
on the walls and door.'

---

[1] ' Hamlet and Ophelia ' and ' Cassandra ' are fully described by Mr.
Sharp at pp. 198-9 and 171, respectively, of his exhaustive monograph
Dante Gabriel Rossetti, a Record and a Study.

Sometimes, when the warmth of the weather permitted the opening of the windows, when the noise in the square was hushed, and the deepening shadows of twilight obscured the too near view of the houses opposite while bringing into yet stronger relief the outlines of several graceful trees in the foreground of the garden of the square, the outlook from her drawing-room became attractive, almost picturesque. Thus it was, I remember, when once I called, somewhat later than my wont, to take her some flowers, and the memory of that evening lingers particularly in my mind because of her especial kindness to me. The weather was warm, and she was reclining on the sofa by the open drawing-room window. She spoke to me anew about the effect the garden at Holmer Green had had on her young imagination. She talked also of her uncle, Dr. Polidori, and told me how disappointed his parents were when he announced his intention to travel with Lord Byron. They thought that in adopting this course, he was doing badly for himself; he ought instead to have taken up a practice that offered at Norwich. A few minutes before seeing Christina Rossetti I had left a somewhat large literary 'at home,' and though this was far from being unenjoyable in its own way, I was struck more than usually by the contrast of the scene I had just quitted, and the serenity, the assured peace, which seemed to dwell around her.

Under ordinary conditions the garden of Torrington Square, enclosed in its prim and somewhat sooty iron railings, looked by no means inviting. It is therefore worth remarking, as an additional instance of Christina's habitual contentment even under circumstances which many people would have deemed depressing, that more than once (when no longer able to walk further) she expressed to me the satisfaction she had felt in walking for a few minutes in this garden supported on the arm of her nurse, Miss (generally styled Mrs.) Read.

One afternoon in the summer of 1894 I called at Torrington Square. I saw by her appearance and learnt incidentally from her words (she never, except on one occasion to be named hereafter, directly alluded to her sufferings), that in all respects she was worse in body than I had ever before seen her, although her cheerful composure was entirely unshaken. The conversation turned upon Mr. Shields and his work, arising, if my remembrance be correct, from my having praised 'The Good Shepherd.' She said what pleasure she felt at my praise of her friend, adding: 'That is the only representation of the subject I ever saw which brings to my mind at all adequately my conception of it.' Then, with the warmth of appreciation not unfrequently her wont in speaking of those who formed her inner circle, she spoke with affection of Mr. Shields, gave utterance to her high opinion of his genius as a painter—especially as a religious painter—and ended: 'You see he does not treat sacred themes merely as an artist; they are part of his life. They are part of his life in a way that I have never known them to be of any other artist, and that is one cause of his marvellous power.' I remarked that the contemplation of such a picture must solace her in hours of pain and weariness, and she said it did.

Christina, in spite of her being somewhat of a recluse, or perhaps the more so because she was somewhat of a recluse, was a keen judge of character. Her own character, if sweetened and purified by the discipline of life, was also strengthened. Although she never used

a harsh word about anyone, she was well able to discrimi-
nate between those she liked and those for whom she
did not care.

Probably the best piece of character-drawing in all
her writings is to be found in the brief poem called ' A
Sketch ' which first appears in her ' New Poems ' :

> The blindest buzzard that I know
>   Does not wear wings to spread and stir ;
>   Nor does my special mole wear fur,
> And grub among the roots below :
>   He sports a tail indeed, but then
>   It's to a coat ; he's man with men :
>
>   .   .   .   .   .
>
> My blindest buzzard that I know
>   My special mole, when will you see ?
>   Oh no, you must not look at me,
>
>   .   .   .   .   .
>
>   . . since your eyes are blind, you'd say,
>   ' Where ?   What ? '   and turn away.

15 August 1864.

Her sympathy in the highest sense of the term was
universal, for she was quick to perceive the good in all.
But it never degenerated into the maudlin weakness
which is the attendant danger of sympathy. Gentleness
was a quality she admired much, and of one friend, Mrs.
Garnett, whose ministrations she valued greatly in her last
illness, she said to me once : ' I like her, she is so gentle.'
Christina Rossetti was also very grateful for the frequent
presence during the same period of Miss Lisa Wilson,[1]
the ' Fior-di-Lisa ' of her lovely poem with that title.

[1] Since Christina Rossetti's death Miss Lisa Wilson has published a
volume of *Verses* dedicated to ' her sweet and gracious memory ' which
conclusively establishes Miss Wilson's own right to rank among lyrical
poets.

Her analysis of motives—her discernment between the apparent and the real is well brought out in her little essay in ' Time Flies ' under date of May 22 respecting an English traveller in Sicily who is everywhere treated with great hospitality and courtesy. At one mansion however, although waited upon with every politeness by a ' depressed staff of domestics,' he ' arrived ' and ' departed ' ' unwelcomed ' by the family.

' He lacked nothing save a welcome.'

.   .   .   .

' This treatment left upon him a gloomy impression. How should meat, drink, shelter suffice and solace an unwelcomed guest ?
' Yet afterwards he saw cause to revise and reverse his estimate, becoming aware that the undemonstrative family who had harboured him laboured at that very time under the anxiety of a bitter grief. Rejoice with him they could not, burden him with a share of their own misery they would not ; all that they had to give they gave, and hid from their guest an irremediable sorrow.
' How often we judge unjustly when we judge harshly. The fret of temper we despise may have its rise in the agony of some great, unflinching, unsuspected, self-sacrifice, or in the sustained strain of self-conquest, or in the endurance of unavowed, almost intolerable pain.
' Whoso judges harshly is sure to judge amiss.'

Touching this quotation from ' Time Flies ' her brother tells me that

' the allusion must be to Edward Lear (author of " Book of Nonsense " etc.) who travelled in Calabria, and who, in his book about the travels makes some statement of the kind—Christina liked his book much towards 1855, finding it full of genial Italian character-drawing and amusement.'

He adds, about another topic :

'I do not consider that C[hristina] was particularly fond of children—In early youth certainly not. As she advanced in years she enjoyed them and their pretty or quaint ways, but still not to any extent comparable to what marks a multitude of women.'

Writing to her brother William under date of March 10, 1887, from Torquay, she says :

'The George Hakes have a little son and it is said that my small Ursula [her goddaughter] on seeing him said " Guy, Guy." '

And again, at a later date from London :

'In talking the other day I never recollected to speak of little Ursula's Bible. If without its being troublesome you could and would oblige me by procuring it at the S.P.C.K. shop, Northumberland Avenue, I should be much pleased. I want a *good print* one with references and Apocrypha, really well bound ; and for such a child should prefer a cheerful binding (red for instance) if there is a choice, but this is of no consequence. So when (D. V.) I see you next Wednesday if you have not seen about it I will set you free from the request ; for although I should in itself prefer your selection, I can get the Bible otherwise.'

Apropos of a friend's funeral she wrote to her brother William :

'It was a relief to me to infer from the newspaper report that cremation had been forborne,'

and in elucidation of the above remark the same gentleman has written to me :

'There seems to be an unmeaning superstition among strict Church-people (I found it so once when speaking to my Mother) that cremation is a device of anti-Christians, to discredit " the resurrection of the body." C[hristina] must have shared this prejudice more or less.'

In relation to his sister's political proclivities he has written as follows :

'My sister knew and cared next to nothing about party politics (apart from questions having a religious bearing) ; in all her later years, however, her feeling leaned more towards the Conservative than the Liberal cause.'

She felt most keenly as to some of the evils in our social system, and wrote thus eloquently in 'The Face of the Deep' on Revelation xviii. 15, 16, 17, 18, and 19 :

' " 15. The merchants of these things, which were made rich by her, shall stand afar off for the fear of her torment, weeping and wailing.

' " 16. And saying, Alas, alas, that great city, that was clothed in fine linen, and purple, and scarlet, and decked with gold, and precious stones, and pearls !

' " 17. For in one hour so great riches is come to nought. And every shipmaster, and all the company in ships, and sailors, and as many as trade by sea, stood afar off,"

' This desolation which we have not yet seen must one day be seen. Meanwhile we have known preludes, rehearsals, foretastes of such as this : so that looking back through the centuries we may take up our lamentation and say :—

' Alas Sodom once full of bread ! From empty fulness, good Lord, deliver us.

' Alas Tyre whose merchants were princes ! From riches but not toward God, good Lord, deliver us.

' Alas the man whose barns sufficed not ! From heart and hands shut close, good Lord, deliver us.

' Alas Dives clothed in purple and fine linen ! From remediless destitution, good Lord, deliver us.

' And looking forward we may say :—

' Alas any whom the unknown day and hour find unprepared ! From the folly of the foolish virgins, good Lord, deliver us.

' And looking around us trembling we needs must say :—

'Alas England full of luxuries and thronged by stinted poor, whose merchants are princes and whose dealings crooked, whose packed storehouses stand amid bare homes, whose gorgeous array has rags for neighbours! From a canker in our gold and silver, from a moth in our garments, from blasted crops, from dwindling substance, from righteous retribution abasing us among the nations, good Lord, deliver us.   Amen.

'" 18. And cried when they saw the smoke of her burning, saying, What city is like unto this great city!'

' If any shipmasters and crews, sailors and sea-traders, have yet to lament and quake, well may arrogant England amid her seas quake and lament betimes.

' " What city is like unto this great city! "—Like what she was, like what she is: her present tallying with her past.

'For purposes of probation height and depth are at once distinguishable and continuous: man, the probationer set midway between these extremities, has it within his option to reclaim either from the other. Probation over, height and depth, whilst still of two aspects, will yet form one evidently undivided sequence ; to the summit or to the base of which consummated man has worked his way.   And why not all the baptised to the summit ?   " Ye did run well ; who did hinder you that ye should not obey the truth ? "

'" 19. And they cast dust on their heads, and cried, weeping and wailing, saying, Alas, alas, that great city, wherein were made rich all that had ships in the sea by reason of her costliness! for in one hour is she made desolate."

' To cast dust on the head with penitence attests death unto sin.   To cast dust on the head with impenitence prefigures the second death.

'Sin conducts all to one goal.   The land sinner finds dust in plenty ; the seafaring sinner shall inherit dust enough.

'Thank God, ample provision is stored for every penitent wheresoever and whatsoever : dust, ashes, are ready to hand for all.

'Lord, array us in spiritual sackcloth, that by penitence we may bear witness to Thy goodness.'

Miss Proctor writes as follows respecting Christina's interest in practical work among the poor :

'In 1886 and 1887 I was engaged in parish work in Ratcliff. My mission was to go on Monday nights to the Factory Girls' Club, London Street, under the special care of the vicar, Rev. R. K. Arbuthnot. Here congregated many of Bryant and May's workers, but ropemakers, satchel-makers, jam-makers, and all the industries of the East End were represented. Many were of Irish parentage and Roman Catholics. The object was to try and interest them in something, and get them into the club after work was over. Miss Rossetti took a deep interest in the welfare of these young people, and would herself have liked to become a working member of the club, had her nursing duties allowed it ; but at that time she had two aunts, invalids, to tend.

'In returning home, which I never did before eleven o'clock p.m., many incidents struck me on the route. I was accustomed to relate all to Miss Rossetti, who specially wished to hear how the evening had been passed. At one time it was the tiny children returning home alone, their part being over at the Theatre, that excited her commiseration, and she said :—

> London makes mirth, but I know God hears
> The sobs in the dark, and the dropping of tears.

'Sometimes my tales were ludicrous scenes at the suppers given, and presided over by Mr. (now Sir) Walter Besant. She was very sympathetic with young people.'

A brief extract may here be made from a letter placed at my disposal as showing her thoughtfulness when even a remote chance occurred of being useful to others :

'Will you kindly add Mr. ——'s No. on the enclosed card, & then allow it to be posted. I had an opportunity of mentioning him to an old-established watchmaker this morning,—tho' I fear nothing will ensue.'

She was never what would be commonly termed an active woman of affairs; yet she was not unpractical and her methodical and carefully arranged account-books of household expenditure were models of neatness.

In 'Time Flies' under date of May 31 she speaks admirably about time and its employment.

'What is meant by "want of time"?   What do I mean by the words?

'It seems that I must mean one of two things: either that I lack time for duties because I devote it to non-duties, or that, devoting it to duties, I feel discontented at lacking leisure for non-duties.

'Non-duties may be attractive; they may even appear on occasion heroic or self-devoted: but we may be sure they are not duties so long as there honestly is not time for them.

'On the contrary, taking the place of duties, they would degenerate into offences.'

She held that possibly we might be near the end of the world and wrote as follows in 'The Face of the Deep':—

'And at the present day when so open-mouthed an antagonism has set in against Christ and Revelation; and when so many "devout and honourable" persons (if following the Inspired text I dare call them so) are arrayed against the truth as it is in Jesus; and when signal virtues of philanthropy, with self-spending and alacrity in being spent, take the field like Goliath the Giant in defiance of the armies of the Living God; I think the pseudo-Christ-like aspect of error becomes prominently urged upon our gravest consideration: especially as of necessity we know not how close upon us may already be the actual personal Antichrist in whom human wickedness appears to culminate; that Antichrist who will, it seems, be a foul human agent and copy of the old original Evil one.   Let us pause a

moment to face this last great adversary, who not as
our open enemy but as one of ourselves, will do this
dishonour.'

Quaintly and characteristically she enforces the
desirability of a sublimated form of courtesy, and under
date of May 24 she writes in ' Time Flies ' :—

' A certain Englishman sojourning in the East, and
by mishap breaking a valuable pipe, the property of his
entertainer, felt abashed, when his host took up the
word : " In a stranger the destruction of so costly an
article might cause displeasure, but in a friend every
action has its charm."
' One friend I once possessed who would, I think, on
occasion have been capable of such graciousness. But
why (if so it be) have I known one such only? And
why am I (alas !) not myself the second?'

The ' friend ' referred to above, Dr. Adolf Heimann,
was Professor of German in University College, London.

With a touch almost of humour she tells in ' Time
Flies,' under date of October 12, how ' a good unobtrusive Christian of my own intimate circle'—the ' good
unobtrusive Christian ' was her aunt Eliza Polidori—
found comfort in the recollection that no day lasted
longer than twenty-four hours. And there is a real but
not an affected humility in the entry in ' Time Flies '
under date of December 4, where she sets before herself
and others, as an example worthy of imitation, the
truth conveyed in the remark of ' an exemplary
Christian ' (her Aunt Charlotte Polidori) that she was
never blamed without perceiving some justice in the
charge.

As might be anticipated Christina had the deepest
love of the masterpieces of English poetry. But, even
when dealing with masterpieces, she was by no means

indiscriminate in her praise. Sometimes, indeed, she admired passages in great poets which are not universally selected for commendation. An example of this is seen in her liking for Milton's sonnet 'To Lawrence' mentioned by her brother in a letter to Mr. Hall Caine. She was an exquisite reader of poetry. Mr. Sharp has told us (*vide* p. 57) how finely she read to him Southwell's 'Burning Babe,' as well as her own work, and from personal knowledge I can confirm the truth of his remarks. Nothing was more delightful than to hear her repeat snatches of poetry, and she was equally able to bring out the subtler rhythm of English prose. I do not think she had ever been taught elocution, and probably she had never even studied it consciously, yet unconsciously its higher rules came to her naturally. Her reading was by no means extensive, but then it was always of the best ; and she could distinguish between verse, however melodious, and poetry. She was generous in her praise of contemporaries—especially when that praise was well merited—as in the case of Augusta Webster's striking drama 'The Sentence.' In the article ('Athenæum,' No. 3,641, August 7, 1897) already referred to appears a letter to Dora Greenwell, dated December 31, 1863, in the course of which Christina says :

'What think you of Jean Ingelow, the wonderful poet ? I have not yet read the volume, but reviews with copious extracts have made me aware of a new eminent name having arisen among us. I want to know who she is, what she is like, where she lives. All I have heard is an uncertain rumour that she is aged twenty-one, and is one of three sisters resident with their mother. A proud mother, I should think.'

And in a letter to Anne Gilchrist, of date 1864, she wrote :

'My acquaintance with Jean Ingelow's poems to which you kindly introduced me, has been followed by a very slight acquaintance with herself. She appears as unaffected as her verses, though not their equal in regular beauty: however I fancy hers is one of those variable faces in which the variety is not the least charm.'

Christina Rossetti's personal habits were of the simplest. She rose early, and dined at one or two o'clock, taking a third meal in the evening. Usually she retired to rest early, though never, I am informed by her brother and others, without passing some time, probably half an hour, in prayer. One day, when at Torrington Square soon after her death, her brother showed me an old-fashioned *prie-dieu*. Even before her last illness she had found the mechanical exertion of kneeling somewhat difficult, and had used this *prie-dieu* as an assistance.

The simplicity and regularity of her life was probably the cause of the considerable recuperative power which frequently surprised her physician, Dr. Stewart, during her last illness. She took Holy Communion twice weekly—on Thursday and Sunday. Probably admirers of her devotional work will recollect her little homilies for special occasions which close ' Time Flies.' The ' holy man ' named by her in the first of these— that for Ember Wednesday, as suggesting a new motive for joining in the service of ' Churching of Women '— was the late Canon Burrows, formerly rector of Christ Church, Albany Street. She was invited to write his life, and wished to do so, only relinquishing the idea owing to the state of her health.

She favoured moderate fasting for religious purposes, and in ' The Face of the Deep ' speaks as follows concerning it : ' God accepts dues as gifts. Man receives gifts as dues,' characteristically and somewhat naively adding, though without mentioning the ' eminent physician ' by name :

' An eminent physician [Sir William Jenner] once told me that there are people who would benefit in health by fasting : a secondary motive, yet surely not an unlawful one. To perform a duty from a motive which is not wrong may prove a step towards performing it from the motive which is right. To leave it unperformed seems the last contrivance adapted to result in its performance.'

Even in the last year of her life, amid constant suffering and much weakness, she was always cheerful and frequently bright, and though a recluse she never spoke to me as such. Here may be introduced some words from Mr. Sharp in a communication to myself :

' A fine phrase of hers that I remember was : " The blithe cheerfulness which one can put over one's sadness like a veil—a bright shining veil. Cheerfulness I consider a fundamental and essential Christian virtue." '

What follows, an extract from a letter to Mrs. Patchett Martin dated November 2, 1891, may be quoted here as describing her ways at a somewhat earlier date. The ' den ' was the little back sitting-room mentioned at p. 143 :

' It is not altogether unsociability which holds me aloof. I live with a quite aged Aunt permanently invalided, and house arrangements and many points have to subserve her convenience. So now friends are very kind in coming to see me without expecting my return visit ; and they take me just as they find me, which in all probability is receiving them into " my den." '

The very tones of her voice, in their slow distinct intonation, were pleasant to hear. Her humorous sonnet-epitaph on the Præraphaelite Brotherhood will be remembered, and also her amusing lines in ' New Poems ' ' On Albina ' and ' Forget Me Not ' written respectively in June, and on August 19, 1844. And as late as June 1894 I recollect her laughing heartily on hearing that a French translation of ' David Copperfield,' which, on a visit to Paris, I had picked up second-hand a few days before, on one of the bookstalls on the *Quais* which line the Seine, was entitled ' Le Neveu de ma Tante.' At all times she was willing to chat about her favourite authors, and her knowledge of literature—even of the by-ways of literature in unexpected quarters—was considerable. For instance, I recollect her telling me on one occasion that though she herself had never read a line of Charles Whitehead, she remembered well her elder brother speaking to her with warm appreciation concerning him, and pointing out to her that probably Whitehead had influenced Dickens's early style.

During the illness of her last surviving aunt, Miss Eliza Harriet Polidori, Christina had secured the services as nurse of Mrs. Read. Finding on the death of her aunt, that she herself required the services of a nurse, and being satisfied in every way with Mrs. Read, she asked her to remain. Two other servants—a cook and a housemaid—had always been kept.

In the morning, and once more towards nine o'clock in the evening, Christina Rossetti gathered the servants around her, reading for a few minutes a passage of Scripture, and then a suitable prayer from the Anglican Prayer-Book, and frequently the Collect for the day. She continued the practice of household devotion twice daily till nearly the close of her life, and when too weak to conduct it herself, she directed what was to be read, and Mrs. Read undertook the duty in her presence. Hymns were never sung on these occasions.

For nearly twenty years she had been a constant worshipper at Christ Church, Woburn Square. A friend informs me that towards the close of her life Christina always sat in the very front pew in church. She remained until the very last before leaving the building, and it was evident from her demeanour that even then she strove to avoid ordinary conversation, evidently feeling that it would disturb her mood of mind.

For certain years previous to 1894 she had suffered from a heart ailment, accompanied by dropsical symptoms, and in May 1892 she was operated on for cancer, successfully it was thought at the time. Early in June 1892, with her brother and a hospital nurse, she went to Brighton, and appeared to gain much benefit from the change. One of her pleasures when there was to hear him read aloud the 'Autobiography of Isaac Williams,' the poet and divine, the friend of John Henry Newman and of Edward Bouverie Pusey, and author of more than one of the 'Tracts for the Times.' She had a great regard for Isaac Williams, who was in some sense a poet of the Tractarian Movement. Dante Gabriel had also a high opinion of this writer's sonnets. Readers of the Prefatory Note to her 'Seek and Find' will recollect her expressions of indebtedness to Williams's 'Harmony.' The letter ensuing shows how she came to read his 'Autobiography':

To Mr. Patchett Martin

30 Torrington Square—W.C.
Thursday. [May 12, 1892.]

' First I thought I would not write till I had something unselfish to write about, but now I feel as if it may look ungracious and ungrateful not to acknowledge your kindness in offering me an occasional book to read.   I shall be very thankful for such a loan when a book is lying absolutely idle, and the particular work you propose (Rev. Isaac Williams) is one I should pick out.

' Very truly your obliged
' CHRISTINA G. ROSSETTI.'

What follows, in a note to Mrs. Patchett Martin, written on June 18, 1892, alludes to the same subject :

' Please hand the enclosed receipt [for 2*l.* 12*s.* 6*d.* in payment of articles contributed to " Literary Opinion "] to Mr. Martin with my thanks and with particular thanks for the books he so obligingly lends me.   I hope to enjoy all three.

' Thank you also for missing me at Church : I hope to refill my seat in a few Sundays.'

To Mr. Patchett Martin

' I took the liberty of taking your loan out of town with me.   Now on my return I send back with my grateful thanks two of the volumes, venturing to retain " Dean Church " as I have not finished reading it.   Mr. Henley's " Hospital " is grim but interesting ; " Isaac Williams " much to my taste.

' Truly your obliged
'CHRISTINA G. ROSSETTI.'

' Dean Church ' means Dean Church's village sermons preached at Whatley, near Frome ; ' Mr. Henley's " Hospital " ' refers to the set of poems in Mr. W. E. Henley's ' Book of Verses.'

About the same date her work had begun to attract attention on the Continent, for her brother tells me that

'Henri Jacottet wrote some good articles about C[hristina], 1893 or 1894, in a Swiss review.'

He has also written to me regarding Christina's attitude towards music—an attitude made interesting psychologically from Dante Gabriel's dislike of elaborate music :

'I don't consider that Christina had any dislike of music : would even say that in a certain sense she liked and admired it—But she had no sort of musical gift of her own, and (sensibly enough) did not cultivate an art towards which she had no vocation.'

There was no piano or musical instrument of any kind in her house, and I never heard her allude in talk in the faintest degree to the pleasure derivable from music.

Towards March or April of 1893 a renewed manifestation of cancer showed itself along her left shoulder and arm, and now any hope of permanent recovery was abandoned.   Her sufferings were great, but her fortitude was even greater.   I often saw her showing visible traces of pain, but never, save once, did she directly allude to it.

On this occasion she said to me, with an inexpressibly pathetic look in her eyes : ' In the letter you wrote to me a little while ago' (she referred to a letter of sympathy I had written to her on the death of a near relative of her own), ' you showed me you believed in prayer.   Will you now promise me to put up one short prayer for me ; I have to suffer so *very* much !'   I promised to comply with her request not once, but many times, and I kept my word. I shall never cease to remember her glance of gratitude.

For the volume entitled 'Verses,' published by the Society for Promoting Christian Knowledge in 1893, and consisting of poems reprinted from her 'Called to be Saints,' 'Time Flies,' and 'The Face of the Deep,' she was at the trouble to copy all the poems out afresh, and to arrange them under separate headings, thus forming one of the most curious and attractive of her manuscripts. Her brother said to her: 'Why do you take the trouble of copying the poems?'

She answered: 'I have plenty of leisure.' In her brother's judgment she copied the poems partly because she liked the mere mechanical act of writing, and partly —and perhaps this was the chief reason—because she was anxious to save all possible expense to the Society. A friend called upon her about ten days after the first large edition of these 'Verses' appeared, and told her it was sold out. Whereupon she exclaimed: 'I'm *so* glad for the sake of the Society. You know that it gets all the profits for the promotion of its work.'

During her last illness and for some time previously, her medical adviser had been Dr. Stewart. In August 1894, owing to serious increase of pain with its resulting weakness, she ceased to attend the public services at Christ Church. Her friend, the Rev. J. J. Glendinning Nash, the incumbent of Christ Church, came to see her weekly, however, usually on the morning of Monday, and held a brief religious service in her room, administering Holy Communion whenever her state permitted. During his absence on a brief holiday his place was taken by the Rev. T. N. Talfourd Major, curate of Christ Church.

Mr. Glendinning Nash informs me that until her last illness she was present at nearly all the weekly services at Christ Church, and received Holy Communion every Sunday and Thursday. ' She took,' he says, ' the deepest interest in Christ Church, its schools, and its district. She subscribed generously, and nearly every Sunday during her illness sent money for the offertory.'

At a late stage of her illness, when her bodily condition necessitated her remaining constantly in bed, her doctor advised her removal into the drawing-room from the bedroom at the back of the drawing-room she had occupied up to that time. The chief purpose of this removal was to obtain the advantage of the greater amount of air, which the increased size of the drawing-room afforded. The appointments of the drawing-room were altered as little as might be, compatible with the change.

To a friend who saw her a few days before her death she said, with a touch of her old contentment, she was so glad to be in bed as she was so ' restful ' there. She further expressed a marked preference for the small bed on which she lay because it was the bed whereon her mother had died. She also said it gave her pleasure to think she used the same sheets and pillows as her mother had used. In spite of the greater convenience of the drawing-room in many respects, it had its disadvantages as a sick room. Chief among these was the fact that it overlooked the square, and that consequently the noise was considerable. I recollect, for instance, calling to inquire after Christina's state on one sultry afternoon in the summer of 1894. As a needful measure, no doubt, the windows were thrust open, and the discordant noise from no fewer than three piano-organs within hearing would, indeed, have been trying to many a sufferer. It is re-assuring, therefore, to learn from her brother, as I have done, that she was not wont to be inconvenienced in the slightest degree by such matters.

Several of her old and most intimate friends have told me that, after she ceased to be able to see them, she sent them very special messages on their calling to inquire after her. Even in my own case, when no longer able to see me, she liked me to call to make inquiries, and liked also to be informed when I called, preferring that I should wait to hear if there was a message. Sometimes she sent me a delicately worded message of thanks, occasionally, though by no means always, making definite inquiries about my own health or other matters requiring a reply. Whenever she sent messages to me they were always couched in different words, but invariably with a pretty turn of expression. Once, I remember, she was ' helped by my sympathy.'

Her brother has said to me, and wishes me to mention, that about a ' couple of years ' before her death Dr. Stewart told him ' she was very liable to some form of hysteria.' For a while in her final illness, though appreciably less in her last fortnight of life, such symptoms were apparent, particularly during semi-consciousness, chiefly manifesting themselves in cries, not so much, as far as could be observed, 'thro' absolute pain ' as 'thro' some sort of hysterical stimulation.'

One of the visits I paid to Torrington Square during the last year of her life (a visit on which I did not see Christina Rossetti) especially lives in my recollection, because of the most memorable conversation I then had with Mr. W. M. Rossetti in the dining-room. Then it was I first came to see, what I have since been very fully conscious of, namely, that beneath his calm, almost judicial manner, there lies a depth of real feeling, and an almost passionate affection for those he loves, qualities not always apparent to those who casually observe his demeanour. After speaking with deep distress of the sufferings of his sister, he told me, (as he has subsequently related in the Preface to the memoir of his brother), that Christina, near to death as she was, had kept him right in many details of the early years, her reminiscences of her childhood being still vivid and accurate.

Under date December 23 in 'Time Flies' there appears this autobiographical allusion :—

'One day I caught myself wishing what I felt convinced would not be the case,—that a certain occupation at once sad and pleasant and dear to me, and at that very moment inevitably drawing towards a close, could have lasted out through the remainder of my lifetime.

'Perhaps no harm in the instinctive wish,—none, I hope : yet what fallacies lay at its root !

'At least two.'

My readers will be interested to learn that the 'occupation' here referred to was the copying out during 1882 for the second volume of the memoir of Dante Gabriel just mentioned, the letters addressed by him to his mother and to Christina herself. In the characteristically written and vivid note by the editor to her posthumous Poems he tells us how, even up to and beyond October 1894, 'she was often extremely conversible.' One day she repeated to him the amusing lines 'In my cottage near the Styx' which are thus preserved to us. Concerning these lines he has written to me as follows :

' I regard it as a jocular outcome of a state of mind which was more dreary than jocular—for C[hristina] did not at all rejoice in her semi-banishment to Frome.'

Despite the marked differences of temperament and of opinion between herself and her brother William, it must have been evident to anyone who had heard her mention him, how deep was her love for him ; and how real was also the respect in which she held him, both on account of his intellectual gifts and because he had been for so long not only the family prop, but, in some sense, the custodian of the family papers and traditions. She evinced this respect in the most practical manner in her power by leaving all her material means to him, and by entrusting to his keeping without reservation of any kind all her manuscripts and papers of whatever sort.

I have his authority for stating that about three months before her death she told him in the course of con-fidential talk that some few years previously, when she had comparatively little to leave, she had made her will in his favour. She added ' that now, being much better off,' she would, *if he* assented, wish to provide 2,000*l.* for religious purposes—but this only in case of his children being, in his opinion, sufficiently well provided for at his death to make this arrangement seem proper to him. He has assented fully to his sister's wish, and has, in his own will (drawn up soon after that interview with his sister), provided for that 2,000*l.* on such conditions regarding his children as make it, in his view, ' practically certain that the 2,000*l.* will go to the uses ' mentioned above.

Even in the last days of her life she did acts of kindness. Not long before her death she gave instructions
that a copy of her volume ' Sing-Song ' should be sent
on New Year's Day as her New Year's gift to the
children of Mr. Robert W. Dibdin, one of the church-
wardens of Christ Church, and at the appointed time
the touching little present duly reached them.

In the late autumn of 1894 Dr. Stewart's own health
required that he should quit England for the south of
France. This was a source of deep regret both to himself and to his patient, as in the circumstances, the part-
ing had the aspect of being final, and Christina had a
warm attachment for him—an attachment heartily
reciprocated. Dr. Stewart left her in charge of Dr.
Abbot Anderson who did all in his power to relieve
her.

It was of course well known that the end was fast
approaching, and could not in any event be much longer
delayed. Nevertheless, her rallying powers had so often
before proved remarkable, that when I reached 30
Torrington Square about half-past one on the afternoon of Saturday, December 29, 1894, it was with an
even greater degree of that curious involuntary surprise
which we generally experience at the presence of Death,
however expected he may be, that I noticed the blinds
were drawn down. Mrs. Read informed me, that about
7 A.M. on the morning of Friday the 28th, Christina had
become very deadly cold, and, with a purple look on the
face. She feared the end had come ; but, using restora-
tives, she sent for Dr. Abbot Anderson. On his
arrival he had found his patient better, and, during the
whole of that day, Friday, little change had been
apparent, Christina Rossetti continuing restful, seeming

to suffer little pain, and taking nourishment. She passed a quiet night, and about 5 A.M. on the morning of December 29, when Emma, the housemaid, who took part of the watching, came as usual into the sick room to relieve Mrs. Read, the latter remarked to her that she thought her mistress's voice (which had grown nearly inaudible) was returning in some measure. Between 6 and 7 A.M. Christina's lips were seen to be moving perpetually in prayer (that it was prayer was shown, though of course the words were unheard, by the frequent inclination of the head as at the name of Jesus) and, as far as could be observed, she was perfectly conscious. At 7.25 A.M., by the watch on the table, the only person actually in the room with her being Mrs. Read, Christina somewhat suddenly gave a faint sigh, and died before her brother William, whose constant and loving ministrations had so often soothed her during the long and weary hours of her last illness, could be summoned.

Mrs. Read asked me to go upstairs, saying her mistress, with characteristic if extraordinary thoughtfulness, had told her that, should I call after her (Christina's) death at any time when it was still possible, I was to be taken to see her. I was touched profoundly by this last and quite unexpected proof of my friend's regard for me, and availed myself at once of the privilege offered to me.

As I entered what had formerly been Christina's drawing-room I thought how unchanged yet how changed was the room. All the pictures, and well-nigh all the pieces of furniture, even to the miscellaneous articles which stood usually on the large drawing-room table, were in the same places as I had been in the

habit of observing them.' This, paradoxical as it may
seem at first sight to say so, added vastly to the sense
of impressiveness, just as the contrast between the commonplace—almost the prosaic—details and the supernatural element indissolubly enlinked with the poem,
adds to the impressiveness of that lyric by Christina
which her brother Gabriel named for her 'At Home.'

The small, narrow, curtainless bed was standing
immediately below Mr. Shields's 'Good Shepherd.'
With the sharpening of the perceptive faculties that
comes to us sometimes, at moments like these, I thought
I had never before seen Dante Gabriel's large chalk
drawing of his sister—that drawn in 1866—appear so
lovely.

Mrs. Read reverently uncovered the dear face, and
as I looked once more upon it, I saw that, though
slightly emaciated, it was not greatly changed since
the last time I had beheld it in life. Perhaps I was
hardly so much struck with the breadth of her brow—I
mean in regard to its indication of intellectual qualities—
as I had been often when conversing with her, but on
the other hand I was struck more than ever before both
by the clear manifestation of the more womanly qualities
and by the strength of purpose shown in the lips. Some
white flowers on a table near at hand gave a sense of
relief. There was pathos, there was solemnity in the
aspect of the room, there was no gloom. My spirit was
moved by the contrast I felt between the holy—almost
the saintly atmosphere of the house and its commonplace surroundings. I remained for a few moments in
the room, while her nurse told me in a subdued voice
the incidents of the past day or two, and how Christina
had often remarked to her of late (very characteristic

was the utterance) : ' This illness has humbled me. I was so proud before.'

I felt how applicable were Christina's own words :

> Weep not ; O friends, we should not weep ;
>   Our friend of friends lies full of rest ;
>   No sorrow rankles in her breast,
> Fallen fast asleep.

Throughout the remainder of that day I did every-thing with the presence of that darkened room ever before me.

To those of us who believe in the blessedness of spiritual assurance—who believe that such an assurance continued up to the latest moments of earthly life is an unspeakable boon—it is always sad to hear of instances where this trust has been lessened or destroyed, or may seem to have been lessened or destroyed, even though by merely physical conditions. Yet even these distressing instances, when they occur, have their aspects of comfort. When we find that some of the most spiritually minded, some of the most holy men and women whom this world has known, have suffered depression, nay even gloom, in their dying moments, we are shown more clearly that our spiritual state does not depend on our own feelings or moods of mind—another useful illustration is thus given us of the constant antagonism between the apparent and the real. I have been led to these reflections because, after much consideration, I have determined to print a communication made to me by Mr. W. M. Rossetti respecting his sister's spiritual condition in the last days of her life He had been good enough to read over the MS. of an article I had written concerning her for one of the periodicals, and it was as to a word or two therein, that he wrote to me as follows :

' In the last three months or so of her [Christina's] life, she was most gloomy on the subject [of her spiritual state], some of her utterances being deeply painful. This of course was beyond measure unreasonable but so it was. *I believe* the influence of opiates (which were indispensable) had something to do with it.

.   .   .   .   .   .

' Assuredly my sister did to the last continue believing in the promises of the Gospel, as interpreted by Theologians ; but her sense of its threatenings was very lively, and at the end more operative on her personal feelings. This should not have been. She remained firmly convinced that her mother and sister are saints in heaven, and I endeavoured to show her that according to her own theories, she was just as safe as they : but this—such was her humility of self estimate—did not relieve her from troubles of soul. If there is any reality in the foundations of her creed, she now knows how greatly she was mistaken.'

Her long and intimate friendship with Mr. Shields continued to the last. I have seen a short letter to him, dated September 5, 1894, which is pathetic both on account of its contents, and because of the handwriting grown shaky. It is of too sacred a character to be given here. I may mention, however, that, after thanking Mr. Shields for the privilege of his friendship, she ends by an almost passionate expression of personal humility couched in a phrase, which, in another, would have appeared exaggerated, even forced, but, in her, seemed only natural.

Much sorrow was felt at her loss, and this was coupled with much praise of her gifts. Seldom indeed has praise been so widespread, never has it been more sincere. As an instance of this a reference here may fittingly be made to what was said about her by two highly distinguished, and, though widely different, very representative men—the first a great poet, the second a great Anglican theologian.   In one of the most touching of his recent elegiac poems Mr. Swinburne wrote :

A soul more sweet than the morning of new-born May
Has passed with the year that has passed from the world away.
  A song more sweet than the morning's first-born song
Again will hymn not among us a new year's day.

Not here, not here shall the carol of joy grown strong
Ring rapture now, and uplift us, a spell-struck throng,
  From dream to vision of life that the soul may see
By death's grace only, if death do its trust no wrong.

Scarce yet the days and the starry nights are three
Since here among us a spirit abode as we,
  Girt round with life that is fettered in bonds of time,
And clasped with darkness about as is earth with sea.

And now, more high than the vision of souls may climb,
The soul whose song was as music of stars that chime,
  Clothed round with life as of dawn and the mounting sun,
Sings, and we know not here of the song sublime :

while Dr. Westcott, Bishop of Durham, sent the following letter to Mr. W. M. Rossetti :—

From The Right Rev. the Bishop of Durham
To Mr. W. M. Rossetti

Auckland Castle
Bishop Auckland
New Year's Day 1895.

  ' Dear Sir,—It may be presumptuous for a stranger to intrude on your solemn quiet, but my debt to Miss Rossetti encourages me to believe a friend who tells me that the simplest expression of sympathy with your loss might not be unwelcome.   It happened that last Christmas Day at our evening gathering I chose "Goblin

Market " to read, and that wonderful story of the power
of a sister's love in the temptations of life touched all
hearts.   On that very day too the friend (Miss Heaton
of Leeds) to whom I owe almost a personal knowledge
of Miss Rossetti, was called to her rest.   Not a week
passes, I think, when I do not find some fresh pleasure
from fragments of your sister's works.   And my experience is, I am sure, that of very many.   Those who
so teach us and reveal themselves to us cannot be lost.
However hard it is to realise as yet that the fact that
they pass out of sight makes them unchangeable, at least
I know—this house with its Chapel tells me so every
day—that some of the friends who are dearest to me
and help me most have entered on a fuller life.   May
you feel the consolation of this eternal companionship
which knows no break in the presence of God.

'Forgive me if I have been too bold, and believe me
to be

'Yrs most faithfully,
'B. F. DUNELM.'

W. M. Rossetti, Esq.
  etc. etc.

In writing to myself under date of Feb. 13, 1896,
the Bishop, after remarking that ' it will be a very great
pleasure' to him if I make 'use' of his letter, goes on
to say that he entertained for Christina Rossetti a
'reverent admiration' which it could not 'adequately
express.'

During the night previous to Christina Rossetti's
funeral, which took place on January 2, 1895, there had
been a slight fall of snow, and the air in the early morning had in it just that suggestion of winter appropriate
to the season.   A preliminary service was held at Christ
Church, conducted by Mr. Glendinning Nash, assisted
by his curate, the Rev. T. N. Talfourd Major.

The service was attended by her brother, his four
children (the Misses Olivia, Helen, Mary, and Mr. Arthur

N 2

Rossetti) who with Mr. Theodore Watts-Dunton, Miss Lisa Wilson, and Mrs. Read were the occupants of the mourning coaches. Among many others present were Mr. John R. Clayton, Mr. and Mrs. F. G. Stephens, Mr. Arthur Hughes, Mr. Frederic Shields, Dr. Abbot Anderson, the Countess Hugo (who married a nephew of the great French writer), Mrs. Garnett, Mrs. Hueffer, Mrs. Virtue Tebbs, Sister Eliza, formerly of St. Margaret's Home, Mrs. Percy Bunting, Mr. William Sharp, Professor Wyndham Dunstan, F.R.S., Mr. Forbes Robertson, Mr. Robert W. Dibdin, Mr. Robert Porter (Superintendent of the eleventh United States census) and Mrs. Porter, Mr. G. A. Garrett, and Mrs. E. T. Cooke ; while among those who sent wreaths were Lady Lindsay, The Countess Hugo, Miss Ursula Christina Gordon Hake, her god-daughter, Sister Eliza, and Dr. Abbot Anderson.

When I entered Christ Church I was struck by the beauty of the edifice—a solemn quiet beauty specially suited to such an occasion. The coffin, brought in a closed hearse from Torrington Square, was met at the western door of the church by the clergymen and the surpliced choir, and, covered by many wreaths of flowers, was solemnly borne to its place in front of the chancel while 'O rest in the Lord' was played on the organ. 'Abide with me' having been sung, Mr. Nash proceeded with the burial service. After that magnificent passage (1 Cor. xv. 20) 'Now is Christ risen from the dead, and become the first-fruits of them that slept' had been read, some stanzas from Christina's poem 'Advent,' beginning

> The Porter watches at the gate,

and ending

> With Jesus Christ our best,

were sung to the tune of St. Ann. Subsequently her

Lord, grant us grace to mount by steps of grace,

set to tasteful and appropriate music composed expressly for the occasion by Mr. F. T. Lowden, organist of Christ Church, was sung. Then, as the coffin was raised from beneath the chancel steps and slowly carried down the aisle, the *Dead March* in *Saul* was played impressively, while many of the congregation waited a moment or two outside the church door, with every token of respect, to see the funeral cortege depart. Her brother, in a letter to Mr. Nash, a word or two of which I am privileged to quote, suitably gave utterance to the general feeling concerning the service held at Christ Church when he spoke of its 'unflawed harmony of manner with its sacred matter.' It was indeed one of those services which will live in the memory of those who took part in it as almost symbolical of the person commemorated. Moreover, as one of Christina Rossetti's most attached friends said to me afterwards, ' there was nothing gloomy about it.'

As far as I am aware, with the exception of one or two persons unknown to me and whom I had not observed at Christ Church, only her brother and his children accompanied by Mr. Nash, Mr. Watts-Dunton, Miss Lisa Wilson, Mrs. Read and myself were present at the interment at Highgate. Her brother, however, informs me that Mr. Sydney Martin attended of his own accord and took some photographs, also that Alice Bloomfield (formerly a housemaid in the service of Christina Rossetti) and a male relative of hers, were there. The family grave of the Rossettis, where Christina was buried with her father and mother and Elizabeth

Eleanor, wife of Dante Gabriel, is in the old portion of Highgate Cemetery. Standing near a pathway on a portion of high ground it is not unpicturesquely situated. A sprinkling of snow had remained on the ground, and, as the closing words of the burial service were being read by Mr. Nash, the winter sunshine, gleaming through the leafless branches of some trees to the right, revealed all their delicate tracery, while a robin sang. Then, after some wreaths from those peculiarly dear to her had been placed on the coffin, and the last look had been taken, we left the cemetery.

I shall close my narrative of Christina's funeral by quoting my friend Mr. Theodore Watts-Dunton's beautiful sonnets descriptive of it, entitled ' The Two Christmastides.'[1] The reference in the closing line of the sestet of the last sonnet is to an incident which took place during her visit to Bognor at Christmas of 1875, a visit mentioned in Chapter III.

THE TWO CHRISTMASTIDES

I

On Winter's woof, which scarcely seems of snow,
  But hangs translucent, like a virgin's veil,
  O'er headstone, monument and guardian-rail,
The New Year's sun shines golden—seems to throw
Upon her coffin-flowers a greeting glow
  From lands she loved to think on—seems to trail
  Love's holy radiance from the very Grail
O'er those white flowers before they sink below.

Is that a spirit or bird whose sudden song
  From yonder sunlit tree beside the grave
Recalls a robin's warble, sweet yet strong,
  Upon a lawn beloved of wind and wave—
  Recalls her ' Christmas Robin,' ruddy, brave,
Winning the crumbs she throws where blackbirds throng?

---

[1] Originally printed in *The Athenæum* for January 12, 1895.

II

In Christmastide of Heaven does *she* recall
  Those happy days with Gabriel by the sea,
  Who gathered round him those he loved, when she
'Must coax the birds to join the festival,'
And said, 'The sea-sweet winds are musical
  With carols from the billows singing free
  Around the groynes, and every shrub and tree
Seems conscious of the Channel's rise and fall'?

The coffin lowers, and I can see her now—
  See the loved kindred standing by her side,
As once I saw them 'neath our Christmas bough—
  And her, that dearest one, who sanctified
  With halo of mother's love, our Christmastide,
And Gabriel too—with peace upon his brow.'

On January 6, 1895, the second Sunday after Christina Rossetti's death, a suitable memorial sermon was preached by Mr. Nash at the morning service of Christ Church from the text 'Her own works praise her,' Prov. xxxi. 31, in the presence of a large and sympathetic congregation. Her death was also fittingly alluded to elsewhere by Dr. Clifford and by others.

Her interest in Christ Church, even in the last days of her life, is strikingly shown by a characteristic request which she made concerning it to her brother William. The following extract of a letter from him to Mr. Nash, dated January 2, 1895, will sufficiently explain to what I refer:

'My sister left a written memorandum worded thus: "The 3 rings on my wedding finger are to be put into a Church offertory unless you, dear William, like to put 1*l.* into the offertory instead of that one of the 3 which is evidently our mother's wedding ring."   I shall of course make the substitution ; and, if you will allow me, convert the 1*l.* into 10*l.*, which will in due course be forthcoming along with the remaining 2 rings.   I have not as yet looked these out, but the matter will not be long delayed.'

The tombstone of the grave wherein Christina Rossetti lies buried is of Portland stone painted white ; and on the neatly kept surface of the grave, strewn with cocoa-nut fibre, when I visited it on September 17, 1896, were laid some beautiful chrysanthemums and autumnal leaves arranged in the form of a cross, the freshness of the flowers showing they had not long been where I saw them.   There is no space left for further lettering on the original headstone, so the words about Christina Rossetti are carved on the slanting face of an additional slab placed across its base, and the initials of the persons interred, and the dates of the interments appear on the back of the footstone.   The inscription in its entirety is as follows :

TO THE

DEAR MEMORY OF

MY HUSBAND

GABRIELE ROSSETTI,

BORN AT VASTO AMMONE

IN THE KINGDOM OF NAPLES

28TH FEB. 1783,

DIED IN LONDON 26TH APRIL 1854.

He shall return no more to see his native country.

Jeremiah xxii. 10.

Now they desire a better country, that is, an heavenly.

Hebrews xi. 16.

Ah Dio—Ajutami Tu.

ALSO OF

FRANCES MARY LAVINIA,

BELOVED WIFE OF THE ABOVE NAMED

GABRIELE ROSSETTI,

BORN APRIL 27TH, 1800, DIED APRIL 8TH, 1886.

Our Saviour Jesus Christ . . . hath abolished death.
Friend go up higher.

ALSO TO THE MEMORY OF

ELIZABETH ELEANOR,

WIFE OF THEIR ELDER SON

DANTE GABRIEL ROSSETTI,

WHO DIED FEB. 11TH, 1862
AGED 30 YEARS.

ALSO OF

CHRISTINA GEORGINA ROSSETTI

DAUGHTER OF

GABRIELE AND FRANCES ROSSETTI

BORN 5TH DECEMBER, 1830.
DIED 29TH DECEMBER, 1894.

Volsersi a me con salutevol cenno.

Give me the lowest place : or if for me
That lowest place too high, make one more low :
There I may sit and see
My God and love Thee so.

About the inscription Mr. W. M. Rossetti writes to me thus :

'" Ah Dio ajutami Tu " [Ah God, do Thou help me] was one of the last exclamations of my Father in his dying moments : I think the last ; " Volsersi a me con salutevol cenno [They turned to me with an act of salutation], a line in Dante's Purgatorio, I put on C[hristina]'s tombstone as suggesting (but not with

such a degree of definiteness as I do not personally
believe) the reunion of the other tenants of that grave
with C[hristina] in the spiritual world.'

In the grave adjoining are buried the wife of Ford
Madox Brown, and Michael Ford Madox Rossetti, the
infant son of Mr. W. M. Rossetti, who died in 1883.
Christina Rossetti's touching poem on the death of this
little child is well known.   Of its four stanzas this is
perhaps the most original :

> Brief dawn and noon and setting time !
>   Our rapid-rounding moon has fled ;
>   A black eclipse before the prime
>   Has swallowed up that shining head.
> Eternity holds up her looking-glass :—
>   The eclipse of time will pass,
> And all that lovely light return to sight.

The motto on the grave is :

> And—if thou wilt—remember.

Christina had the quiet simplicity of real greatness,
and this simplicity was doubtless in itself an evidence
of genius.   In intercourse with her one lost consciousness of being in the presence of a distinguished poet,
because one became conscious of being in the presence
of a woman distinguished in the more noble womanly
qualities.   Nature evidently had endowed her not only
with the gifts proper to a poet, and these in a lavish
degree, but also with choicest gifts of the heart and
soul.   But if this was so, it was equally true that she
had herself matured and perfected her natural gifts by
that sublimest education of all—the education of the
soul.

Personally she was warmly attached to the Church

of England.   Respecting it she said in ' The Face of the Deep ' :

' To myself it is in the beloved Anglican Church of my Baptism : a living branch of that one Holy Catholic Apostolic Church which is authoritatively commended and endeared to every Christian by the Word of God.'

But she had too noble a soul to be narrow.   A single practical example of the truth of this remark, out of many that might be cited, will suffice here.   An intimate friend of hers said to me soon after her death, ' The fact of my being a Wesleyan made no difference to Christina.'   But, indeed, Christina Rossetti's own writings confirm this view of her character.   In ' The Face of the Deep,' while deprecating needless schism, she writes :—

' Strength attaches to union, resource to multiplicity. The kingdom of death (notwithstanding that death is dissolution) retains strength while it coheres ; for our Lord Himself declared that were Satan divided against himself his kingdom could not stand.   How much more would the kingdom of life, which is the Church Catholic, wax invincibly strong if all Christendom were to become as at the first of one heart and one mind !   Alas ! for the offences of former days and of this day, for our fathers' offences and our own, which have torn to shreds Christ's seamless vesture.

' Nevertheless inasmuch as multiplicity is allied to resource, let us, until better may be, make capital even of our guilty disadvantage.   Let us be provoked to good works by those with whom we cannot altogether agree, yet who many ways set us a pattern.   Why exclusively peer after defects while virtues stare us in the face ?   Cannot we—I at least can learn much from the devotion of Catholic Rome, the immutability of Catholic Greece, the philanthropic piety of Quakerism, the zeal of many a " Protestant."   And when the Anglican Church has acquired and reduced to practice each virtue from every such source, holding fast meanwhile her own goodly heritage of gifts and graces, then may those others likewise learn much from her : until to every Church, congregation, soul, God be All in all.'

And again, in the same volume, she writes in her commentary on the text 'His eyes were as a flame of fire,' &c. (Rev. xix. 12) :

'Moreover in the surpassing rapture of that day recognition will not be all : discovery likewise (please God !) awaits us.   As one has strikingly suggested : some that glanced at afar off appear stones, when viewed close at hand may turn out to be sheep.   God all along has beheld them as sheep, and sheep they were : the misapprehension (thank God) was ours.
'To-day I read " Samaria " ; to-morrow I may redecipher the selfsame letters as " Sᵃ. Maria."

Passing away the bliss,	Clean past away the sorrow,
The anguish passing	The pleasure brought back to
away :	stay :
Thus it is	Thus and this
To-day.	To-morrow.'

In an article contributed to 'The Athenæum' of February 15, 1896, on her 'New Poems'—an article referred to already—Mr. Watts-Dunton, with his accustomed keen penetration and delicacy of touch, gives the following admirable analysis of certain aspects of her character :

'Mr. W. M. Rossetti speaks of "the very wide and exceedingly strong outburst of eulogy" of his sister which appeared in the public press after her death. Yet that outburst was far from giving adequate expression to what was felt by some of her readers—those between whom and herself there was a bond of sympathy so sacred and so deep as to be something like a religion.   It is not merely that she was the acknowledged queen in that world (outside the arena called

" the literary world ") where poetry is " its own exceeding great reward," but to other readers of a different kind altogether—readers who, drawing the deepest delight from such poetry as specially appeals to them, never read any other, and have but small knowledge of poetry as a fine art—her verse was, perhaps, more precious still. They feel that at every page of her writing the beautiful poetry is only the outcome of a life whose almost unexampled beauty fascinates them.

'Although Christina Rossetti had more of what is called the unconsciousness of poetic inspiration than any other poet of her time, the writing of poetry was not by any means the chief business of her life. She was too thorough a poet for that. No one felt so deeply as she that poetic art is only at the best the imperfect body in which dwells the poetic soul. No one felt so deeply as she that as the notes of the nightingale are but the involuntary expression of the bird's emotion, and, again, as the perfume of the violet is but the flower's natural breath, so it is and must be with the song of the very poet, and that, therefore, to write beautifully is in a deep and true sense to live beautifully. In the volume before us, as in all her previously published writings, we see at its best what Christianity is as the motive power of poetry. The Christian idea is essentially feminine, and of this feminine quality Christina Rossetti's poetry is full. In motive power the difference between classic and Christian poetry must needs be very great. But whatever may be said in favour of one as against the other, this at least cannot be controverted, that the history of literature shows no human development so beautiful as the ideal Christian woman of our own day. She is unique, indeed. Men of science tell us that among all the fossilized plants we find none of the lovely family of the rose, and in the same way we should search in vain through the entire human record for anything so beautiful as that kind of Christian lady to whom self-abnegation is not only the first of duties, but the first of joys. Yet, no doubt, the Christian idea must needs be more or less flavoured by each personality through which it is expressed. With regard to

Christina Rossetti, while upon herself Christian dogma imposed infinite obligations—obligations which could never be evaded by her without the risk of all the penalties fulminated by all believers—there was in the order of things a sort of ether of universal charity for all others. She would lament, of course, the lapses of every soul, but for these there was a forgiveness which her own lapses could never claim. There was, to be sure, a sweet egotism in this. It was very fascinating, however.'

She never obtruded her piety, yet I felt instinctively that I was in the company of a holy woman. In a copy of her ' Verses,' given to me, she wrote in her own clear handwriting—handwriting firm until four months before the end—

Faith is like a lily lifted high and white ;

and throughout life she no more doubted the existence of a state of coming blessedness than the traveller doubts the existence of the place for which he is bound, when setting out on a journey ; to her the persons and things' of the future life were realities. Probably this confidence, together with the conviction that God's angel Death would soon release her from pain, was the reason of her wonderful—her heroic endurance of suffering ; while (except during the brief period of melancholy mentioned previously) she cherished an earnest hope of heaven for herself in spite of her vivid sense of her own shortcomings. I shall always feel proud and glad that I knew personally one of the most lovable women who ever lived.

CHAPTER VI

GENERAL POEMS

'Verses' 1847—Italian Poems—'Death's Chill Between' and 'Heart's Chill Between' ('Athenæum' 1848)—'The Germ'—'Goblin Market and other Poems'—'The Prince's Progress and other Poems'—'A Pageant and other Poems'—'New Poems,' edited by Mr. William Michael Rossetti, 1896, (containing 'A Triad,' 'Cousin Kate,' and 'Sister Maude' reprinted from 'Goblin Market and other Poems')—Italian Poems.

IN my account of Christina Rossetti's poems I shall in most cases adhere to the order in which she herself placed them in the various volumes of her verse, reserving the consideration of the devotional poems in her respective volumes, 'Goblin Market and other Poems,' 'Prince's Progress and other Poems,' 'A Pageant and other Poems,' and her posthumous 'New Poems,' to my chapter on her devotional verse.

Christina Rossetti's first verses, addressed to her mother on her birthday, were written on April 27, 1842, and from that date she wrote verse frequently. By 1847 a considerable quantity of poetry had accumulated, and in that year her grandfather, Gaetano Polidori, printed privately a small volume of her compositions under the title of 'Verses,' all of the poems being dated. The book consists of sixty-six pages, 12 mo. size, and when first printed, it had only some slight 'paper cover;' the various recipients therefore bound their copies in accordance with their individual taste.   As the volume is now very rare, and becoming increasingly valuable, it may be of interest to reproduce the type of the title-page in facsimile :—

VERSES

BY CHRISTINA G. ROSSETTI

DEDICATED TO HER MOTHER.

Perchè temer degg' io?   Son le mie voci
Inesperte, lo so : ma il primo omaggio
D' accettarne la MADRE
Perciò non sdegnerà ; ch' anzi assai meglio
Quanto a lei grata io sono
L' umil dirà semplicità del dono.
METASTASIO.

PRIVATELY PRINTED
AT G. POLIDORI'S, NO. 15, PARK VILLAGE EAST,
REGENT'S PARK, 'LONDON. 1847.

Next comes 'A Few Words to the Reader,' signed 'G. Polidori,' in which that gentleman, after remarking that the contents of the volume had been ' composed from the age of twelve to sixteen,' says :

' As her maternal grandfather, I may be excused for desiring to retain these early spontaneous efforts in a permanent form, and for having silenced the objections urged by her modest diffidence, and persuaded her to allow me to print them for my own gratification at my own private press ; and though I am ready to acknowledge that the well-known partial affection of a grandparent may perhaps lead me to overrate the merit of her youthful strains, I am still confident that the lovers of poetry will not wholly attribute my judgment to partiality.'

The foregoing words are dictated by commonsense, and it is noteworthy that Gaetano Polidori, affectionate grandparent as he undoubtedly was, did not lack critical discrimination on occasion.   Dante Gabriel, with the mature judgment of fourteen, in a letter to his mother, called two of Christina's pieces, ' Rosalind ' and ' Corydon's Resolution,' composed at the age of twelve, ' very good.'   Gaetano Polidori did not insert these pieces, however.

Christina's grandfather was justified in printing her early verses for other reasons than merely grandfatherly predilection, for these early poems show in a quite unusual degree, when we recollect the author's age, the qualities which individualised subsequently all her work, but more especially all her work in verse.   They have distinct originality of conception and of presentation, a certain indefinable aloofness from the objects described, while, at the same time, they manifest a remarkable clearness in the delineation of these objects, conjointly with sumptuousness of imagery.

' The Dead City,' the opening poem, dated April 9,

1847, runs to ten pages, and has all the qualities just enumerated. The following are the first five stanzas:

> Once I rambled in a wood
> With a careless hardihood,
> Heeding not the tangled way;
> Labyrinths around me lay,
> But for them I never stood.
>
> On, still on, I wandered on,
> And the sun above me shone;
> And the birds around me winging
> With their everlasting singing
> Made me feel not quite alone.
>
> In the branches of the trees
> Murmured like the hum of bees
> The low sound of happy breezes,
> Whose sweet voice that never ceases
> Lulls the heart to perfect ease.
>
> Streamlets bubbled all around
> On the green and fertile ground,
> Through the rushes and the grass,
> Like a sheet of liquid glass,
> With a soft and trickling sound.
>
> And I went, I went on faster,
> Contemplating no disaster;
> And I plucked ripe blackberries,
> But the birds with envious eyes,
> Came and stole them from their master.

Here it may be noted that the word 'master,' perhaps unconsciously introduced for rhyme purposes, shows the uncertain touch of the beginner. But how beautiful are the stanzas that quickly succeed, how charged with foreshadowings of her later, her more mature, style!

Happy solitude, and blest
With beatitude of rest ;
Where the woods are ever vernal,
And the life and joy eternal,
Without death's or sorrow's test.

O most blessed solitude !
O most full beatitude !
Where are quiet without strife
And imperishable life,
Nothing marred, and all things good.

And the bright sun, life begetting,
Never rising, never setting,
Shining warmly overhead,
Nor too pallid nor too red,
Lulled me to a sweet forgetting—

Sweet forgetting of the time ;
And I listened for no chime,
Which might warn me to begone ;
But I wandered on, still on,
'Neath the boughs of oak and lime.

Equally poetic, and perhaps more remarkable, as its
author was only thirteen at the time it was written, is 'The
Water Spirit's Song,' dated 1844, where are these lines :

In the silent hour of even,
When the stars are in the heaven,
When in the azure cloudless sky
The moon beams forth all lustrously ;
When over hill and over vale
Is wafted the sweet scented gale ;
When murmurs thro' the forest trees
The cool refreshing evening breeze ;
When the nightingale's wild melody
Is waking herb and flower and tree
From their perfumed and soft repose
To list the praises of the rose

> When the ocean sleeps deceitfully ;
> When the waves are resting quietly ;
> I spread my bright wings, and fly far away
> To my beautiful sister's mansion gay :
> I leave behind me rock and mountain,
> I leave behind me rill and fountain,
> And I dive far down in the murmuring sea
> Where my fair sister welcomes me joyously ;
> For she's Queen of Ocean for ever and ever,
> And I of each fountain and still lake and river.

'Summer,' belonging to 1845—her fifteenth year—and dated December 4, is more conventional in conception and treatment, yet none but a poet could have written such a line as

> Round her float the laughing hours.

Less satisfactory is 'The Ruined Cross,' appertaining to her sixteenth year, and dated April 22, for it shows traces of the influence of Felicia Hemans and Lætitia Landon in their worst—their most sentimental moods. More successful is 'Love Ephemeral' (dated February 25, 1845), while Dante Gabriel was of opinion that 'Mother and Child' (dated January 10, 1846),—so touching in its mingled simplicity and sweetness—might have been written by Blake. The somewhat minute analysis of emotion in 'Love Attacked' and 'Love Defended,' (dated respectively April 21, and April 23), is very striking when we recollect that the two poems were produced in 1846 when the poet was only fifteen.

'Divine and Human Pleading,' belonging also to 1846, and dated February 8—March 30, is very noticeable if we remember its author's age. A 'trembling contrite man' pleads 'wearily' :

> I would the Saints could hear our prayers !
>   If such a thing might be,
> O blessed Mary Magdalene,
>   I would appeal to thee !

Presently he has a vision of Mary Magdalene, and after some fine lines of description, the poem proceeds :

> Long time she looked upon the ground ;
>   Then raising her bright eyes,
> Her voice came forth as sweet and soft
>   As music when it dies:
>
> O thou who in thy secret hour
>   Hast dared to think that aught
> Is faulty in God's perfect plan,
>   And perfect in thy thought !
>
> Thou who the pleadings wouldst prefer
>   Of one sin-stained like me,
> To His who is the Lord of Life,
>   To His who died for thee !
>
> In mercy I am sent from heaven :
>   Be timely wise, and learn
> To seek His love who waits for thee,
>   Inviting thy return.

Afterwards, in some stanzas, vigorously worded, though somewhat unsatisfactory in metre, Mary Magdalene tells her own experience, ending :

> In hope and fear I went to Him,—-
>   He broke and healed my heart ;
> No man was there to intercede.
>   As I was, so thou art.

As we have seen, the young Rossettis, during childhood, read eagerly the best English fiction and poetry of their day, and two of the poems here, 'Sir Eustace

Grey,' descriptive of Crabbe's character of that name, and 'Eva' from Maturin's novel 'Women' (dated respectively October 14, 1846, and March 18, 1847) are very vivid transcripts by Christina of the supposed emotions of two widely different personages. Probably the best known of the poems contained in the 'Verses' of 1847 is the sonnet entitled 'Vanity of Vanities.' 'Vanity of Vanities' has received much and deserved praise from competent critics. Personally I recognise to the full its poetic merit. Nevertheless, and I express the opinion with diffidence, it appears to me slightly morbid and insincere. It must be remembered, however, that it only purports to be what ' the Preacher saith,' and may not therefore convey what the author really felt.

As might have been expected occasional instances of imperfect workmanship occur in these immature efforts. Here and there also are examples of unusual phrasing, very natural in the case of English poems written at so early an age by one accustomed from infancy to hear Italian spoken, and who very often spoke it herself. 'Love Attacked' (dated April 21, 1846) ends with this stanza :

> In answer to my crying,
>   Sounds like incense
> Rose from the earth, replying,
>   'Indifference.'

An English girl would in all likelihood have been prevented from using 'incense' as a rhyme word with accent on the second syllable by a recollection of its other significance.

In the line

> Flowers soon must fade away

('Love Ephemeral,' dated March. 18, 1847, p. 22) the opening word becomes a dissyllable. But we must not forget that this tendency was common among versifiers of the period.

There are two Italian poems in the book—'Amore e Dovere' ('Love and Duty') and 'Amore e Dispetto' ('Love and Scorn'), inscribed respectively 'Begun February 25, 1845,' and 'Folkestone, August 21, 1846.' Both are tuneful, and, as Christina Rossetti's metrical essays in the language of her ancestors, deeply interesting.

Here may be introduced, on account of their intrinsic merit, two poems, 'Death's Chill Between' and 'Heart's Chill Between.' They appeared in 'The Athenæum' of October 14 and 21, 1848. 'Heart's Chill Between' does not seem to have been reprinted ; and 'Death's Chill Between' has not appeared since its publication, in 1853, in a book called 'Beautiful Poetry.'

HEART'S CHILL BETWEEN

I did not chide him, though I knew
  That he was false to me,
Chide the exhaling of the dew,
  The ebbing of the sea,
The fading of a rosy hue —
  But not inconstancy.

Why strive for love when love is o'er ?
  Why bind a restive heart ?—
He never knew the pain I bore
  In saying : 'We must part ;
Let us be friends and nothing more.'
  —Oh, woman's shallow art !

But it is over, it is done,—
  I hardly heed it now ;

So many weary years have run
  Since then, I think not how
Things might have been,—but greet each one
  With an unruffled brow.

What time I am where others be,
  My heart seems very calm —
Stone calm ; but if all go from me,
  There comes a vague alarm,
A shrinking in the memory
  From some forgotten harm.

And often through the long, long night,
  Waking when none are near,
I feel my heart beat fast with fright,
  Yet know not what I fear.
Oh how I long to see the light,
  And the sweet birds to hear !

To have the sun upon my face,
  To look up through the trees,
To walk forth in the open space
  And listen to the breeze,—
And not to dream the burial-place
  Is clogging my weak knees.

Sometimes I can nor weep nor pray,
  But am half stupefied :
And then all those who see me say
  Mine eyes are opened wide
And that my wits seem gone away :—
  Ah, would that I had died !

Would I could die and be at peace,
  Or living could forget !
My grief nor grows nor doth decrease,
  But ever is :—and yet
Methinks, now, that all this shall cease
  Before the sun shall set.

DEATH'S CHILL BETWEEN

Chide not ; let me breathe a little,
   For I shall not mourn him long ;
Though the life-cord was so brittle,
   The love-cord was very strong.
I would wake a little space
Till I find a sleeping-place.

You can go,—I shall not weep ;
   You can go unto your rest.
My heart-ache is all too deep,
   And too sore my throbbing breast.
Can sobs be, or angry tears,
Where are neither hopes nor fears?

Though with you I am alone
   And must be so everywhere,
I will make no useless moan,—
   None shall say ' she could not bear' :
While life lasts I will be strong,—
But I shall not struggle long.

Listen, listen ! Everywhere
   A low voice is calling me,
And a step is on the stair,
   And one comes you do not see.
Listen, listen ! Evermore
A dim hand knocks at the door.

Hear me ; he is come again,—
   My own dearest is come back,
Bring him in from the cold rain ;
   Bring wine, and let nothing lack.
Thou and I will rest together,
Love, until the sunny weather.

I will shelter thee from harm,—
   Hide thee from all heaviness.

Come to me, and keep thee warm
  By my side in quietness.
I will lull thee to thy sleep
With sweet songs :—we will not weep.

Who hath talked of weeping ?—Yet
  There is something at my heart,
Gnawing, I would fain forget,
  And an aching and a smart.
—Ah ! my mother, 'tis in vain,
For he is not come again.

Christina Rossetti's surviving brother furnishes me with some information about these poems :

'The former was first called The Last Hope, 22 Sept. [18]47 ; the latter, Anne of Warwick, 29 Sept. [18]47. The 2 titles printed in the Athenæum must have been adopted with a view to giving the poems, when printed, a certain flavour of interdependence (Gab[riel]'s suggestion perhaps).'

'The Germ,' where Christina Rossetti's verse next appeared in print, has received already so much attention elsewhere that much space need not be devoted to it here ; while the facts concerning this magazine, now famous, though it attracted little attention on its first appearance, may be summarised briefly. It ran for two numbers only under the title of 'The Germ,' subsequently appearing for two more numbers as 'Art and Poetry,' and then ceasing to exist. 'The Germ' was the organ of the Præraphaelite Brotherhood, a band of young, some of them very young men, and most of them destined to be celebrated. Four things are chiefly remarkable about the periodical. First, that so many of its contributors became eminent ; secondly, the high character of its contents both from the artistic and the literary point of view ; thirdly,—although perhaps this is what might have been expected—its lack of immediate success ; and fourthly, that in spite of the extreme youth of some of its literary contributors, they had already written and contributed to it work that might now almost be called classic. As instances of this may be named Dante Gabriel's ' My Sister's Sleep,' (there entitled ' Songs of One Household,' and marked No. 1), ' The Blessed Damozel,' and his vivid prose story ' Hand and Soul ' ; William Michael's sonnet ' The Evil under the Sun,' since called ' Democracy Downtrodden ' ; and Christina's songs ' Dream Land,' and ' Oh roses for the flush of youth.'   It is noteworthy that in

Before in the old time,

the last line of this exquisite song, not only is the stress laid upon the article ' the,' but the accentuated word is followed by a vowel whereby a hiatus occurs, which renders the line almost immetrical and unscannable.

The first number of ' The Germ ' appeared in January 1850, when Dante Gabriel had not completed his twenty-second year ; William Michael, acting as editor, and also as a large contributor, was little more than twenty, and Christina only nineteen. The names of the contributors to ' The Germ ' were not published in the text of the magazine, but, beginning with the third number, were printed on the outside wrapper. Concerning Christina's pseudonym in ' The Germ ' of ' Ellen Alleyn,' Mr. William Rossetti has written to me :

' My impression is that C[hristina] placed her poems at the disposal of G[abriel], to be used (whether with or without real name) much as G[abriel] chose. He invented and inserted the name " Ellen Alleyn," and only after he had done this did C[hristina] know anything about it.'

The last stanza of the poem called 'Dream Land' runs thus in 'The Germ':

> Rest, rest, for evermore
> Upon a mossy shore,
> Rest, rest, that shall endure,
> Till time shall cease ;—
> Sleep that no pain shall wake,
> Night that no morn shall break,
> Till joy shall overtake
> Her perfect peace,

while in Christina Rossetti's 'Goblin Market and other Poems' and her collected 'Poems' it stands as :

> Rest, rest, for evermore
> Upon a mossy shore ;
> Rest, rest at the heart's core
> Till time shall cease :
> Sleep that no pain shall wake,
> Night that no morn shall break,
> Till joy shall overtake
> Her perfect peace.

The lyric can hardly be said to be improved, however, by the substitution of

> Rest, rest at the heart's core

for

> Rest, rest, that shall endure.

Among Christina's other contributions to 'The Germ' are her powerful poem 'A Testimony' founded on Ecclesiastes ii. 1, 2, and perhaps better known by its opening line

> I said of laughter it is vain ;

'An End'; and 'A Pause of Thought.'

'Goblin Market and other Poems' was published in 1862 by Messrs. Macmillan. It contained two designs drawn on wood-blocks by her brother Dante Gabriel, both illustrative of lines in the title-poem. The wood-cut of the first of these designs, facing the title-page, and illustrating 'Buy from us with a golden curl,' was, it has often been said, cut by William Morris, and was his first experiment as a wood engraver. This is an error, however, for William Morris himself told me that the design was cut not by him, but by the late Charles Joseph Faulkner, formerly Fellow and Tutor of University College, Oxford. Mr. Faulkner was at the time a partner in the artistic firm of Messrs. Morris, Marshall, Faulkner & Co. The firm's initials, M. M. F. & Co., appear on the design, and William Morris thought that this was why it had been supposed, mistakenly, that he had himself cut the design. Dante Gabriel's second design forms the title-page, the centre of it illustrating the words 'Golden head by golden head'; as it has been described at considerable length[1] I shall not further refer to it here beyond saying that the wood-block was cut by Mr. W. J. Linton.

'Goblin Market and other Poems' at once achieved success, and established its author's position as a poet, though it must be remembered that poems like 'Up-hill,' 'A Birthday,' and 'An Apple Gathering,' all of which had previously appeared in 'Macmillan's Magazine,' had already done much to attract attention to Christina Rossetti as a poet of both marked performance and promise. It does not always happen that contemporary criticism respecting a volume of poems has qualities of abiding truth, but the verdict on these poems in 'The

---

[1] See Mr. Sharp's *Dante Gabriel Rossetti: a Record and Study*, p. 106.

British Quarterly Review ' has, as her brother William points out, ' stood the test of time.' That organ of critical opinion said :

' All [the poems] . . . are marked by beauty and tenderness : they are frequently quaint, and sometimes a little capricious.'

' Goblin Market ' was received immediately into especial favour, and perhaps remains to this day the most genuinely popular of all Christina Rossetti's writings. Mrs. Norton, soon after its appearance, compared it to Coleridge's ' Ancient Mariner.' ' Goblin Market '—the title was suggested by Dante Gabriel —may be described briefly as the story of two sisters, Laura and Lizzie, who are besought by ' Goblin merchantmen ' to partake of their fruits. One sister refuses, while the other sister eats. The goblins —' malignant spirits '—by the law of their temptation do not appear again to anyone who has once partaken of their fruits. The person who thus partakes is doomed irrevocably, for this first taste wastes him or her down to the grave in the longing for a second taste, which alone can bring restoration to well-being. In this story the girl who would not herself eat, meets the goblins once more for the sake of her dying sister, and some juices from their ' goblin fruits ' restore that dying sister to health.

James Ashcroft Noble, in a penetrative essay called ' The Burden of Christina Rossetti ' in his subtly-wrought volume, ' Impressions and Memories,' after pointing out that 1862 witnessed also the publication of the ' Last Poems ' of Elizabeth Barrett Browning, says that ' Goblin Market ' may be

‘ read and enjoyed merely as a charming fairy-fantasy, and as such it is delightful and satisfying ; but behind the simple story of the two children and the goblin fruit-sellers is a little spiritual drama of love’s vicarious redemption, in which the child redeemer goes into the wilderness to be tempted of the devil, that by her painful conquest she may succour and save the sister who has been vanquished and all but slain. The luscious juices of the goblin fruit, sweet and deadly when sucked by selfish greed become bitter and medicinal when spilt in unselfish conflict.’

This is admirable, and eloquently put, but it may be questioned whether the critic has not perhaps somewhat overstated the case for didacticism in the poem.

‘Goblin Market’ was written in April 1859, and the MS. was entitled originally ‘‘A Peep at the Goblins—To M. F. R,’ thus showing the close connection in the author’s mind with her sister, ‘ M. F. R.’ being of course Maria Francesca. Concerning the poem her surviving brother writes to me :

‘ I don’t remember that there were at that time [the date at which the poem was written] any personal circumstances of a marked kind : but I certainly think (with you) that the lines at the close, “ There is nothing like a sister,” etc., indicate *something* : apparently C[hristina] considered herself to be chargeable with some sort of spiritual backsliding, against which Maria’s influence had been exercised beneficially. I have more than once heard C[hristina] aver that the poem has not any profound or ulterior meaning—it is just a fairy story : yet one can discern that it implies at any rate this much—That to succumb to a temptation makes one a victim to that same continuous temptation ; that the remedy does not always lie with oneself ; and that a stronger and more righteous will may prove of avail to restore one’s lost estate.’

As the design illustrative of the words ‘ Buy from us

with a golden curl' has been dealt with fully by Mr. Sharp in his monograph recently mentioned, it is needless to discuss it here at great length. One aspect of the design demands however a moment's comment. Not infrequently I have heard the artist censured because he had made the goblin animals of hideous aspect, whereas vice is usually made seductive at least in appearance. But such an observation comes from misconception of the facts, for, as the artist's younger brother remarked very properly when I told him of these cavils:

'It is C[hristina] who says what the Goblins were like—wombat, ratel, etc., etc.—Gabriel figures a cat, an owl, and a cockatoo—3 beautiful animals—and figures them properly; also a wombat and a rat, which are animals far from ugly. Between wombat and cockatoo comes a speckled animal, not exactly pretty, nor meant to be so: it is a sunfish which belonged to my brother, and the like of which, (gilded) is at this moment hanging above my head—C[hristina] does not tell us that the *animals* were seductive in aspect, nor is there any reason why they should be (rather the contrary)—but that their *fruits* were seductive.'

I suggested to the same gentleman that perhaps the great fondness of Dante Gabriel for all animals, and not less for animals with something grotesque or eccentric about them, might have caused his sister, when arranging in her mind what forms her 'goblin merchantmen' were to assume, to recollect the strange animals, such as the wombat and the ratel—which, had it not been for her brother's predilection, probably would never have come under her notice—and to give to her 'goblin merchantmen' some of their characteristics. But he answered immediately:

'It would be a mistake to think that C[hristina] caught from Gabriel a fancy for odd-looking animals— She had it equally herself—She knew Wombat and Ratel at the Zoological Gardens : Gabriel never possessed a Ratel, nor a Wombat until several years after C[hristina] wrote "Goblin M[arket]."—It was C[hristina] and I who jointly discovered the Wombat in the Zoological Gardens—From us (more especially myself) Gabriel, [Sir Edward] Burne-Jones, and other wombat enthusiasts, ensued, such is my reminiscence and belief.'

In 1893 Messrs. Macmillan issued 'Goblin Market' separately in 8vo. form, illustrated by Mr. Laurance Housmann. Thus presented, it makes a dainty little volume in its green and gold cover, and, though the illustrations have not the unique interest belonging to the two illustrations Dante Gabriel did for the poem, they are not without interest of their own. The title-page of this edition is noteworthy. In the centre, and above, we see the goblin merchantmen, who display their wares, invitingly, while at the foot of the picture Laura and Lizzie are seated. Laura looks at the fruit, longingly, while Lizzie covers her eyes, presumably to keep out the too seductive sight.

Opposite the passage in the poem containing an enumeration of the various fruits, and opening with the lines

> Apples and quinces
> Lemons and oranges,

we have a full page illustration representing the gathering of the fruit. The picture gives effectively the subtle atmosphere of the poem. The conflict with the goblins is excellently rendered, and the flight of Lizzie, in order that Laura might get some of the juice after the goblins had squeezed the fruit on her mouth, is well

done. Set to music by the competent hands of Mr.
Aguilar 'Goblin Market' has become also a fine cantata.
Under the title of 'Il Mercato de' Folleti,' it was trans-
lated into Italian by Christina Rossetti's cousin, Signor
Teodorico Pietrocola Rossetti, and published in Florence
in 1867.

Christina Rossetti's consummate skill in setting forth
diverse moods of poetry—moods rarely found in the
same poet—is seen strikingly in such a poem as 'When
I was dead my spirit turned,' a poem for which her
brother Dante Gabriel suggested the not very happy title
of 'At Home.'   We feel almost the presence of the dis-
embodied spirit in such verses as :—

> I listened to their honest chat :
>   Said one : ''To-morrow we shall be
> Plod, plod along the featureless sands
>   And coasting miles and miles of sea.'
> Said one : ' Before the turn of tide
>   We will achieve the eyric-seat.'
> Said one : 'To-morrow shall be like
>   To-day, but much more sweet.'
>
> .   .   .   .   .
>
> I shivered comfortless, but cast
>   No chill across the table-cloth ;
> I all-forgotten shivered sad
>   To stay and yet to part how loth :
> I passed from the familiar room ;
>   I who from love had passed away,
> Like the remembrance of a guest
>   That tarrieth but a day.

This is the result of the blending of a realism equal to,
or even greater, than that of Crabbe with a deep though
indefinable mysticism.   Other poems of the same class,
though with a more distinct love interest, are the sonnet
'After Death,' (remarkable for vivid presentment of

ordinary objects and the quaint Italian touch of the last line

    To know he still is warm though I am cold) ;

' The Hour and the Ghost,' revealing, in addition to these qualities, command over dialogue, a difficult form to write in; and ' Dead before Death.'

Love poetry is a conspicuous feature in the volume under consideration.   In the original manuscript, dated in Christina's own handwriting ' 12th December 1848,' of ' When I am dead, my dearest' now in my possession, and appearing in facsimile on p. 147, the stanzas are written without a break, and the fourteenth line runs

    That doth nor rise nor set

instead of

    That doth not rise nor set

in the printed version.   There are, besides, six variations in punctuation.   Some critics have held that the metre of this song is a glad metre, and the metre is used to imply a certain chastened gladness in the thought of death.   But such an opinion savours of super-subtlety. One afternoon, when I was speaking to Mr. William Rossetti about this song, he quoted the lines

    Haply I may remember,
    And haply may forget,

and added : ' You see Christina does not say there will not be recognition after the Resurrection, for then she was quite certain there would be recognition.   She only expresses uncertainty on the point during the intermediate state after death and before the Resurrection.'

' Do you think,' I said, ' that your sister, a great poet, always subordinated the wording of her poems to her views as to theological doctrine?'

' I do not say,' he answered, ' that Christina never used a merely poetic phrase ; but I do say that in the main she kept strictly to what she considered theological truth.'

Dated August 9, 1854, ' The Convent Threshold ' has, presumably, a reference to an Italian blood feud, and has been truly called by Dante Gabriel a ' <u>splendid piece of feminine ascetic pass</u>ion.' Despite, however, my profound admiration for this really great poem, I cannot help thinking that the phrase ' My lily feet ' in the line

My lily feet are soiled with mud

gives a touch of insincerity to the passage where it occurs. Surely no woman in actual life, leaving her lover in such tragic circumstances, would so describe her feet—the emotion—the passion, would entirely do away with the thought which this language expresses. I make no apology for my word of demur. Admiration has called it forth, for, as Mrs. Meynell has truly said :

' In this poem—it is impossible not to dwell on such a masterpiece—without imagery ; without beauty except that which is inevitable (and what beauty is more costly ?) ; without grace, except the invincible grace of impassioned poetry ; without music, except the ultimate music of the communicating word, she utters that immortal song of love and that cry of more than earthly fear ; a song of penitence for love that yet praises love more fervently than would a chorus hymeneal.'

' The Convent Threshold ' is not based on any real incident.

Among other love poems are the exquisite sonnets called ' Rest ' and ' Remember ' ; the lyrics entitled ' An End ;' ' A Birthday,' written November 18, 1857 ; the unspeakably beautiful lines beginning 'Come to me in the silence of the night;' 'Three Seasons,' and 'May.' The brief ballad ' Maude Clare ' renders vividly a strong situation, and shows a keen perception and insight into the love passion.   Readers of his ' Letters ' will recollect that her brother Dante Gabriel did not admire ' No thank you, John,' a lyric depicting a woman's total indifference towards a suitor for her hand, couched (a rare thing with Christina!) in a light vein, but many—myself among the number—will not agree with him.

Three notable poems—the sonnet, ' A Triad,' and two remarkable ballads, ' Cousin Kate ' and ' Sister Maude '—which appeared in this volume, were omitted by the author from her collected works from conscientious reasons.   She was perhaps unduly sensitive in this matter.   Concerning ' A Triad ' Mr. W. M. Rossetti has written to me :

' I don't remember having heard her make any express statement about her motives for burking Triad ; but am clear that they proceeded more or less on a notion that the sonnet might be misconstrued, or unfavourably construed, from a moral point of view ; the perfectly respectable wife, who "bloomed like a tinted hyacinth at a show," was "a sluggish wife," and "droned in sweetness,' being evidently regarded with less sympathy than her less decorous colleagues.   There was a painter, George Chapman, known to Gabriel and me, and in a minor degree to C[hristina].   He painted a picture of the Triad : and I think it quite possible that something may have been said by him, or in his set, which impressed C[hristina] with this notion of contingent misconstruction. Of course I consider that she was wrong in suppressing the poem ; wiredrawn scrupulosity was one of her manifest infirmities, if also of her quasi-virtues.'

My correspondent includes ' A Triad,' ' Cousin Kate ' and ' Sister Maude ' in ' New Poems.'

One of the most striking examples of nature poetry
is 'Twilight Calm,' which, though in motive quite
original, shows the influence of Wordsworth. Here is
a touch of Wordsworthian realism :

> The cock has ceased to crow, the hen to cluck,
> Only the fox is out, some heedless duck
> Or chicken to surprise.

The rather weak inversion of

> some heedless duck
> Or chicken to surprise

mars somewhat the beauty of the passage. Fine examples of Christina's unconventional treatment of conventional themes are seen in ' Winter Rain,' and ' Another
Spring.'

Mr. Watts-Dunton has pointed out how excellent is
' An Apple Gathering' in its perfect presentment of a
moral conception, and certainly the poem must take
rank among Christina Rossetti's masterpieces. It is,
however, too well known to require detailed analysis
here. She wrote as follows in an annotated copy of the
volume as to that powerful poem ' My Dream ':

' " My Dream " was merely a poetic fancy and was
not a dream at all.'

This note is all the more interesting from the fact that
the poem has every appearance of being a veritable dream.
' Up-hill,' another masterpiece, written June 29, 1858,
might have been regarded as one of her ' Devotional
Pieces,' had not the poet elected to place it among her
secular poems. A brief sixteen-line poem, it reveals
quaintly, with one flash of genius, a whole philosophy of
life.

In 1866 Messrs. Macmillan published her second

volume of verse, 'The Prince's. Progress and other Poems.' Reference has already been made to Mr. Edmund Gosse's article on Christina Rossetti in his 'Critical Kit Kats.' Therein Mr. Gosse very justly expresses surprise that 'The Prince's Progress,' 'where the parable and the teaching are as clear as noonday,' has never been popular. Even in literal fact there is enough truth in this statement to make it needful to say briefly that the poem describes how a prince, lured from his rightful path at first by light pleasures, and afterwards by the pursuit of the elixir of life, fails to reach his destined bride until she is dead. The greatness of this noble poem lies in its subtle poetic atmosphere—a poetic atmosphere which is beyond the reach of exact definition, but which enshrines it among the great poems of the century. It gains in intensity of passion as it proceeds until we forget its occasional metrical ruggednesses. The title-page of the volume and the design opposite were drawn by Dante Gabriel and engraved by Mr. W. J. Linton.

An early version of the closing stanzas of 'The Prince's Progress,' beginning with the line 'Too late for love, too late for joy,' were printed in 'Macmillan's Magazine' for May 1863, under the title of 'The Fairy Prince who arrived too late.' In this version there are three noteworthy variants from the final form. The lovely stanza :—

> Ten years ago, five years ago,
>   One year ago,
> Even then you had arrived in time,
>   Though somewhat slow ;
> Then you had known her living face
>   Which now you cannot know :

> The frozen fountain would have leaped,
> The buds gone on to blow,
> The warm south wind would have awaked
> To melt the snow—

there ran as follows :

> Ten years ago, five years ago,
> One year ago,
> Even then you had arrived in time,
> Though somewhat slow.
> The frozen fountain would have leaped,
> The buds gone on to blow,
> The warm south wind would have awaked
> To melt the snow,
> And life have been a cordial ‘ Yes,’
> Instead of dreary ‘ No.’

This is obviously an inferior form, while the lines—

> Now these are poppies in her locks—

and

> Lo, we who love weep not to-day

begin respectively

> Now those are poppies in her locks,

and

> So, we who love weep not to-day.

The exquisite love poetry contained in the book under consideration must next claim our attention. Chief among the poems of this class is ‘ Maiden-Song,’ the story of Margaret, Meggan and May, a sprightly lyric of not inconsiderable length—full of joy and unshadowed by grief—so full of joy, indeed, that for this reason alone, it stands out pre-eminently among its author's best work. About it is a touch of fairy lore, that distinguishing touch of fairy lore rare even in good poetry, rare even in Christina Rossetti's poetry, a something present only in poetry of a certain class, and even then only in the highest poetry of that class.   Take the first stanza :

> Long ago and long ago
>   And long ago still,
> There dwelt three merry maidens
>   Upon a distant hill.
> One was tall Meggan,
>   And one was dainty May,
> But one was fair Margaret,
>   More fair than I can say,
> Long ago and long ago.

Apparently by the simple expedient of the repetition

> Long ago and long ago.

a fascinating sense of remoteness is conveyed ; I say *apparently*, advisedly, for in truth there is art of an ethereal sort in the arrangement of the poem—a perfect poem, in spite of its seeming negligence, both as to rhymeless lines and as to metre.   Particularly noticeable also is the influence which ' birds ' ' beasts ' and ' fishes ' exercise in this as in others of Christina's poems.   How daring, yet how successful is this simile respecting Margaret, when Meggan and May go on their quest, in search of

> Strawberry leaves and May-dew.

Margaret is described as

> Fragrant-breathed as milky cow,
>   Or field of blossoming bean.

Meantime ' light-foot May ' with her companion rested during the heat of the day, while

> Creeping things among the grass,
>   Stroked them here and there ;

Presently the sisters sing, and ' honey-mouthed ' is ' the double flow.'

Then follows a declaration of love to Meggan by 'a herdsman from the vale' and to May by 'a shepherd from the height.' Both accept their lovers. By-and-by, Margaret, awaiting her sisters' return, leant on the garden gate :

> The slope was lightened by her eyes
>   Like summer lightning fair,
> Like rising of the haloed moon
>   Lightened her glimmering hair.

Later she also sang. 'The King of all that country' heard her, and

> claimed her for his bride.
> So three maids were wooed and won
>   In a brief May-tide,
> Long ago and long ago.

It is interesting to find from the 'Family Letters' of Dante Gabriel that Mr. Gladstone once recited this poem, and it is easy to fancy how vivid the poem must have seemed as heard from his lips.

Entirely in a different key is 'Songs in a Cornfield,' full of forcible description, though occasionally marred by prosaic lines, such as

> He'll not find her at all.

Christina Rossetti, in a published letter, designates 'Songs in a Cornfield' as one of the most successful pieces in her 'Prince's Progress' volume.

A 'Ring Posy' and 'Beauty is Vain' should be mentioned in this connection. The former treats the love sentiment with a playful humour, which, as has been indicated before, is seldom employed by this poet ; the latter perhaps can hardly be properly called a love poem at all. Yet inferentially it deals with the love sentiment in that mournful (some would call it morbid) vein peculiar to its author.

Here, as in her previous volume, she deals with the supernatural. 'The Poor Ghost,' and 'The Ghost's Petition,' for instance, bring out vividly the contrast between the living and the dead, and show a power of depicting—almost revealing—the supernatural, which of itself would place Christina Rossetti high among poets. Probably none of her idyls—idyls showing always a real narrative gift—are finer than 'Lady Maggie' and 'Jessie Cameron' or 'A Farm Walk.' 'Twice,' a poem full of devotional feeling, may here be alluded to. Its passion is none the less intense from being expressed so simply.

In a brief note, which lies before me, written from 166 Albany Street probably in 1861 or 1862, addressed to Dante Gabriel, Christina says :—' I am taking your advice and leaving *Twice* amongst the miscellaneous : thank you so heartily for all kind trouble.'

This implies that it was her first intention to place *Twice* (now among the ' Miscellaneous Pieces ') among the ' Devotional Poems ' at the close of the volume. The note is a further evidence of the advice which, as mentioned before, was given to her by Dante Gabriel regarding the arrangement of her two first volumes of poems.

Sympathy with the poor Christina always had, and, were her poems more concerned with social problems, it would be more apparent in them. ' A Royal Princess ' is, however, the single instance I know where Christina Rossetti frankly avows democratic sentiments. For although the poem is dramatic, there can be little doubt that a certain degree of personal predilection is exhibited. The poem incisively shows the satiety which arises from ceaseless luxury. The vigorous narrative poem, ' Under the Rose,' composed perhaps at as late a date as July 1866, is written in the first person. It tells, with much strength of delineation, the familiar story of a high-born woman's shame and the suffering entailed on her innocent child. In the volume of Christina's collected ' Poems ' published in 1875, and in all subsequent editions of her collected works, the title was changed to 'The Iniquity of the Fathers upon the Children.' During one of my interviews with her brother subsequent to Christina Rossetti's death, in answer to a question I had put to him respecting this· change, he said :

' I think the reason why Christina changed the title of " Under the Rose " was because she felt that that title might expose her to the inference of having treated a serious subject somewhat lightly. Gabriel suggested " Upon the Children," but she thought that somewhat ambiguous, and in this I agree with her, although I also agree in thinking " The Iniquity of the Fathers upon the Children " is too long. But as I told you before, [he had previously alluded to it] I think the story is probably based ·on some recollection of " Bleak House." " Bleak House " had appeared before the poem was written.'

Then, turning to her own annotated copy of her poems, on a bookshelf near, he opened it, and read to me the following note about the poem in her own handwriting :

' This was all fancy, but Mrs. Scott [Mrs. William Bell Scott] afterwards told me of a somewhat similar fact.'

In reference to the lyric addressed to L. E. L., Mr. W. M. Rossetti has written to me:

'I regard L. E. L. as the merest *fancy* title—In my opinion the poem is a dejected outpouring of C[hristina]'s own—When the question of publishing it arose, she did not want it to figure as strictly personal, and so called it L. E. L.'

Of the many lovely Nature poems in this volume my preference lies with 'Child's Talk in April' from which I cannot refrain from quoting some stanzas.

> I wish you were a pleasant wren,
>   And I your small accepted mate ;
> How we'd look down on toilsome men !
>   We'd rise and go to bed at eight
>   Or it may be not quite so late.
>
> .   .   .   .   .   .
>
> Perhaps some day there'd be an egg
>   When spring had blossomed from the snow :
> I'd stand triumphant on one leg ;
>   Like chanticleer I'd almost crow
>   To let our little neighbours know.
>
> Next you should sit and I would sing
> Through lengthening days of sunny spring ;
>   Till, if you wearied of the task,
> I'd sit ; and you should spread your wing
>   From bough to bough ; I'd sit and bask.
>
> Fancy the breaking of the shell,
>   The chirp, the chickens wet and bare,
> The untried proud paternal swell ;
>   And you with housewife-matron air
>   Enacting choicer bills of fare.
>
> Fancy the embryo coats of down,
>   The gradual feathers soft and sleek ;
> Till clothed and strong from tail to crown,
>   With virgin warblings in their beak,
>   They too go forth to soar and seek.

Other notable nature poems are 'Gone for Ever,' 'Spring Quiet,' and 'A Chill.' 'Autumn' is perhaps one of the most striking examples we possess of Christina's characteristic melancholy. Its pensive cadences, so exquisite in their rhythmical flow, linger in the mind. Doubtless the poem is highly symbolical. Listen to these opening stanzas. The remarkable metrical effects that result from the rhyming of the first and seventh lines may possibly have attracted Mr. Swinburne's attention, and caused him to attempt cadences, somewhat similar in measure, though even more difficult.

> I dwell alone—I dwell alone, alone,
>   Whilst full my river flows down to the sea,
>   Gilded with flashing boats
>   That bring no friend to me :
> O love-songs gurgling from a hundred throats,
>   O love-pangs, let me be.
>
> Fair fall the freighted boats which gold and stone
>   And spices bear to sea :
> Slim, gleaming maidens swell their mellow notes,
>   Love promising, entreating—
>   Ah ! sweet, but fleeting—
>   Beneath the shivering, snow-white sails.
>   Hush ! the wind flags and fails—
> Hush ! they will lie becalmed in sight of strand—
>   Sight of my strand, where I do dwell alone ;
> Their songs wake singing echoes in my land—
>   They cannot hear me moan.

The curious sympathy she felt with inhabitants of the earth other than mankind is brought out forcibly in the subjoined lines from 'Eve.'

> Thus she sat weeping,
> Thus Eve our Mother,
> Where one lay sleeping
> Slain by his brother.

Greatest and least
Each piteous beast
To hear her voice
Forgot his joys
And set aside his feast.

The mouse paused in his walk
And dropped his wheaten stalk ;
Grave cattle wagged their heads
In rumination ;
The eagle gave a cry
From his cloud station ;
Larks on thyme beds
Forbore to mount or sing ;
Bees drooped upon the wing ;
The raven perched on high
Forgot his ration ;
The conies in their rock,
A feeble nation,
Quaked sympathetical ;
The mocking-bird left off to mock ;
Huge camels knelt as if
In deprecation ;
The kind hart's tears were falling ;
Chattered the wistful stork ;
Dove-voices with a dying fall
Cooed desolation.

Christina Rossetti's mental attitude towards death—an unusual, and somewhat morbid attitude—will be seen strikingly in this first stanza from the strong nature poem 'Life and Death':

Life is not sweet.   One day it will be sweet
    To shut our eyes and die :
Nor feel the wild flowers blow, nor birds dart by
    With flitting butterfly,
Nor grass grow long above our heads and feet
Nor hear the happy lark that soars sky high,

> Nor sigh that spring is fleet and summer fleet,
>   Nor mark the waxing wheat,
> Nor know who sits in our accustomed seat.

'A Pageant and other Poems' was published by Messrs. Macmillan in August 1881 as has been already mentioned. Concerning the title-poem 'The British Quarterly Review' said :

'The "Pageant" is full of grace and fancifulness ; there is a playful freshness in it ; it abounds in delicate pictures, which claim for themselves a place apart in the imagination,'

while 'The Guardian' remarked respecting its author :

'She breathes habitually the atmosphere of wonder and aspiration. But she is also a student of high literary models, and can express herself on an occasion with the clearness, directness, and precision which are the usual indications of a thoroughly trained mind.'

'The Westminster Review' perceived :

'Very good work in Miss Rossetti's new volume of poems,'

while 'The Daily News' found that

'A more finished grace, however, is perhaps traceable in some of these pieces than she has hitherto attained. . . Characterized by a grave tenderness.'

A sonnet addressed to the author's mother designated rightly by Dante Gabriel as 'lovely in its heartfelt affection,' and a brief lyric called 'The Key Note' revealing both the poet's sadness and her consolation in the contemplation of nature open the book. The title-poem called 'The Months: A Pageant' runs to twenty-two pages, and is in the form of a masque, in which the 'personifications' of January, March, July, August, October, and December are assumed by boys, and February, April, May, June, September, and November, by girls. The stage directions are ample and interestng, and, properly mounted, it should be a very picturesque little play for children. It has been played in America at least once, and probably elsewhere. Each of the months from January to December has suitable attributes, and many of the interspersed lyrics have special beauty. Here and there, however, some of the lines are rugged. 'A Pageant' holds a unique place among Christina's long poems; it is cheerful throughout, with not a single note reminding the reader of sorrow. Among a group of poems descriptive of nature, 'Freaks of Fashion '—a humorous recital of how the birds met and discussed as to what were the more fashionable garments to wear—is prominent. The beautiful lyric, ' An October Garden,' is pervaded by subtle mournfulness; while the last stanza of the lovely and pathetic ' Death Watches ' merits quotation :

> The cloven East brings forth the sun,
>   The cloven West doth bury him.
> What time his gorgeous race is run
>   And all the world grows dim ;
> A funeral moon is lit in heaven's hollow,
> And pale the star-lights follow.

The somewhat longer poem ' An Old-World Thicket,' having Dante's phrase '. . . Una selva oscura ' as motto, is full of chastened symbolism.

Christina had a distinct faculty for writing simple, direct tales in verse, with a touch of half-unconscious regret in them, and it is a pity that she has given us so few of these. ' Johnny,' which appears in this volume

—an anecdote of the first French Revolution—is a
fine example. Very powerful are the ballads here.
'Brandons Both' tells the love story of Milly Brandon
and her cousin Walter. Though necessarily dramatic
in form, it would not, I think, be unwarrantable to conclude that in—

Milly has no mother ; and sad beyond another
  Is she whose blessed mother is vanished out of call :
Truly comfort beyond comfort is stored up in a Mother
  Who bears with all, and hopes through all, and loves us all—

there is an allusion to the mother who was never long
absent from Christina's thoughts. The first line of
each stanza has occasionally an internal rhyme, and the
metre is the same as in Jean Ingelow's exquisite
'Requiescat in Pace.' Is it unreasonable to suppose
that the measure was suggested by a poem which first
appeared in November 1863, nearly eighteen years
before the publication of 'The Pageant and other
Poems'? Somewhat similar in motive to 'Sleep at
Sea' is 'A Ballad of Boding,' where the writer has a
vision of three ships—'Love ship,' 'Worm ship,' and a
'third ship,' and what befell them and their crews. The
poem ends finely thus:

There was sorrow on the sea and sorrow on the land
When Love ship went down by the bottomless quicksand
To its grave in the bitter wave.
There was sorrow on the sea and sorrow on the land
When Worm ship went to pieces on the rock-bound strand,
And the bitter wave was its grave.
But land and sea waxed hoary
In whiteness of a glory
Never told in story
Nor seen by mortal eye,
When the third ship crossed the bar
Where whirls and breakers are

And steered into the splendours of the sky;
That third bark and that least
Which had never seemed to feast,
Yet kept high festival above sun and moon and star.

Two of the chief glories of this volume are the noble sonnet sequences named respectively, 'Monna Innominata,' and 'Later Life.' 'Monna Innominata' suggests comparison with Elizabeth Barrett Browning's 'Sonnets from the Portuguese.' But such a comparison may be reserved to Chapter X., where a critical survey of Christina Rossetti's work is attempted.

'Monna Innominata' is a series of fourteen sonnets supposed to be written by one of the 'unnamed ladies, "donne innominate," sung by a school of less conspicuous poets' than Dante and Petrarch. Prefixed to it is a very interesting prose note, the close of which is given below :

'Had such a lady spoken for herself, the portrait left us might have appeared more tender, if less dignified, than any drawn even by a devoted friend. Or had the Great Poetess of our own day and nation only been unhappy instead of happy, her circumstances would have invited her to bequeath to us, in lieu of the Portuguese Sonnets, an inimitable " donna innominata " drawn not from fancy but from feeling, and worthy to occupy a niche beside Beatrice and Laura. '

Each of the fourteen sonnets is introduced by an appropriate quotation from Dante and Petrarch.

It was indeed a happy inspiration to make this 'donna innominata' speak for herself. When all are so beautiful it is difficult to select special sonnets for mention. The second, and one of the most lovely sonnets of the series, has an almost identical motive to that of Mrs. Meynell's strong poem, ' An Unmarked

Festival.   It is merely a literary coincidence, however
for Mrs. Meynell informs me that it was only when
writing the essay on Christina Rossetti's poetry, mentioned
elsewhere, that she first read the sonnet in question.
Then she was herself impressed by the identity of the
fundamental idea.

Here are the opening lines of Sonnet 4.

' Poca favilla gran fiamma seconda.'—DANTE.
' Ogni altra cosa, ogni pensier va fore,
   E sol ivi con voi rimansi amore.'—PETRARCA.

I loved you first : but afterwards your love
    Outsoaring mine, sang such a loftier song
As drowned the friendly cooings of my dove.
    Which owes the other most? my love was long,
    And yours one moment seemed to wax more strong.

The concluding lines of No. 5 are the perfect
expression of a noble woman's love-passion :

So much for you ; but what for me, dear friend?
    To love you without stint and all I can
To-day, to-morrow, world without an end ;
    To love you much and yet to love you more,
    As Jordan at his flood sweeps either shore ;
Since woman is the helpmeet made for man.

How delicately worded is the thought here.   I quote
again, this time the closing lines of Sonnet 6 :

Yet while I love my God the most, I deem
    That I can never love you overmuch ;
    I love Him more, so let me love you too ;
Yea, as I apprehend it, love is such
I cannot love you if I love not Him,
    I cannot love Him if I love not you.

But to my thinking the noblest sonnet of the whole is
No. 12.   It reveals the absorbing love which casts out

selfishness. An excerpt is not made from it merely because it seems to me that the sonnet ought to be read in its entirety. The exquisite love sonnet, 'Touching Never,' which occupies a separate place in the volume deserves mention ; while ' Passing and Glassing ' has a somewhat similar central idea to ' Beauty is Vain.'

In Chapters II. and X. some attention has been given to the fine sequence of twenty-eight sonnets entitled 'Later Life'; therefore a comparatively brief reference must suffice here. The fifteenth sonnet suggests Christina's views respecting the problem of the sexes. How noble is the conclusion :

> Did Adam love his Eve from first to last ?
> I think so ; as we love who works us ill,
> And wounds us to the quick, yet loves us still.
> Love pardons the unpardonable past :
> Love in a dominant embrace holds fast
> His frailer self, and saves without her will.

' An " Immurata " Sister,' one of the poems in this volume not in sonnet form, has the following characteristic reference to women :

> Men work and think, but women feel ;
> And so (for I'm a woman, I)
> And so I should be glad to die
> And cease from impotence of zeal.

It is worthy of note that the foregoing lines were originally written as part of Christina's ' En Route '—a poem which did not appear in full until the publication of her posthumous ' New Poems.'

The final sonnet of ' Later Life ' is a worthy climax to the exalted train of thought throughout the sequence. Listen to the music of these lines, lines original and strong, about death :

> In life our absent friend is far away :
>   But death may bring our friend exceeding near,
>
>   .   .   .   .
>
> The dead may be around us, dear and dead ;
>   The unforgotten dearest dead may be
>   Watching us with unslumbering eyes and heart
> Brimful of words which cannot yet be said,
>   Brimful of knowledge they may not impart,
>   Brimful of love for you and love for me.

Though Christina's sonnets are in the Petrarchan form in none of them is there a separation between the octave and the sestet, and in one of the noblest of them, 'After Communion,' there are certain divergences from the customary position of the respective rhymes. It is however unnecessary to dwell here at length on minute points of sonnet construction ; let us recall her brother Gabriel's remark that fundamental brain-work in a sonnet far outweighs any irregularity of construction.

The arrangement of the contents of Christina Rossetti's first collected edition of general 'Poems' (1875) requires some little elucidatory remark. The book consisted of the poems which had appeared in the 'Goblin Market' and the 'Prince's Progress' volumes, the chief poems in point of length and importance being usually placed first, followed by the devotional poems not arranged in a section by themselves as formerly.

Christina included here for the first time some notable poems which had previously been published in magazines. The chief of these is, perhaps, her choicest lyrical masterpiece, 'Amor Mundi.' As its title suggests, this poem is an allegory of how love of the world leads inevitably to destruction. Printed originally during 1865 in the first volume of 'The Shilling Magazine, it was there illustrated by Mr. F. A. Sandys. Mr. Sandys's wood-cut illustration, though somewhat hard in some of its details, has many excellent qualities. The lovers are seen advancing, the man playing on a lute, the woman gazing into a looking-glass. In front, but as yet unseen by them, are the 'scaled and hooded worm,' creeping among the brushwood, and the 'thin dead body'—the latter effectively though not repulsively delineated. The woman is turning and will soon catch a glimpse of 'seven' small masses of 'grey cloud-flakes' just at the rainy 'skirt.' Besides some variations in punctuation, not of sufficient moment to be dealt with, the first two lines of the last stanza appear as:

Turn again, O my sweetest,—turn again, false and fleetest :
This way thereof thou weetest I fear is hell's own track.

Students of Christina Rossetti will recollect that the corresponding lines in the 1875 edition of her 'Poems,' as well as in the 1884 and 1888 editions and also in the general 'Poems' of 1890, are:

Turn again, O my sweetest,—turn again, false and fleetest :
This beaten way thou beatest, I fear is hell's own track.

Something may be said in favour of 'the way thereof thou weetest' rather than 'the beaten way thou beatest.'

Another of the poems included for the first time is the lovely sonnet, 'Venus's Looking Glass,' written in the Elizabethan manner ; and especially noticeable for various reasons are the nature poem, 'Bird Raptures,' and the sonnets, 'Love Lies Bleeding' and 'To-day's Burden.' 'To-day for Me' has been described by her brother Dante Gabriel as 'the greatest of all her poems.' The expression of individual opinion from so competent a critic must of course have weight. Nevertheless it seems to me that neither in intensity of feeling nor in sublimity of subject does the poem reach her highest level.

In the first complete edition of her general 'Poems' (1890) the arrangement of the 1875 edition was preserved and entitled 'First Series,' while the contents of the volume called 'A Pageant and other Poems' (1881) followed them, and were called 'Second Series.' To the 1890 volume she added a vivid narrative poem 'Brother Bruin,' a story of a dancing bear. This poem is particularly interesting as betokening her versatility, and as showing that she could be as quietly realistic as Cowper. The bear's master is cruel, and the poor dancing bear dies sadly. His master,

> His idle working days gone past,

goes to the workhouse.

> There he droned on—a grim old sinner
> Toothless and grumbling for his dinner,
> Unpitied quite, uncared for much
> (The ratepayers not favouring such),
> Hungry and gaunt, with time to spare :
> Perhaps the hungry gaunt old Bear
> Danced back, a haunting memory.
> Indeed I hope so : for you see
> If once the hard old heart relented
> The hard old man may have repented.

This definitive edition also contained for the first time 'To-day's Burden.'

The question as to whether a poet ought to give to the world only his best, or whether, his or her rank being assured, it is permissible to print work which, though it reaches a certain standard of metrical craftsmanship, may yet in some cases fall short of perfect excellence, is a question that has been asked often, and will continue to be asked.   To this, as to most, if not all, of the questions in higher criticism, no final answer can be returned.   The answer in each case ought to depend on the position of the poet, and it will also be determined in each case to a large extent by the idiosyncrasy of the critic.   Personally I am of opinion that Christina Rossetti's place as a poet warrants the publication of much, if not all, the work included in the posthumous 'New Poems,' already briefly referred to ; and I am grateful to Mr. W. M. Rossetti for having given students of his sister's poetry so many additional lovely examples of it.   In these 'New Poems' there are not many failures, but even if these were far more numerous than they are, the failures of a great poet, besides their biographical value, are deeply instructive to students of poetry, and useful as warnings to those who seek to write it.

'New Poems ; hitherto unpublished or uncollected,' has opposite to the title-page a portrait of Christina from a pencil drawing by Dante Gabriel, probably a preliminary study for 'Ecce Ancilla Domini.'   On the title-page itself are the lines

> I rated to the full amount
> Must render mine account

and the book is dedicated to

ALGERNON CHARLES SWINBURNE

A GENEROUS EULOGIST OF

CHRISTINA ROSSETTI

WHO HAILED HIS GENIUS AND PRIZED HIMSELF
THE GREATEST OF LIVING BRITISH POETS
MY OLD AND CONSTANT FRIEND
I DEDICATE THIS BOOK
W. M. R.

Her brother contributes a characteristic and interesting Preface of seven pages. After calling attention to the 'strong outburst of eulogy' of his sister which followed her death, he goes on to state the principles upon which he has arranged the poems he has given to the world. He does not attempt any detailed criticism of the poetic work he lays before the public, but proceeds to give some valuable particulars about his sister's habits as a poet and writer—particulars already alluded to. His explanation of the reasons why his sister did not herself print many of the verses may be quoted in his own words :

'It may be asked why did she not publish these verses herself? As to most of the items I see no special reason, unless it be this—that, in point of subject or sentiment, they often resemble, more or less, some of those examples which she *did* print; and she may have thought that the public, while willing to have one such specimen, would be quite contented to lack a second.'

Aided by his sister's notebooks mentioned before, in which, with the exception of one or two casual omissions, all the poems are dated, he has been able to place the date after each poem. And, in the case of these omissions, he has himself supplied probable dates. The volume under consideration is divided into various sections with the respective titles of ' General,' ' Devotional,' and ' Italian Poems,' followed by ' Juvenilia.' The first section contains one hundred and eighty, the second seventy-nine, the third thirty-four, and the fourth seventy-one pages. The ' Italian Poems ' comprise verses in that language by Christina ; while ' Juvenilia ' comprehends most, but not all, of the poems printed in the ' Verses ' of 1847 as well as numerous other youthful efforts. The editor's valuable notes, spoken of before, many of them of some length, occupy twenty-one pages and conclude the book.

'General Poems' opens with a sonnet entitled 'The whole head is sick and the whole heart faint,' the date of which shows that it was written after the author had completed her seventeenth year. It is noticeable on account of its intrinsic merits, and because of its early anticipation of the author's mature style. The poet in the last four lines is depicting those who are experiencing a well-known phase of feeling:

> For them there is no glory in the sky,
>   No sweetness in the breezes' murmuring:
> They say, 'The peace of heaven is placed too high,
>   And this earth changeth and is perishing.'

'Repining,' contributed by Christina to 'The Germ,' is here reprinted for the first time. In view of her brother's comprehensive note on the subject it will be needless for me to dwell at length on the poem. In the main one must agree with the strictures he passes upon it, though it is redeemed by passages like this:

> Death—death—oh let us fly from death!
> Where'er we go it followeth;
> All these are dead; and we alone
> Remain to weep for what is gone.
> What is this thing? thus hurriedly
> To pass into eternity;
> To leave the earth so full of mirth;
> To lose the profit of our birth;
> To die and be no more; to cease,
> Having numbness that is not peace.
> Let us go hence; and, even if thus
> Death everywhere must go with us,
> Let us not see the change, but see
> Those who have been or still shall be.

'Lady Montrevor,' relating to the character of that **name in Maturin's 'Wild Irish Boy,'** mentioned on another occasion, is a good example of her early work. The series of sonnets, twelve in number, composed at seventeen to *bouts-rimés* supplied by her brother William, show great metrical skill and command over language in one so young—when we bear in mind the rapidity with which they were composed—Sonnet IX. was written in five minutes. But the editor would have acted more wisely had he omitted Sonnet VII. Such phrases as 'It's too wet for that' and 'Fire not allowable' are hardly permissible in verse of this kind, even although that verse was written by Christina Rossetti. One of the most beautiful of these sonnets is Xb, instinct with true inspiration. There is vision in the lines :—

> I fancy the good fairies dressed in white,
> Glancing like moonbeams through the shadows black.

The humorous 'Vanity Fair,' numbered Xc, was much admired by Coventry Patmore at the time it was written. Mr. W. M. Rossetti properly calls attention to the power of his sister in utilising the same rhymes in Xa, Xb, and Xc for totally different trains of thought. 'On Keats,' the sonnet which immediately follows the sonnets above named, is not in *bouts-rimés*.

'Three Nuns,' a poem in three divisions, is a passionate outburst of ascetic fervour. Presumably the utterance of three dying nuns, it is worthy of the writer who afterwards wrote 'The Convent Threshold.' 'The End of the First Part' is vivid and striking ; though dated as early as April, 1849, it is remarkable as being a religious poem almost in her later manner. This is especially seen in the closing stanzas, the last of which is as follows :

> There other garden-beds shall lie around,
>   Full of sweet-briar and incense-bearing thyme :
> There I will sit, and listen for the sound
>   Of the last lingering chime.

The song beginning

> We buried her among the flowers,

' Annie,' and the ' Song,' the opening lines of which are—

> It is not for her even brow
>   And shining yellow hair,
> But it is for her tender eyes
>   I think my love so fair :—

are all exquisite love lyrics, and not the least quality of their charm is their utter simplicity. But perhaps the poet reaches her highest note in the perfect stanza which closes the third of the lyrics just named :

> So in my dreams I never hear
>   Her song, although she sings
> As if a choir of spirits swept
>   From earth with throbbing wings :
> I only hear the simple voice
> Whose love makes many hearts rejoice.

The long poem, ' To what Purpose is this Waste ? ' is not particularly noteworthy, except as containing the line

> A silent praise as pain is silent prayer,

a line so original that I doubt not it will take its place among familiar quotations ; nor will her admirers ever cease to remember the sonnet called ' A Pause,' which, for passionate though subdued beauty, must be placed in the first rank among her masterpieces. ' Cor Mio,' a sonnet, is conspicuously interesting, for it shows that sometimes Christina made very considerable alterations in her work—the poem having already appeared, with a much changed octave, as Sonnet 18 of ' Later Life ' in her ' Pageant ' volume. ' How one chose ' and ' Seeking Rest ' are tender and touching poems, while the two sonnets entitled ' Two Thoughts of Death ' are very sombre, and the excessive, even repulsive, realism of the first, is extenuated, if not pardoned, when we see that it is intentionally heightened, to give the effect of contrast to the second sonnet. ' Three Moments ' is likewise a strong, almost dramatic, poem. Both ' A Dirge ' and Summer is ended ' are admirable. The third stanza of the last-named aptly shows Christina Rossetti's conception of death—

> Weep not for me when I am gone,
> Dear tender one, but hope and smile :
> Or, if you cannot choose but weep,
>   A little while weep on,
>   Only a little while.

Throughout the present work Christina Rossetti has been regarded as an English poet, and I do not purpose therefore to give here any detailed commentary on the Italian poems in her posthumous book. These compositions, however, are not in my judgment unworthy of their author. I may perhaps be allowed to quote respecting them the opinion of a far more competent critic than myself—a critic who, moreover, even in this case, would, I think, be impartial. Concerning them the editor has written :

' I consider that her Italian verses are, from a poetical point of view, every bit as good as her English verses, while the exquisite limpidity of the Italian language adds something to the flow of their music. There are likely to be some inaccuracies and blemishes of diction, but perhaps only a native eye would detect these—mine barely does.'

Appended to the Italian poems are fourteen pages of 'Ninna-Nanna,' a name originally given by Christina Rossetti's cousin, Signor Teodorico Pietrocola-Rossetti, to some translations he had made into Italian from her 'Sing-Song.' Her brother has applied the term 'Ninna-Nanna' here to translations or paraphrases made by herself about 1879 of certain of the poems in 'Sing-Song' already published.

CHAPTER VII

DEVOTIONAL POEMS

rom 'Annus Domini'—'Called to be Saints'—'Time Flies'—'The Face
of the Deep'—'Goblin Market and other Poems'—'The Prince's
Progress and other Poems'—'A Pageant and other Poems'—'Verses'
(1893)—'New Poems'—List of poems, mainly devotional, included
neither in her general 'Poems,' nor in her religious 'Verses' (1893).

MANY of Christina Rossetti's devotional Poems—some
of them are roundels—are very short, and are concerned with religious themes which are almost trite.
In nothing is her undoubted power so much shown as in
the fact that so few of them are commonplace.   Had she
not had genius they might have sunk to the level of
much religious verse—respectable in purpose, excellent
in execution, nothing more.

Christina Rossetti often achieves fine effects by a
skilful use of internal rhymes, and also by a no less
adroit handling of the same phrase turned in a diverse
manner.

It is difficult for a commentator to choose an order
in classification of poems so similar in style and in
aim.   The method pursued shall be to mention
the opening lyrics in her prose volumes; then the
religious verses in 'Goblin Market and other Poems,'
'The Prince's Progress and other Poems,' and 'A Pageant
and other Poems,' in the order of those three volumes;
and subsequently to discuss the religious poems which she

included first in the original edition of her collected poems—that published in 1875. Afterwards shall follow an analysis of her 'Verses' (1893), together with a list of her metrical compositions that appear in her devotional prose works, but not in 'Verses' (1893), with some remarks on these compositions; and finally the devotional section of 'New Poems' shall be dealt with.

'Annus Domini,' her first volume of devotional prose, opens with a devotional lyric which has no title, and of which the first stanza may be given :

> Alas my Lord,
> How should I wrestle all the livelong night
> With thee my God, my Strength and my Delight?

A copy of the volume now in my possession belonged to Christina herself. It was given to her on her birthday, December 5, 1880, by her aunt, Miss Eliza Polidori, and remained with her until her death.

Between stanzas six and seven in this copy is written the following interpolated stanza in Christina Rossetti's own handwriting :

> Gulped by the fish,
> As by the pit, lost Jonah made his moan ;
> And Thou forgavest, waiting to atone.

A facsimile is given at p. 242. Her brother Dante Gabriel much admired this poem. Unlike in motive or in substance to George Herbert's 'Affliction,' it is yet somewhat akin to it in pensive thought.

Her next devotional work, 'Seek and Find,' contains no verse.

'Called to be Saints,' the ensuing volume, has a lyric without title appended to a brief devotional meditation called 'The Key to my Book.' Here are the first four stanzas :

R

This near-at-hand land breeds pain by measure
That far-away land overflows with treasure
      Of heaped-up good pleasure.

Our land that we see is befouled by evil :
The land that we see not makes mirth and revel,
      Far from death and devil.

x

      Yet Jacob did
So hold Thee by the clenched hand of
      prayer
That he prevailed, and Thou didst bless
      him there.

      Elias prayed,
And sealed the founts of Heaven ; he
      prayed again
And lo, Thy Blessing fell in showers of
      rain.

      All Nineveh
Fasting and girt in sackcloth raised
      a cry,
Which moved Thee ere the day of grace
      went by.

      Thy Church prayed on
And on for blessed Peter in his strait,
Till opened of its own accord the gate.

[Facsimile of p. x of a Copy of 'Annus Domini' showing
      an inserted Stanza in Manuscript.]

This land hath for music sobbing and sighing :
That land hath soft speech and sweet soft replying
      Of all loves undying.

This land hath for pastime errors and follies :
That land hath unending, unflagging solace
      Of full-chanted 'Holies.'

Some objection may possibly be felt to the somewhat monotonous metrical effect of a poem in a stanza of three consecutive double rhymes. Conceivably the measure may have been suggested by George Herbert's 'Sepulchre' beginning

> O blessed bodie ! Whither art thou thrown ?
> No lodging for thee, but a cold hard stone ?
> So many hearts on earth, and yet not one
>   Receive thee ? '

There, however, the consecutive rhymes are single not double.

'Letter and Spirit,' the next in chronological order of her devotional works, contains no verse, so we pass to 'Time Flies' where, although there is much verse there is no opening general lyric. 'The Face of the Deep,' her latest and longest, and, as many think, her finest prose work, contains a notable lyric couched in a most characteristic manner. The first stanza is subjoined :

> O, ye who love to-day,
> Turn away
> From Patience with her silvery ray :
> For Patience shows a twilight face :
> Like a half-lighted moon
> When daylight dies apace.

'Goblin Market and other Poems' contains at least five religious poems of the highest rank, 'The Three Enemies,' 'Passing Away,' 'Advent,' 'Symbols,' and 'Up-hill '—for the last named is properly a religious poem though not classed by its author as such. All are masterpieces in somewhat varying ways. Of 'Passing Away,' which appeared in a section entitled 'Old and New Year Ditties,' some lines may be quoted :

Passing away, saith my Soul, passing away.
With its burden of fear and hope, of labour and play ;
Hearken what the past doth witness and say :
Rust in thy gold, a moth is in thine array,
A canker is in thy bud, thy leaf must decay.
At midnight, at cockcrow, at morning, one certain day
Lo, the Bridegroom shall come and shall not delay :
Watch thou and pray.
Then I answered : Yea.

Passing away, saith my God, passing away :
Winter passeth after the long delay :
New grapes on the vine, new figs on the tender spray,
Turtle calleth turtle in Heaven's May.
Though I tarry wait for Me, trust Me, watch and pray.
Arise, come away, night is past, and lo, it is day.

Mr. Swinburne (my authority for the statement is her
brother Dante Gabriel) regards ' Advent ' as ' perhaps
the noblest of all her poems.' Its metre, the familiar
iambic alternate eight and six feet set in stanzas of eight
lines, is a metre seldom adopted by its author. In
inferior hands this measure grows wearisome, but in the
hands of a great poet it is very noble. 'Symbols,'
written on January 7, 1849, is inserted in an earlier form
in her prose story ' Maude,' where the third line of the
second stanza and the second line of the third stanza
appear respectively as

> Wherein three little eggs were laid,

and

> That I had tended with such care ;

while in ' Goblin Market and other Poems ' the same
lines are given as

> Wherein three speckled eggs were laid,

and

> That I had tended so with care

—a considerable improvement. The sonnets 'Dead before Death' and 'The World' require no especial mention. The less known 'Amen' of which the opening stanza is :

> It is over. What is over ?
>   Nay, how much is over truly !—
> Harvest days we toiled to sow for ;
>   Now the sheaves are gathered newly,
>   Now the wheat is garnered duly,

deserves a brief allusion on account of some of its metrical effects. The measure is regular trochaic in lines of four feet with alternate rhymes, a fifth line of equal length with the others, and rhyming with the second and fourth, being added, presumably, for the sake of variety.

Let us now turn to the devotional section of 'The Prince's Progress and other Poems.' Here we may observe that if 'The Lowest Place' has not the gorgeousness of diction nor the brilliance of poetic imagery we find in 'Advent' and others of her poems of this class, it has qualities which in Christina Rossetti are more unusual than mere poetic attributes. In it there is, besides, a certain homeliness and directness of utterance to which we are unaccustomed. As these characteristics are combined with poetic fire, the piece becomes specially noteworthy. Many of Christina Rossetti's devotional poems, fine as they are as devotional verse, could only be used as such in reading. 'The Lowest Place,' on the other hand, has, if I am not mistaken, been placed in not a few hymnals. 'If only' has distinct beauty. In such a phrase as

> If I might only love my God and die !
> But now He bids me love Him and live on,

there is one of those individual touches sometimes

mistakenly considered signs of her morbidity—an error arising from want of apprehension of Christina Rossetti's point of view.

There is much noble and inspiring devotional verse in 'A Pageant, and other Poems,' the only one of her separate poetic volumes which contains no section termed 'Devotional Poems.'   'For Thine own Sake, O Lord,' gives a cheering view of human aspirations and of Divine goodness :

> Wearied of sinning, wearied of repentance,
>   Wearied of self, I turn, my God, to thee ;
> To thee, my Judge, on Whose all-righteous sentence
>   Hangs mine eternity :
> I turn to Thee, I plead Thyself with Thee,—
>   Be pitiful to me.
>
> .   .   .   .
>
> I plead Thyself with Thee Who art my Maker,
>   Regard Thy handiwork that cries to Thee ;
> I plead Thyself with Thee Who wast partaker
>   Of mine infirmity,
> Love made Thee what Thou art, the love of me,—
>   I plead Thyself with Thee.

The sonnet aptly called 'Why' expresses with succinct beauty an inquiry made at some time by each devout soul :

> Lord, if I love Thee and Thou lovest me,
>   Why need I any more these toilsome days :
>   Why should I not run singing up Thy ways
> Straight into heaven, to rest myself with Thee ?

This may be compared with Crashaw's fine lyric (Dr. Grosart's edition of this poet in 'The Fuller Worthies' Library' is quoted from) :

A SONG OF DIVINE LOVE

Lord, When the sense of Thy sweet grace
Sends up my soul to seek Thy face,
Thy blessed eyes breed such desire,
I dy in Loue's delicious fire.
    O Loue ! I am thy Sacrifice ?
Be still triumphant, blessed eyes !
Still shine on me, fair suns ! that I
Still may behold, though still I dy.

And, in Christina Rossetti's poem, no less perfect is the Saviour's answer.   ' A Pageant and other Poems ' is fitly closed by the tender lyric ' Love is strong as Death.'

Certain noteworthy religious poems were added by Christina Rossetti to the first edition of her collected poems issued in 1875.   Chief among these is ' Paradise '—a masterpiece among the limited class of poems in English literature which are descriptive as well as devotional.   Her picture of heaven is as vivid as though of some place actually seen with bodily eyes, and yet not a phrase, not a word, jars because of excessive realism. ' They desire a better country ' has an individual though not an unpleasing mournfulness.   ' When my Heart is vexed I will complain,' a dialogue between the soul and its Redeemer, is remarkable for motive and for metrical qualities ; and the skill with which the dialogue form is handled must not be overlooked.

' Verses ' (1893) consisted entirely of religious poetry. Many of these ' verses ' were the work of her later years, and were reprinted, as mentioned before, from ' Called to be Saints,' ' Time Flies,' and ' The Face of the Deep.' She divided the pieces into eight sections, termed respectively ' Out of the Deep have I called unto Thee, O Lord,' ' Christ our All in All,' ' Some Feasts and Fasts,' ' Gifts

and Graces,' 'The World. Self Destruction,' 'Divers
Worlds.   Time and Eternity,' 'New Jerusalem and its
Citizens,' and 'Songs for Strangers and Pilgrims,' the
poems being classified according to subject. In analysing
this book her own order shall be adhered to.

The first section, 'Out of the Deep have I called unto
Thee, O Lord,' extends to nine pages and contains
seventeen sonnets.   In placing them in the foreground
of her volume she displayed considerable critical discernment as they splendidly show the devout side of her
genius.   The opening sonnet begins thus :

> Alone Lord God, in Whom our trust and peace,
> Our love and our desire, glow bright with hope ;
> Lift us above this transitory scope
> Of earth, these pleasures that begin and cease,
> This moon which wanes, these seasons which decrease :
> We turn to Thee ; as on an eastern slope
> Wheat feels the dawn beneath night's lingering cope,
> Bending and stretching sunward ere it sees.

All these sonnets have an especial beauty, but perhaps the most beautiful of all is that with the heading

> Where neither rust nor moth doth corrupt

beginning

> Nerve us with patience, Lord, to toil or rest,

or the opening lines of the second of the two sonnets
with the inscription ' As the Sparks fly upwards ' :

> Lord, make us all love all : that, when we meet
> Even myriads of earth's myriads at Thy Bar,
> We may be glad as all true lovers are
> Who having parted count reunion sweet.

The magnificent sonnet

> Weigh all my faults and follies righteously

ought also to be named. The succeeding section 'Christ our All in All' extends to twenty-nine pages and contains a dialogue poem beginning.

O Lord when Thou didst call me, didst Thou know

which is a considerable achievement, for it is exceedingly difficult to treat poetically a subject of saintly aspiration, in such a form. The eight lines which close the page with the general title of 'King of Kings and Lord of Lords,' are concise and lovely. The opening line

Thy Name, O Christ, as incense streaming forth

is an instance of her infrequent revision, and is a vast improvement on

Thy Name, O Christ, as ointment is poured forth

as it stood when it first appeared in 'The Face of the Deep.'

The section 'Some Feasts and Fasts' extends to forty-eight pages, and contains the lyric 'Herself a Rose' that was inserted originally in 'Called to be Saints.' It is full of the exquisite symbolism which makes Christina Rossetti a great poet. In the same section she has appropriated a fine sonnet to the Vigil of St. Bartholomew, a sonnet which occurs originally in 'The Face of the Deep' in the midst of her commentary on the words

'And he saith unto me, Write, Blessed are they which are called unto the marriage supper of the Lamb. And he saith unto me, These are the true sayings of God.'

It is additionally interesting because introduced by some remarks on symbolism—remarks very instructive as coming from her.

'Symbolism affords a fascinating study: wholesome

so long as it amounts to aspiration and research ; unwholesome when it degenerates into a pastime. As literal shadows tend to soothe, lull, abate keenness of vision ; so perhaps symbols may have a tendency to engross, satisfy, arrest incautious souls unwatchful and unprayerful lest they enter into temptation.'

Under the heading of ' All Saints : Martyrs ' we have an otherwise fine sonnet which is remarkable, as containing the line

All luminous and lovely in their gore.

'Gore' in serious poetry is now almost inadmissible, and its employment here, even by Christina Rossetti, will not reconcile other poets to its use.

The section entitled ' Gifts and Graces ' extends to eighteen pages, and possesses a singularly beautiful poem with the heading ' When I was in trouble I called upon the Lord ' that recalls to some extent, though without any imitation, Donne's ' Hymn to the Father.' Christina Rossetti's poem is beautiful not only for the ideas expressed but for delicacy of rhythm. Quotation may be made of the first and fourth stanzas.

> A burdened heart that bleeds and bears
>   And hopes and waits in pain,
> And faints beneath its fears and cares,
>   Yet hopes again :
>
> . . . . .
>
> Or if Thou wilt not yet relieve,
>   Be not extreme to sift :
> Accept a faltering will to give,
>   Itself Thy gift.

The section called ' The World. Self Destruction ' extends to six pages, and is succeeded by a section, entitled ' Divers Worlds. Time and Eternity,' that reaches to nineteen pages. Under the sub-title of

'Awake, thou that sleepest' it contains a poem beginning:

> The night is far spent, the day is at hand:

The closing stanza is as follows:

> Far, far away lies the beautiful land :
>   Mount on wide wings of exceeding desire,
>   Mount, look not back, mount to life and to light,
>   Mount by the gleam of your lamps all on fire
>   Up from the dead men and up from the night.
> The night is far spent, the day is at hand.

The lyric originally formed part of its author's
exposition of the text, 'The night is far spent, the
day is at hand' in 'The Face of the Deep.' The characteristic 'Time passes away' is also included in
this section. It may be well to point out here that in
this, as well as in some others of her poems in French
verse-forms, written in her later years, she uses succeeding
rhymes (in 'Time passes away' the rhymes in question
are 'pain' and 'bay') which are open to the objection of
containing similar vowel sounds. The poem beginning

> Time lengthening, in the lengthening seemeth long :

the second of the two poems with the sub-title, 'The
earth shall tremble at the look of Him,' is solemn in
subject, and has a correspondingly solemn metre whose
rhythm gives it majesty and force. How expressive are
the lines

> Time lengthening, in the lengthening seemeth long

and

>   Eternity still rolling forth its car,
>   Eternity still here and still to come.

· The noble eight-line poem beginning

> Heaven's chimes are slow, but sure to strike at last

is placed as the second poem under the sub-title of
'All Flesh is Grass,' in this section.   In Christina
Rossetti's 'New Poems' appear ten stanzas to which
the editor has given the title 'Restive.'   The third
stanza,

> These chimes are slow, but surely strike at last :
>   This sand is slow, but surely droppeth through :
> And much there is to suffer, much to do,
>   Before the time be past,

will be seen to be an early version of

> Heaven's chimes are slow, but sure to strike at last :
> Earth's sands are slow, but surely dropping thro' :
> And much we have to suffer, much to do,
>   Before the time be past.

It is probable that she wrote the fine concluding
stanza :

> Chimes that keep time are neither slow nor fast :
>   Not many are the numbered sands nor few :
> A time to suffer, and a time to do,
>   And then the time is past,

when composing 'Time Flies.'   This shows that even
Christina Rossetti, who is supposed to have revised so
little, sometimes acted like the poets of elaboration, a
class to whom she cannot be said to belong, and built
up a fine poem from some comparatively unimportant
lines having originally an altogether different connection.

The seventh of the sections into which 'Verses' of
1893 is divided, is entitled 'New Jerusalem and its
Citizens.'   From 'The Face of the Deep,' comes the
first of the three poems with the sub-title 'She shall
be brought unto the King.'   Its opening line, 'The
King's daughter is all glorious within,' is noticeable

metrically, because the first foot must be made 'The King's dau', to scan—a somewhat daring licence.

In the same section a sonnet beginning :

> Dear Angels and dear disembodied Saints
> Unseen around us, worshipping in rest,
> May wonder that man's heart so often faints
> And his steps lag along the heavenly quest,

is inserted in the course of her commentary on the words,

' And after these things I saw four angels standing on the four corners of the earth, holding the four winds of the earth, that the wind should not blow on the earth, nor on the sea, nor on any tree.'

(' The Face of the Deep,' Chap. VII.).   This sonnet has a vivid, almost an autobiographical touch.

Not infrequently in many of her devotional poems, and perhaps noticeably in this sonnet, we are reminded of the quaintness and intensity of Quarles, though in Christina Rossetti we rarely perceive the realism bordering on the ludicrous apparent in some of his ' Emblems.' Elsewhere in her writings, (notably in passages of ' Time Flies,' and also in the lyric in this book ' Lord whomsoever Thou shalt send ' under the title of ' Are they not all Ministering Spirits,' and likewise in ' The Face of the Deep,') she expresses her views about guardian angels.

In the last section of this book, headed ' Songs for Strangers and Pilgrims,' under the title ' Whither the tribes go up, even the tribes of the Lord,' we have a poem of ten lines.   The first stanza begins :

> Where never tempest heaveth,
> Nor sorrow grieveth,

and the second stanza :

> Where never shame bewaileth,
> Nor serpent traileth.

The fifth line of the first stanza is 'Sleep' and the fifth line of the second stanza is 'Reap.' Another poem in 'Verses,' cast in the antique mould, is one of twelve lines, originally in 'The Face of the Deep,' and beginning :

Day and night the Accuser makes no pause,

in which the same rhyme is continued throughout. In these poems, and others of her religious verses, the influence of Donne and Wither would seem to be traceable, different as were these seventeenth century poets in some aspects of poetic art.

Under date of April 13, in 'Time Flies,' there is a sweet little nature lyric of eight lines beginning :

A cold wind stirs the blackthorn
To burgeon and to blow,
Besprinkling half-green hedges
With vegetable snow.

It is placed in the section with the sub-title of 'Endure Hardness,' the last line of the stanza being :

With flakes and sprays of snow,

a marked improvement on

With vegetable snow,

a phrase not altogether happy.

In the same section are the fine verses beginning :

Our life is long. Not so, wise Angels say

which may be compared with Horatius Bonar's lines on the same subject beginning :

He liveth long who liveth well :
All other life is short and vain.

'Home by different ways' may be alluded to, and the

delicately wrought poem, worthy of George Herbert,
'Praying always.' The latter is in three stanzas, of
which the first is given below :

PRAYING ALWAYS.

> After midnight, in the dark
> 　The clock strikes one,
> 　New day has begun.
> Look up and hark !
> With singing heart forestall the carolling lark.'

In the poem of considerable length, 'To what purpose
is this Waste,' dated January 22, 1853, and first published
in ' New Poems,' occur the lines :

> And other eyes than ours
> 　Were made to look on flowers,
> Eyes of small birds and insects small :
> 　The deep sun-blushing rose
> 　Round which the prickles close
> Opens her bosom to them all.
> 　The tiniest living thing
> 　That soars on feathered wing,
> Or crawls among the long grass out of sight,
> 　Has just as good a right
> To its appointed portion of delight
> 　As any King.

This is the earlier form of the charming stanza
so full of sympathy with animals, which appears in
' Time Flies,' and begins :

> Innocent eyes not ours,
> 　Are made to look on flowers,
> Eyes of small birds and insects small.

It will be readily seen from the above that Christina
Rossetti's alterations, comparatively infrequent though
they were, were sometimes important, and that she

always achieved a higher poetic excellence in her finished poem than in her first draft.

The brief lyric

> Before the beginning Thou hast foreknown the end,

which originally appeared in 'The Face of the Deep' as part of her commentary on the text Rev. xix. 18,

' That ye may eat the flesh of kings, and the flesh of captains, and the flesh of mighty men, and the flesh of horses, and of them that sit on them, and the flesh of all men, both free and bond, both small and great,'

is a striking instance of a certain morbidity she shows again and again in dwelling on the concomitants of death, or perhaps it might be more just to say in a too frequent dwelling on the idea of death. A similar remark can be made with regard to the otherwise lovely lyric beginning

> Young girls wear flowers,

though the fancy she there works out, that perchance angels resort to grave-yards, is in itself a beautiful one.

Some metrical qualities of the poems included in 'Verses' (1893) may be indicated at this point. There are, for example, several instances of a very successful use of internal rhymes. Here is one :

> He speaks with Dove-voice of exceeding love,
> And she with love-voice of an answering Dove.

And again :

> Trembling before Thee we fall down to adore Thee,
> Shamefaced and trembling we lift our eyes to Thee :
> O First and with the last ! annul our ruined past,
> Rebuild us to Thy glory, set us free
> From sin and from sorrow to fall down and worship Thee.

And once more in the solemn lyric 'Life that was born to-day,' the first stanza of which may serve for purposes of illustration, the same feature is discernible:

Life that was born to-day
Must make no stay,
But tend to end
As blossom-bloom of May.
O Lord, confirm my root,
Train up my shoot,
To live and give
Harvest of wholesome fruit.

The two sonnets under the sub-title of 'Heaviness may endure for a night, but joy cometh in the morning' are notable specimens of her work, despite these lines in the first sonnet that border too closely on the ridiculous:

Thus I sat mourning like a mournful owl,
And like a doleful dragon made ado.

The analysis of a noble volume—the greatest contribution to religious verse of our century—must not close without mentioning the perfect lyric beginning:

We know not a voice of that river,

printed previously in 'The Face of the Deep' after her commentary on the passage in the twenty-second chapter of Revelation,

'And he showed me a pure river of water of life, clear as crystal, proceeding out of the throne of God and of the Lamb,'

nor must it conclude without mentioning the heartfelt lines beginning

As froth on the face of the deep

whose beautiful rhythm suggests the metre of Mr. Swinburne's memorable 'Dedication' to the first series of

S

his 'Poems and Ballads.' Finally, allusion must be made to Christina Rossetti's characteristic conception of the goodness of God, embodied in the opening lines that follow her remarkable sonnet on the passage:

'And one of the four beasts gave unto the seven angels seven golden vials full of the wrath of God, Who liveth for ever and ever.'

> Seven vials hold Thy wrath : but what can hold
>   Thy mercy save Thine own Infinitude
>   Boundlessly overflowing with all good,
> All lovingkindness, all delights untold ?
> Thy love, of each created love the mould ;
>   Thyself, of all the empty plenitude.

The following is a list of the poems which appeared in 'Time Flies' and in 'The Face of the Deep,' but were not included by Christina Rossetti either in her collected 'Poems' of 1890 or in her 'Verses' of 1893. These poems are chiefly devotional. Two of them however which begin respectively 'A handy Mole who plied no shovel' and 'Contemptuous of his home beyond,' (descriptive of the death of a frog), show her love for animals, and have flashes of gentle humour. The poems having no titles, the opening line is given in each case.

'TIME FLIES'

> 'Love is all happiness, love is all beauty'—p. 34.
> 'A handy Mole who plied no shovel'—p. 40.
> 'A Rose which spied one swallow '—p. 85.
> 'Contemptuous of his home beyond'—p. 129.

'THE FACE OF THE DEEP'

> 'What will it be, O my soul, what will it be ? '—p. 35.
> 'Lord, Thou art fullness ; I am emptiness'—p. 36.
> 'O Lord, I cannot plead my love of Thee '—p. 84.

'Lord, comest Thou to me ?'—p. 224.
'Love us unto the end, and prepare us'—p. 248.
'Lord, grant us eyes to see'—p. 285.
'I sit a queen, and am no widow, and shall see no sorrow'—
    p. 417.
'Passing away the bliss'—p. 448.
'As one red rose in a garden when all other roses are white'—
    p. 450.
'Love builds a nest on earth and waits for rest'—p. 513.
'Jesus alone :—if thus it were to me'—p. 549.

Though not markedly different in tone or in sentiment from the devotional poems which Christina
Rossetti published in her lifetime, the devotional poems
contained in the 'New Poems' are a worthy complement to them.   As an instance of her succinct work,
when her poetic inspiration reached its most exalted
point, the lovely eight-line lyric entitled ' A Christmas
Carol' may be mentioned.   It begins :

> Whoso hears a chiming for Christmas at the nighest
>   Hears a sound like Angels chanting in their glee,
> Hears a sound like palm-boughs waving in the highest,
>   Hears a sound like ripple of a crystal sea. .

When a poet chooses a most hackneyed subject, and
employs a rhyme-word like ' glee,' to do the work of
' rapture ' or some such word, and then achieves notable
success, we may take it as a sure sign of poetic inspiration.   Poetic achievement is often the result of attention
to small details, often the vanquishing of small difficulties—difficulties, however, which are none the less haras-
sing because they are small.

Among other excellent religious verses in these' New
Poems' are 'Yea I have a goodly Heritage,' and ' I
know you not,' of which the last stanza is as follows :

> But Who is this that shuts the door,
>   And saith—I know you not—to them?
>   I see the wounded hands and side,
>   The brow thorn-tortured long ago :
>   Yea, This who grieved and bled and died,
>   This same is He who must condemn ;
>   He called, but they refused to know ;
> So now He hears their cry no more.

Very pathetically beautiful also is one of her early sonnets, dated December 18, 1853, and beginning :

> When I am sick and tired it is God's will :
>   Also God's will alone is sure and best :—
>   So in my weariness I find my rest,
> And so in poverty I take my fill.

A further poem showing mastery over dialogue, a form not easy to handle satisfactorily in the treatment of spiritual subjects, is that under the somewhat infelicitous title of 'Conference between Christ, the Saints, and the Soul.' [1]

[1] When the present work was about to be printed off, and when, unfortunately, it was too late to make further alterations in the text, or to adopt his suggestion made in the following communication respecting 'Conference between Christ, the Saints, and the Soul,' Mr. W. M. Rossetti wrote to me :

'It is true that, thro' failing to trace the poem by its title, I put it into the New Poems : but that was a mistake of mine, for the poem was published by Christina [who had e-named it " I will lift up mine eyes to the Hills "] in her Poems of 1875 and 1891. If you make any observation on the poem, it would seem more proper that your observation should come among your remarks on poems published by Christina herself, and not among your remarks upon the New Poems which were published by me after her death.'

CHAPTER VIII

CHILDREN'S BOOKS AND PROSE STORIES

'Sing-Song'—'Speaking Likenesses'—'Commonplace, and other Short
Stories'—'Maude.'

IN this chapter I shall deal first with Christina Rossetti's books for children, subsequently discussing 'Commonplace, and other Short Stories.'   And, it may be, that in doing so I shall call attention to certain aspects of her genius in its lighter moods—aspects and moods overlooked too frequently.

One of the strongest ties between her and Mr. Swinburne was their love of children.   And Mr. Swinburne's fine child-poem ' Olive,' (on a little niece, nine years old, of his friend Mr. Watts-Dunton)—a child-poem full of beautiful description—was an especial favourite of hers.

To one, who, like myself, knew Christina Rossetti in her solitude, a solitude that must sometimes have been loneliness, it is curious and interesting, and from some points of view even a little pathetic, to think of the popularity of her children's books, such, for instance, as ' Sing-Song,' in numberless nurseries throughout the world, while its author saw so little of children.   For when I knew Christina Rossetti her liking for children was not seldom made evident by word or by look.

Anne Gilchrist has prettily said concerning ' Sing-

Song,' in a letter to Mr. W. M. Rossetti, that its brief lyrics are 'as sweet and spontaneous as a robin's song : . . . melody of the right kind indeed for the little ones ; who want it as much as they want air and sunshine, or laughter and kisses.'   And this praise is not ill-bestowed.

It is observable that both Christina Rossetti and Jean Ingelow, two of the greatest poetesses of our age, have excelled in writing for children.   Jean Ingelow has given us children's stories both in prose and in verse, such as the ' Stories told to a Child ' and the lovely poem ' Echo and the Ferry,' showing subtle knowledge of the heart of a child, and marvellous power of depicting it.   In ' Sing-Song,' the volume now to be treated of, Christina Rossetti has given terse and brief lyrical utterance to the feelings and aspirations of children—utterance which is as realistic in the higher sense as the best poems in Robert Louis Stevenson's ' Garden of Verses,' while full of a dramatic imagination that lifts them to a higher level of insight and aspiration than is reached even by that delightful writer in those delightful child-poems. But ' Sing-Song,'—though, of course, it has an affinity to the work for children of Jean Ingelow and Robert Louis Stevenson—has also its points of difference, but this difference is precisely one of those which are more easily felt than exactly defined in words.   At first sight the lyrics in ' Sing-Song ' seem so simple as to demand neither thought nor artistic workmanship on the part of their author, and yet, spontaneous as they seem, looked at more closely, they reveal considerable thought, and not a little technical workmanship.   Many of the brief bird-like songs in this volume are perfectly expressed, and it is by no means easy to attain perfect expression within brief limits.   To judge by the number of volumes written for children it would appear not hard to write a children's book, and yet to me at least it has always seemed that to write a book for children, which would not only be loved by them, but would be regarded in the well-nigh unanimous opinion of the best judges among their elders as a classic in its own department, must require both real and especial genius. Such a volume is 'Sing-Song.' Its lessons are not enforced by dull didacticism, and even its teaching is elevated into poetry.

'Sing-Song, a nursery rhyme book, with one hundred and twenty illustrations by Arthur Hughes, engraved by the brothers Dalziel,' was published in 1872, and the dedication page is as follows :

Rhymes
Dedicated
Without permission
To
The Baby
Who
Suggested them.

This 'baby' was the son of Professor Arthur Cayley, the celebrated Cambridge mathematician.

When illustrating 'Sing-Song' Mr. Arthur Hughes lived for some time at a cottage on Holmwood Common, Surrey, and he has given me some interesting particulars respecting his illustrations and the localities from which they were drawn.

Opposite the title-page is a full-page design representing a baby in its peasant mother's lap who, seated at the foot of an old oak tree, is knitting. At their side, though unseen of any, except possibly the child, sits a tiny rabbit with raised forepaws in attitude of mild entreaty.   At some little distance off are sheep at rest. In the foreground two lambs gaze upon the mother and child, and so does a donkey's foal, standing on a little bridge spanning a stream, from which its mother drinks. On the banks of the stream are birds. Behind the mother and child, and unseen by them, some cherubs peep.   This design, so lovely in its touching simplicity, drawn from Holmwood Common, is perhaps uncon-sciously a sort of allegory of innocent childhood attract-ing to itself what is innocent, youthful, and harmless in the lower creation. It may be questioned, however, whether the introduction of the cherubs does not detract from the harmony of the picture by recalling the onlooker's mind from this idyllic country scene to something essentially incompatible with it. The land-scape here, be it remembered, is real, not a painter's convention.

The old well illustrating the lines beginning

> Kookoorookoo ! kookoorookoo !
> Crows the cock before the morn ;

was sketched at Cookham Dene, near Maidenhead ; the pretty old cottage window half thrown open to the frosty air with the kindly little girl throwing out

> A crumb for robin redbreast
> On the cold days of the year,

from a cottage window at Holmwood Common ; the delightful ingle nook descriptive of

> There's snow on the fields,
> And cold in the cottage,

from an old farm cottage at Holmwood ; and the dead thrush lying beside the rush basket at head of the lines

> Dead in the cold, a song-singing thrush,
> Dead at the foot of a snowberry bush—

from a rush basket made by children at the same place.

> My baby kisses and is kissed,
> For he's the very thing for kisses,

is a portrait of the wife and baby son of the artist. The drawing associated with

> If all were rain and never sun,
> No bow could span the hill ;

represents a rainbow that spans an extensive country, while behind the rainbow is a hill. This is also a picture of Holmwood Common ; and the hill behind the rainbow portrays Redlands Woods. Dante Gabriel much admired this drawing, more especially the ' bent old woman and the child,' in the foreground ' as illustrating the effect of sorrows and troubles and their teaching during the progress of life.' A sketch of a pigeon cote on a farm off Holmwood Common is linked to one of the most delightful little lyrics in the volume, ending

> The summer days are short
>   Where southern nights are long :
> Yet short the night when nightingales
>   Trill out their song.

The picture of a little girl doing a hem ; of the little boy and the toy horse ; of another little girl teaching another little boy arithmetic on a blackboard, and of a little boy looking at a sun-dial, interpreting respectively the lines :

> A pocket handkerchief to hem—
>   Oh dear, oh dear, oh dear !
> How many stitches it will take
>   Before it's done, I fear.

> Seldom 'can't,'
> Seldom 'don't';
>
> 1 and 1 are two—
> That's for me and you.
>
> How many seconds in a minute?
> Sixty, and no more in it,

were drawn from the artist's youngest daughter; his youngest son; his eldest daughter and youngest son; and from a sun-dial in an old garden at Maidstone.

To accompany the poem that follows is a spirited drawing figuring donkeys, pigs, and geese on Holmwood Common, and the next sketch, representing a stile and tree, was also executed in the same locality. The belfry at page 94 was sketched by the artist when staying at a house lent to him by a friend, near Cæsar's Camp on Wimbledon Common. The drawing at the head of the lines beginning:

> Who has ever seen the wind?
>   Neither I nor you:
> But when the leaves hang trembling,
>   The wind is passing thro',

showing a horse and pigs with a background of trees, was sketched at Holmwood. In it the artist represents the pigs as running from the wind. Does he mean to suggest the Yorkshire saying that 'pigs can see t' wind'? The drawing figuring a mole was drawn from a mole seen on Holmwood Common by the artist; that of an old woman in a chair was sketched from a chair in a cottage in the same neighbourhood; and that showing a sweet cottage window with the moon peeping through was delineated from the actual window of the artist's Holmwood lodging.

One of the most fascinating of Christina's brief lyrics in this volume is that beginning :

> Boats sail on the rivers,
>   And ships sail on the seas ;
> But clouds that sail across the sky
>   Are prettier far than these.

The delightful, characteristic landscape which accompanies it represents the outlook over the Thames on the road to Rochester near a village called Stone, just before coming to Greenhithe ; while the drawing that represents a ship's deck illustrative of the song commencing :

> I have a little husband
>   And he is gone to sea,
> The winds that whistle round his ship
>   Fly home to me,

was appropriately made by the artist at the London docks.   The pretty picture of Willie and Margery in the swing represents his youngest son and daughter.

Not the least graceful of Christina Rossetti's lyrics says whimsically that the 'bee' 'brings home honey' ; 'the father' 'money' which 'mother' expends ; while 'baby' 'eats the honey.'   The sketch at the head of it represents 'baby' on 'mother's' lap being fed with a spoon.   In the background are the beehives, while 'father' looks on.   Mr. Hughes informs me that this sketch 'delighted Dante Gabriel Rossetti very much,' and that 'he spoke of the "silly happy sort of" expression of the man.'

Mr. Shields, who has a very high opinion of Mr. Arthur Hughes both as a painter and as a book illustrator, has pointed out to me in conversation the very fine qualities and admirable symbolism of the design associated with the quasi-humorous lines wherein little Molly although

> All the bells were ringing
> And all the birds were singing,

sat down to cry just because she had broken her doll. Molly is seated on the ground at the foot of a little tree. Her left hand holds the remains of her doll, its decapitated head being in front of her, the back of her right hand is thrust into her right eye presumably to check the tears ; from the boughs of the trees many birds, with visibly open bills, seem, almost audibly, to sing, while at the top of the picture is a scroll of bells. In the judgment of Mr. Shields this same scroll of bells most successfully intensified the symbolism, and he added ' Such a design as the bells would never have occurred to me, I often quote the lines to people in small troubles.'

One does not usually think of Christina Rossetti as humorous, yet a light, playful humour is often present in ' Sing-Song.' What playful fancy could be better conceived and worked out than in the lines :

> If a pig wore a wig
> What could he say ?
> . . . . .
> If his tail chanced to fail
> . . . . .
> Send him to the tailoress
> To get one new ;

or than in the quaint enumeration beginning

> A pin has a head, but has no hair ;

and concluding

> And baby crows, without being a cock.

Were space available much might be said about the comical conceit respecting fishes and lizards, beginning

> When fishes set umbrellas up,

with its inimitable woodcut, and similar conceits concerning mice, crows, and sprats!

Christina Rossetti dedicates to the 'garden-mouse' (whom she designates as 'poor little timid furry man') a tuneful lyric akin to Burns's fine ode to the same 'Wee, sleekit, cow'rin, timorous beastie.' Both poets were equally fond of animals, and both in the poems just named regard the creature whom they address with a fondness akin to pity. The pretty representation of a field-mouse at the head of Christina Rossetti's lyric was drawn from a field-mouse found by Mr. Hughes on Holmwood Common.

A little later on Christina Rossetti's love of nature bursts forth, and she compares the condition of a linnet in a 'gilded cage' with the hard fate of a linnet at liberty during severe weather, and asks the child to answer which is best. The reply might be doubtful, but she ends by saying:

> But let the trees burst out in leaf
> And nests be on the bough,
> Which linnet is the luckier bird,
> Oh who could doubt it now?

The lines commencing:

> Hope is like a harebell trembling from its birth,
> Love is like a rose the joy of all the earth;
> Faith is like a lily lifted high and white,
> Love is like a lovely rose the world's delight;

might possibly be regarded as somewhat beyond a child's comprehension. Christina Rossetti herself

evidently liked these lines much, for she wrote respectively :

> Hope is like a harebell trembling from its birth,

and (as mentioned before in an allusion to her strong
religious convictions)

> Faith is like a lily lifted high and white,

in copies of her general 'Poems' (1890) and of her
'Verses' (1893) now owned by me.

The only objection that can be urged against the
otherwise lovely lyrics beginning :

> Fly away, fly away over the sea,
> Sun-loving swallow, for summer is done

and

> When a mounting skylark sings
> In a sunlit summer morn,

is that their full significance lies beyond the understanding of children. In a collected edition of her poetical
works these lyrics ought to be included. The beautiful
poem about stars and flowers whose final lines are :

> Winged angels might fly down to us
> To pluck the stars,
> But we could only long for flowers
> Beyond the cloudy bars—

has a wistful touch in it.

The volume next to be dealt with was originally
called 'Nowhere,' but Dante Gabriel pointed out that a
'free-thinking book' had been 'called "Erewhon," which
is "Nowhere" inverted,' so it became 'Speaking Likenesses.' Like 'Sing-Song' the volume is illustrated by
Mr. Arthur Hughes.

'Speaking Likenesses,' issued in 1874, and presumably a series of stories told to some girls by their

aunt to while away the hours of sewing, cannot be ranked high among its author's books. It is not comparable with the best work of the same kind by 'Lewis Carroll' and Jean Ingelow. Nevertheless it is not without some good qualities. The following extract, which may be called 'Flora's Entrance into the House of her Dreams,' shows vivid fancy, and perhaps it is characteristic of Christina Rossetti that here she introduces, with obvious moral intent, the looking-glasses throughout the room.

FLORA'S ENTRANCE INTO THE HOUSE OF HER DREAMS.

'The door opened into a large and lofty apartment, very handsomely furnished. All the chairs were stuffed arm-chairs, and moved their arms and shifted their shoulders to accommodate sitters. All the sofas arranged and rearranged their pillows as convenience dictated. Footstools glided about, and rose or sank to meet every length of leg. Tables were no less obliging, but ran on noiseless castors here or there when wanted. Tea-trays ready set out, saucers of strawberries, jugs of cream, and plates of cake, floated in, settled down, and floated out again empty, with considerable tact and good taste: they came and went through a square hole high up in one wall, beyond which I presume lay the kitchen. Two harmoniums, an accordion, a pair of kettledrums and a peal of bells played concerted pieces behind a screen, but kept silence during conversation. Photographs and pictures made the tour of the apartment, standing still when glanced at and going on when done with. In case of need the furniture flattened itself against the wall, and cleared the floor for a game, or I daresay for a dance. Of these remarkable details some struck Flora in the first few minutes after her arrival, some came to light as time went on. The only uncomfortable point in the room, that is, as to furniture, was that both ceiling and walls were lined throughout with looking-glasses; but at first these did

not strike Flora as any disadvantage ; indeed she
thought it quite delightful, and took a long look at her
little self full length.'

As 'Commonplace, and other Short Stories' has been
long out of print, and is therefore the least accessible of all
Christina Rossetti's works, and moreover as this book
widely differs from those with which her name is usually
associated, somewhat fuller attention shall be devoted to
it than might otherwise have been thought needful.

It is noteworthy not only that one family should
have produced two eminent poets—Dante Gabriel and
Christina Rossetti—but that these great poets should
have left behind them some very noble imaginative
prose work, small though the quantity be. It is further
remarkable that both Dante Gabriel's ' Hand and Soul '
and Christina's ' Lost Titian ' are stories concerned with
Art and artists. Both ' Hand and Soul ' and ' The Lost
Titian ' will live because of the creative ardour shown in
them. If we except the prose tales of William Morris
(which, fine though they are, are in substance so different
that they cannot properly be discussed in this connection), none other of the great poets of the later years of
the century—Tennyson, Robert Browning, Mr. Swinburne and Matthew Arnold—ever wrote, or at any
rate ever published, any signed prose stories.

The volume under consideration seems to indicate
that at one period of her life Christina Rossetti had a
tentative purpose of becoming a novelist. I am unaware
that Elizabeth Barrett Browning or Felicia Hemans ever
published prose stories. But students of literary history
know, of course, that Lætitia Landon did so, as did
also Augusta Webster, an infinitely greater poet ; while,
among other prominent women poets, the stories of Jean

Ingelow are familiar, and full of evidences of her genius. This would seem to suggest that in the feminine mind the art of writing verses and the art of writing stories are somewhat akin. But notable objective poets like Sir Walter Scott have also been notable novelists. In truth viewed in some aspects the art of writing poetry and the art of writing stories do not seem so dissimilar as might at first sight appear. But the question is a wide one and cannot profitably be dealt with at length here.

Although 'Commonplace, and other Short Stories' did not appear until 1870 when the authoress reached her fortieth year we are told in the opening words of a brief 'Prefatory Note,' dated April 1870, that

'The earliest of these tales dates back to 1852, the latest was finished in 1870.'

Concerning the interesting point of the date of these various stories her brother has written to me as follows :

'"Nick" was an early performance, and seems to me the most likely story to have been written in 1852. "The Lost Titian" was also earlyish, but more (I should say) towards 1855. I incline to think that "Commonplace" may have been the latest of all, and therefore the one finished in 1870.'

Let us take them in the order in which they are printed in the volume. 'Commonplace,' the longest, evinces considerably more ability in construction than any of the others, though in other respects it is not the best. Its fair degree of originality can hardly be questioned, yet I should have been disposed to find in it traces of the influence of Mrs. Gaskell, and even of Mrs. Oliphant in her quieter moods, had not Mr. W. M. Rossetti informed me that in all probability his sister never read the last-named of these two great novelists. 'Commonplace' is a tale of three sisters, Catherine, Lucy, and Jane, whose several characters are differentiated carefully and stand out clearly before us, while in Miss Drum, their old school-mistress, Christina Rossetti shows that she could depict successfully a personage with humorous traits.

In my judgment, for clear and natural colouring 'The Lost Titian' is the finest story in the book. Written somewhat later than Dante Gabriel's 'Hand and Soul,' it has, like that story, much atmosphere of its own, and real mediæval colour combined with absolute fidelity in its delineation of the scenes depicted. Titian at the height of his artistic power and fame, has completed what he regards as his masterpiece, and summons two of his friends, Gianni and Giannuccione, to look at it on the day before all Venice is to behold it. The two friends vie with each other in its praise, and, before they part, arrange that they shall meet again in the evening, for Titian himself bids them

'"Rehearse to-morrow's festivities, and let your congratulations forestall its triumphs."

'"Yes, *evviva !*" returned the chorus, briskly ; and again "*evviva !*"

'So, with smiles and embraces, they parted. So they met again at the welcome coming of Argus-eyed night.

'The studio was elegant with clusters of flowers, sumptuous with crimson, gold-bordered hangings, and luxurious with cushions and perfumes. From the walls peeped pictured fruit and fruit-like faces, between the curtains and in the corners gleamed moonlight-tinted statues ; whilst on the easel reposed the beauty of the evening, overhung by budding boughs, and illuminated by an alabaster lamp burning scented oil. Strewn about the apartment lay musical instruments and packs of cards. On the table were silver dishes, filled with leaves and choice fruits ; wonderful vessels of Venetian glass, containing rare wines and iced waters ; and footless goblets, which allowed the guest no choice but to drain his bumper.

'That night the bumpers brimmed. Toast after toast was quaffed to the success of to-morrow, the exaltation of the unveiled beauty, the triumph of its author.'

The evening hours pass swiftly in merriment, despite the fact that Titian feels secret uneasiness which Gianni tries vainly to dispel by his skill in lute playing and in singing, for he is an adept in both arts. At length it is proposed that the three should gamble, the stakes being high. 'Gianni the imperturbable' has lost, and continues to lose ; his money, his pictures, his gondola, his jewels, all have gone. Then, laughing, he turns to Titian and says :

'Amico mio, let us throw the crowning cast. I stake thereon myself ; if you win, you may sell me to the Moor to-morrow, with the remnant of my patrimony ; to wit, one house, containing various articles of furniture and apparel ; yea, if aught else remains to me, that also do I stake : against these set you your newborn beauty, and let us throw for the last time ; lest it be said cogged dice are used in Venice, and I be taunted with the true proverb,—" *Save me from my friends, and I will take care of my enemies.*"

'"So be it," mused Titian, "even so. If I gain, my friend shall not suffer ; if I lose, I can but buy back my treasure with this night's winnings. His whole fortune will stand Gianni in more stead than my picture ; moreover, luck favours me. Besides, it can only be that my friend jests, and would try my confidence."

'So argued Titian, heated by success, by wine and play. But for these, he would freely have restored his adversary's fortune, though it had been multiplied tenfold, and again tenfold, rather than have risked his life's labour on the hazard of the dice.

'They threw.

'Luck had turned, and Gianni was successful.

'Titian, nothing doubting, laughed as he looked up from the table into his companion's face ; but no shadow of jesting lingered there. Their eyes met, and each read each other's heart at a glance.

'One, discerned the gnawing envy of a life satiated : a thousand mortifications, a thousand inferiorities, compensated in a moment.

'The other, read an indignation that even yet scarcely realised the treachery which kindled it ; a noble indignation, that more upbraided the false friend than the destroyer of a life's hope.'

Venice wondered what had become of Titian's great painting. Titian kept silence as to his friend's treachery because 'branding Gianni as a traitor ... would expose himself as a dupe.' Giannuccione, the third reveller, overcome by 'drunken sleep' had seen 'little ; and what he guessed Titian's urgency induced him to suppress.' Time wore on, everything seemed to prosper with Gianni, but by-and-by his former fondness for play returned, and he lost everything. For that night all his possessions —and among them Titian's masterpiece—were his own, on the morrow they would pass inevitably into other hands. That splendid work he had hitherto kept in secret, hoping when Titian was dead to proclaim himself the painter of it, and so win 'world-wide fame.' Gianni was a craftsman of some little skill and much resource. His resolution was taken. Seizing coarse pigments, such as could be removed at pleasure, he covered over Titian's work, and then painted on the top a dragon suitable for an inn-sign. The next day, at the meeting of his creditors, among whom Titian appeared for the first time, intent on regaining his picture, Gianni said that some of the more valuable of his effects had recently been destroyed accidentally by fire, and that the tavern sign (pointing to the dragon) had been painted for an inn-keeper just deceased. This he remarked presumably hoping to be allowed to retain it as valueless. At this point the dragon was claimed, somewhat unexpectedly, by a creditor, who was also an inn-keeper. With much show of politeness Gianni endeavoured to dissuade him from his purpose, alleging that the dragon was not yet in a suitable condition to leave his studio. But the inn-keeper was determined and carried it off immediately. Gianni, in his subsequent obscurity, devoted all his energies to ' concocting a dragon superior in all points to its predecessor.' He intended to induce the inn-keeper to take this and to give back the dragon he now possessed. But, when the new dragon was nearly finished, Gianni suddenly died, and knowledge of the lost painting ' died with him.'

In her Prefatory Note Christina Rossetti writes respecting all the tales that are included in the volume, but especially as to ' The Lost Titian ' :

' Not one of the stories is founded on fact.

.' This might not seem worth stating, had I not reason to fear that one or two of my kindest friends have viewed " The Lost Titian " somewhat in the light of an imposture. I therefore take this opportunity of putting on record that I am not conversant with any tradition which points to the existence of a lost picture by that great master with whose name I have made free.'

As to these remarks of his sister, Mr. William Rossetti points out to me :

' The reason why " The Lost Titian " might be viewed as an imposture must be that somebody might suppose the story to be a narrative of real fact : indeed I have a rather clear impression that someone in our circle *did*

so suppose.   I think Christina had also, to some extent,
in her mind the fate which befell Gabriel's old " Germ "-
story named " Hand and Soul " ; for it is a fact that more
persons than one really believed what Gabriel says about
the picture in the Pitti &c., and actually made enquiry
for it on the spot.'

'Nick' and 'Hero,' which follow 'The Lost Titian'
are fairy stories.   Both are good, but the latter reveals
perhaps a higher order of imagination, and was much
admired by Dante Gabriel.   'Vanna's Twins,' that
succeeds these, is a pretty and touching story of child-
life and evinces considerable power in delineating Italian
character of the lower middle class.   It used to be a
great favourite with Mr. Swinburne.   'A Safe Investment' might be termed an allegory of the relative
advantages of, and difference between, heavenly and
earthly commerce, if 'commerce' be a permissible word
in such a connection.   'Pros and Cons,' and 'The Waves
of this Troublesome World' (which concludes the
volume), are interesting only as illustrative of Christina
Rossetti's theological views and position ; indeed she
herself tells us that each of these stories was composed
with a special object.

Evidently in her later years Christina Rossetti
looked with disfavour on the book we are now discussing.
For, in September 1891 when sending a list of her
books to Mr. Patchett Martin, at his request, in prospect
of an article upon her in 'Literary Opinion,' she remarked :

'Commonplace and other Short Stories.   [Out of
print and not worth reprinting].'

It is impossible to concur with her judgment in this
instance.

I share her younger brother's regret that we do not now possess 'Folio Q,' in his opinion the best prose story his sister ever wrote. Of this he spoke in his 'Memoir' of Dante Gabriel (vol. ii. p. 162):

'It dealt with some supernatural matter—I think, a man whose doom it was not to get reflected in a looking glass (a sort of alternative form, so far, of " Peter Schlemihl "),'

and on the same subject to myself:

'The story, as written by C[hristina], had not, either in intention or in fact the remotest savour of immorality: but it contained some incident (I forget what) which some readers, more knowing than C[hristina] might have supposed to mean something or other which it did not in the least mean—Gabriel noticed this and either he or I conveyed the hint to C[hristina]. She without further ado destroyed the MS.'

I have been permitted to examine the original manuscript of 'Maude,' mentioned before, and to make what extracts seem desirable. The manuscript is a quarto size notebook of ruled blue paper, with a stiff paper cover, greyish in colour. The author's corrections, few and unimportant in themselves, are interesting because they are in the firm and bold handwriting of her after years—handwriting so widely different from the neat penmanship, deficient in individuality, in which the body of the tale is written. Thus it is clear from internal evidence that these alterations were made at a considerably later date than that at which the rest of the narrative was composed, and therefore, at least once, she looked through it in mature life.[1] The title-page is as follows:

[1] Mr. W. M. Rossetti states that this revision was made probably in 1870 or 1875.

MAUDE :

Prose and Verse,

By Christina G. Rossetti,

London 1850.

Viewed from the artistic standpoint 'Maude' is far from being altogether satisfactory, and its didactic tendencies are frequently too obvious ,for success even in a didactic direction. Nevertheless, bearing in mind the age at which it was produced, its good qualities are not seldom manifest ; and throughout there is a directness of purpose, combined with a simplicity of diction, that sometimes is really touching.

Elsewhere are mentioned certain of her early poems which, in their original form, appeared in 'Maude.' Here it will be sufficient to give a brief summary of, and some extracts from, the tale.

Maude Foster, 'just fifteen' when the story opens, is described as having 'features' which

'were regular and pleasing, as a child she has been very pretty ; and might have continued so but for a fixed paleness, and an expression, not exactly of pain, but languid and preoccupied to a painful degree. Yet even now if at any time she became thoroughly aroused and interested, her sleepy eyes would light up with wonderful brilliancy, her cheeks glow with warm colour, her manner become animated, and drawing herself up to her full height she would look more beautiful than ever she did. as a child. So Mrs. Foster said, and so unhappily Maude knew. She also knew that people thought her clever, and that her little copies of verses were handed about and admired. Touching these same verses, it was the amazement of every one what could make her poetry so broken hearted as was mostly the case. Some pronounced that she wrote very foolishly about things she could not possibly understand ; some wondered if she really had any secret source of uneasiness ; while some simply set her down as affected. Perhaps there was a degree of truth in all these opinions.’

Partly for the benefit of her health, Maude is taken on a short visit to the country house of her aunt where she becomes very intimate with her cousins Agnes and Mary Clifton.[1] At a birthday party given in honour of the latter, she excels all competitors in making *bouts-rimés* sonnets, and becomes acquainted with Magdalen Ellis who eventually enters a Sisterhood. Some time elapses, and Maude, going to be a bridesmaid to Mary Clifton, meets with a serious accident from which she never recovers. During her lingering illness Agnes comes to nurse her. The tale goes on :

‘ A burning sun seemed baking the very dust in the streets, and sucking the last remnant of moisture from the straw spread in front of Mrs. Foster’s house, when the sound of a low muffled ring was heard in the sick room ; and Maude, now entirely confined to her bed, raising herself on one arm, looked eagerly towards the door ; which opened to admit a servant with the welcome announcement that Agnes had arrived.

‘ After tea Mrs. Foster, almost worn out with fatigue, went to bed ; leaving her daughter under the care of their guest. The first greetings between the cousins had passed sadly enough. Agnes perceived at a glance that Maude was, as her last letter hinted, in a most alarming state : while the sick girl, well aware of her condition, received her friend with an emotion which showed she felt it might be for the last time. But soon her spirits rallied.

‘ “ I shall enjoy our evening together so much, Agnes ; ” said she, speaking now quite cheerfully : “ you must tell me all the news. Have you heard from Mary since your last despatch to me ? ”

---

[1] According to Mr. W. M. Rossetti these girls were, ‘ to some extent, limned from two young ladies, Alice and Priscilla Townsend.’

' " Mamma received a letter this morning before I set off; and she sent it hoping to amuse you.   Shall I read it aloud ? "

' " No, let me have it myself."   Her eye travelled rapidly down the well-filled pages, comprehending at a glance all the tale of happiness.   Mr. and Mrs. Herbert were at Scarborough ; they would thence proceed to the Lakes ; and thence most probably homewards, though a prolonged tour was mentioned as just possible.   But both plans seemed alike pleasing to Mary ; for she was full of her husband, and both were equally connected with him.

' Maude smiled as paragraph after paragraph enlarged on the same topic.   At last she said : " Agnes if you could not be yourself, but must become one of us three : I don't mean as to goodness, of course, but merely as regards circumstances,—would you change with sister Magdalen, with Mary, or with me ? "

' " Not with Mary, certainly.   Neither should I have courage to change with you ; I never should bear pain so well : nor yet with sister Magdalen, for I want the fervour of devotion.   So at present I fear you must even put up with me as I am.   Will that do ? "

' There was a pause.   A fresh wind had sprung up and the sun was setting.

.   .   .   .

' " Agnes [said Maude] it would only pain Mamma to look over everything if I die ; will you examine the verses, and destroy what I evidently never intended to be seen.   They might all be thrown away together, only Mamma is so fond of them.—What will she do ? "— and the poor girl hid her face in the pillows.

' " But is there no hope, then ? "

' " Not the slightest, if you mean of recovery ; and she does not know it.   Don't go away when all's over, but do what you can to comfort her.   I have been her misery from my birth till now ; there is no time to do better.   But you must leave me, please ; for I feel completely exhausted.   Or stay one moment : I saw Mr. Paulson [the clergyman] again this morning, and he promised to come to-morrow to administer the Blessed Sacrament to me ; so I count on you and mamma receiving with me, for the last time perhaps: will you?"

'"Yes, dear Maude. But you are so young, don't give up hope. And now would you like me to remain here during the night? I can establish myself quite comfortably on your sofa."

'"Thank you, but it could only make me restless. Goodnight, my own dear Agnes."

'"Goodnight, dear Maude. I trust to rise early to-morrow, that I may be with you all the sooner."

'So they parted.

'That morrow never dawned for Maude Foster.

———

'Agnes proceeded to perform the task imposed upon her, with scrupulous anxiety to carry out her friend's wishes. The locked book she never opened: but had it placed in Maude's coffin, with all its records of folly, sin, vanity; and she humbly trusted, of true penitence also. She next collected the scraps of paper found in her cousin's desk and portfolio, or lying loose upon the table; and proceeded to examine them. Many of these were fragments, many half-effaced pencil scrawls, some written on torn backs of letters, and some full of incomprehensible abbreviations. Agnes was astonished at the variety of Maude's compositions. Piece after piece she committed to the flames, fearful lest any should be preserved which were not intended for general perusal: but it cost her a pang to do so; and to see how small a number remained for Mrs. Foster. Of three only she took copies for herself. The first was dated ten days after Maude's accident.

.   .   .   .

'The second, though written on the same paper, was evidently composed at a subsequent period:

Fade, tender lily,
   Fade, O crimson rose,
Fade, every flower,
   Sweetest flower that blows.

Go, chilly Autumn,
  Come O Winter cold ;
Let the green stalks die away
  Into common mould.

Birth follows hard on death,
  Life is withering.
Hasten, we shall come the sooner
  Back to pleasant Spring.—

.   .   .   .

'Agnes cut one long tress from Maude's head ; and on her return home laid it in the same paper with the lock of Magdalen's hair. These she treasured greatly : and gazing on them, would long and pray for the hastening of that eternal morning which shall reunite in God those who in Him, or for His sake, have parted here.

'Amen for us all.'

CHAPTER IX

DEVOTIONAL PROSE

Annus Domini —'Seek and Find'—'Called to be Saints'—'Letter and Spirit'—'Time Flies'—'The Face of the Deep.'

'ANNUS DOMINI,' which was issued in 1874, through the publishing house of Messrs. James Parker & Co., Oxford and London, is the first in point of date of Christina Rossetti's devotional prose works, and deserves particular attention, as it presents many features showing the inception of her later devotional prose style. 'Annus Domini' is called on the sub-title page 'a prayer for each day of the year, founded on a text of Holy Scripture.' Following the title-page is a brief commendatory note by the Rev. William Henry Burrows mentioned before. Next comes a short Prefatory Note by the author, and then two pages occupied by what she names a 'Calendar' wherein the numbers are given of certain of the prayers which presumably she considered appropriate to memorable periods of the Christian year, such as Advent, Christmas, Epiphany, Septuagesima, Lent, Passiontide, Holy Week, Easter, Ascension, Whitsuntide, Holy Trinity, Saints' Days, Feast of the Blessed Virgin, S. Michael and All Angels, Ember Weeks, and Rogation Days. Each prayer is addressed to Christ. These prayers are not so imaginative as Christina's later devotional work. Perhaps this restraining of the imagination may have arisen on her part from her deep reverence for prayer as prayer, and her feeling, once or twice expressed to me, that no human creature, however skilful, ought wantonly to embroider with his own ability petitions to the Almighty. It may also have arisen partly from the fact that her symbolism became more developed in later life. But even in this book we find her remarkable power of evoking spiritual sublimity from Biblical passages which at first sight do not appear to contain it in a great degree. As an example of her writing here page 354 may be quoted in its entirety :

'Rev. xv. 4.

'" *Who shall not fear Thee, O Lord, and glorify Thy Name? for Thou only art Holy.*"

'O Lord Jesus Christ, Who only art Holy, forgive, I implore Thee, forgive and purge the unholiness of Thy saints, the unholiness of Thy little ones, the unholiness of Thy penitents, the unholiness of the unconverted, the unholiness of me a sinner. God be merciful to us sinners. Amen.'

Occasionally we see the influence of the Book of Common Prayer and it is not too much to say that she has sometimes caught much of its well-ordered grandeur. Perhaps there is almost an excessive realism in these words, part of a petition to Christ :

'By virtue of Thy victory give us also, I entreat Thee, victory. Let Thy pierced Heart win us to love Thee, Thy torn Hands incite us to every good work, Thy wounded Feet urge us on errands of mercy, Thy crown of thorns prick us out of sloth, Thy thirst draw us to thirst after the Living Water Thou givest : let Thy life be our pattern while we live, and Thy death our triumph over death when we come to die. Amen.'

But how beautiful, how full of the true rhythm of the finest English prose is the following:

'O Lord Jesus Christ, King of Kings, draw, I beseech Thee, all Kings of the earth to come and worship before Thee. Bless them who for our sakes are burdened with responsibility and cares; teach us to reverence, love, and obey them in all things lawful; and in the next world of Thy goodness give them with us rest. Amen.'

'Seek and Find' was published in 1879, and on the title-page is termed by its author 'A double series of short studies of the Benedicite.' In a 'Prefatory Note' on the succeeding page, she tells us that in writing her book she consulted the 'Harmony' by the late Isaac Williams (presumably his work entitled 'A Harmony of the Four Evangelists'). She goes on to say that, as she is unacquainted with either Hebrew or Greek, any 'textual elucidations' were obtained from 'some translation,' and that she discovered 'many valuable alternative readings' 'in the Margin of an ordinary Reference Bible.'

Following the 'Prefatory Note,' under the general heading of 'The Benedicite,' are five pages of small type setting forth the contents of the volume, each of the five pages being divided into three columns, as seen in the illustrative extract given below:

THE BENEDICITE.

THE PRAISE-GIVERS ARE	GOD'S CREATURES,	CHRIST'S SERVANTS.
O all ye Works of the Lord, bless ye the Lord: praise Him, and magnify Him for ever.	God saw everything that He had made, and, behold, it was very good. (Gen. i. 31.)	The Word was God. All things were made by Him; and without Him was not anything made that was made. (St. John i. 1, 3.)

The ' first series ' of ' studies,' called on the sub-title-page ' Creation,' occupy one hundred and fifty-three pages ; while the ' second series,' termed ' Redemption,' fill one hundred and fifty-nine pages.

In a letter to Christina, (October 8, 1879), her brother Dante Gabriel says that he finds ' Seek and Find ' ' full of eloquent beauties,' and then adds :

' I am sorry to notice that—in my own view—it is most seriously damaged, for almost all if not for all readers, by the confusion of references in the text, which they completely smother. Surely these should all have been marginal, and not nearly so numerous. [Mr. Frederic] Shields, who was of course much interested in seeing the book, took quite the same view in this.'

The volume might certainly have been better arranged. But, this objection stated, little but praise ought to be given to a work that contains so many noble prose sequences. ' It is the Spirit that quickeneth '—Christina Rossetti, without knowing Hebrew and Greek, was, nevertheless, frequently able to flash light on a Scriptural phrase, or series of phrases, owing to a devout use of her poet's intuition, for, generally speaking, she approaches even her prose work from the standpoint of a poet. Throughout ' Seek and Find ' her characteristic inclination towards symbolism is everywhere displayed and mainly with happy effect, although once and again, as in her disquisition on the connection between fishes and men, she appears to carry her symbolism a little too far. Perhaps the finest disquisition in the book is that on angels—a disquisition valuable not only for the ideas set forth therein, but because some of these ideas seem to be more fully the outcome of her personal experience than is usual even with Christina Rossetti.

and mainly with happy effect, although once and again, as in her disquisition on the connection between fishes and men, she appears to carry her symbolism a little too far. Perhaps the finest disquisition in the book is that on angels—a disquisition valuable not only for the ideas set forth therein, but because some of these ideas seem to be more fully the outcome of her personal experience than is usual even with Christina Rossetti. The excerpt that follows, sets forth some of these ideas :

'Since we believe that even in this life we dwell among the invisible hosts of angels,—since we hope in the life to come to rejoice and worship without end in their blessed company, let us collect what we already know of these our unseen fellows, that by considering what are their characteristics, we ourselves may be provoked unto love and to good works.' (Heb. x. 24).

'Seek and Find' is not one of Christina Rossetti's great books, but it is not unworthy of her, and is further noticeable as exhibiting her great knowledge of the Bible.

'Called to be Saints : The Minor Festivals Devotionally Studied,' was published in 1881. The saints and festivals dealt with in the volume are St. Andrew, 'Apostle'; St. Thomas, 'Apostle'; St. Stephen, 'Deacon'; St. John, 'Apostle and Evangelist'; The Holy Innocents ; St. Paul, 'Apostle'; The Presentation and Purification ; St. Matthias, 'Apostle'; The Annunciation ; St. Mark, 'Evangelist'; St. Philip and St. James the Less, 'Apostles'; St. Barnabas, 'Apostle'; St. John, 'Baptist'; St. Peter, 'Apostle'; St. James the Great, 'Apostle'; St. Bartholomew, 'Apostle'; St. Matthew, 'Apostle and Evangelist'; St. Michael and

All Angels ; St. Luke, ' Evangelist ' ; St Simon and St. Jude, ' Apostles ' ; and All Saints.

Prefixed to the volume is ' The Key to my Book, a short essay ending with the lyric ' This near-at-hand-land ' to which reference has been made at the beginning of Chapter VII. To each of the saints a separate section is given. Each of these sections is again sub-divided into brief dissertations, and in the contents each of these has a separate heading. The first of these headings is always styled ' The Sacred Text ' ; the second, ' Biographical Additions ' ; the third, ' A Prayer,' a composition written wholly by Christina Rossetti, and partly based on the characteristics of the especial saint commemorated. Then comes what is designated as ' A Memorial.' These ' memorials ' are noteworthy in many ways, and are often of considerable length, the memorial of St. Andrew, for example, extending to ten pages of fairly close type. They show their author's intimate acquaintance with the Bible, and her great power in bringing the passages she cites to bear on the particular subject she has in hand. Each of the pages in these ' memorials ' is divided midway into two portions. At the opening of the left-hand column are the first words of some brief commentatory matter, supplied by Christina Rossetti, and printed in block type, and these commentatory words are interspersed in the left-hand column of the ' memorials ' throughout the book. For purposes of example this commentatory matter in the first three pages of the memorial to St. Andrew has been given below, and printed consecutively, but, to save space, more closely than in the author's text, asterisks being placed where breaks occur in the original :

' St. Andrew of Bethsaida * * * learns of St. John Baptist, follows Christ and abides with him that day,

* * * brings to our Lord his brother, * * * on whom a new name is bestowed, * * * is called from the nets to be fisher of men, * * * is ordained Apostle.'

Following each of these detached phrases, and set in the same type as the rest of the volume, are Scripture passages relating either to the Saint's history, or mainly interpreting it. In the right-hand column are texts from the Bible also in usual type illustrative of, but not directly referring to, the saint. Further there is a little treatise, often most delicately phrased, relating to some flower, and to each of the saints she appropriates some particular flower. To St. Andrew, for instance, she appropriates the daisy. She adds likewise, in the case of the Apostles, a short disquisition on each particular precious stone with which she associates them, the disquisitions in their case being suggested by Rev. xxi. 14 :

'And the wall of the city had twelve foundations, and in them the names of the twelve apostles of the Lamb.'

She follows the order of the precious stones given in the same chapter of Revelation, verses 19 and 20, and, adopting the Ecclesiastical Calendar in the assignment of the stones, gives the jasper to St. Andrew and, proceeding in regular order, gives the amethyst, the last of the stones mentioned, to St. Jude—the latest apostle in the Ecclesiastical Calendar. Scattered throughout the prose text moreover are some of her most exquisite and solemn lyrics, fervid and intense in their piety, ecstatic in their rapture, but these, as they are discussed in Chapter VII., need not be referred to in detail here.

Following Rev. iv. 7 :

' And the first beast was like a lion, and the second beast like a calf, and the third beast had a face as a man, and the fourth beast was like a flying eagle,'

and the traditions of many centuries, she appropriates the fourth living creature, the eagle, to St. John, with a few words charged with fitting symbolism ; while in a similar manner she gives the first living creature, a lion, to St. Mark ; the third living creature, an angel, to St. Matthew ; and the second living creature, an ox, to St. Luke.

The prose of ' The Key to my Book ' is full of that rhythmical beauty noticeable especially in much of her devotional prose,—perhaps, because the mental qualities required in order to write such prose with a high degree of excellence, were precisely the qualities she possessed. Her simple yet sensuous mind —a mind stored with poetic imagery—found in such work a stimulus to lofty achievement.   Nor, in her case, is this lofty achievement ever gained by elaborate artifice.   Her arrangement and choice of words are as unartificial as the wild flowers of England, which she prefers to associate with the saints she loves, rather than the flora of Palestine.   Very tender and touching are these opening words :

' How beautiful are the arms which have embraced Christ, the hands which have touched Christ, the eyes which have gazed upon Christ, the lips which have spoken with Christ, the feet which have followed Christ.
' How beautiful are the hands which have worked the works of Christ, the feet which treading in his footsteps have gone about doing good, the lips that have

spread abroad his name, the lives which have been counted loss for him.'

Her description of 'Hepaticas' which she allocates to Matthias is an excellent example of her admirable power of idealising a merely botanical description. Work such as this is exceedingly difficult. If ordinary language be used, then the effect is commonplace and dull. If overmuch symbolism be employed, then the result seems strained and unreal. In this instance, however, the result is most successful. The passage which follows is especially pretty and fanciful:

'Hepaticas favour a light soil, and love to meet the morning sun rather than to endure a more continuously sunny exposure. They do not well bear moving, or at the least they bear it not always with indifference: an instance is quoted of one changing from blue to white when transplanted, whilst on returning to its former soil the enduring plant resumed its original tint. Humble in height, the hepatica may be termed patient in habit; for during one whole year the blossom, perfect in all its parts, lurks hidden within the bud.

'This plant belongs to the family of Anemones or Wind-flowers; and, as a wind-flower, seems all the more congruous with St. Matthias; . . . When, the lot having already fallen on him, "suddenly there came a sound from heaven as of a rushing mighty wind," that wind which "bloweth where it listeth," and on him as on the rest the Fiery Tongue of consecrating power lighted and sat.

'Kindly as the hepatica thrives amongst us, it yet is no native of England, but comes to us from Switzerland. Thus if hepaticas prefer repose, they yet submit to transference, blooming cheerfully in their allotted sphere.'

Mention may be made of an exquisite little homily on violets; of her 'Prayer for Conformity to God's Will'; and of her disquisition on 'Arbutus and Grass,' which she designates as 'great and small,' and assigns to All Saints Day. In the discourse last-named there is one of the autobiographical touches which, when they occur in her work, are always interesting.

'Often as I have let slip what cannot be regained, two points of my own experience stand out vividly; once, when little realising how nearly I had despised my last chance, I yet did in bare time do what must shortly have been for ever left undone ; and again, when I fulfilled a promise which beyond calculation there remained but scant leisure to fulfil.'

As to this passage Mr. William Rossetti has sent me the following communication :

'[Concerning] those references made by Christina in " Called to be Saints."　As to " doing in bare time what would shortly have been un-do-able," the natural inference seems to be that she did something or other in relation to a person who soon afterwards died.　As to a promise which was fulfilled, but only just in time, a similar inference again suggests itself.　It is just as likely as not that the incidents were in themselves of the very slightest consequence possible ; for C[hristina] often bore such matters in mind, if any sort of principle seemed to be involved in them.'

The last quotation that shall be made from 'Called to be Saints ' is from her meditation on St. Michael and All Angels, and may be said to be a complement to the passage concerning angels in 'Seek and Find ' lately referred to.　The extracts which here follow show how deep was the spirituality of her nature.

'Now of all which is, that which is made known unto us is undoubtedly made known for our profit. Let us not fail to love God all the more because He hath given His Angels charge concerning His own to keep them in all their ways ; because the armies of heaven pitch their camp around the faithful when need arises ; because blessed spirits minister to the heirs of salvation ; because they rejoice over one sinner that. repenteth :—for all this we know assuredly, whether or not with a multitude of pious souls we solace ourselves by the thought of one Angel guardian assigned to each baptised person. . . . When it seems (as sometimes through revulsion of feeling and urgency of Satan it may seem) that our yoke is uneasy and our burden unbearable, because our life is pared down and subdued and repressed to an intolerable level : and so in one moment every instinct of our whole self revolts against our lot, and we loathe this day of quietness and of sitting still, and writhe under a sudden sense of all we have irrecoverably foregone, of the right hand, or foot, or eye cast from us, of the haltingness and maimedness of our entrance (if enter we do at last) into life,—then the Seraphim of Isaiah's vision making music in our memory revive hope in our heart.'

Probably with the single exception of ' The Face of the Deep,' ' Called to be Saints ' is more thoroughly and beautifully built up through symbolism than any other of Christina Rossetti's devotional books.

Lady Mount-Temple ' found joy in ' ' Called to be Saints ' (to use Mr. Shields's happy phrase). He told this to Christina who, in a letter to him now before me, expresses her great satisfaction at hearing it.

' Letter and Spirit : Notes on the Commandments,' published in 1883, is dedicated

To
My Mother
in thankfulness for her
dear and honoured
example.

—a dedication specially interesting in view of some words to Mr. Shields, which may here be inserted. Writing

As there are celestial bodies & bodies terrestrial, but the glory
of the celestial is one, & the glory of the terrestrial is another, & as
one star differeth from another star in glory, so do the Holy Gospels
differ in glory of their symbols in glory. Each Gospel displays its proper
& unique splendour in harmony with its fellows, while each
symbol special gift & grace of its own Gospel.
St. Augustine points out how a Man, Lion, Ox, tread earth &
to conform with the first 3 Gospels these throw forth the humanity of
Christ, record His practical precepts of righteousness, His
winning parables drawn from things visible, His miracles of
mercy wrought on flesh & blood, the standard by which our
daily conduct must be regulated & will be judged.

[FACSIMILE OF A MANUSCRIPT PAGE OF ONE OF CHRISTINA ROSSETTI'S DEVOTIONAL WORKS.]

from 'Church Hill, Birchington-on-Sea,' under date August 23, 1883, Christina says :

'Thank you for welcoming "Letter and Spirit"—my Mother's life is a far more forcible comment on the Commandments than are words of mine.'

As its title is doubtless meant to indicate, 'Letter and Spirit' is a treatise on the inner meaning of the Commandments. Christina places in full on the first page of her book Christ's exposition of the Decalogue as it is given in Mark xii. 28–30, and Matt. xxii. 39–40, and then quotes the entire Decalogue itself, the rest of the work being an exposition of it. The volume ends with a Harmony on I. Corinthians xiii. and in the right column parallel sayings of Jesus culled from the Gospels.

On a first glance at this book one is apt to think that, in form at least, it partakes too much of the character of the ordinary religious commentary. Not till we have looked further into it do we perceive it filled with the same qualities which have made her other devotional prose remarkable—the qualities I mean of symbolism and a chastened form of imagination.

'Letter and Spirit' is the only one of her books, except 'Seek and Find,' and Speaking Likenesses,' which contains no verse of her own. It is likewise noteworthy from the fact that only two lines of verse of other writers are quoted—the lines of Bishop Heber :—

> Richer by far is the heart's adoration,
> Dearer to God are the prayers of the poor.

Seldom in her books did she quote the verses of other poets. Probably this was because, in her case, it was so easy to write verse. But was there another reason? It is a somewhat interesting field of speculation.

In none of her books does she approach more nearly to theological disquisition than in the volume at present under discussion. A conspicuous instance of this is to be seen in her remarks about the Trinity. A portion of these remarks may be quoted to show her in a polemical mood—a mood unusual with her:

'"Hear, O Israel; The Lord our God is one Lord: and thou shalt love the Lord thy God with all thy heart, and with all thy soul, and with all thy mind, and with all thy strength."

'This first, "the Great," Commandment is characterised by unity. Whatever else we find in it, this is one of its essential features, if not its leading feature. And, in fact, within this unity is bound up the entire multitude of our duties; out of this one supreme commandment have to be developed all the details of every one of our unnumbered obligations.

'"Hear, O Israel; the Lord our God is one Lord." While "the Christian verity" declares to us the mystery of the All-Holy Trinity, "the Catholic religion" asserts the inviolable Unity of the Godhead [Athanasian Creed]. And touching these two mysteries, it seems that to grasp, hold fast, adore the Catholic Mystery leads up to man's obligation to grasp, hold fast, adore the Christian Mystery; rather than this to the other. What is Catholic underlies what is Christian: on the Catholic basis alone can the Christian structure be raised; even while to raise that superstructure on that foundation is the bounden duty of every soul within reach of the full Divine Revelation. In God's inscrutable Providence it has pleased Him that millions of the human race should live in unavoidable ignorance of Christian doctrine: to that fundamental doctrine of God's unity, from which the other is developed, He has graciously vouchsafed a freer currency; so that while the Jewish Church knew it by revelation, multitudes of the Gentile world knew or

at least surmised it by intellectual or spiritual enlightenment.   Let us thank God that this main point of knowledge we hold in common with so vast a number of our
dear human brothers and sisters, children along with
ourselves of the all-loving Father ; let us thank Him
through Jesus Christ that we Christians are instructed
how thus acceptably to thank Him ; let us beseech Him
in that all-prevailing Name to add to each of us, whatsoever we be, every lacking gift and grace.

'Whilst Unity appears the sole existence essential to
be conceived, our conceiving it as separate from ourself
attests at once our likeness and our unlikeness to it.
That which we conceive is on our own showing other
than ourselves who conceive it : yet to conceive that
which has no existence is (I reverently assume) the
exclusive attribute of Almighty God, Who out of
nothing created all things.   To modify by a boundless
licence of imagination the Voice of Revelation, or of
tradition, or our own perceptions, concerning the universe,
its Ruler, inhabitants, features, origin, destinies, falls
within the range of human faculties.   And thus may not
light be thrown on that mass of bewildering error (whose
name is legion) which at every turn meeting us as man's
invention, is after all a more or less close travestie of
truth ? So like in detail, so unlike as a whole, to the
truth it simulates, that alternately we incline to ask : If
so much is known without immediate revelation, wherefore reveal ?   If truth pervades such errors, if such errors
can be grafted upon truth, is truth itself distinguishable
or is it worth distinguishing ?

'At first sight and apparently the easiest of all
conceptions to realise, I yet suppose that there may
in the long run be no conception more difficult for
ourselves to clench and retain than this of absolute
Unity ; this Oneness at all times, in all connexions, for
all purposes.'

The following passage has importance both because
it shows the strength of her convictions and because
it comes from the pen of a great poet with a poetic
environment almost unique—from a poet moreover

whose intense love of beauty was perhaps as great as that of any poet of our century:

'And if that be not mere fancifulness which seeks to trace a parallel between the Second and Seventh Commandments, it seems to follow by parity of reasoning that as regards whatever leads to sensual temptation a rule of avoidance, rather than of self-conquest or even of self-restraint, is a sound and scriptural rule. For the Jews were bidden not to degrade or defile, but absolutely to do away with all idols, and to obliterate every trace of idolatry; not one image might they hoard as a curiosity or an antiquity or a work of art; neither were they encouraged, even if under any circumstances it might be lawful for them, so much as to investigate the subject of heathen rites: "When ye are passed over Jordan into the Land of Canaan; then ye shall drive out all the inhabitants of the land from before you, and destroy all their pictures, and destroy all their molten images, and quite pluck down all their high places" (Num. xxxiii. 51, 52); "Thus shall ye deal with them; ye shall destroy their altars, and break down their images, and cut down their groves, and burn their graven images with fire. For thou art an holy people unto the Lord thy God" (Deut. vii. 5, 6); "When the Lord thy God shall cut off the nations from before thee, whither thou goest to possess them, and thou succeedest them, and dwellest in their land; take heed to thyself that thou be not snared by following them, after that they be destroyed from before thee; and that thou enquire not after their gods, saying, How did these nations serve their gods? even so will I do likewise. Thou shalt not do so unto the Lord thy God: for every abomination to the Lord, which he hateth, have they done unto their gods" (Deut. xii. 29–31).

'"Beloved, now are we the sons of God, and it doth not yet appear what we shall be: but we know that, when He shall appear, we shall be like Him; for we shall see Him as He is. And every man that hath this hope in Him purifieth himself, even as He is pure" (1 St. John iii. 2, 3). Blessed indeed are the pure in heart, for they shall see God. With such a beatitude in view, with so inestimable a gain or loss at stake, with such a prize of our high calling in Christ Jesus to yearn for, all we forego, or can by any possibility be required to forego, becomes—could we but behold it with purged impartial eyes—becomes as nothing. True, all our lives long we shall be bound to refrain our soul and keep it low : but what then ? For the books we now forbear to read, we shall one day be endued with wisdom and knowledge. For the music we will not listen to, we shall join in the song of the redeemed. For the pictures from which we turn, we shall gaze unabashed on the Beatific Vision. For the companionship we shun, we shall be welcomed into angelic society and the communion of triumphant saints. For the amusements we avoid, we shall keep the supreme Jubilee. For the pleasures we miss, we shall abide, and for evermore abide, in the rapture of heaven. It cannot be much of a hardship to dress modestly and at small cost rather than richly and fashionably, if with a vivid conviction we are awaiting the "white robes" of the redeemed. And indeed, this anticipation of pure and simple white robes for eternal wear may fairly shake belief in the genuine beauty of elaborate showiness even for such clothes as befit us in "the present distress" ; Solomon in all his glory was outdone by a lily of the field, and all his glory left him a prey to sensuality : and this launched him into shameless patronage of idol-worship ; until the glory of his greatness and the lustre of his gifts, combined with heinousness of his defection, have remained bequeathed to all ages as an awful warning beacon.'

Nothing is more unreasonable than the opinion so often expressed and apparently truly felt that the poetic mind is deficient in practical attributes. The exact reverse is not seldom the case with the higher types of poetic genius, and certainly nothing could be more practical than the exhortations of Christina Rossetti in this book. She refers to England by name, and is persuaded 'that our national honour, wealth, credit, already impaired' probably implies, 'unless we repent' the commencement 'of our chastisement.' By and by she remarks that it is 'no light offence to traduce the dead.' If we believe that every man and woman born into the world since its beginning still lives a life unbroken by death—still retains 'one continuity of individual existence from birth to this moment, from this moment to the Day of Judgment'—if we feel assured that, with them, we shall ourselves be judged, then must we realise in full that to cherish 'malice' towards them is 'simply devilish'—then must we realise what 'a solemn thing it is to write history'; and she concludes by this personal reference, striking in its graceful homeliness :

'I feel it a solemn thing to write conjectural sketches of Scripture characters ; filling up outlines as I fancy, but cannot be certain, may possibly have been the case ; making one figure stand for this virtue and another for that vice, attributing motives and colouring conduct. Yet I hope my mistakes will be forgiven me, while I do most earnestly desire every one of my personages to be in truth superior to my sketch.'

We have likewise some carefully thought out remarks on the arrangement of daily life ; on the relative importance of rest and work ; and on what really constitutes work, what rest.

The beautiful ' Harmony,' alluded to already, opens with a little note, in which she tells her readers that it ' was in part if not wholly suggested to me,' and though the person who made the suggestion is not certainly known, it was most probably her sister Maria.

She approaches, as said before, in ' Letter and Spirit ' more nearly than in her other writings to theological disquisition. She was not a professed theologian. She had too distinct a bias to the symbolical—to the poetic

—and was too little touched by the merely intellectual, to excel in theological disquisition. Occasionally, however, particularly in her prose devotional works, we come upon passages in which her natural commonsense and her natural eloquence enable her to deal with themes more or less theological with much power.

'Time Flies : A Reading Diary,' with the appropriate motto ' A day's march nearer home ' from James Montgomery, was published in 1885. It was dedicated thus :

To

My Beloved Example, Friend,

MOTHER.

' Her children arise up, and call her blessed.'

' Time Flies ' has the distinction of containing more frequent personal references than any other of her books, unless it be ' The Face of the Deep.' Indeed it may almost be called a kind of spiritual autobiography. For even when there are no obvious personal allusions many of the original thoughts and pregnant sayings that enrich the book must have had their root in her own spiritual experience. Probably having to write something about each day in the year, something that must necessarily be short, and that ought also to be concise and pithy, she fell back, unconsciously, on her own wide experience, wide, not in the outer but in the inner sense. Be this as it may, what has just been said gives an added and peculiar value to 'Time Flies,' altogether apart from the remarkable literary merit of the book.

As showing Christina Rossetti's breadth of mind and ample charity, despite her firm and unwavering faith not only in religion but in dogma, it is worthy of note, that very often in the course of these books we encounter passages which none could have written but a woman who had thought for herself, and who had not reached her present standpoint without much deep meditation. Seldom does she allow her passion for symbolism to carry her too far, and thus her symbolism rarely becomes, as we have often seen it become in the hands of lesser writers, something almost ridiculous. This in itself is a great achievement. For, as may easily be imagined, in a volume of brief devotional essays such as this 'reading diary' is in effect, it is most difficult to discuss in a few words, and without a sense of the ridiculous, such questions, for instance, as whether the association of 'tapers and bonfires' with St. Blaise arose or did not arise out of a quibble on his name. To January 24, she allocates the sonnet beginning :

> 'Give Me thy heart.' I said : Can I not make
> Abundant sacrifice to Him Who gave
> Life, health, possessions, friends, of all I have,
> All but my heart once given ?

terming the sonnet 'devotional.' She further adds that a 'friend' gave it to her many years before, and that she now reproduces it from memory. The 'friend' was James Collinson.

Sometimes Christina Rossetti introduces in a characteristic manner her opinions respecting subjects only indirectly connected with the theme which she is treating at the moment. Thus under date of February 5, and in relation to the Feast of St. Agatha, Virgin Martyr (who is supposed to have 'suffered death' about the year 251) she tells how Catania and Palermo claim to be the birthplace of 'this heroine of piety'; how Quintianus, 'Consular of Sicily' loved Agatha ;

and how, when he found that Agatha remained a Christian and repelled his overtures, his affection towards her became repugnance. She narrates further how he 'exhausted cruelty and torture' on her in vain, and how subsequently Agatha died in prison. Then she discusses anew, with simplicity and force, the familiar problem of how far a man or a woman may differ on important points and yet love one another. Her conclusion is that much real affection may exist despite important differences of opinion, and she closes her remarks by quoting St. Paul's words at Athens ' I found an altar with this inscription, " To the Unknown God." '

'Time Flies' contains many sayings of Christina's full of striking commonsense such as this : ' For many are they of whom the world is both "not worthy" and ignorant,' or this under date of February 18, where she adduces some excellent lessons from the ' quaint remark ' of a friend who said, concerning her own—not Christina Rossetti's—feet, that it was a good thing they were so large for thus anyone could wear her boots. Then we have a neat and sensible little homily, with considerable freshness, on the 'square man in a round hole.' Later we have a cheerful little exhortation on the subject of ' dirt' as the symbol of 'something out of place.' Still later there is a timely disquisition on the relative duties of hospitality in which she points out that

' In many cases the person who annoys and the person who is annoyed are both in the right, or (if you please) are both in the wrong '—

illustrating her proposition by the differing standards of courtesy of an Arab chief and his English guest.

In response to an enquiry as to whether the poem allocated to February 15 beginning

> My love whose heart is tender, said to me,

and ending

> And still she keeps my heart and keeps its key,

refers to her sister, her younger brother writes to me :

'I certainly regard it as applying to Maria. The 2nd line, "a moon lacks light" &c., is conclusive to me. Maria had a very round face, and Christina was much in the habit of calling her Moon, Moony, &c. I have no doubt that Maria on some occasion made this her cue for saying something very like what appears in the poem. However I never knew her to call C[hristina] her "Sun," or anything of the sort.'

At February 8 are some subtle and carefully differentiated remarks respecting heaven and music, in the course of which Christina points out that music to be music must not be monotonous, and that therefore 'a heaven of music,' even if that conception of heaven be not somewhat narrow and unreasonable, would be a place of variety, not of monotony. Under date of March 28 and April 16, she shows conclusively that, what she aptly calls physical 'grievous besetments,' may not relatively be disadvantageous ; she also at the second date avers how even our most cherished opinions almost inevitably are modified by time, drawing therefrom this cheerful moral :

'If even time lasts long enough to reverse a verdict of time, how much more eternity ?

'Let us take courage, secondary as we may for the present appear. Of ourselves likewise the comparative aspect will fade away, the positive will remain.'

At March 7 we meet with a few words about Vivia

Perpetua, the martyr, on the subject of whose pathetic career the author of 'Nearer my God to Thee' wrote a drama full of force and poetical enthusiasm. Christina Rossetti's special powers of reasoning are admirably used in her moralisings on the Feast of St. George, Martyr. The entry under May 8 has peculiar interest, and reveals her love of William Blake :

'There is a design by William Blake symbolic of the Resurrection. In it I behold the descending soul and the arising body rushing together in an indissoluble embrace : and the design, among all I recollect to have seen, stands alone in expressing the rapture of that reunion :'

—an opinion worth quoting when we recollect how great, apparently, was the influence of Blake on her own work, though it is right to add what Mr. William Rossetti tells me :

'It would I think be an error to suppose that C[hristina] at any time read B[lake] much or constantly—certainly she prized the little she did read.'

The entry under May 8 closes with a suitable quotation from Cayley's translation of Dante's 'Paradise,' Canto XIV.

Under date of August 30 tact is discussed shrewdly. Her entry for the following day, (where she dwells on the resemblance, once pointed out to her, between a grey parrot and an elephant) seems at first sight to have a quality akin to humour, were it not for the grim seriousness of the words with which she concludes :

. 'It is startling to reflect that you and I may be walking about unabashed and jaunty, whilst our fellows observe very queer likenesses amongst us.

'Any one may be the observer : and equally any one may be the observed.

'Liable to such casualties, I advise *myself* to assume a modest and unobtrusive demeanour.

'I do not venture to advise *you*.'

In a right sense she had a fearlessness, almost a contempt of current opinion, and, under date of September 30, she recalls with approval the saying of Jerome to the lady Asella : 'I know we may arrive at heaven equally with a bad, as a good name.' There is deep spiritual teaching in the following words which occur under date of December 20 :

'St. Thomas doubted.

'Scepticism is a degree of unbelief : equally therefore it is a degree of belief. It may be a degree of faith.

'St. Thomas doubted, but simultaneously he loved. Whence it follows that his case was all along hopeful.'

'The Face of the Deep : a Devotional Commentary on the Apocalypse' has as motto 'Thy judgments are a great deep'—Psalm xxxvi. 6. It was dedicated

To

My Mother

for the first time

to her

beloved, revered, cherished memory,

and was published in 1892 by the Society for Promoting Christian Knowledge.

In the simple and touching account given by Mr. William Rossetti (in his memoir of Dante Gabriel) of the early education of his brother and sisters we are told how their good mother instructed them in the Bible, and in this connection the Apocalypse is especially mentioned. There is therefore fair ground for supposing that Christina Rossetti's knowledge of the Book of the Revelation, and her fondness for it, had their origin in very early days, probably, in Mr. William Rossetti's opinion, by the age of eight or nine. Should such be the case, and the inference is just, it is striking and beautiful to think that her last, and in some respects her greatest literary achievement, was a commentary on the Book she had loved as a child.

'The Face of the Deep' deals systematically with the entire 'Book of the Revelation of St. John,' a chapter in the commentary being devoted to each Chapter of the Book. One, two, or three verses of the chapter under consideration are placed in block type, being followed by a paragraph or paragraphs of comment.

Two and a half, or perhaps three years elapsed between the date at which she first commenced to write her treatise and the date on which she handed the completed manuscript to her publishers.

The commentary, as indicated by the sub-title, is of course largely devotional. No effort of set purpose is made on the author's part to expound prophecy, nor does she make any fixed attempt at exegesis. Throughout, the reader is impressed by her childlike humility and by her unconsciousness of the fact that she possessed, in addition to her other gifts, no small share of miscellaneous learning. Very frequently when a word or phrase suggests something to awaken her lyrical gift, she breaks forth into snatches of exquisite song. Throughout the commentary we have also many noble prose litanies (to use the apt word by which Mr. Shields spoke of them to me). In these sequences her rich diction and fine ear for the rhythm of prose enable her to excel. Some of these, indeed most of them, are choice examples of rhythmically-balanced and delicate prose. Once and again, indeed, she reaches such a high level of style that her work is comparable with the finest masterpieces of prose composition in the English language—with the work, for example, of the translators of the authorised version of the English Bible of James the First's time—of the compilers of 'The Book of Common Prayer'—and with great writers like Hooker and Jeremy Taylor.

Her 'Prefatory Note,' with its reference to her sister Maria, has been spoken of in Chapter II. at page 63. It is couched in that characteristic vein of dignified humility (the phrase is used for lack of a better) with which students of her writings are familiar. This, indeed, is the secret of her wide influence. Very original likewise are the opening words wherein she implies that if she cannot 'dive' and 'bring up pearls' she may at least 'collect amber.' 'Though,' she adds, 'I fail to identify Paradisaical " bdellium," I still may hope to search out beauties of the "onyx stone." ' These words are the keynote of the entire commentary.

Of a commentary of such considerable length as 'The Face of the Deep,' (extending to five hundred and fifty-two pages) it is manifestly undesirable, even if space permitted, to give a full and detailed analysis. The interspersed verse has been discussed in Chapter VII., and it will therefore be sufficient to advert to some of the more important prose passages.

She bases her opening sentences on the first two verses of chapter i. of the Revelation, and writes:

'" Things which must shortly come to pass."—At the end of 1800 years we are still repeating this "shortly," because it is the word of God and the testimony of

Jesus Christ; thus starting in fellowship of patience with that blessed John who owns all Christians as his brethren (*see* ver. 9),'

so emphasising anew what she regards as the central idea of the book. In the course of her remarks on Rev. i. 12–16, we have one of the first outbursts of devotional feeling which, noticeable in all Christina Rossetti's religious works, are especially so in 'The Face of the Deep.' And these outbursts of devotional—of ecstatic feeling grew in intensity as she proceeded in the writing of this treatise—as the sublimity of her theme gradually took a deeper hold of her mind. Nothing shows more clearly her essential sanity, her essential commonsense —qualities in which her mind was akin to the greatest minds of all ages—than that never throughout 'The Face of the Deep' has she once departed either from sanity or commonsense. And remembering the temptations which the obscurity, as well as the abounding symbolism of the theme, must have had for her, who was at once so devout, so poetic, and so prone to symbolism, to say this of 'The Face of the Deep' is to say much, and yet not to laud it unduly.

Conspicuous examples of her litanies are to be found on pages 132, 151, 155, 175, 209, 226, 265, 280, 282, 323, 398, 407, 408, 426, 456, 472, and 474. One of the shortest, though not less expressive of these, is that on the page first named :

'O Saviour, show compassion !
'Because if Thou reject us, who shall receive us ?
'O Saviour, show compassion.
'Because we are half dead, yet not wholly dead,
'O Saviour, show compassion,

'Because Thou art the Good Samaritan, the Good

Physician; bind up our wounds pouring in Thine oil and Thy wine, take care of us, provide for us, set us forward on our way, bring us home. And because Thou lovest us, even for Thine own sake,

'O Saviour, show compassion.'

Students of style will observe the carefully balanced sound of the modulated cadences. Very different, yet equally beautiful, is that other somewhat longer litany addressed to Christ, from which this is an extract :

'Lord Jesus, lovely and pleasant art Thou in thy high places, Thou Centre of bliss, whence all bliss flows. Lovely also and pleasant wast Thou in Thy lowly tabernacles, Thou sometime Centre wherein humiliations and sorrows met.
'Thou Who wast Centre of a stable, with two saints and harmless cattle and some shepherds for Thy Court,
'Grant us lowliness.
'Thou Who wast Centre of Bethlehem when Wise Men worshipped Thee,
'Grant us wisdom.
'Thou Who wast Centre of the Temple, with doves or young pigeons and four saints about Thee,
'Grant us purity.
'Thou Who wast Centre of Egypt, which harboured Thee and thine in exile,
'Be Thou our refuge.
'Thou Who wast Centre of Nazareth where Thou wast brought up,
'Sanctify our homes.
'Thou Who wast Centre of all waters at thy Baptism in the River Jordan,
'Still sanctify water to the mystical washing away of sin.
'Thou Who wast Centre of all desolate places during forty days and forty nights,
'Comfort the desolate.
'Thou Who wast Centre of a marriage feast at Cana,
'Bless our rejoicing.

'·Thou Who wast Centre of a funeral procession at
Nain,
        ' Bless our mourning.
' Thou Who wast Centre of Samaria as Thou sattest
on the well,
        ' Bring back strayed souls.
' Thou Who wast Centre of all heights on the Mount
of Beatitudes,
        ' Grant us to sit with Thee in heavenly places.
' Thou Who wast Centre of sufferers by the Pool of
Bethesda,
        Heal us.
' Thou Who wast Centre of all harvest ground when
Thou wentest through the cornfields with Thy disciples,
        ' Make us bring forth to Thee thirty, sixty, a
        hundredfold.'

The litany beginning,

' Jesus Who didst touch the leper,
        Deliver us from antipathies ;
Who didst dwell among the Nazarenes,
        Deliver us from incompatibility,'

is introduced by what the author terms 'Purlieus and
Approaches which tend towards or border upon Hatred
of the Righteous ' part of her commentary on the text,

**'Saying, Hurt not the earth, nor the sea, nor the
trees, till we have sealed the servants of our God in
their foreheads.'**

She tabulates and numbers eight of these 'purlieus and
approaches ' aforesaid under various headings.   Some
of these headings are notably original, as this :
    6. ' Reciprocal angles, yours always in the wrong,'
or this :
    7. ' Reciprocal soreness, I always in the right,'
and the paragraph succeeding these headings is quaintly
effective :

'Taking one a day, you will require a week and a day for your self-reform. I, alas ! foresee requiring much more than a week and a day for mine.'

Equally quaint is her diction in the passage concerning the 'transcendent riches of poverty,' where the 'holy woman,' unmentioned by name, was her sister Maria, who had given her a piece of their mother's needlework.

Somewhat further on, we have this thoughtful observation—giving a glimpse into her own mind :

'Absolute darkness engulfs me when I attempt to realise the origin of evil. Yet even in that darkness which may be felt and which I feel, one point I dare not hesitate to hold fast and assert : evil had its origin in the free choice of a free will. Without free will there can be neither virtue nor vice ; without free choice neither offence nor merit.'

The litany which follows her exposition of Rev. xviii. 22, 23, and which seems suggested also by Mark viii. 36, 37, is not quite so successful in literary qualities, for it does not reach the high level of style of some of its predecessors. Students of Christina Rossetti should not, however, fail to read and study noble examples of litanies at pages 456, 472, and 474, in which they will find fine instances of the skilful use of antithesis.

The remarkable phrase 'There was no more sea' (Rev. xxi. 1) has often caused perplexity not unmingled with a vague feeling of regret. Is the phrase to be taken literally, or is 'the sea' to be regarded merely as an emblem of sorrow—sorrow that is to be 'done away'? St. John wrote the Apocalypse in Patmos—an island—the sea would therefore necessarily seem to him (each time that, with weary heart, he looked upon it) as something that separated him from those he loved best. Thus by a mental process, with which all thinkers are familiar, the cause would appear eventually to stand for the effect, and the sea itself would become unconsciously an emblem of separation. Nor must we forget that the passion for the sea is a passion of comparatively modern times. It was a passion unfelt by the ancients.

Christina Rossetti's observations on this point are so fraught with her own peculiar symbolism, so full of the idiosyncrasies of her own mental attitude in regard to interpretation, that they are well worthy of quotation. She says in the course of her commentary on Chapter xxi.

'**1. And I saw a new heaven and a new earth : for the first heaven and the first earth were passed away ; and there was no more sea.**

'Heaven and earth are to be renewed. Not so the sea : "There was no more sea." And wherefore not the sea :

'Regarding the first creation as symbolical, one answer (however inadequate, please God, not contradictory of truth) suggests itself. The harvest of earth ripened, was reaped, was garnered : the sea nourished and brought up no harvest. It bore no fruits which remain, it wrought no works which follow it. It was moreover originally constituted as a passage, not as an abode : across it man toiled in rowing to the haven where he would be, but itself never was and never could become that haven. Thus it presents to us a picture of all which must be left behind.

.   .   .   .

'Yet how shall we be consoled for our lost sea with its familiar fascination, its delights, its lifelong endearedness ? Lo ! heaven enshrines its own proper sea of glass as it were mingled with fire, and the uplifted voice of the redeemed is as the sound of many waters. There at last is fulness of that joy, whereas the sea never yet was full ; there plenteousness of pleasures as a river. There music unheard hitherto, unimaginable, in lieu of the long-drawn wail of our bitter sea.

'Or if after all we cannot during our actual weakness be thoroughly and consciously consoled on this point, let it at least bring home to us that better it is to enter into life, halt, or maimed, or one-eyed, than having two feet, hands, eyes, to be shut out. To suffer loss and be saved is better than to forego nothing and be lost.

'"There was no more sea."—As in a far different matter, "For our sakes, no doubt, this is written."'

Here is an explanation showing the analytical faculty of the explainer. It occurs in her remarks on 'And he opened his mouth in blasphemy against God, to blaspheme His Name, and His tabernacle, and them that dwell in heaven' (Chap. xiii. 6).

'Devils are not atheists : we are emphatically certified that they believe and tremble. During our Lord's earthly ministry, devils even proclaimed Him in the audience of men.

'Atheism appears to be a possibility confined to a lower nature. A body seems to be that which is capable of blocking up spirit into unmitigated materialism. "No man has seen God at any time :" that flesh and blood which cannot inherit the kingdom of God may, if it will, deny His existence.'

The love, the gentleness, which abode with her are never more evident throughout her writings than in 'The Face of the Deep,' yet she was stern and uncompromising in her views as to sin itself, as is seen by the closing words of a portion of her remarks as to 'So he carried me away in the spirit into the wilderness,' &c. (Chap. xvii. 3).

'To each such imperilled soul, Angel and Apostle here set a pattern. If we too would gaze unscathed and undefiled on wickedness, let us not seek for enchantments, but set our face towards the wilderness. Strip sin bare from voluptuousness of music, fascination of gesture, entrancement of the stage, rapture of poetry, glamour of eloquence, seduction of imaginative emotion ; strip it of every adornment, let it stand out bald as in the Ten stern Commandments. Study sin, when study it we must, not as a relishing pastime, but as an embittering deterrent. Lavish sympathy on the sinner, never on the sin. Say, if we will and if we mean it, Would God I had died for thee : nevertheless let us flee at the cry of such, lest the earth swallow us up also.'

The passage immediately ensuing is given here chiefly because of its autobiographical allusion and its characteristic admission of error. How few authors would have been equally candid! The person referred to was probably her sister Maria :

'It was once pointed out to me, that in the Bible the first mention of a lamb occurs in connection with Abraham's virtual sacrifice of Isaac: " Isaac spake unto Abraham his father, and said, My Father : and he said, Here am I, my son. And he said, Behold the fire and the wood : but where is the lamb for a burnt offering? And Abraham said, My son, God will provide Himself a lamb for a burnt-offering." And I think the observation is essentially correct, despite the " seven ewe lambs " of the preceding chapter ; inasmuch as these do not belong (so to say) to the same spiritual context. Yet, had I been aware of both texts, I should not (in *Seek and Find*) without a modifying clause have referred to Isaac's words as absolutely *first*.

'[Which oversight invites me to two wholesome proceedings : to beg my reader's pardon for my errors ; and ever to write modestly under correction.]'

Mr. Shields has pointed out to me how naive, yet how charmingly individual, is this sentence which she placed at the close of ' The Face of the Deep '—her latest and, as I cannot help thinking, in virtue of many fine qualities both of thought and of style, her noblest prose work :—

' If I have been over-bold in attempting such a work as this, I beg pardon.'

CHAPTER X

CRITICAL SURVEY

Remarks respecting various aspects of Christina Rossetti's work, and
reasons why it is likely to retain its value.

IT is not possible to accentuate overmuch the influence on Christina Rossetti of her Italian lineage, her early surroundings, and the fact that, when quite young, her mind was saturated with Italian literature. She was probably influenced first by her father, and, at a little later date, by Metastasio the lyric poet. Her surviving brother tells me that she never cared much for Petrarch : and 'of Boccaccio,' he remarks, ' she never, I should say, read a dozen lines.'

He adds :

' But she was greatly fascinated by Tasso when she first read that poet about 1848. She also enjoyed parts of Ariosto though she forebore to read him freely for fear of coming upon " improper " passages.'

She was as deeply influenced by Dante as was any other member of the Rossetti family, but this was not until a subsequent period. In mature life her knowledge of Dante, and even of Petrarch was great, as is shown by the skilfully chosen quotations from both these writers, prefixed to each of the sonnets in her noble sonnet-sequence ' Monna Innominata.'

Her elder brother told Mr. Arthur Hughes, and,

several of his other early friends, that he regretted the morbidity of his sister's work. And there can be no doubt that there is some ground for the regret. Many, even of the finer of her earlier poems, have an atmosphere, which, in another poet, we should consider unreasonably sad. Greatness, however, is justified of its results, and we are tempted to feel that even Christina Rossetti's most morbid strains ('the skeletons of Christina's various closets,' to quote a droll phrase from a letter by her brother, the poet, to her mother, a letter distinguished because of its rather grim humour) were right and reasonable merely because they were hers. Nor must it be forgotten that many young poets, Tennyson is a familiar example, had a tendency towards morbidity, or at least to melancholy, in their early work. It may be, as Mr. J. S. Cotton, the well-known scholar, once said to me when discussing this subject, that sadness in itself is sometimes a sign of the possession of the higher poetic qualities in imperfect development.

The critic of the far future, of whom we hear so much and think so little, will accord a high place among the great poets of this century to the poet to whom we owe 'Amor Mundi,' 'An Apple Gathering,' 'Maude Clare,' 'The Convent Threshold,' and 'Maiden-Song.' He will single out as amongst the finest love songs in our language such a flawless lyric as 'When I am dead, my dearest'—a lyric so full of atmosphere, so perfect in its tenderness and in its portrayal of affection.

Christina Rossetti was akin to Blake, and her kinship to some of the Elizabethan poets, such as Southwell, was hardly less near. Her own symbolism was allied to the symbolism of Blake, notably in such a piece as his poem entitled 'The Lamb;' and she felt likewise the same kind of sympathy with Nature as he did. She had not, like Blake, those visions of the supernatural which our practical commonsense rejects as hallucinations, but, like him, she abode in London, the 'most earthly of earthly cities,' to quote a phrase of Mr. Alfred H. Miles in his excellent article on Blake in 'The Poets and the Poetry of the Century,' and, like Blake also, she was often 'away in Paradise.'

Since the death of Christina Rossetti it has several times been asserted that Elizabeth Barrett Browning was the greater poet of the two, because her poems dealt with themes of more widespread human interest. Possibly Christina Rossetti thought that some of the subjects handled by Elizabeth Barrett Browning were not suitable for treatment in poetry. Certainly what has been said in Chapter III. as to Christina Rossetti's attitude respecting vivisection, minors' protection, and other such measures, shows as keen interest on her part in social and philanthropic projects as that evinced by Elizabeth Barrett Browning, though she did not, like the author of 'The Cry of the Children,' write a great poem on any such theme.

No formal adjudication on two poets so eminent as Elizabeth Barrett Browning and Christina Rossetti shall be attempted here. Henceforward lovers of English literature will feel gladness that our language is enriched by the masterpieces of both poets, and will probably feel equally grateful for both. It may not, however, be out of place to state certain points of agreement or of contrast between them.

Elizabeth Barrett Browning and Christina Rossetti were alike in their ardent affection for Italy, and both

women were equally firm believers in the essential truths
of Christianity. No doubt Elizabeth Barrett Browning
was the more learned of the two, in the academic sense
of the word, for, unlike the author of 'Wine of Cyprus,'
Christina Rossetti was unacquainted with Greek or
Hebrew, nor had she that intuitive sympathy with the
classic attributes, temper, and mood of mind which is
sometimes apparent in the work of Elizabeth Barrett
Browning. Certainly the outlook on life of the
two great writers under consideration was not a little
different; the last named was naturally disposed to
broader views both in social and ethical matters than
was Christina Rossetti.

Though, as just indicated, both had great fondness
for Italy, their views as to liberty in general, and possibly
as to liberated Italy, were not the same. The author
of 'Casa Guidi Windows' held strongly the conception
of liberty almost as a good in itself (which was one of
the tenets of a certain group of thinkers among whom
she moved in later life) rather than as merely a means
to an end.

The finest work of Christina Rossetti in verse reaches
a higher point of technical excellence than the finest
work of Elizabeth Barrett Browning; indeed, it might
be said that Christina's verse as a whole is of higher
technical excellence than that of Elizabeth Barrett
Browning. In religion the latter had a much wider
view than had Christina, for her mind was less concerned
with the doctrinal aspects of faith than with problems,
such as the problem of the mystery of suffering, which lie
just beyond the sphere of devotion—problems such as
that which she dealt with in 'Cowper's Grave.'

It is well worthy of note that both Elizabeth Barrett

Browning and Christina Rossetti were distinguished as writers of sonnets. The latter's elder brother is reported to have said that his sister could not have written the 'Sonnets from the Portuguese.' The justice of the remark may appear doubtful when we recollect the superb and individual series of sonnets, called 'Monna Innominata '—sonnets charged with the most etherealised love passion in its most spiritual development. In all coming time it will be one of the chief glories of Christina Rossetti that 'Monna Innominata,' though based on the same general theme as the 'Sonnets from the Portuguese,' should show no indebtedness to them in thought or in metrical resource.

Perhaps No. xliii. of the 'Sonnets from the Portuguese' beginning—

> How do I love thee?   Let me count the ways.
> I love thee to the depth and breadth and height
> My soul can reach,—

is most akin to Christina Rossetti's method ; and this, and that yet more noble sonnet by Elizabeth Barrett Browning, entitled ' Perplexed Music,' commencing :

> Experience, like a pale musician, holds
> A dulcimer of patience in his hand—

a sonnet in theme, conception, and execution, one of the most perfect in the language—should be examined carefully by the student of poetic form who wishes to see the aspects of similarity and of difference between our two more famous women poets. Such a comparison will show furthermore that it is simple, elemental emotion, adequately expressed, which makes a poem really great, not Art alone, though, of course, Art when properly used, is an invaluable aid. Dante Gabriel passed some severe strictures on certain of his sister's poems owing to what he called the 'falsetto muscularity ' of their ' Barrett-Browning style.' [1]   Personally I am not of opinion that these strictures were justifiable.   In my view, hardly any, if any, trace of the influence of Elizabeth Barrett Browning is discernible in Christina Rossetti's work.

Had space permitted it would have been well to give a detailed analysis, accompanied by full quotations, of the way in which Christina Rossetti's treatment of the love passion varies from that of Elizabeth Barrett Browning.   Possibly it may be admitted that the latter writer has, in some respects, a greater human interest in poems like ' The Rhyme of the Duchess May,' ' Bertha in the Lane,' and ' The Lay of the Brown Rosary.'   This is because her way of looking at life was broader than Christina Rossetti's, and she had perhaps a deeper insight into ordinary social intercourse.   For this reason I do not think Christina Rossetti could have given us poems like ' The Lady's Yes,' ' A Man's Requirements,' or ' Amy's Cruelty '—poems which show great knowledge of the *nuances* which go to make up everyday conduct.   ' A Man's Requirements ' might almost be called a satire on the disposition of the conventional male when contemplating love-making.   ' Amy's Cruelty ' again, though instinct with equal fidelity and truth, goes deeper, and tells us, as only a woman of genius could tell us, a woman's feelings with regard to love.   But, after all, these poems owe their success not to their qualities as poems but to their vividness and insight in depicting the conditions they describe.   Readers of

[1] See *Dante Gabriel Rossetti: His Family Letters, with a Memoir*, vol. ii. p. 323.

Chapter III., will have observed what were Christina Rossetti's opinions on the much-debated question of the equality of the sexes. Here it may be noted that Elizabeth Barrett Browning disagreed with her absolutely, for, as Mr. W. T. Stead says aptly, in his preface to the selection from Elizabeth Barrett Browning's poems in his 'Masterpiece Library':

'No one more keenly resented than Mrs. Browning the comparative praise, implying positive blame, that eulogises her work merely as woman's work, and not on its merits as work. "Please to recollect," she wrote once to a friend, "that when I talk of women I do not speak of them as many men do . . . according to a separate peculiar and womanly standard, but according to the common standard of human nature." As with life, so with art, and the work which is the product of artistic life. It is good in itself, or bad in itself, irrespective of the sex of its author.'

Few who had the high privilege of knowing Christina Rossetti personally, or who have even a thorough acquaintance with her work, can doubt either the profound influence which Italy exercised over her, or her deep sympathy with the cause of Italian liberation. It is therefore significant of the essential divergences of temperament between the two women that it is to Elizabeth Barrett Browning, the Englishwoman by descent and association, not to Christina Rossetti, that we owe stirring poems of the liberation of Italy such as 'First News from Villafranca' and 'A Tale of Villafranca,' and especially that vivid poem, full of the pathos of a woman's grief, called 'Parted Lovers.' In Christina Rossetti's 'Italia, io ti saluto !' there is pathos also, but it is the personal, not the national note, that we hear in this exquisite last stanza :

> But when our swallows fly back to the South,
> To the sweet South, to the sweet South,
> The tears may come again into my eyes
> On the old wise,
> And the sweet name to my mouth.

I am tempted irresistibly to make some comparison, however short, between Christina Rossetti's work and that of Jean Ingelow. Both poets have given us remarkable poems which deal with varying aspects of the supernatural. Though Christina Rossetti's ' The Hour and the Ghost,' and Jean Ingelow's ' Requiescat in Pace ' are dissimilar in much, they are similar in this, that both achieve the difficult task of introducing the supernatural by simple means ; in both poems the fine effects are the result of atmosphere, of intuition, rather than of definite statement. No poem of the supernatural can be really effective unless it reaches its higher effects by suggestion. It is so with Coleridge's ' Christabel,' and it is this quality in the two poems under discussion which gives them a rank almost classic.

Both poets are firm believers in the verities of the Christian faith, though Jean Ingelow has less symbolism, and looks on religion from a somewhat different and perhaps a more English standpoint.

The present monograph is a record as well as a study ; therefore it may not be unfitting if certain critical remarks by contemporary writers as to Christina Rossetti are introduced here. Mr. Swinburne's admiration is well known, and is expressed in these lines taken from his ' Ballad of Appeal ' to her :

> Blithe verse made all the dim sense clear
> That smiles of babbling babes conceal :
> Prayer's perfect heart spake here : and here

> Rose notes of blameless woe and weal,
> More soft than this poor song's appeal.
> Where orchards bask, where cornfields wave,
> They dropped like rains that cleanse and lave,
> And scattered all the year along,
> Like dewfall on an April grave,
> Sweet water from the well of song.

When writing to Mr. Hall Caine, her elder brother says :

'[Mr.] Swinburne, who is a vast admirer of my sister's, thinks the "Advent" perhaps the noblest of all her poems, and also specially loves the "Passing Away." I do not know that I quite agree with your decided preference for the two sonnets of hers you signalise,—the "World" is very fine, but the other, "Dead before Death," a little sensational *for her*. I think "After Death" one of her noblest, and the one "After Communion." In my own view, the greatest of all her poems is that on France after the siege—"To-day for Me." A very splendid piece of feminine ascetic passion is "The Convent Threshold."'

In a Preface contributed to Mr. A. C. Pollard's edition of Herrick, Mr. Swinburne writes (and this further praise is emphatic on account of its connection) :

'It has often been objected that he [Herrick] did mistake himself for a sacred poet : and it cannot be denied that his sacred verse at its worst is as offensive as his secular verse at its worst ; nor can it be denied that no severer sentence of condemnation can be passed upon any poet's work. But neither Herbert nor Crashaw could have bettered such a divinely beautiful triplet as this :—

> We see Him come, and know Him ours,
> Who with His sunshine and His showers
> Turns all the patient ground to flowers.

'That is worthy of Miss Rossetti herself : and praise of such work can go no higher.'

Mr. W. M. Rossetti never achieved better critical work than when, in his spirited defence of his old friend, Mr. Swinburne,[1] he wrote characteristically, and with admirable and subtle perception, about his own sister :

'The reader will find in one place a reference to the writings of a member of my own family. I advisedly keep this exactly as it stood, being *better* pleased that it should be published with my name to it than (as would have been done according to the original scheme) anonymously. I should not have shirked to have the anonymous tribute traced home to me ; and am still less loth to avow that tribute—saying in it, as I have done, nothing beyond what I know or believe to be true. The last man who need love the anonymous system is a self-respecting critic acquainted with many of the persons concerning whom it is his lot to write.

'The last of our present poetic quartett, Christina Rossetti, is a singer of a different order from all these, reaching true artistic effects with apparently little study and as little of mere chance—rather by an internal sense of fitness, a mental touch as delicate as the finger-tips of the blind. She simply, as it were, pours words into the mould of her idea ; and the resultant effigy comes right, because the idea, and the mind of which it is a phase, are beautiful ones, serious, yet feminine and in part almost playful. There is no poet with a more marked instinct for fusing the thought into the image, and the image into the thought : the fact is always to her emotional, not merely positive, and the emotion clothed in a sensible shape, not merely abstract. No treatment can be more artistically womanly in general scope than this, which appears to us the most essential distinction of Miss Rossetti's writings. It might be futile to seek for any points of direct analogy or of memorable divergence between Mr. Swinburne and Miss Rossetti. The prevalent cadence of the poem " Rococo," and the lyrical structure of " Madonna Mia," may, however, suggest that the poet is a not unsympathetic reader of

[1] *Swinburne's Poems and Ballads. A Criticism.*

the poetess's compositions ; nor is " The Garden of Proserpine " much unlike some of these so far merely as lyrical tone is concerned.'

In his striking essay entitled ' Reminiscences of Christina Rossetti,' to which allusion has been made elsewhere, Mr. Watts-Dunton remarks respecting her poetic art :

' Of all contemporary poets, she had seemed to me the most indubitably inspired. I had made a life-long study of poetic art, yet Christina's art-secret had baffled me. Her very uncertainty of touch, as regarded execution, seemed somehow to add to the impression she made upon me of inspiration. She never (as her brother William, who has gratified me by reading these pages, reminds me) " made up her mind that she would write something, and then proceeded to write it. She always wrote just as the impulse and the form of expression came to her, and if these did not come, she wrote not at all." But it was not her inspiration which over-awed me at the idea of meeting her. It was the feeling that her inspiration was not that of the artist at all, and not that of such dramatic passion as in other poets I had been accustomed to, but the inspiration of the religious devotee. It answered a chord within me, but a chord that no poet had theretofore touched.

' It seemed to me to come from a power which my soul remembered in some ante-natal existence and had not even yet wholly forgotten.'

Mr. Andrew Lang in ' The Cosmopolitan Magazine ' for June, 1895, wrote as follows :

' There can be little doubt that we are now deprived of the greatest English poet of the sex which is made to inspire poetry, rather than to create it. Except Mrs. Browning, we have no one to be named with Miss Rossetti in all the roll-call of our literary history . . . . We have had, it is true, in Scotland, lady lyrists whose songs, like Lady Nairne's and Lady Anne Lindsay's, I myself prefer to all the works of Miss Rossetti, Mrs.

Browning, Miss Proctor, and Mrs. Hemans. But for the quality of conscious. art, and for music and colour of words in regular composition, Miss Rossetti seems to myself to have been unmatched. The faults of Mrs. Browning she did not follow, and curious it is that the more learned lady shows most of the errors which learning is supposed to counteract. Things of Miss Rossetti's will live with things of Carew's and Suckling's.'

Dr. Richard Garnett in 'The Dictionary of National Biography' said :

'Her " Goblin Market" is original in conception, style, and structure, as imaginative as the " Ancient Mariner," and comparable only to Shakespeare for the insight shown into unhuman and yet spiritual natures.'

In 'The New Review' of February 1895, Mrs. Meynell spoke finely thus :

'To the name of poet her right is so sure that proof of it is to be found everywhere in her " unconsidered ways," and always irrefutably. How does this poet or that approach the best beauties of his poem ? From the side of poetry, or from the side of commonplace ? Christina Rossetti always drew near from the side of poetry : from what to us, who are not altogether poets, is the further side. She came from beyond those hills. She is not often on the heights, but all her access is by poetry. Of few indeed is this so true.'

Mr. Arthur Christopher Benson, in 'The National Review' of February 1895, remarked discerningly about her :

'Some writers have the power of creating a species of aërial landscape in the minds of their readers, often vague and shadowy, not obtruding itself strongly upon the consciousness, but forming a quiet background, like the scenery of portraits, in which the action of the lyric or the sonnet seems to lie. I am not now speaking of pictorial writing, which definitely aims at producing, with more or less vividness, a house, a park, a valley, but lyrics and poems of pure thought and feeling, which have none the less a haunting sense of locality in which the mood dreams itself out.

'Christina Rossetti's *mise-en-scène* is a place of gardens, orchards, wooded dingles, with a churchyard in the distance. The scene shifts a little, but the spirit never wanders far afield ; and it is certainly singular that one who lived out almost the whole of her life in a city so majestic, sober, and inspiring as London, should never bring the consciousness of streets and thoroughfares and populous murmur into her writings. She, whose heart was so with birds and fruits, cornfields and farmyard sounds, never even revolts against or despairs of the huge desolation, the laborious monotony of a great town. She does not sing of the caged bird, with exotic memories of freedom stirred by the flashing water, the hanging groundsel of her wired prison, but with a wild voice, with visions only limited by the rustic conventionalities of toil and tillage. The dewy English woodland, the sharp silences of winter, the gloom of low-hung clouds, and the sigh of weeping rains are her backgrounds.'

In 'The Poets and the Poetry of the Century' Mr. Arthur Symons has pointed out certain aspects of her genius with much lucidity and force :

' The secret [of her style]—which seems innocently unaware of its own beauty—is, no doubt, its sincerity, leading to the employment of homely words where homely words are wanted, and always of natural and really expressive words ; yet not sincerity only, but sincerity as the servant of a finely touched and exceptionally *seeing* nature. A power of seeing finely beyond the scope of ordinary vision : that, in a few words, is the note of Miss Rossetti's genius, and it brings with it a subtle and as if instinctive power of expressing subtle and yet as if instinctive conceptions ; always clearly, always simply, with a singular and often startling homeliness, yet in a way and about subjects as far removed from the borders of commonplace as possible. This power is shown in every division of her poetry ; in the peculiar

witchery of the poems dealing with the supernatural, in
the exaltations of the devotional poems, in the particular charm of the child-songs, bird-songs, and nature
lyrics, in the special variety and the special excellence
of the poems of affection and meditation. The union
of homely yet always select literalness of treatment with
mystical visionariness or visionariness which is sometimes
mystical, constitutes the peculiar quality of her poetry
—poetry which has, all the same, several points of
approach and distinct varieties of characteristic.'

Mr. Lionel Johnson, in ' The Academy ' of July 25,
1896, has remarked concerning her with true critical
acumen :

'Doubtless her poems, now comprised in three collected volumes, include many a piece of airy fantasy,
many a laughing lyric, many a poem born of external circumstance ; but her characteristic greatness lies in her
most intimate, most severe, most passionate and sacred
poems : in the work which sets her in the company
of Herbert, Vaughan, the converted Donne, Crashaw,
Father Southwell, the divine Herrick, Cardinal Newman.
And by this it is not meant that her obviously and osten-
sibly sacred poems are alone her greatest : many
others, poems of meditation or of passion, with no distinct
Christian cry in them, stand side by side with the
poems divine and devout. Her fair and stern philosophy of life, which never fails to draw to itself her
choicest powers of art, is that which marks out her
poetry for distinction and for admiration. Her more
external work, with its gaieties and beautiful imaginings,
is full of delights.'

Christina Rossetti was not always happy in her choice
of titles, though occasionally, in titles like ' Amor Mundi,'
like 'The Hour and the Ghost,' or like 'The Face of
the Deep,' her choice was particularly good. I have
reason to suppose that she experienced some difficulty
in finding titles which pleased her. But, whether my

supposition in this respect be correct or no, it is clear that 'Echo' is a feeble and unmeaning title for the exquisite lines beginning :

Come to me in the silence of the night

in 'Goblin Market and other Poems,' and that 'The End of the First Part' is not a felicitous title for an ecstatic religious lyric. Occasionally throughout her work we have phrases which sound somewhat un-English ; perhaps also in her verse she uses too often contractions like 'I'd.' Not seldom some of her critics have cavilled at her frequent use of unrhymed lines. Such critics must not forget that many of our best poets introduced similar unrhymed lines when using the same metrical forms as she has done. But even if we admit that such objections contain a certain degree of truth, we must not fail to recollect that

'a special quality of her verse is a *curiosa felicitas* which makes a metrical blemish tell as a suggestive grace'

(to quote a good phrase in Mr. Watts-Dunton's article on Christina Rossetti in 'The Athenæum' of January 5, 1895).

Regarding the ruggedness for which some of her later poetical work has been censured, Mr. W. M. Rossetti has written to me :

'The so-called ruggedness depends I fancy to some. extent upon the fact that C[hristina] was extremely prone to writing (and this was of course intentional—and very gracefully managed) lines differing in *length*: a tendency originating possibly in the structure of the Italian "canzone."'

As an argument against the value of Christina Rossetti's work, both in verse and in prose, it may be

urged (and I have heard it so urged) that her narrowness
of range, and her tendency to dwell too much on one set
of emotions, make her work monotonous.   In such a con-
tention there is a 'residuum of truth.'   And, if for this
reason alone, her work is the less likely ever to become
popular, as a whole, in the strict sense.   Nevertheless,
we must remember that there is in our literature a group
of writers of whom, in recent times, she is perhaps the
chief representative,—writers who unburden their full
hearts without thought of artifice, or of artistic restraint,
and who are content if a portion of their work is read,
dwells in the memory, or is looked at again in quiet hours.
Such writers do not always concern themselves with the
general effect of their work considered in its entirety.

It has been said that in giving so much time,
thought, and labour to religious poems, and to devotional and other prose work, she impaired her poetic
gift.   Our opinion as to the importance of this remark
must depend mainly on the view we take as to what
constitutes poetry, and as to what is its chief value.   Is it
to be chiefly valued as an exhibition of metrical high Art
or for its message ?   Is an author to be judged by the
value of his message, and not merely by the form in
which he expresses it ?   Is he to feel that the responsibility of the life of letters is grave, and that by his influence on others his place will finally be determined ?   If
we hold the message to be the really important thing—
so important, indeed, that if the writer thinks he can best
deliver that message in prose it is his duty to write prose
—then we must hold her blameless in any case.   If, on
the contrary, we hold the message unimportant, then
we must condemn her if it be true, as perhaps it is, that
she lost some of her poetic faculty by writing so much

devotional matter. But, even if such be our opinion, we cannot fail to admire the noble purposes of her sacred lyrics, or the fine qualities of her sacred prose.

Elsewhere in this monograph I have made allusions to, or suggested the comparison of her work with that of various other poets of religion. But nevertheless it may not be out of place at this point to make some further observations on this topic. She was as conscious of the teaching power in poetry, and believed as strongly in it, as the most unimaginative verse writer. But her natural aptitude for symbolism and her large poetic vocabulary prevented her from ever becoming prosaic—a notable thing to say when we remember that some of our finest English poets have often been prosaic. I do not find in her religious verse the influence of authors like Cowper and Newton, though in some degree she was at one with them in having a didactic aim ; but to Keble, to Faber, and particularly to Newman, she had, in my judgment, much poetic kinship, though Mr. W. M. Rossetti informs me that ' she thought *nothing* of Keble as a poet.'

Her father's volume of sacred verse, ' L'Arpa Evangelica,' given to the world, it will be recollected, when he was nearing the close of his striking career, had a marked effect upon her. Such poems as ' L'Annunzia-zione ' and ' La Pentecoste ' were certain to touch and unconsciously shape her thoughts. Of both Keats and Shelley she was very fond. And if, unlike most of our sacred poets, she was always poetic, it was in a large measure because she infused into sacred themes the same passionate intensity, the same beauty both of language and of substance, which these poets used in their most lofty secular verse.

In virtue of the stately, the dignified prose sequences in 'The Face of the Deep,' which I have ventured to call litanies, I claim for Christina Rossetti a high place among the very few great masters of that rare kind of English prose, which, while distinct from poetry, yet seems to stand on its threshold.

Without possessing profound erudition she had sufficient of the learning of fact for the purposes of those of her books which she consecrated absolutely to religion. Moreover what she lacked in dry-as-dust erudition was far more than made up by an exceptional, an almost unsurpassed gift of insight into the inner meaning of passages. This was partly, no doubt, the result of her poetic intuition, and this feature makes her work of this kind a new glory of Protestant theology.

I should have deemed that her sacred prose gave evidence of her deep study of seventeenth century religious writers, and that her study of volumes like the prose treatise called 'The Mount of Olives,' by the poet best known under the name of Henry Vaughan, the Silurist, had noticeably done much to form her style, had not her younger brother, after reading over my manuscript, written to me :

'"Deep study of 17th century religious writers"— Did she study them at all? Jeremy Taylor was a great favourite with our mother, and I suppose C[hristina] had some knowledge of him—Vaughan's "Mount of Olives" was I fancy absolutely unknown to her—and I question whether she can have read a line of V[aughan]'s *poetry* earlier than 1875 or so.'

That an author's personality is generally to be traced in his or her work has so frequently been remarked that the remark has become a truism. But it is especially applicable to Christina Rossetti, and, as has been indicated before, nowhere in her writings are personal touches more evident than in 'Time Flies' and in 'The Face of the Deep.' Perhaps in 'The Face of the Deep' this arose from the fact that she regarded it as her last book, and, indeed, spoke of it as such. As we grow in years we become usually more and more personal in our writings. And properly so, for in this way our experience is placed at the service of others.

Like us all, Christina Rossetti had her sorrows, some of them deep and life-long, and yet she was a fortunate woman. She was fortunate in her parents; she was fortunate in her early surroundings; she was fortunate, as she advanced in life, in the other members of her family; and when she came to die she was fortunate in the warm praise of herself and of her work which was unanimously expressed.

Mr. Aubrey de Vere, in the last of his valuable 'Essays Chiefly on Poetry,' the essay entitled 'Recollections of Wordsworth,' says of Wordsworth that he

'frequently spoke of death as if it were the taking of a new degree in the University of Life. "I should like," he remarked to a young lady, "to visit Italy again before I move to another planet—"'

a striking utterance, which shows the poet's settled conviction as to the certainty of a future life. Some such feeling was perhaps the cause of the placidity apparent in Christina Rossetti's work—a placidity which was one, though not of course the only one of the great qualities that characterised it. We must also remember, as 'The Daily News' well remarked a day or two after her death, 'Her noblest books were those books without words that she lived.' Nor must we forget that Christina Rossetti—whether we look to the quality or to the quantity of her poetry of devotion—was pre-eminent among the illustrious English poets who have enriched the literature of Christian teaching by their genius. As long as Christianity remains the most vital force in the lives of millions of English-speaking people, the memory of that poet of their faith who gave them such a poem as ' Passing away, saith the world passing away,' or ' Paradise,' with its exquisite las stanza, the very quintessence of Christian expectation —who gave them that beautiful hymn, part of which, beginning ' The Porter watches at the gate,' was sung so fittingly at her funeral service—who gave them the perfect lines, beginning ' Thy lovely saints do bring Thee love '—will be cherished and honoured.

BIBLIOGRAPHY

By J. P. ANDERSON, British Museum

CONTRIBUTIONS TO MAGAZINES ETC

ATHENÆUM. Poem. 'Death's Chill Between.' Oct. 14, 1848, p. 1,032. Reprinted in vol. i. of *Beautiful Poetry*, 1853, p. 248.

Poem. 'Heart's Chill Between.' Oct. 21, 1848, p. 1,056.

Poem. 'Mirrors of Life and Death.' March 17, 1877. Reprinted in *A Pageant, and other Poems*, 1881, p. 25.

Poem. 'An October Garden.' Oct. 27, 1877. Reprinted in *A Pageant, and other Poems*, 1881, p. 103.

Sonnet. 'Resurgam.' Jan. 28, 1882, p. 124. Reprinted in *Poems*, 1891, p. 378.

Poem. 'Birchington Churchyard.' April 29, 1882, p. 538. Reprinted in *Poems*, 1891, p. 318.

Poem. 'Michael F. M. Rossetti.' Feb. 17, 1883, p. 214. Reprinted in *New Poems*, p. 181.

Poem. 'Cardinal Newman.' Aug. 16, 1890, p. 225. Reprinted in *New Poems*, p. 261.

THE GERM. Poem. 'Dream Land.' By Ellen Alleyn, No. i. Jan. 1850, p. 20. Reprinted in *Goblin Market, and other Poems*, 1862, p. 33.

Poem. 'An End.' By Ellen Alleyn. No. i. Jan. 1850, p. 48. Reprinted in *Nightingale Valley*, edited by William Allingham, 1859, and in *Goblin Market, and other Poems*, 1862, p. 60.

Poem. 'A Pause of Thought.' By Ellen Alleyn. No. ii. Feb. 1850, p. 57. Reprinted in *Goblin Market, and other Poems*, 1862, p. 94.

Song. By Ellen Alleyn. No. ii. Feb. 1850, p. 64. Reprinted in *Goblin Market, and other Poems*, 1862, p. 65.

Poem. 'A Testimony.' By Ellen Alleyn. No. ii. Feb. 1850, p. 73. Reprinted in *Goblin Market, and other Poems*, 1862, p. 160.

Poem. 'Repining.' By Ellen Alleyn. No. iii. March 1850,
p. 111. Reprinted in *New Poems*, p. 4.

Poem. 'Sweet Death.' By Ellen Alleyn. No. iii. March
1850, p. 117. Reprinted in *Goblin Market, and other Poems*,
1862, p. 153.

THE BOUQUET CULLED FROM MARYLEBONE GARDENS. Poem
'Versi' (Italian). June 1851 to Jan. 1852, p. 175. Reprinted in *New Poems*, p. 269.

Poem. 'L'Incognita' (Italian). June 1851 to Jan. 1852,
p. 216. Reprinted in *New Poems*, p. 270.

'Corrispondenza Famigliare.' Jan. to July 1852, pp. 120, 121,
218, 219; July to Dec. 1852, pp. 14, 15, 55-57.

AIKEN'S YEAR (probably contributed to). Poem. 'Behold I
Stand at the Door and Knock.' 1852-54. Reprinted in
New Poems, 1896, p. 198. (*See* Notes by W. M. Rossetti
at p. 389 of *New Poems*.)

MEMOIRS OF MALLET DU PAN. Translated by Mr. W. M.
Rossetti and Mr. Benjamin H. Paul. Part of the translation
was executed by Christina Rossetti 'towards 1855.'

IMPERIAL DICTIONARY OF BIOGRAPHY (1857-63). Edited by
Dr. Waller. Contains many articles by Christina Rossetti
on Italian writers and other celebrities.

THE CRAYON (New York). 'The Lost Titian.' (This tale appeared in *The Crayon* about 1856.) Reprinted in *Commonplace, and other Short Stories*, 1870, pp. 145-163.

ONCE A WEEK. Poem. 'Maude Clare.' Vol. i. Nov. 5, 1859,
pp. 381, 382. Reprinted in *Goblin Market, and other Poems*,
1862, p. 76.

MACMILLAN'S MAGAZINE. Poem. 'Up-hill.' Vol. iii. Feb. 1861
p. 325. Reprinted in *Goblin Market, and other Poems*, 1862
p. 128.

Poem. 'A Birthday.' Vol. iii. April 1861, p. 498. Reprinted
in *Goblin Market, and other Poems*, 1862, p. 56.

Poem. 'An Apple-Gathering.' Vol. iv. Aug. 1861, p. 329.
Reprinted in *Goblin Market, and other Poems*, 1862, p. 73.

Poem. 'Light Love.' Vol. vii. Feb. 1863, p. 287. Reprinted
in *The Prince's Progress, and other Poems*, 1866, p. 92.

Poem. 'The Bourne.' Vol. vii. March 1863, p. 382. Reprinted
in *The Prince's Progress, and other Poems*, 1866, p. 107.

Poem. 'The Fairy Prince who Arrived too Late.' Vol. viii.
May 1863, p. 36.

Poem. 'A Bird's-eye View.' Vol. viii. July 1863, p. 207.
Reprinted in *The Prince's Progress, and other Poems*, 1866,
p. 86.

Poem. 'The Queen of Hearts.' Vol. viii. Oct. 1863, p. 457. Reprinted in *The Prince's Progress, and other Poems*, 1866, p. 82.

Poem. 'One Day.' Vol. ix. Dec. 1863, p. 159. Reprinted in *The Prince's Progress, and other Poems*, 1866, p. 84.

Poem. 'Sit Down in the Lowest Room.' Vol. ix. March 1864, pp. 436-439. Reprinted in *Goblin Market, The Prince's Progress, and other Poems*, 1875, p. 107.

Poem. 'My Friend.' Vol. xi. Dec. 1864, p. 155. Reprinted in *Goblin Market, The Prince's Progress, and other Poems*, 1875, p. 175.

Poem. 'Spring Fancies.' Vol. xi. April 1865, p. 460. Reprinted in *The Prince's Progress, and other Poems*, 1866, p. 52, under the title of 'Spring Quiet.'

Poem. 'Last Night.' Vol. xii. May 1865, p. 48. Reprinted in *New Poems*, 1896.

Poem. 'Consider.' Vol. xiii. Jan. 1866, p. 232. Reprinted in *Goblin Market, The Prince's Progress, and other Poems*, 1875, p. 234.

Poem. 'Helen Grey.' Vol. xiii. March 1866, p. 375. Reprinted in *New Poems*, p. 138.

Poem. 'By the Waters of Babylon.' Vol. xiv. Oct. 1866, pp. 424-426. Reprinted in *Goblin Market, The Prince's Progress, and other Poems*, 1875, p. 238.

Poem. 'Seasons.' Vol. xv. Dec. 1866, pp. 168, 169. Reprinted in *New Poems*, p. 71.

Poem. 'Mother Country.' Vol. xvii. March 1868, pp. 403, 404. Reprinted in *Goblin Market, The Prince's Progress, and other Poems*, 1875, p. 257.

Poem. 'A Smile and a Sigh.' Vol. xviii. May 1868, p. 86. Reprinted in *Goblin Market, The Prince's Progress, and other Poems*, 1875, p. 184.

Poem. 'Dead Hope.' Vol. xviii. May 1868, p. 86. Reprinted in *Goblin Market, The Prince's Progress, and other Poems*, 1875, p. 122.

Poem. 'Autumn Violets.' Vol. xix. Nov. 1868, p. 84. Reprinted in *Goblin Market, The Prince's Progress, and other Poems*, 1875, p. 88.

Poem. 'They desire a better Country.' Vol. xix. March 1869, pp. 422, 423. Reprinted in *Goblin Market, The Prince's Progress, and other Poems*, 1875, p. 95.

Poem. 'A Wintry Sonnet.' Vol. xlvii. April 1883, p. 498. Reprinted in *Poems*, 1891, p. 370.

POEMS : An Offering to Lancashire. Edited by Isa Craig, 1863.

Poem. 'A Royal Princess,' pp. 2–10. Reprinted in *The Prince's Progress, and other Poems*, 1866, p. 123.

A WELCOME : Original contributions in poetry and prose. London, 1863. Poem. 'Dream-Love,' pp. 63-66. Reprinted in *The Prince's Progress, and other Poems*, 1866, p. 59.

LYRA EUCHARISTICA. Edited by Rev. O. Shipley, 1863. Poem. 'The Offering of the New Law, the One Oblation once Offered,' p. 48. Reprinted in *New Poems*, p. 247.

Poem. 'Conference between Christ, the Saints and the Soul, p. 167. Reprinted in *Goblin Market, The Prince's Progress, and other Poems*, p. 260, under the title of 'I will lift up mine eyes unto the Hills.'

LYRA EUCHARISTICA. Second edition. Edited by Rev. O. Shipley, 1864. Poem. 'Come unto Me,' p. 5. Reprinted in *New Poems*, p. 255.

Poem. 'Jesus, do I love Thee,' p. 355.

LYRA MESSIANICA. Edited by Rev. O. Shipley, 1864. Poem 'I know you not,' p. 28. Reprinted in *New Poems*, p. 258.

Poem. 'Before the paling of the Stars,' p. 63. Reprinted in *New Poems*, p. 244.

Poem. 'Good Friday,' p. 236. Reprinted in *The Prince's Progress, and other Poems*, 1866, p. 214.

Poem. 'Easter Even,' p. 251. Reprinted in *New Poems*, p. 245.

LYRA MESSIANICA, 1865. Poem. 'Within the Veil.' Reprinted in *New Poems*, p. 250.

Poem. 'Paradise in a Symbol.'

Poem. 'Paradise in a Dream.'

LYRA MYSTICA. Edited by Rev. O. Shipley, 1865. Poem. 'After this the Judgment,' p. 33. Reprinted in *The Prince's Progress, and other Poems*, 1866, p. 210.

Poem. 'Martyr's Song,' p. 427. Reprinted in *The Prince's Progress, and other Poems*, 1866, p. 206.

THE SHILLING MAGAZINE. Poem. 'Amor Mundi.' With a drawing by F. Sandys. Vol. i. 1865, p. 193. Reprinted in *Goblin Market, The Prince's Progress, and other Poems*, 1875, p. 192.

THE ARGOSY. 'Hero : a Metamorphosis.' Vol. i. Jan. 1866, pp. 156–165. Reprinted in *Commonplace, and other Short Stories*, 1870, pp. 183–211.

Poem. 'Who shall deliver Me?' Vol. i. Feb. 1866, p. 288. Reprinted in *Goblin Market, The Prince's Progress, and other Poems*, 1875, p. 263.

Poem. 'If' (with an illustration by F. A. Sandys). Vol. i. March 1866, p. 336. Reprinted in *New Poems*, p. 145.

Poem. 'Twilight Night.' Vol. v. Jan. 1868, p. 103. Reprinted in *Goblin Market, The Prince's Progress, and other Poems*, 1875, p. 180.

Two Sonnets. I. 'Venus's Looking Glass.' II. 'Love Lies Bleeding.' Vol. xv. Jan. 1873, p. 31. Reprinted in *Goblin Market, The Prince's Progress, and other Poems*, 1875, p. 156.

Poem. 'A Dirge.' Vol. xvii. Jan. 1874, p. 25. Reprinted in *Goblin Market, The Prince's Progress, and other Poems*, 1875, p. 89.

Poem. 'A Bride Song.' Vol. xix. Jan. 1875, p. 25. Reprinted in *Goblin Market, The Prince's Progress, and other Poems*, 1875, p. 102.

CHURCHMAN'S SHILLING MAGAZINE. 'The Waves of this Troublesome World: a Tale of Hastings Ten Years Ago.' Vol. i. 1867, pp. 182–193, 291–304. Reprinted in *Commonplace, and other Short Stories*, 1870, pp. 271–329.

Story. 'Some Pros and Cons about Pews.' Vol. i. 1867, pp. 496–500. Reprinted in *Commonplace, and other Short Stories*, 1870, pp. 257–267.

Essay. 'Dante, an English Classic.' Vol. ii. 1867, pp. 200–205.

Story. 'A Safe Investment.' Vol. ii. 1867, pp. 287–292. Reprinted in *Commonplace, and other Short Stories*, 1870, pp. 241–253.

SCRIBNER'S MONTHLY. (CENTURY.) Poem. 'A Christmas Carol.' Vol. iii. Jan. 1872, p. 278. Reprinted in *Goblin Market, The Prince's Progress, and other Poems*, 1875 p. 221.

Poem. 'Days of Vanity.' Vol. v. Nov. 1872, p. 21. Reprinted in *Goblin Market, The Prince's Progress, and other Poems*, 1875, p. 68.

Poem. 'A Bird Song.' Vol. v. Jan. 1873, p. 336. Reprinted in *Goblin Market, The Prince's Progress, and other Poems*, 1875, p. 184

THE CENTURY. Essay. 'Dante. The Poet illustrated out of the Poem.' Feb. 1884, pp. 566–573.

Poem. 'One Sea-side Grave.' May 1884, p. 134. Reprinted in *Poems*, 1891, p. 339.

PICTURE POSIES, poems chiefly by living authors, 1874. Poem. 'An English Drawing-room,' p. 50. Reprinted under the title of 'Enrica,' 1865, in *Goblin Market, The Prince's Progress, and other Poems*, 1875.

Poem. 'By the Sea,' p. 59. Reprinted in *Goblin Market, The Prince's Progress, and other Poems*, 1875, p. 59.

DUBLIN UNIVERSITY MAGAZINE. Poem. 'Yet a Little While.' Vol. i. N.S., 1878, p. 104. Reprinted in *A Pageant, and other Poems*, 1881, p. 42.

A MASQUE OF POETS. Bost. 1878. Poem. 'Husband and Wife,' pp. 42-44. Reprinted in *New Poems*, p. 154.

NEW AND OLD. Edited by Rev. C. Gutch. 'A Harmony on First Corinthians,' xiii. Vol. vii. Feb. 1879, pp. 34-39.

THE CHILDREN'S HYMN BOOK. Compiled chiefly by Mrs. Carey Brock (1881). Poem. 'Thou art the same, and Thy years shall not fail,' p. 260. Reprinted in *New Poems*, p. 260.

SONNETS OF THREE CENTURIES. Edited by T. Hall Caine, 1882. Sonnet. 'To-day's Burden,' p. 190. Reprinted in *Poems*, 1891, p. 380.

DAWN OF DAY. 'True in the Main.' Two Sketches. May 1, 1882, pp. 57-59, and June 1, 1882, pp. 69-70.
Poems. 'Ash Wednesday.' 'Lent.' Reprinted from *Verses* (1893), Feb. 1894, p. 40.

CENTURY GUILD HOBBY HORSE. Poem. 'A Christmas Carol.' Vol. ii. 1887, p. 1. Reprinted in *Poems* 1891, p. 429, and in *New Poems*, 1896, p. 261.
Poem. 'A Hope Carol.' Vol. iii. 1888, p. 41. Reprinted in *Poems*, 1891, p. 427.
Poem. 'There is a Budding Morrow in Midnight.' Vol. iv. 1889, p. 81. Reprinted in *Poems*, 1891, p. 382.

ATALANTA. Poem. 'Yea I have a Goodly Heritage.' Oct. 1890, p. 3. Reprinted in *New Poems*, p. 262.

MAGAZINE OF ART. Poem. 'An Echo from Willowwood.' Drawing by C. Ricketts. Vol. xiii. Sept. 1890, p. 385. Reprinted in *New Poems*, p. 164.
Poem. 'The Way of the World.' With an illustration by W. E. F. Britten. July 1894, p. 304. Reprinted in *New Poems*, p. 183.

LITERARY OPINION. Poem. 'A Death of a First-born.' Jan. 14, 1892. Feb. 1892, p. 227. Reprinted in *New Poems*, p. 263.
Poem. 'Faint, yet Pursuing.' Vol. ii. 1892, p. 67. Reprinted in *New Poems*, p. 264.
Essay. 'The House of Dante Gabriel Rossetti.' (With a sketch by Miss Margaret Thomas.) Vol. ii. 1892, pp. 127-129.

DANTE GABRIEL ROSSETTI, HIS FAMILY LETTERS, 1895. Verse. 'The Chinaman.' Vol. i. p. 79.
Sonnet. 'The P. R. B.' Vol. i. p. 138.

Poem. 'The Eleventh Hour' (appeared in some Magazine; *see* Mr. W. M. Rossetti's notes to *New Poems*, p. 389). Reprinted in *New Poems*, p. 214.

Poem. 'A Visitor from the South.' Illustrated by Alfred Boyd Houghton.

MUSICAL SETTINGS

'Goblin Market,' as a cantata, by E. Aguilar.

'All Thy works praise Thee, O Lord. A Processional of Creation,' Selected stanzas from. Adapted by the Rev. J. J. Glendinning Nash, and set to music by Mr. Frank T. Lowden. Performed for the first time at Christ Church, Woburn Square, London, October 21st, 1897.

'Songs in a Cornfield,' as a cantata, by Sir G. A. Macfarren. Numerous settings by Mary Grant Carmichael and other composers.

WORKS

To my Mother on the Anniversary of her birth, April 27, 1842. (Privately printed at G. Polidori's, London, 1842) s. sh. 8vo. Christina Rossetti's first verses. Included in the volume of 'Verses,' 1847.

Verses by Christina G. Rossetti. Dedicated to her mother. Privately printed at G. Polidori's, No. 15, Park Village East, Regent's Park, London, 1847, 12mo.
Printed by her maternal grandfather, G. Polidori.

Goblin Market, and other Poems. With two designs by D. G. Rossetti. Macmillan & Co. Cambridge, 1862, 192 pages, 8vo. Bound in dark blue cloth.

Goblin Market, and other Poems. Second edition. Macmillan & Co. Cambridge, 1865, 12mo.

The Prince's Progress, and other Poems. With two designs by D. G. Rossetti. Macmillan & Co. London, 1866, 8vo. Bound in green cloth.

Poems. Roberts Bros. Boston, 1866, 16mo.

Poems. New edition enlarged. Roberts Bros. Boston, 1876, 16mo.

Outlines for illuminating. 'Consider.' A Poem. (Designed by A. Donlevy.) A. D. F. Randolph & Co., New York, 1866, obl. 4to.

Il Mercato de' Folletti ('Goblin Market'); poema tradotto in Italiano da T. P. Rossetti. Firenze, 1867, 8vo.

Commonplace, and other Short Stories. F. S. Ellis, London, 1870, 8vo.

Commonplace, and other Short Stories. Roberts Bros. Boston, 1870, 8vo.

Sing-Song, a nursery rhyme book. With 120 illustrations by Arthur Hughes, engraved by the Brothers Dalziel. George Routledge and Sons, London, 1872, 8vo.

Sing-Song. Roberts Bros. Boston, 1872, 8vo.

Sing-Song. Another edition. George Routledge and Sons, London, 1878, 16mo.

Sing-Song. Another edition. Macmillan & Co. London, 1893, 8vo.

Annus Domini, a prayer for each day of the year, founded on a text of Holy Scripture. (Edited by [the Rev.] H. W. Burrows.) James Parker & Co. London, 1874, 32mo.

Annus Domini. Roberts Bros. Boston, n.d. 18mo.

Speaking Likenesses. With pictures thereof by Arthur Hughes. Macmillan & Co. London, 1874, 8vo.

Speaking Likenesses. Roberts Bros. Boston, 1874, 12mo.

Goblin Market, The Prince's Progress, and other Poems. With four designs by D. G. Rossetti. New edition. Macmillan & Co., London, 1875, 8vo. Reprinted 1879, 1884, 1888.

Seek and Find. A double series of short studies of the Benedicite. Society for Promoting Christian Knowledge, London, 1879, 8vo.

A Pageant, and other Poems. Macmillan & Co. London, 1881, 8vo.

Called to be Saints : the Minor Festivals devotionally studied. Society for Promoting Christian Knowledge, London, 1881, 8vo. Passages from the Bible relating to the Saints, with meditations.

Poems. Roberts Bros. Boston, 1882, 8vo.
The frontispiece is the portrait of Christina G. Rossetti, from the original drawing by Dante G. Rossetti in the possession of Mr. W. M. Rossetti.

Letter and Spirit. Notes on the Commandments. Society for Promoting Christian Knowledge, London, 1883, 8vo.

Time Flies : a reading Diary. Society for Promoting Christian Knowledge, London, 1885, 8vo.

Time Flies. Roberts Bros. Boston, 1886, 12mo.

Poems. (With four designs by D. G. Rossetti.) New and enlarged edition. Macmillan & Co. London, October 1890, 8vo. Reprinted December 1890, February and August 1891, 1892, 1894, 1895, 1896.

The Face of the Deep : a devotional commentary on the Apocalypse. (With the Text.) Society for Promoting Christian Knowledge, London, 1892, 8vo.

The Face of the Deep. E. and J. B. Young & Co. New York, 1892, 8vo.

Goblin Market. Illustrated by Laurence Housman. Macmillan, & Co. London, 1893, 8vo. One hundred and sixty copies of a large paper edition were printed.

Verses. Reprinted from 'Called to be Saints,' 'Time Flies,' and

'The Face of the Deep.' Society for Promoting Christian Knowledge, London, 1893, 8vo.

New Poems, by Christina Rossetti hitherto unpublished or uncollected. Edited by William Michael Rossetti. Macmillan & Co. London and New York, 1896, 8vo.

The Rossetti Birthday Book. Edited by Olivia Rossetti. Macmillan & Co. London and New York, 1896, 16mo.

Maude. With an introduction by W. M. Rossetti. James Bowden, London, 1897, 8vo.

ANA

Eyles, F. A. H. Popular Poets of the Period. London, 1889, 8vo. 'Miss Christina G. Rossetti.' By John Walker, pp. 234-240. (Selections from her poems, with a notice.)

Forman, H. Buxton. Our Living Poets ; an Essay in Criticism. London, 1871, 8vo. 'Christina Gabriela Rossetti,' pp. 231-253.

—— Article in Celebrities of the Century, edited by Lloyd C. Sanders, on Christina Rossetti.

Garnett, Richard. Dictionary of National Biography, Vol. XLIX. Article on Christina Rossetti.

Gilchrist, H. Harlakenden. Anne Gilchrist, Her Life and Writings. London, 1887, 8vo. Numerous references to Christina Rossetti.

Gosse, Edmund. Critical Kit-Kats. London, 1896, 8vo. 'Christina Rossetti,' pp. 133-162.

—— A Short History of Modern English Literature, London, 1898, 8vo. 'Christina Rossetti,' pp. 380-382.

Hake, Dr. Gordon. Memories of Eighty Years. London, 1892, 8vo. Contains references to Christina Rossetti.

Hill, George Birkbeck. Letters of Dante Gabriel Rossetti to William Allingham 1854-1870. London, 1897, 8vo. ; New York, 1898 (before their publication in book form a portion of these letters appeared in *The Atlantic Monthly* May-August 1897). Contains references to Christina Rossetti.

Hueffer, Ford M. Ford Madox Brown ; a Record of his Life and Work. London, 1896, 8vo. Contains several references to Christina Rossetti.

'M.' 'The Athenæum' August 7, 1897. Article entitled 'A Poetic Trio,' containing a letter by Christina Rossetti, pp. 193-194.

Miles, Alfred H. The Poets and the Poetry of the Century, vol. vii. entitled 'Joanna Baillie to Mathilde Blind,' London, 1893, 8vo. Christina G. Rossetti. By Arthur Symons, with selections from her poetical works, pp. 417-448.

Nash, Rev. J. J. Glendinning. A memorial sermon preached at

Christ Church, Woburn Square, for the late Christina Georgina
Rossetti. London, 1895, 8vo.

Noble, James Ashcroft. Impressions and Memories. London,
1895, 8vo. ; ‘The Burden of Christina Rossetti,’ pp. 55–64.

Proctor, Ellen A. A Brief Memoir of Christina G. Rossetti. With
a preface by W. M. Rossetti. London, 1895, 8vo.

Robertson, Eric. S. English Poetesses. London, 1883, 8vo.
‘Christina Rossetti,’ pp. 338–348.

Rossetti, Dante Gabriel, his Family Letters. With a memoir by
William Michael Rossetti. 2 vols. London, 1895, 8vo.
Contains numerous references to Christina Rossetti, with a
portrait painted by Dante G. Rossetti, and several letters to her.

Rossetti, William M. Dante Gabriel Rossetti as Designer and
Writer. London, 1889, 8vo.
Numerous references to Christina Rossetti.

Rossetti, William M. Swinburne’s Poems and Ballads. A Criticism. London, 1866, 8vo.
Contains references to Christina Rossetti.

— ‘Chambers’s Encyclopædia.’ Article, ‘Christina G. Rossetti.’
London, 1895, vol. viii., p. 815.

Scott, William Bell. Autobiographical Notes of the Life of William
Bell Scott. Edited by William Minto. London, 1892, 8vo.
Contains references to Christina Rossetti.

Stedman, Edmund Clarence. Victorian Poets. London, 1887, 8vo.
‘Christina Rossetti,’ pp. 280, 443.

Swinburne, Algernon Charles. A Midsummer Holiday and other
Poems. London, 1884, 8vo. ‘A Ballad of Appeal to Christina
G. Rossetti,’ p. 112.

—— ‘A Century of Roundels,’ London, 1883, 8vo. ‘Dedication
to Christina Rossetti.’

Symons, Arthur. ‘Studies in Two Literatures.’ London, 1897,
8vo. Essay on Christina Rossetti, pp. 135–149.

Taylor, Bayard. Critical Essays and Literary Notes. New York,
1880, 8vo. ‘Christina Rossetti,’ pp. 330–332.

Walker, Hugh. The Age of Tennyson, London, 1897. ‘Christina
Rossetti,’ pp. 244–246.

Wood, Esther. Dante Rossetti and the Pre-Raphaelite Movement.
London, 1894, 8vo. References to Christina Rossetti.

REVIEWS, CRITICISMS, MEMORIAL POEMS, ETC

Rossetti, Christina G.—*The Catholic World*, by F. A. Rudd, vol. iv.
1867, pp. 839–846. *Tinsley’s Magazine*, vol. v., 1869, pp. 59–67.
The Fortnightly Review, by William Sharp, vol. xxxix. N.S.,

1886, pp. 427-429; same article, *The Eclectic Magazine*, vol. cvi., pp. 599, 600, and *Littell's Living Age*, vol. clxix., pp. 169, 170. *The London Quarterly Review*, by Arthur Symons, July 1887, pp. 338-350. *Woman's World* (with portrait), by Amy Levy, 1888, pp. 178-180. *The Sun*, by Elspeth H. Barzia, June 1890, pp. 615-618. *Literary Opinion* (with portrait), by James Ashcroft Noble, Dec. 1891, pp. 155-157. *The Century* (with portrait), by Edmund Gosse, vol. xlvi., 1893, pp. 211-217. *The National Review*, by A. C. Benson, Feb. 1895, pp. 753-763. *The Athenæum*, by Theodore Watts [Dunton], Jan. 5, 1895, pp. 16-18. *The Academy*, Jan. 5, 1895, p. 12. *The Saturday Review*, by Arthur Symons, Jan. 5, 1895, pp. 5, 6. *The Dial* (Chicago), Jan. 16, 1895, pp. 37-39. *The New Review*, by Alice Meynell, Feb. 1895, pp. 201-206. *The Bookman* (with portrait), by Katherine Tynan (Mrs. Hinkson), Feb. 1895, pp. 141, 142. *Cassell's Family Magazine* (with portrait), by Alexander H. Japp, Feb. 1895, p. 227. *Great Thoughts* (with portrait), by Frances E. Ashwell, Feb. 2, 1895, pp. 288-290. *The Leisure Hour* (with portrait), by Mrs. Watson, Feb. 1895, pp. 245-248. *The Author*, by Mackenzie Bell, March 1895, pp. 269, 270. *The Primitive Methodist Quarterly Review*, by M. Johnson, vol. xxxvii., 1895, pp. 469-481. *Good Words*, by Grace Gilchrist, Dec. 1896, pp. 822-826.

— Called to be Saints. *The Academy*, by G. A. Simcox, Nov. 5, 1881, p. 341.

— Character Sketch of. *The Young Woman* (illustrated with portraits, &c.), by Sarah A. Tooley, Nov. 1894, pp. 37-44. By an error the portrait at p. 43 represents Mrs. W. M. Rossetti, not Christina Rossetti.

— Child's Recollections of Rossetti, A. *The New Review*, by Lily Hall Caine (Mrs. Day). Sep. 1894, pp. 246-255. Contains references to Christina Rossetti.

— Commonplace, and other Short Stories. *The Athenæum*, June 4, 1870, pp. 734, 735.

— Goblin Market, and other Poems. *The Eclectic Review*, vol. ii. N.S., 1862, pp. 493-499; same article, *Littell's Living Age*, vol. lxxiv., pp. 147-150. *Macmillan's Magazine*, by Mrs. C. E. Norton, vol. viii., 1863, pp. 401-404; same article, *Littell's Living Age*, vol. lxxix., pp. 126-129. *The Athenæum*, April 26, 1862, pp. 557, 558.

— In Memoriam (Poem). *The Manchester Quarterly*, by Rowland Thirlmere, [Mr. John Walker], Jan. 1896, pp. 39-45.

— Letter and Spirit. *The Academy*, by G. A. Simcox, June 9, 1883, pp. 395, 396.

Rossetti, Christina G.   Letters of D. G. Rossetti.   *The Atlantic Monthly*, May–Aug. 1896, by George B. Hill.

— New Poems, 1896.   *The Athenæum*, Feb. 15, 1896, pp. 207–209.   *The Saturday Review*, Feb. 22, 1896, pp. 194–197.   *The Spectator*, Feb. 29, 1896, pp. 309, 310.   *Poet-lore*, March, 1896, pp. 149, 150.   *The Guardian*, March 18, 1896, p. 432.   *The Atlantic Monthly*, April, 1896, pp. 570, 571.   *The Academy*, by Lionel Johnson, July 25, 1896, pp. 59–60.

— New Year's Eve, A.   *The Nineteenth Century*, by Algernon Charles Swinburne, Feb. 1895, pp. 367, 368.

— Pageant and other Poems, A.   *The Academy*, by T. Hall Caine, Aug. 27, 1881, p. 152.   *The Athenæum*, by Theodore Watts [Dunton], Sep. 10, 1881, pp. 327, 328; same article, *The Eclectic Magazine*, vol. xxxiv.   N.S., pp. 708–712.

— Poems of.   *The Saturday Review*, June 23, 1866, pp. 761, 762 ; same article, *The Eclectic Magazine*, vol. iv. N.S., 1866, pp. 322–325.   *The Spectator*, Sep. 1, 1866, pp. 974, 975.   *The Catholic World*, vol. xxiv., 1877, pp. 122–129.   *The Nation*, by J. R. Dennett, vol. iii., 1866, pp. 47, 48.   *The London Quarterly Review*, vol. lxviii., 1887, pp. 338–350.   *The Academy*, by Richard Le Gallienne, Feb. 7, 1891, pp. 130, 131.

— Poetry of.   *The Bookman* (with portrait), by Katherine Tynan (Mrs. Hinkson,) Dec. 1893, pp. 78, 79.   *The Monthly Packet*, by C. R. Coleridge, March, 1895, pp. 276–282.   *The Westminster Review*, by Alice Law, April, 1895, pp. 444–453.

— Prince's Progress, and other Poems, The.   *The Athenæum*, June 23, 1866, pp. 824, 825.

— Reminiscences of.   *The Nineteenth Century*, by Theodore Watts [Dunton], Feb. 1895, pp. 355–366.

— The Rossettis.   *The London Quarterly Review*, Oct. 1896, pp. 1–16.

— Short Tales of.   *The Spectator*, Oct. 29, 1870, pp. 1292, 1293.

— Sing-Song.   *The Athenæum*, Jan. 6, 1872, p. 11 ; *The Academy*, by Sidney Colvin, Jan. 15, 1872, pp. 23, 24.

— Some Reminiscences of.   *The Atlantic Monthly*, by William Sharp, June, 1895, pp. 736–749 ; *The Bookman*, by Katherine Tynan (Mrs. Hinkson), Feb. 1895, pp. 141, 142.

— To. (Verse), *Good Words*, by Dora Greenwell, vol. xvii. 1876, p. 824.   *The Literary World*, by Mackenzie Bell, Jan. 4, 1895, p. 21.   *The Academy*, by Michael Field, April 4, 1896, p. 284.

— 'Two Christmastides,' *The Athenæum*, by Theodore Watts-Dunton, Jan. 12, 1895, p. 49.

— Verses (1893).   *The Athenæum*, Dec. 16, 1893, pp. 842, 843.   *The Sunday at Home* (with portrait), by Lily Watson, May 1894, pp. 435–428.

CHRONOLOGICAL LIST OF WORKS

CHRONOLOGICAL LIST OF PORTRAITS,
PHOTOGRAPHS, ETC.

By MACKENZIE BELL

Portrait (watercolour) by Filippo Pistrucci, 1838. Reproduced in the present volume, p. 8.

Etching from the above watercolour by William Bell Scott, *circa* 1860.

Another watercolour by Filippo Pistrucci (very bad), *circa* 1840.

Pencil-drawing by Dante Gabriel Rossetti, 1847—being a frontispiece to a copy of 'Verses,' 1847, now in the possession of Mr. William Michael Rossetti.

Portrait (oil) by Dante Gabriel Rossetti, 1848. Processed in 'Dante Gabriel Rossetti : his Family Letters.'

Head (pencil) by Dante Gabriel Rossetti, *circa* 1848. It now belongs to Mr. Sydney Morse. Reproduced in the present volume, to face p. 15.

Head (profile), a tracing of a drawing by Dante Gabriel Rossetti. Reproduced to face p. 259 of 'Dante Gabriel Rossetti's Letters to William Allingham, 1854–1870.' It is stated in that volume that 'Mr. Arthur Hughes, in whose possession the tracing is, believes that the drawing is made as a study for the head of the Virgin in Rossetti's first Præraphaelite picture, *The Girlhood of Mary Virgin*, painted in 1848-49.'

Head of Mary in 'The Girlhood of Mary Virgin,' by Dante Gabriel Rossetti, 1849.

Head by Dante Gabriel Rossetti (perhaps preliminary study for 'Ecce Ancilla Domini,' 1849. Processed in 'New Poems,' 1896.

Portrait (oil) by James Collinson, 1849. Reproduced for the first time in the present volume, to face p. 17.

Head in 'The Annunciation' by Dante Gabriel Rossetti, 1850.

Pencil-drawing by Dante Gabriel Rossetti, executed in October, 1852, in the possession of W. M. Rossetti. Reproduced for the first time in the present volume, to face p. 27.

Pencil-drawing (profile) by Dante Gabriel Rossetti, in the possession of Mr. W. M. Rossetti, *circa* 1855.

Dante Gabriel Rossetti's design of King Arthur and the Weeping Queens in illustrated edition of Tennyson's *Idylls of the King*, published by Edward Moxon (1856-7). One of the female heads is Christina Rossetti.

Photograph (full-length), 1861.

Photograph of Christina Rossetti and her mother, now in the possession of Mr. W. M. Rossetti, taken by 'Lewis Carroll' (the Rev. Charles Lutwidge Dodgson) in the garden of Tudor House, 16 Cheyne Walk, towards 1863. Reproduced in the present volume, to face p. 135.

Photograph of Christina Rossetti, in a family group consisting of her mother, her sister Maria, her brothers Dante Gabriel and William Michael, and herself, also taken by 'Lewis Carroll,' in the garden of Tudor House, *circa* 1864 or 1865.

Chalk drawing by Dante Gabriel Rossetti (face resting on hands), 1866. Reproduced in the present volume as frontispiece.

Portrait (in chalk) of Christina Rossetti and Mrs. Rossetti by Dante Gabriel Rossetti, 1877, now in National Portrait Gallery.

Two heads (in chalk) by Dante Gabriel Rossetti, 1877.

Photograph (Messrs. Elliott and Fry)—Full-face, 1877.

Photograph (Messrs. Elliott and Fry)—Downcast eyes, 1877.

Christina Rossetti sat for Lady Jane Beaufort in William Bell Scott's distemper painting at Penkill Castle, representing James I. of Scotland, his first sight of Lady Jane Beaufort.

Note by Mr. W. M. Rossetti after reading foregoing list of portraits :

'I have lately been handling 2 other portraits by G[abriel] wh[ich] seem worth mentioning. 1 is a profile, not later than

1846, or maybe 1845 : it is a goodish piece of work for that early time, but is of course not marked by G's finer qualities. A very direct literal rendering, and, from that point of view, highly interesting pencil drawing. 2 is a graceful pencil drawing, towards 1852 or perhaps earlier : Christina in a large easy chair, full length : clearly a study of her from the life, but the face is not strongly defined nor greatly like.'

'There are various other sketches of Christina by Dante Gabriel[1]—not any, I think, of marked importance.'

.   .   .   .

'A few pages of M.S., consisting of notes upon various passages in Genesis and Exodus, were found among the papers left by Christina at the time of her death. The notes (which may date towards 1865) relate to Old Testament types of the New Testament dispensation, and to other matters. They are at present (Oct. 1897) consigned to the Society for Promoting Christian Knowledge, with a view to publication.'

[1] One of these appears as frontispiece to ' Maude.'

9 783337 099138